ABOUT THE AUTHORS

LINDA P. BAKER is the author of the DRAGONLANCE novels *The Irda* and (with Nancy Varian Berberick) *Tears of the Night Sky*. She contributed to previous DRAGONLANCE short story collections and *The History of DRAGONLANCE*. She lives with her husband Larry in Mobile, Alabama.

NANCY VARIAN BERBERICK is the author of six fantasy novels as well as a few dozen short stories in the fantasy genre. Among her recent work is *Tears of the Night Sky* (with Linda Baker). She is hard at work on another DRAGONLANCE novel, a solo flight. She lives with her husband, architect Bruce A. Berberick, and their two dogs in a fascinating and flourishing inner city neighborhood in Charlotte, North Carolina.

GILES CUSTER and TODD FAHNESTOCK met in high school eleven years ago. Within an hour of meeting, they started a philosophical conversation they haven't yet been able to finish. Their nomadic lifepaths have crisscrossed over the years, and they have managed to collaborate on four novels and a smattering of short stories. They currently live on opposite ends of California.

JEFF GRUBB is among those who walked the surface of Krynn as its molten surface congealed into continents, and welcomed the first dragons that arrived on Ansalon's shores. He writes for many worlds, but has a soft spot in his heart (some would say head) for the Gnomes. His latest book is *The Gathering Dark*, set in the world of MAGIC: THE GATHERING.

MIRANDA HORNER lives in the Seattle area with her husband Shaun and three cats. She has been editing for TSR for over three years and has worked as the game and newsletter editor for the DRAGONLANCE product group for approximately two of those three years.

KEVIN JAMES KAGE resides hither and yon: mostly yon. He is an aspiring bard, which basically means that he writes music and sings a lot but doesn't get paid for doing either. He currently attends the University of Illinois at Urbana-Champaign. "Much Ado About Magic" is his first published work.

RICHARD A. KNAAK's novels, including the *New York Times* best-seller *The Legend of Huma*, and his Dragonrealm series, have sold well over a million copies in several languages. His short fiction has appeared in nine DRAGONLANCE anthologies. Among his most recent novels are *Land of the Minotaurs*, the modern fantasy *Dutchman*, and *The Horse King*. At present, he is at work on several projects, including a new DRAGONLANCE novel about the minotaurs and *Black Flame*, a novel set in the world of Shattered Light, a new CD Rom game. His web site can be accessed at www.sff.net/people/knaak.

ROGER E. MOORE enjoys gainful employment as an editor and sometime designer of GREYHAWK and FORGOTTEN REALMS campaign products for Wizards of the Coast. His ever-changing interests currently include model rocketry, fiction writing, and looking for stuff on the Internet. If he could ever get his plan to build a 1:5-scale Mercury-Redstone off the ground, he would be content, but he has a great family and is plenty happy with that.

DOUGLAS NILES has been involved in the DRAGONLANCE line since its inception, writing novels including *The Last Thane*, *The Puppet King*, *Fistandantilus Reborn*, *The Dragons*, *The Kagonesti*, *Emperor of Ansalon*, and *The Kinslayer War*. Recently he has finished the Watershed trilogy, an epic series published by Ace Fantasy. He is a lifelong Wisconsin resident, and lives in the boondocks with his wife Chris and their two children.

NICK O'DONOHOE has been a mystery, science fiction and fantasy writer. His Crossroads novels about veterinarians treating fantasy animals include *The Magic and the Healing* (selected by the American Library Association as Best Book for Teens), *Under the Healing Sign* and *The Healing of Crossroads*. His first science fiction novel was *Too, Too Solid Flesh* for TSR, about an all-android acting company of Hamlet. He has also written *The Gnomewrench in the Dwarfworks*, a World War II home front fantasy, due out in the summer of 1999.

Williams Bay, Wisconsin resident JANET PACK is fondly remembered by GEN CON Game Fair® convention attendees for her portrayal of Tasselhoff Burrfoot with the Weis and Hickman Traveling Road Show. She has also sung her original music from *Leaves from the Inn of the Last Home*, *The History of Dragonlance*, and The Deathgate Cycle during Gen Con seminars. Her latest publication is "Money Well Spent" in *Mob Magic*. Look for her new music in the forthcoming *Leaves from the Inn of the Last Home, Volume II*.

JEAN RABE is the author of the Dragons of a New Age Trilogy: *Dawning of a New Age*, *Day of the Tempest*, and *Eve of the Maelstrom*, and co-author of *Maquesta Kar-Thon* in the DRAGONLANCE series. Her other novels include *Red Magic, Secret of the Djinn*, and *Night of the Tiger*. She has published numerous short stories. In her spare time she feeds goldfish, pretends to garden, and edits magazines.

PAUL B. THOMPSON is a freelance writer with nine novels and numerous shorter works to his credit. Five of his books are DRAGONLANCE novels, written in collaboration with Tonya Carter Cook. His newest book, a MAGIC: THE GATHERING novel, will appear in May 1999 from Wizards of the Coast. Paul also writes for the offbeat Internet news service ParaScope (www.parascope.com). He lives in Chapel Hill, North Carolina, with his wife Elizabeth.

MARGARET WEIS and DON PERRIN still live in a barn in Wisconsin with three dogs and three cats. They have recently completed work on the sequel to *The Soulforge* called *Brothers in Arms*, dealing with the first months of Raistlin's and Caramon's military training. Margaret is currently working with Tracy Hickman on the first Volume of the War of Souls trilogy, *Dragons of a Fallen Sun*, for 2000. Don is putting the finishing touches on the new roleplaying game Sovereign Stone, a game based on a world created by artist Larry Elmore. The game is being published by Corsair Press. Visit them at their web site at www.mag7.com.

Heroes & Fools

Tales of the Fifth Age

Edited by
Margaret Weis
and Tracy Hickman

HEROES AND FOOLS
TALES OF THE FIFTH AGE

First Printing: July 1999
Printed in the United States of America.
Library of Congress Catalog Card Number: 98-88144

9 8 7 6 5 4 3 2 1

T21346-620

ISBN: 0-7869-1346-0

U.S., CANADA,	EUROPEAN HEADQUARTERS
ASIA, PACIFIC & LATIN AMERICA	Wizards of the Coast, Belgium
Wizards of the Coast, Inc.	P.B. 2031
P.O. Box 707	2600 Berchem
Renton, WA 98057-0707	Belgium
+1-800-324-6496	+32-70-23-32-77

Visit our website at www.tsr.com

TABLE OF CONTENTS

Introduction

It is always a pleasure to work on a new DRAGONLANCE anthology for many reasons. We have a chance to read and edit interesting and entertaining stories, and we have the fun of working with such talented authors as we have represented in *Heroes and Fools*. Some of these authors are old friends, others are new to DRAGONLANCE. All have done an exceptional job in this collection of stories.

The Fifth Age has been seen as a dark and mysterious age, wherein the gods have departed and gigantic dragons rule the world. Heroes arise to try to bring light back to the world, but, as we find in some of these stories, the fools have their place too, for is laughter really just another kind of magic? Perhaps it is the best kind.

Our first story is by an author well-known to DRAGONLANCE fans, Janet Pack. She brings back her wonderful Solamnic knight and his kender companion to deal with a fearsome monster in "Boojum, Boojum."

"Tree of Life" is by an author new to anthologies but not to those who enjoy playing the DRAGONLANCE roleplaying game. Miranda Horner tells the touching story of a dryad's efforts to save her dying tree.

"Songsayer" by Giles Custer and Todd Fahnestock brings us the story of a young bard in search of a hero. What he finds isn't exactly what he expects.

"Gnomebody" by Jeff Grubb is a gnome story. There, you've been warned!

"The Road Home" by Nancy Berberick, another author well-known to DRAGONLANCE readers, is a chilling tale of murder and revenge.

Paul Thompson, best known for his work on the Elven Nations Trilogy, brings us a story of a would-be knight endeavoring to trap a daring bandit in "Noblesse Oblige."

"Much Ado About Magic" is by an author new to DRAGONLANCE, Kevin James Kage, also known as "the Bard" to his friends on the Internet. He tells the wild tale of a kender, a gully dwarf, and several gnomes who all believe that they can bring magic back to Krynn.

"A Pinch of This, A Dash of That" by Nick O'Donohoe is the story of traveling actors who become mixed up (literally) with a seller of magical potions to the hilarious confusion of everyone, including the audience.

"The Perfect Plan" by Linda Baker is the story of a sorceress's obsessive love for a man and the predicament she faces when her rival for his love returns from the dead.

Richard Knaak, longtime DRAGONLANCE author, writes the intriguing tale of "The Ghost in the Mirror" about a thief trapped by a wizard and forced to do his master's bidding.

"Reorx Pays a Visit" by Jean Rabe is the story of a draconian who takes on the aspect of his victim and unintentionally becomes the hit of the party.

"The Bridge" by Doug Niles is a story of a clan of dwarves seeking a new homeland, who find their way blocked by a rival clan.

"Gone" by Roger E. Moore is a strange and eerie tale of a band of adventurers who set off in search of treasure only to find it guarded by Chaos monsters.

"To Convince the Righteous of the Right" by Margaret Weis and Don Perrin continues the story of Kang and his band of draconians told in the novel The Doom Brigade. In this tale, the draconians, hoping to find a safe haven in which to raise their young, take refuge in a Temple of Paladine.

"Boojum, Boojum"
Janet Pack

The proprietor of the Crossroads Inn looked nervous. He had good reason. Besides his regular noon patrons and the usual handful of strangers in his establishment, there were also eight Dark Knights and a kender. The regulars and guests sat to the left in loose knots around small tables, whispering to each other and throwing furtive glances toward the dark forces; the Knights lounged around a trestle board to the right, intently listening to their leaders; and the kender roamed the bar, occasionally bursting forth in song in a voice rendered seventeen times louder than normal by the amount of dwarven spirits he'd imbibed.

The innkeeper shook his balding head. Not an auspicious day, although the ale the Knights were drinking had lent an extra jingle to his money drawer. He wiped down the bar with a damp rag, making a detour around the kender who had finally fallen asleep with head curled on his arms. He tried not to listen to scraps of conversation, especially those coming from Takhisis's troop.

"We need to post notices for maps of this area," Khedriss Mennarling, commander of the strike force of Dark Knights, was saying. "A good target is rumored nearby. If these rumors prove to be true, then we will have the test we require."

The kender stirred groggily. "Mapsh?" he muttered into the bar, his pronunciation still under the influence of dwarven spirits.

"The reconnaissance will take time," continued Thrane Gunnar, burly second-in-command of the troop. "So we'll need to be patient. Luck will be as important as a good map. Maps with information this specific are not common." The big man's eyes glittered maliciously as he happened to connect looks with the merchant seated nearest him. His rusty-hinge voice rattled the windows. "You have an interest in our business?"

Everyone in the room tensed. The merchant looked away immediately, shaking his balding head. "No. No interest," he squeaked.

"Good," replied Gunnar. "Make sure it stays that way." He surveyed the rest of the patrons for a challenge. No one met his eyes.

"I got mapsh." Suddenly motivated, the kender swung up onto the bar and danced across it singing:

I know of the boojum, boojum, monster of the glade.
It swings a club made of a tree, and is silent on its raid.
It has a treasure ages old laid up within its cave,
And it laughs a great and rumbly laugh as it guides you to
*   your grave . . . ulp!*

Thanks to Gunnar's swift muscular reach, the small being found himself suddenly sitting in the middle of the Dark Knights' table, surrounded by eight calculating glares.

"Let's find out what he knows," said Mennarling. "Hold him, Drethon."

Firm hands closed about the kender's upper arms. He squinted at the fingers, but couldn't believe that pale sausages possessed such strength.

"Even if he knows nothing, we can have some fun with him," growled Gunnar, slapping the captive hard enough to make his ears ring. "He's probably not worth our time. Kender only take up space that can be occupied by better people." He leaned toward the short creature, threatening. "What's this boojum you're singing about, and where does it live?"

"Hi, my name's Thistleknot Tangletoe." With his eyes slightly crossed, the kender thought the Dark Knights looked truly peculiar. Thistleknot tried to fix his sight by pulling at the corners of his eyes, but it didn't work.

"What? Oh, yesh, the boojum. Well, it's huge and furry, and very fierce. Everybody knows that." His voice dropped to a conspiratorial whisper. "An' everybody knows its favorite dessert ish kender. More's the compliment!"

One of Mennarling's eyebrows cocked. "Where is this legendary beast?"

"Oh, you're close, it's right around thish area. Thash why the trade route changed. There washn't much left of a certain caravan after the last boojum raid, so they moved the road south. The old way runs deep in the forest. No one 'ardly goes there anymore."

Gunnar rumbled, "Do you happen to have a map?"

"I thought you'd never askh!" caroled Thistleknot, reaching for a bulging pouch and spreading out a beautifully detailed parchment. "We're right here, at the Crossroadsh Inn." His finger wobbled. "The boojum haunts thish vicinity." They could see it was not far away, labeled simply "Boojum" in red, underlined twice. "The 'X' marks its cave. An' you gotta be careful when you get there." He brought his fingers to his lips and whispered. Mennarling leaned forward slightly to hear and to examine the tiny but precise printing. "There are lots and lots of trapsh!"

Mennarling looked at Gunnar. "Can we trust him?"

"Kender maps are some of the best on Krynn."

"Is the monster real, or just a legend, though? You come from this area, Relthas. What say you?"

The woman warrior considered. "As I told you, I've heard of this boojum all my life, sir. It may be legend, but things have happened to livestock and people that have never been thoroughly explained. Piles of bones have been found next to trails. Persons have disappeared. Sometimes the bodies are found with expressions suggesting they died of fright. I've never seen it," she said slowly, "but I, for one, believe the boojum does exist."

Tangletoe danced next to the map. "I know of the boo-jum, boojum—" he started to sing. Drethon silenced him with a cuff to the ear.

Mennarling nodded, satisfied, and rose. "Then it is decided. This boojum will become the test subject for Her Dark Majesty's new death machine. We've saved a lot of time by discovering this kender and his map." He threw a few coins on the table, grabbed up the chart, turned toward the door, and added, "If boojums like kender so much, bring this one along for bait."

"Heeeyyyyyyy!" Thistleknot howled as Drethan hauled him backward off the table by collar and belt. When the Dark Knight shifted his grip, however, Tangletoe scooted for the portal, leaving a ragged piece of collar in Drethan's hand.

"Stop him!" boomed Gunnar.

Thistleknot managed to dodge the only Dark Knight between him and the outside. He skidded across the porch and raced toward a hand-drawn cart with a big closely swathed burden, the only refuge in sight despite being guarded by three—no, four—humans.

Tangletoe dove beneath the canvas, instantly intrigued by his whereabouts. He worked his hands beneath the ropes at the largest end. "Metal," he muttered. "Heavy. It'sh bigger'n me. Wonder if it's hollow. Whatsh thish, writing? Too dark. Wunnder what it shays? Yeoww!"

One of the guards had him by his heels and dragged him out. "We've got him," he announced to the rest of the Dark Knights as they charged from the inn.

Gunnar grinned through large, square teeth. Mennarling nodded. Tangletoe tried to duck but was too slow. Gunnar's fist slammed into his chin, and the kender saw multicolored stars.

"Boootiful," he managed to say, and knew no more.

* * * * *

Tangletoe awoke abruptly, his sense of being in a different place than before tingling along his nerves. Blearily he tried to think where he had been and where he was going. Certain clues presented themselves to his dwarven spirits-befuddled brain.

The first was that he dangled from a rope tied tightly around his middle affixed to a springy pole that bounced him up and down, up and down, in the darkening woods. The rope also caused him to spin around, which gave him only occasional glimpses of the trees looming suddenly before him, as well as a queasy stomach. Or was the latter an aftereffect of the dwarven spirits? He didn't know, and at the moment, didn't care.

The pole was held by Thrane Gunnar, who grinned wickedly after glancing upward and noticing the late afternoon light bouncing off of Tangletoe's slitted eyes.

"Here boojum, boojum, boojum," he called. The rest of the troop laughed, except for Khedriss Mennarling.

"Quiet," the Dark Knight commander snapped. Behind him, the eight men and two women pulling the canvas-draped death machine on a small two-wheeled wooden cart hushed their catcalls. "According to the kender's map we're now well into boojum country. The monster could be anywhere. Be vigilant."

"My m-m-map!" wailed Thistleknot mournfully from the rope end of the springy pole, his enunciation still beyond perfect control. "You owe me for th-that map. It's my very besht one!"

Mennarling smiled without humor, his pale blue eyes resembling ice. He replied in a low voice that made the kender think of edged steel being pulled from a scabbard.

"You tried to steal our Queen's experimental machine. I still wonder how, in your inebriated state and in such little time, you managed to work yourself under without loosening any of the ropes. But that's a mystery I'll save to ponder later. Meanwhile, you are making a valuable sacrifice toward the great goals of Her Dark Majesty. Remember that."

"But . . . but I wasn't stheal—watch ou—oooofffff!"

A sudden shift of the pole in Gunnar's hands brought the kender into unfriendly proximity with a tree. He tried to fend it off with his fists, but Gunnar jounced the pole and sent him whacking against the trunk not once, but twice. Tangletoe left some skin on its rough bark. His new abrasions stung. The pain helped his mind to clear a little.

"Ouch! Hey, I could help if I really wanted to. I know important information that could lead you right to—"

"Silence, kender," Mennarling barked. "We have your precious map and all the meticulous notations you made on it. There's only one more thing we require of you, and that's to keep smelling like a kender. Bleed a little, and attract the boojum. . . ."

Of course Tangletoe smelled like a kender, and mighty proud he was of it. But the bleeding he could do without. He used sore hands to fend off a branch trying to snag him.

"I don't write everything down on my maps, you know. There isn't always enough room, and—"

Without hesitation Gunnar whirled Thistleknot around and whacked him into the nearest large branch, temporarily stunning him. "Let's try quiet bait," he grinned.

"Don't kill him … yet," one of the Dark Knights warned.

"If he dies, we could turn him into a kender projectile," said Gunnar thoughtfully.

"I'll consider that seriously," Mennarling said softly, speaking mainly to Gunnar. "That would be an intriguing fallback."

Gunnar momentarily spared a hand from grasping the pole to massage one ear. "He deserves all the punishment we can devise. My hearing will never be the same: his singing is worse than any screech owl." His hand returned to the pole, and he gave the kender a harsh jolt.

"Ow! Hey! Who are you calling a screech owl?"

"Just making sure you're still up there and on the job, boojum bait," Gunnar chuckled.

"I worry that the fuel is not quite right," Mennarling muttered, "and that the troop is not drilled well enough in the loading procedures." Thistleknot strained to hear.

"You saw me train them," Gunnar protested. "We trained for days. I ran them through the steps until it takes only moments to get ready. Every one of them can perform his or her duty. Even on a moonless night, I swear, they could do it backward if you ordered it. Nothing has been left to chance. All that remains is finding the boojum."

"We may only have moments to react. By all reports, this boojum is fast for his size. And what if there are casualties among the operating squad?"

"You know these people," stated Gunnar. "They're among the best of the Dark Queen's forces in Ansalon: loyal, quick, and dedicated. They'll perform, and well."

"But this is a weapon that has only been fired twice, and never during battle. . . ."

That is when Mennarling's hand in the air stopped the troop. He pulled Thistleknot's map from the breast of his tunic and studied it before turning to them, his voice still pitched low. They leaned forward to hear every important word.

"According to the kender's scribblings, we've reached the vicinity of this boojum's lair. It is reputedly set with many traps. Be extra wary from now on. Anything can happen. I'm slowing the pace. We don't want to lose Her Dark Majesty's new death weapon to a pit trap." He waited for the murmurs of assent to die down. "Right, then. Forward, carefully."

They crept onward, picking their way gingerly down the path, stout sticks, bow ends, and spear butts waving like feelers on bugs. Dirt stirred into the air and coated them with pale dust sometimes festooned with long green tendrils of weed and fern.

Thistleknot was grinning from his overhead vantage. Preoccupied as they were, at least the pole held by Gunnar no longer slapped him against every tree they passed.

"Lieutenant." A soft hail came from middle rank of the troop. Mennarling whirled, hand on the pommel of his sword, and sprinted back in that direction.

Relthas stood frozen with the wooden haft of her spear stuck deep into the dirt near the side of the path. With Mennarling watching, she pulled it up to show there was no resistance, and then stabbed around until she could trace the outline of a corner.

"Pit trap. Good work, Relthas. Proceed everyone, but be watchful." The commander returned to the head of his troop as the others labored to maneuver the covered cart bearing the Dark Queen's new death weapon safely past the hazard.

"Lieutenant." Mennarling hurried to investigate again, this time finding an ingenious spring-snare covered with forest detritus. He peered upward into the arching trees, but couldn't resolve anything sinister in the fading light.

"Lieutenant." This time it was a partially hidden rope snaking off into the bracken. Mennarling didn't investigate further. The soldiers gave it wide berth.

This boojum was wily. He would prove an excellent adversary, a perfect test target, if they could just lure him into sight.

"Looks like we got to the right place," Gunnar said with a satisfied nod as Mennarling caught up to him again.

"Indeed. The map is excellent. I had expected traps, but not so many and so diverse."

"You know, there's a big outcropping of granite near the boojum's cave," Thistleknot said conversationally. "That's how you know you're getting really close."

"Keep your mouth shut, kender. We're busy," snapped Gunnar. He'd almost forgotten the diminutive one. He gave the pole a whirl and a whack just for good measure.

Thistleknot grumbled, "Ow! I was just trying to be helpful."

"We don't need that kind of help from you," replied Khedriss tartly. "What we need is the boojum."

Now the soldiers wended their way in cautious silence. Late-day crickets fell silent, too, as did those little birds that normally chirped through anything save the fiercest thunderstorms and full darkness. The Dark Queen's minions concentrated on avoiding the boojum's traps and transporting their new weapon without dire incident.

Something, a peculiar clicking noise, made Thistleknot look up and to his right. His eyes widened at what he saw there, and he tried to clear his suddenly constricted throat. "Uh—"

"I told you to shut up, kender," Gunnar ordered.

"But there's—"

"When I want information from you, I'll beat it out of your ugly little body," the second-in-command thundered, beginning to jostle the pole in preparation to flinging the kender against another tree.

Two huge hairy hands reached down. One grabbed the kender's rope where it dangled from the pole, the other sliced it cleanly through with an overlarge knife.

"Whoaaaaa—uuulllppppppppp!" was all Thistleknot could manage as he vanished into the canopy.

"The boojum!" Gunnar cried.

"Ready the weapon!" shouted Mennarling at the same time.

The Dark Knights swirled with activity, ripping off the canvas shrouding their death machine. Then they rolled in a big round shape, poured liquid from skins down its throat, and tamped it all with a large padded stick. Two men stood at each wheel to turn the mechanism on orders from their commander. Relthas and her sister soldier stood waiting to ignite the wick with a torchlight. Everyone seemed to be holding their breaths.

"I think you confused them," whispered Thistleknot to his companion. "Thanks for finally getting me off that rope. It hurt!" He gingerly rubbed his stomach.

"Shift your location, so that when they fire nothing will perish but leaves." The big hairy thing beckoned. Thistleknot nimbly followed his rescuer along the branches—good thing, too. Moments after, several arrows flew into the foliage where they'd stood.

"Predictable," whispered the tall costumed man. He stepped down to another branch, grabbed a bunch of bloody bones secreted there, and cut one of two cords holding them to a branch. They dropped among the Dark Knights with a muted *thwop* and left a sticky dark stain on Gunnar as one glanced off his leather armor. The big hairy thing stepped to a large cone-shaped contraption and spoke into the small end, sending his voice through the forest much amplified from its normal pleasant baritone.

"I AM BOOJUM. YOU TRESPASS IN MY DEMESNE. THE PENALTY IS DEATH DESPITE THE TASTY KENDER!"

Lifting his face from the cone and the hairy hood from his sweaty face, the mild-featured Solamnic Knight with curly brown hair grinned at the kender and shifted his position, whispering, "Now we'll see what transpires."

More arrows answered his pronouncement. Fortunately they were off target.

"That was good," Thistleknot commented, impressed with his friend's improvisations. "I didn't know you were going to get all dressed up and everything."

"I admit to being truly inspired by counterfeiting the boojum." The Solamnic Knight scratched. "Yet this weave is vexing. I hope to be rid of it very soon. Ah, they've come within range. Prithee, draw on that cordage next your right foot."

"This one?" The kender heaved. A number of buckets filled with mud and pea-sized gravel upended, pouring their contents onto the hapless beneath. Curses and howls rose from the squad, along with a few arrows, which fortunately missed by far.

"Save the fuel!" Thistleknot heard Gunnar holler. "Wait for a good shot!"

Thistleknot giggled in delight. "This is working out better than I'd hoped."

"As long as we can purloin that weapon for study," grunted the Knight, making his way back to the conical voice expander, "we will have achieved success."

"SURRENDER NOW. SAVE YOURSELVES FROM CERTAIN AND PROLONGED DESTRUCTION."

"They never will, you know," stated the kender, watching the scurrying below. "Uh ohhhh. Run!"

The night filled with a flash brighter than lightning, brighter than day. A massive roar was followed by splintering of branches as a projectile the size of his head ripped past. The iron ball—for that is what it was—eventually struck a substantial tree and lodged there. Only moments after embedding itself, it exploded, blowing the entire crown from the forest patriarch and flinging its woody shards all around and on the ground.

"Wow!" was all Thistleknot could muster. His ears rang with concussion.

"By my father's sword, that weapon has a god's voice." The Solamnic Knight sounded very far away to the kender, although the man in the hairy costume stood right beside him.

"In the name of Her Dark Majesty Takhisis, we demand your immediate surrender, boojum," called Mennarling in his best indomitable tone.

Thistleknot looked at his partner. The Knight shrugged, indicating a stalemate. Biting his lip, the kender forced himself to think and preferably to think fast.

"Yeeeooowwwww!" The branch he stood on suddenly dipped violently, sending Thistleknot plummeting into the midst of the Dark Knights. He landed hard but scrambled out of the way as his tall associate in the hemp costume minus its disguising hood thumped down a moment later, nearly on top of him.

Although the Solamnic Knight's expression reflected surprise, he recovered quickly, leaping to his feet to face Gunnar as the rest of the enemy. Looking equally surprised, if not confused, the Dark Knights closed a circle around him and the kender, their weapons bristling. The Solamnic's hand curled around his cherished ancestor's sword hilt, and he drew the ancient weapon from its scabbard. The warriors were at a stand-off and took each other's measure for several heartbeats as the forest maintained silence about them.

Above, something rustled. Thistleknot looked up and felt his eyes go wider than ever as his muscles jellied. The grinning countenance staring into his appeared to be savoring an excellent joke. His eyes finally tore away from those huge brown ones in the foliage, and he shuffled over to where the Solamnic Knight stood ready for battle.

"Uh . . . uh . . ." was all he could stutter, tugging at the Knight's sagging costume.

"Not now," hissed his tall partner. "Can you not see I am engaged?"

A dark bass laughed, its roar seemingly coming from the bowels of the earth as well as the ceiling of the sky. It filled the forest without aid from the conical voice-enhancer. The Dark Knights froze. Everyone, even the Solamnic Knight, looked up.

"BOOJUM IMPERSONATOR. PITIFUL PLAYACTOR. NOW ENCOUNTER THE REAL BOOJUM!"

The sound of a huge bowstring's thrum capped the end of the monster's statement. One of the Dark Knights hissed suddenly and folded forward with an overlarge arrow stuck in his chest. Three feet of said arrow appeared to protrude from his back.

"BUT HERE IS NO SPORT. YOU ARE AS DYNAMIC AS DUCKS FROZEN ON A POND. I WILL MAKE ME SOME FUN."

A rope snaked down, dropping over the head of the soldier standing closest to the secret weapon, and pulled tight. This Dark Knight was quickly hoisted into the trees, so fast he couldn't even raise a weapon. A moment later was heard a yelp and the distinctive sounds of bones cracking.

A huge arrow struck the ground near Relthas. She moved back a step, then a few more when another arrow followed. The third missile caused her to leap aside. She flailed the air as dirt crumbled beneath her feet and a pit trap yawned to engulf her. Her pitiful moans were heard every few minutes, until eventually they ceased entirely.

"Come on, fill in there!" Mennarling snapped a command as he stepped bravely to the front, peering up at the trees, finding no trace of the mysterious foe. His voice was sharp, and it brought his soldiers' concentration back into focus. "Ready that machine!"

His team bent to the task, fed fuel to the barrel of the cannon, tamped down the ball, and aimed the death machine into the canopy, all with impressive speed and precision. Except for the Dark Knight, who stumbled over Thistleknot, and Gunnar, who was looking daggers at the Solamnic Knight, there was little wasted movement.

Mennarling shouted, "Fire!"

Steel slid from two scabbards at the same instant the death weapon roared. Gunnar and the Solamnic Knight staggered from the concussive noise, but still managed to trade slices. Thistleknot was thrown to the ground, hands clapped over his much-abused ears. From flat on his back he noticed movement above him in the trees.

"WHAT IF I THROW THIS BACK AT YOU? IT IS NO THREAT TO ME," the boojum's voice thundered, stirring the leaves.

"Uuuhhh ohhhhh!" The kender scrambled up and away as the explosive projectile, shooting sparks, thudded back down into the center of the knot of Dark Knights.

It went off almost immediately, hurling shot, shrapnel, and dirt into the bodies of those soldiers too slow to take cover. Four were wounded. It also dismembered the wheels of the wagon supporting the death machine, tilting it crazily and burying the nose of the barrel among leaves and pine needles. A nearby tree burst into flame as pieces of the cannonball made contact, bringing a lurid light to the darkening scene.

Clashing steel continued as the explosion faded. Thistleknot saw that his friend in disguise was well matched. The Solamnic Knight's reach and quickness were balanced by the Dark Knight's impressive fighting skills. It seemed the two could duel forever.

As well they might, or at least to exhaustion, unless Mennarling interfered. The troop leader slunk around the edge of the firelight with sword at the ready, angling to come to the aid of his cohort. Crouching, Thistleknot aimed himself in the Dark Knight commander's direction and poised to take off at a good clip.

Something clamped over his ankle. Dropping face first, the kender then twisted to see what caught him. A hand belonging to one of the Dark Knights held him in an iron grip. The man's grin looked spectral in the light from the burning tree.

"Saw what you intended," the soldier rasped. "Can't let you sneak up on my commander." He lifted a short sword and maneuvered to his knees without letting go of his prisoner. Firelight glinted along his blade. "I confess I'm going to enjoy this."

"HUMAN OFFAL."

Something huge swept down from the trees and disappeared just as quickly, swatting the Dark Knight away from the kender as if the warrior were a pesky gnat. The man went flying one direction, his sword another. His scream trailed off.

"THAT TINY BEING IS MY DESSERT!"

Thistleknot didn't wait to see what would happen next. Risking a glance over his shoulder, he jumped up and ran directly into something warm and unyielding. It grunted. Tangletoe looked up past leather scale armor into the cold eyes of Khedriss Mennarling.

"Just who I wanted to bump into," the troop leader said, knotting his fingers over the back of Thistleknot's leather vest. "Your timing is perfect. I—"

"CHILDREN SHOULD ESCHEW AMUSING THEM-SELVES WITH SHARP OBJECTS. THIS DANCE NO LONGER DELIGHTS ME. I WILL MAKE AN END."

Gunnar oofed out air as an arrow buried itself in his chest. He staggered backward until he collided with the death machine, sat down hard, and sighed out his last breath.

"My friend," choked out Mennarling, before regaining his martial composure. "I will kill you first, kender, and then the trickster and I will finish this travesty of a battle."

"I WILL FINISH THIS!"

The being that dropped out of the tree and landed lightly despite his enormous frame was as big as his voice. Completely awed, an unusual emotion for a kender, Thistleknot estimated the creature's height at somewhere around ten feet, possibly more. Thick long brown and sorrel fur covered most of his body. Shorter hair highlighted his facial features, notably dark eyes that gleamed with intelligence. His domed head was topped with two upstanding rounded ears. He carried a huge longbow made from a thick tree branch, with tremendously long arrows riding in a quiver made from bull hide. A club hung opposite the quiver, both dangling from a thick leather belt, the only clothing he wore.

"The boojum!" Thistleknot whispered loudly, as the Dark Knight closest to him turned and ran into the forest without a word, vanishing in the night.

"LET US SEE IF THIS COUNTERFEIT CAN SKIRMISH WITH THE AUTHENTIC," the monster said, hurting everyone's ears with his thunderous laughter.

"But you're putting up no weapon," protested the Solamnic Knight, trying not to breathe hard and look particularly beleaguered in his unravelling hemp disguise. Mennarling, temporarily ignored and glad for the oversight, inched away from the monster.

" 'TIS YOU WHO NEEDS WEAPONS, NOT I." The monster reached out a finger and tapped the Solamnic Knight's outstretched sword. It wavered despite the young man's best efforts to hold it firmly in place. "COME, MAKE YOUR PLAY."

"Very well." The Solamnic Knight showed granite determination, making him appear much older than his years as he settled into a fighting stance. "Ready."

"I've got to help him!" Thistleknot muttered to himself. His feet scrabbled forward, as a hand on his leather vest yanked him back. "Oooooofffff!"

"You've got to help *me*." Mennarling turned and dragged the kender toward the death machine, signaling to the remaining quartet of his squad with a wave of his sword. "This is our last chance to fulfill the mission. One exploding sphere remains—and if that doesn't work, there's always the kender."

"But—" Thistleknot began, before choking cut him off.

"All right, start loading."

Thistleknot was enlisted to help as the Knights righted the machine. Mennarling stood over him with threats. The kender was distracted, especially when he heard the Solamnic Knight's sword crunch against something, followed by a heavy grunt. He managed to spill quite a bit of the fuel before one of the Knights noticed, shoved him away, and added more, tamping the whole mess down the machine's maw.

Mennarling exhorted the Dark Knights. Because the wheels were broken, they were going to have to hold the cart up during firing. They swung the machine around and aimed at the Solamnic Knight and the real boojum, who were still skirmishing. Thistleknot didn't much like being forced to crouch beneath the barrel, helping to hold the metal tube aloft. The Dark Knight standing opposite him looked equally skeptical.

"I'd almost rather be inside," said the kender. "I can imagine what it feels like hurtling out of that thing—"

"Fire!" ordered Mennarling, touching flame to the hole in the top.

Thistleknot didn't know when he took off running or what prompted him to do so. The kender only knew that by the time the death weapon had sucked down the flame, coughed, hesitated a moment, and then exploded, he was already in full flight.

He tripped over something and sprawled, feet flying, as shrapnel whizzed by. The weave beneath his elbows looked familiar. Thistleknot turned, looked, and choked.

The Solamnic Knight lay in a pool of blood, his face shadowed by bruises and peaceful in death. Strings of hemp were clotted around a gaping wound in his chest. One hand still clutched the hilt of his precious sword, its blade now badly nicked and broken in two.

Kenders don't cry as a rule, but Thistleknot Tangletoe thought his brave dead partner deserved some tears. He looked at the still-burning tree, hoping its brightness might help his eyes water, and squeezed them half-shut tightly. "We sure had great times," he sniffed. His friend had been a rare man, strong and gentle, with a sly sense of humor equal to his own. Considering everyone else the kender had met throughout his life had demanded his maps, taken him for granted, beaten him up, or just plain tried to ignore him, Thistleknot gave the Solamnic Knight his highest rating:

"Having adventures with you was really, really fun."

One teardrop dampened the corner of his right eye. He looked around, saw no sign of Mennarling (probably blown to bits) or the other Knights (ditto). No sign either of the real boojum, whom he would have liked to shred slowly. Shrugging, Thistleknot did one of the things kender are best at: He put sorrow behind him.

"There's no way I can take even a piece of that death weapon back to the Solamnic enclave," he mused, looking at the twisted metal. "It's too bad. I'd like to, it would be the honorable thing to do and all that. But it's all curled back on itself, like dying flower petals. I'd have to get another cart, and have someone help me hoist it on. That'd slow me down considerably. The Knight commander might just have to do with a description.

"Hey, that's it! I can make a drawing—just like a map. I can present the Solamnics with a map of the death machine!" He turned back to the Knight's body, coaxing forth another sorrowful sniff. "I promise you that I'll finish our assignment and tell everybody a wonderful story of your death. Your Lord Dulth-what's-'is-name will *really* honor your memory after I'm done." He frowned, chewing on his lip. "Come to think of it, I'd better take something of yours back so they know I'm telling the truth."

Thistleknot stepped over to where the Knight's out-flung fist still gripped his weapon. Grasping the cross-piece, he pulled once, then again. Even in death, the young man wouldn't (or couldn't) abandon his grandfather's legacy. His fingers remained firmly locked about the hilt.

"And he called *me* stubborn," the kender muttered, yanking again. "Ulp!"

Something snatched him by the back of the vest. Thistleknot found himself confronting the grinning visage of the boojum. "Uh, hello," he managed without too much tremble in his voice. "My name's Thistleknot Tangletoe. What's yours?"

"Told you I'd leave you for last," laughed the boojum in a voice that was oddly normal. "Didn't I, friend Knight?"

"Dessert was your word precisely," a familiar voice answered. "Pardon me if I say so, but I don't know how you abide such furry covering. I may have to drown myself in healing muds for a tenday before I wash away the irritation from that carpet."

Thistleknot tried to crane his head over his shoulder. "But you . . . you're—"

"Sincerely dead," stated the Solamnic Knight, sitting up and picking loose hemp from his armor, "to which deception I owe gratitude to my friend boojum, a stage natural." He reached behind a fallen log to replace the broken sword reverently with his own, antique whole one.

"I followed a traveling theatrical troupe around for a while," the monster said deprecatingly, "and studied their techniques." He had a slight lisp, caused, Tangletoe speculated, by his overlong canines. "Over time, I've practiced and improved upon them."

The kender squirmed. "Oh, pardon. I forgot," said the furry being, setting Thistleknot gently on the ground. "By the way, the expression on your face when you thought your friend here was dead was . . . ah . . . truly dramatic. I only wish I could master the expression of such delicate emotions. Especially the moment when you tried to squeeze out that tear. Brilliant. It would make inspired stagecraft."

"That's one I'll treasure long," the Knight murmured. "Imagine, a kender crying! And over me!"

Thistleknot felt anger rise from the tips of his toes to the ends of his pointed ears. "You tricked me!"

"Ah, but 'twasn't a hurtful tricking," consoled the boojum.

"Certes, only good fun between friends," stated the Knight, rising to peel off his "wound" and buffing where it had been stuck. "This prevarication allowed me an excellent retribution for your insisting on being the bait, while I was made to suffer in costume." He patted the boojum on the arm. "Fortunately, this noble beast and I chanced to cross paths and made friends, and the rest is . . . well, you know the rest."

Thistleknot glared at him unforgivingly.

"Kender, put away your wounded pride," said the Solamnic Knight. "Here stands another one such as we. Remember you that ambitious plan that we discussed over our campfire nary a week gone by?"

"The one about sneaking into the Dragon Highlord's library and changing all his war maps for new ones with little mistakes dropped into them?"

"No, the one where . . . never mind. The point, little friend, is that if we join with the boojum, we can, in the future, venture much more complicated sorties."

The boojum beamed proudly. Thistleknot beamed back, warming up to the fellow.

"Now the three of us can take the remains of the death machine back to my Lord Dulthan. On the way, we can plot our next operation." The Knight bowed his head respectfully toward the boojum. "That is, if you are so inclined, friend boojum."

"I must admit I did enjoy myself tonight," said the grinning monster. "Let us do as you say. But first we must adjourn to my cave for some delicious tea and dessert."

"Dessert?" asked a worried Thistleknot. "But what about . . .? The legends? The legends say boojums eat kender for dessert."

"Never," the boojum shuddered. "Although some kender do make good appetizers."

"Hold," the knight said thoughtfully. "Think you this might be a gnome-wrought machine? And if so, it functioned extremely well?"

"There's some writing on the big part," Tangletoe stated. "I found it when . . . hey, wait for me!"

Monster and Solamnic sprinted for the ruined weapon, which lay in the area fitfully lit by the still-burning tree. The boojum hefted the back end of the barrel and rotated it with help from the curly-haired human as the kender scampered up.

"Ah, there it is." The legendary being squinted at the script. " 'Made by A. Diddlethompermarium, Gnome Inventor Extraordinaire.' " The boojum stopped in surprise, nearly dropping the cannon.

Thistleknot laughed with delight as the knight finished the memorial in an awed voice.

" 'Popcorn Popper. Patent Pending.' "

Tree of Life
Miranda Horner

The sun beat down on the face of the dryad, causing her to lick her dry lips. She looked over at the blue dragon and its crushed rider for the hundredth time. The last skeletal remains of dried-out trees had been knocked down by the dragons' fall from the skies, so the area looked even more desolate and sun-scorched than before. To the dryad, the landscape looked so alien to the way it used to be. Now, instead of the cool grove and the sun-dappled meadows, seared land with dead grass, the exposed bones of rock, and the splinters of dry trees met her once-green eyes. No rain had fallen on this land for quite a while, and the dryad knew that if this weather continued, she and her tree would die within the day.

Peeking out from under the rider's chest was a large skin of water. The dryad silently cursed the fact that the two had fallen just out of reach of her and her withered tree. If the dragon battle had started a bit earlier and the blue dragon had fallen a little closer, she thought, I might have been able to save my tree with that waterskin. As it was, her reach fell short by a foot.

She turned back to her tree and despaired. The weakness that she felt mirrored that of the dried-out oak tree that had birthed her so many seasons ago. Just a few moon cycles back, the land had been green and fertile, with birds, trees, deer, and other forest life. Now they were all gone . . . all dead. And, as the landscape had changed, so too had she. As the leaves fell off the trees and the grass had crisped under the too-hot sun, her skin had changed from pale to tan. Her long glorious hair that had once been a vibrant green had changed to a brittle, dull brown. "How can I protect the land from this horrible drought? It's not natural," she whispered to her tree. No response met her aching question. She laid her hand gently down on an exposed root. "You're the last tree standing, but not for much longer. If only I could get the water from that human before we both die. We could figure something out. I know we could."

A slight breeze picked up and blew the dryad's hair around her face. A few dead leaves rustled halfheartedly and then settled down again. The limbs of her tree looked stark against the hot sky. A few withered leaves clung to the oak. In an effort to think past the fatigue and despair that washed over her, the dryad looked past her tree. In the distance, waves of heat distorted the ruined land into something from the dryad's deepest nightmare. She gazed at the scene, mesmerized, until a gasp of pain broke her reverie.

"Bolt?" a man's voice cried out. "Get up," he ordered weakly.

The dryad got up onto her knees and watched as the man struggled to pull himself out from under the large blue dragon. She had seen the dragon try to twist at the last moment to protect his rider, but it hadn't worked. Instead, the dragon's body crashed over the man's legs, crushing them. The heavy plate armor that covered the man didn't help matters any, she knew. Not only did it impede his movement, but its dark, lily-engraved bulk also attracted the heat of the sun. The human is already very hot, she noted, but things would certainly get worse before the day ended.

"Bolt?" The man had managed to pull the waterskin out from under him and yank his helm off of his head, but that was it. "Are you hurt badly?"

The dryad decided to step in. "Human, the dragon is dead. The silver dragon raked its underside badly. It was a glorious battle," she added, "if you like such things." It was hard to make her voice loud enough, she discovered.

"I will remember the flash of the silver parrying the grace of the blue for as long as I live," she declared.

The man turned toward her quickly. "Who are you?" he demanded. His face had a harsh cast, and his hair was matted with dried blood, making it look darker than the sandy brown that must be its natural color. The dryad noted that he was clean-shaven.

"No enemy of yours, unless you intend to harm my tree," the dryad responded rather curtly. Then, realizing that this man held something in his hands that was invaluable to her, she added more reasonably, "Of course, your cares rest elsewhere, like in your cities or in the skies above."

The man looked as if he was about to say something, but started coughing instead. Once he was done, he unscrewed the cap off of his waterskin and gulped a mouthful.

"Noooo!" the dryad cried out before she could stop herself.

He looked up and slowly screwed the cap back on. "What, are you thirsty, too? Well, you won't get any of this until you tell me who you are and what you're doing here." His stare pierced her with its coldness.

The dryad readjusted her position, sitting cross-legged. Her head reeled a bit. It won't do to faint right now, she told herself crossly. She smiled slightly and said, "I'm the guardian of this area." She gestured to the desiccated trees that surrounded her. Only her own oak tree still stood completely upright. The rest were leaning or had been broken in the dragon's fall. "I live here."

The man looked around as much as he was able to. "Not much of a place to live," he stated, clearly unimpressed.

The dryad kept an enticing smile on her face, but inwardly she cringed at the offense. "It used to be a forest with many glades and brooks, but some unnatural drought has caused it to die."

The man's expression didn't change. "Well, then. I'm not going to tell you what a fool you are for staying here, but . . . oh, look. I just did," he added sardonically. "But I do need your help to get out from under Bolt."

A look of sadness crossed his face. "I'll give you some water for your help."

The dryad allowed herself to look as if she were considering the offer. In the past, her gentle, playful words and smile were enough to charm humans into doing what she wanted them to do. That didn't seem to be working now, though. Briefly she looked down at her seared skin and realized that she probably didn't look half as nice as she used to. The lack of moisture showed in her prominent bones and dry skin. Even her hair seemed parched. Another wave of weakness and despair rolled over her, not allowing her to think clearly. Soon, she realized, I won't be able to move at all.

"Well?" the human asked archly. He tried to shift position to look at her more comfortably, but the pain must have been too intense, for he grimaced and closed his eyes.

"May I have that drink you promised me?" she finally asked. "I answered your questions."

Her response garnered no reaction from the man. He must have passed out from the pain, she thought. "Human? Wake up," she called out in a rough voice.

No response. She reached out as far as she could and was able to pat the dirt near his head. "Wake up." Nothing. Gently she kneaded the root under her hand and sought contact with her tree. "What if he doesn't wake up?" she murmured. "I will have lost my chance to keep you alive." She bowed her head in concentration, trying to reach out to her tree's consciousness. She felt a vague presence, but it was too sapped of energy. "Everything around me dies," she whispered brokenly. She would have wept, if she had any tears left.

Another grunt of pain brought her attention to the human. "Wake up," she encouraged him.

The man pushed himself up a little on his right arm. "Get me out from under this," he demanded harshly. His expression was pained and hostile at the same time.

The dryad shook her head. "You told me that you'd give me a drink of water if I answered your questions."

He simply stared at her for a moment, then nodded.

"Very well." He settled himself down and unscrewed the waterskin. He poured some of the water into the cap and reached back with his left arm, careful to hold the full waterskin upright with his right hand so as not to spill it.

"That's it?" the dryad asked. She had hoped that he would pass back the whole waterskin.

"Take it."

The man's tone of voice allowed for no argument, so she reached out for the cap. Instead of drinking it, though, she carefully spilled it over the exposed root under her hand. The man's expression grew incredulous. "What are you doing?" he asked.

She waited until every last bit of water had dripped from the lid before handing it back to him. "I must protect my tree," she answered. She looked up pleadingly. "Please, give me the waterskin so that my tree may live."

The man shifted to close the waterskin. "Why should I do that? Your tree is dead. I'm not. You're not. If you help me get out from under my dragon, I'll give you more than a sip of this water. You must help me start back to my rendezvous point. I'm sure that my fellow Knights will be looking for me along that path soon."

The dryad looked down at the root, noticing that the water had already soaked through. She didn't feel any stronger, so it must not have been enough. "I can't help you," she declared softly.

The Knight pushed himself up and looked at her angrily. "Why? Do you so oppose the goals of the Knights of Takhisis that you won't help me out from under a dead mount?" he asked. "You mourn for the lost life of this forest, but you won't help someone not of the forest maintain his hold on life?"

"I simply can't help you, human," she said sadly. "I am not what you think I am."

He frowned and said, "Well, you look like an elf, except for the dark skin. I don't recall ever seeing a wild elf with skin that dark and without any tattoos. What are you if you're not an elf?"

"I am a dryad. I was born of that tree back there," she

stated simply. Another hot breeze stirred the hair around her face.

"And how does that prevent you from helping me? Or taking from me this waterskin that you so desire?" he asked.

"Normally, I cannot leave the area around my tree without dying slowly. Because of the state of my parent tree, I have found my boundaries to be even harsher and more limited," she told him. If I had more strength, she reflected, I could stand over him and threaten him to get that waterskin. Now I have to use truth to get what I need, she thought.

"So that is as far as you can go," he deduced.

She nodded. His contorted position must be causing him great pain, and his armor must be very hot, for he was sweating profusely now, she noticed. "When you first fell, I tried to come nearer, but I didn't have the strength to approach any closer than this spot."

The Dark Knight nodded slowly. "Then I guess I shouldn't waste my strength talking to you, since you aren't of any help to me. I will just stay here and wait for the others in my talon to find me." He unscrewed the cap of the waterskin and took another sip of water. He looked sadly at the dragon that pinioned his legs. He seemed as greatly sorrowed by the creature's death as he was frustrated by his own predicament.

"Are your friends within a day's flight from here?" Judging by the wounds that the Knight evidenced, he might not live through the night. She knew that her tree wouldn't.

"Why should it matter to you?" the Dark Knight returned as he screwed the cap back onto the waterskin.

"Your wounds are bad enough that I don't think they'll get to you soon enough," the dryad explained.

With his left arm the Knight gestured at his legs. "My legs are crushed, not bleeding."

"But already you roast under this sun. You've several more hours to go before the sun begins its descent," the dryad noted.

"And I've enough water to get me through this," the Knight said through clenched teeth. "Now enough of your incessant patter. Leave me be."

"I can't. My tree is dying. I desperately need the little water you have to restore it to health," she argued.

The Knight settled onto his back. "Surely you don't think that this bag of water will bring your dead tree back to life? Besides, I need the water more. I must survive until my talon finds me," he replied harshly.

The dryad rested her throbbing forehead on her cradled palms. The heat was getting stronger. If she could just get the Knight to give over the waterskin, everything would be fine again. Her tree would live and she could recuperate in its shade. "The water will heal my tree," she said defiantly. "You're the one who is as good as dead. This talon of yours won't ever find you amidst the ruin of this place."

"Enough, dryad. I must rest, and your words will do me no good in that regard," the Knight declared, sounding tired and angry at the same time.

The dryad raised her head. "From what little I know of humans, I'd think it would be rather stupid of you to sleep after the injuries you have suffered—hitting your head."

"Really? And what makes you think that?"

She almost laughed at how he kept answering her even though he told her to stay silent. "Many seasons ago, when there were still three moons in the sky, a human dressed a little differently than you passed through my glade. He had similar metal fittings, but they didn't form the pattern of skulls and lilies like yours. His helm still sat upon his head, though it had lost one of its metal wings and was greatly dented." She paused to determine if he was listening. "He wandered about randomly, clearly dazed by something. I saw him sit down with his back against a tree not too far from here and then go to sleep. The next morning, when I sent a sylph over to check on him, the sylph discovered that the human had died in his sleep."

"Was he wounded in any other way?" the Knight asked finally. The dryad was afraid that she'd lost him to sleep for a minute or two. "And what is a sylph?" he added.

She decided to answer the second question first. "Sylphs look a little like elves, except they have wings and consist of magic and air. And as for the wounds, since the human was completely covered by metal, except for his face, I don't know," she admitted. "Sometime during the next season a kender came by and discovered the human. By then nature had reclaimed its own, so the kender found only a skeleton and the metal. She dragged the remains farther off into the forest."

The Knight grunted, amused. "So, even you have suffered the presence of kender, eh?"

"They came through every now and again," the dryad admitted. "They have never tried to destroy this forest, like you humans often do."

"I beg to disagree," the Knight countered. He raised himself back onto his right arm in order to peer at her. "Even kender cut down trees to gain farmland and grow crops."

The dryad shrugged. "They never did here."

"That's as it may be." He stared at her for a moment. "So, if you're as isolated as you seem, how do you know that kender are kender and not just little humans? For that matter, how do you know anything about humans?"

If I keep answering his questions, the dryad thought, maybe he'll give me some more water for my tree. "My tree is hundreds of seasons old. Shortly after its first seeding, it bore me. Over the passage of the seasons, I've seen many different forms of life. Mostly forest animals, but I have encountered humans, kender, elves, and even those bearded people called dwarves. I have tried to pay attention, and learn about the world around me," she finished. "Now, I ask again, may I have your water? You're not going to live past nightfall, and I could certainly put it to use."

The Knight snorted, then worked to free the cap from the waterskin again. "Okay, I'll give you another capful, but you'd better drink it yourself this time. None of this spilling it on your dead tree." He handed over the cap, his outstretched hand trembling.

The dryad took the cap and deliberately poured it over the root as he watched. "Don't you understand how nature works, human? This tree bore me. If I can save it, we can help bring this forest back to its normal state." She gave the cap back to him. This time, their fingers brushed briefly because of his shaking hand. The Dark Knight snatched the cap away and quickly closed the waterskin.

"How could your silly dead tree save what's left of this forest?" the human asked roughly.

He didn't like revealing his weakened state, the dryad noticed. "You should never underestimate the power of nature. Even droughts as bad as this one do come to an end. If I can make my tree last another week, or even another day, it might be enough time for rain to come."

"I don't think you realize what has been going on around here over the last few years," the Knight declared, his tone tinged with amusement. "The gods have left Krynn to our care. Great dragons have come to take control of the lands. In some places, the land itself is changing to conform to the power of these dragons. You are probably sitting on some dragon's land even now, helpless to resist what is happening."

The dryad wanted to look away from the Knight's imposing stare, but she couldn't back down now. She felt a certain stirring in the back of her mind, indicating that her beloved tree had registered the small trickle of water this time. "If that's the case, then so be it," she began, her voice rising in volume. "Either way, I expect you will die, and your blood will water the ground upon which you lay. That alone could help my tree for a few hours. However, that's not enough. What I really need is your water before you die. Your sacrifice could allow the land to flourish again. Think on that while the sun beats down on your reddening skin and your so-called talon heads off to another destination, not even noticing your absence. Think on that when your last breath leaves you and you realize that you could have given yourself a shaded place to rest your body for all eternity. Think on that when you understand that your selfishness has deprived the rest of the world of hope. Hope for life. Hope for the future. You humans understand hope, at least the twisted hope of acquiring land, possessions, and all else you hold dear."

Silence greeted her harsh words. The dryad lowered her head, wishing that she could weep, for her tears were never salty and they might help her tree live longer. Clearly she had failed, and the Dark Knight had chosen to ignore her until he passed out again—if he hadn't already passed out.

"You may think whatever you like, dryad, but I have my own beliefs and my own honorable goals to achieve," he said, finally. "When I became a Dark Knight, I had a Vision of what my Dark Queen wished for me. This Vision spoke of battles won for her sake. Never did it say that I should give my last hope of survival to a nature spirit who sits next to a dead tree. I cannot fail my Queen by surrendering to you this water. Once my fellow Knights come and rescue me out from under my Bolt, I can heal and once again ride to victory for Takhisis."

The dryad raised her head and gazed at his expression. It spoke of pain and duty. "So, your hopes for the future differ from mine, human," she whispered and sighed. "I always find you humans to be so full of determination to get your way. You don't take the time to look around and realize that others also walk through life. Never do you think that the trees do their job by providing shade for you or that the birds should be thanked for chattering overhead. If there were no trees or birds, you wouldn't be able to achieve these goals that your mistress has set for you."

The Knight settled onto his back again, biting back a gasp of pain. He looks so very pale under the redness caused by exposure to sun, the dryad thought. He must be losing blood. "Are those the birds you speak of?" he asked once he got comfortable.

She looked up and noticed several vultures flying overhead. "Even carrion eaters serve a purpose, Knight."

"Yes, they eat the flesh of the fallen. My talon usually shoots them down. They are foul beasts, always hovering over the battlefield," he declared in an annoyed tone. "I suppose they've come for Bolt. I wish my crossbow was at hand."

She sighed and shook her head. "If something didn't eat the dead, we would be surrounded by carcasses."

"So, you don't mind?" the Knight asked, clearly trying to get a rise out of her. "You don't care if they tear away pieces of flesh, fight over your body. It doesn't bother you?" He laughed without humor. "Vultures are disgusting creatures who prey on those whose passing should be honored in a more fit manner. I know of one fellow Knight who wore a family ring that he wished to pass on to his daughter. The ring had been handed down from one generation to the next ever since before the First Cataclysm. It bore the symbol of a wild boar, which signified an event that gave honor to his family. Evidently, a great boar had almost gored a member of the Ergothian nobility, and the man's forebear saved the noble's life by killing the boar, thus gaining the gratitude of the noble's family. The man's ancestor received the ring from the noble's family. Ever after that it was passed down from firstborn to firstborn. Because of a few vultures, though, I was unable to retrieve the ring from the Knight's body and deliver it to his daughter. The vultures must have eaten it before I could get to him."

The dryad pondered the story for a few moments, then answered. "First of all, you place too much emphasis on the trappings of honor." An expression of annoyance flickered across his face. "Secondly, if I die outside my tree, then it is fitting that my body becomes part of the circle of life," she said calmly. "However, I intend to crawl back inside my tree before I die."

"And if your tree dies with you inside? What then?"

The dryad watched the vultures land on the ground several yards away. "My body ceases to exist when I'm part of my tree," she said absently. She looked at him sharply. "Are you offended by my honesty?"

The Knight shook his head weakly. "Telling the truth is an admirable trait. I do not get offended if I ask a question and you give a truthful response. By asking the question, I open myself up to both falsehoods and truths. While a falsehood may make me feel more comfortable, I prefer to hear the truth. That way, I know where I stand."

The dryad looked over at the gathering vultures. "I prefer to tell the truth whenever possible. Often, humans follow the exact opposite behavior, I've discovered. At least, that is true of the ones I've talked to."

The Knight frowned. "You haven't spoken to many Knights, have you? Though we serve an Evil mistress, our honor requires truth."

The dryad smiled wryly. "Then the truth couldn't offend you." The heat of the sun must be getting to me, she thought. She looked down at her skin. It seemed as dead and dry as the surrounding land. I won't survive much longer, she realized. Neither will my tree.

"No, it couldn't," he agreed. He was no longer sweating, but he should be, she thought.

The vultures hopped nearer. Slowly they were moving closer, the dryad noted. If nothing challenged them, they would continue to edge closer until they could tear at the blue dragon's flesh. The silver had raked its side, slicing open a great wound, making things easier for the carrion birds. "If you die here because your talon doesn't show up like you insist it will, won't you have stained your honor by lying to yourself?" she asked wearily.

He remained silent for a bit before answering. To the dryad, time seemed to slow down and then stretch out interminably. I'm slowly dying, she thought.

"My talon moved on ahead of me just as I was ambushed by the silver and its rider," the Knight revealed. "We fought a fierce battle in the skies, then Bolt took a bad hit from the rider's lance. After that, the silver dragon grazed my Bolt and then we both fell from the sky," he said. His voice too was not much more than a whisper now, she thought.

"So the rest of your talon flew somewhere and they expect you to catch up? How do you think they'll know where to come back and find you?"

The Knight sighed. "They know what path we took. They can guess where I fell behind. They should be coming along soon, as a matter of fact."

"Are you sure that you aren't lying to yourself?" the dryad queried in a weak voice. "And don't you stain your honor if you tell a falsehood, even to yourself?"

"I hadn't thought of that before," he admitted. "I would have to say yes." He slowly raised himself to a position where he could get a drink of water from the waterskin. When he was done, he almost dropped to the ground, wincing with pain. "And you? Are you lying to yourself when you say that this waterskin will help your tree and this forest to live?"

"Maybe not the forest. But the tree," she said, "the tree has remarkable powers. It had enough magic in it to birth me. I have no doubt that your sacrifice of water would help revive the tree. And with the tree alive and growing, perhaps others would follow—even in the face of your great dragons and their destructive magic."

The two of them remained silent, watching the vultures creep toward their feast. Just when they were about to slip out of sight and attack the dragon's gaping wound, the dryad made an effort, calling on her last reserves, and got up on her knees to yell as loudly as she could, "Heeeeyaaaah!"

The startled birds flapped their wings and scattered to a spot farther away. The Knight too was jolted and turned around to look at her. The dryad sank down and stretched out, exhausted. "Why did you do that?" the Knight asked softly.

The dryad shrugged. Even though her link to her tree had been slightly strengthened by the small doses of water, she was too weak even to speak.

"Here, have some water." The Knight held out another capful. His hand trembled worse, causing some of the water to spill onto the ground. The dryad reached out slowly and took the cap. She immediately dashed the water over her tree's roots and handed the cap back. Immediately she felt a little better. Gradually she sat up again. The Knight was looking at her, puzzled.

"Why did you scare away the vultures?" he asked again.

She shrugged. "You dislike them so."

"After your little speech on how they serve as part of a natural cycle, you decided to scare them away?" he asked. "You must have a reason." He sounded wary. "You did it just to get some water, didn't you?"

Her head hurt. The sun was high in the sky now, so the

heat was at its worst. "Since you prefer the truth, I must answer 'yes' to your question."

The Knight's face expressed doubt, so she looked beyond him and noticed the vultures starting their approach again. "Watch the vultures," she told him. "My energy is almost gone, then you will be on your own." He looked at her in concern. "Did you expect that I would out-live you, Knight? I would need a lot more water to do that," she pointed out, her voice not much more than a rasp.

"You are in better condition than me," he argued half-heartedly. "Come now, sit up and talk. It is like you say: If I go to sleep, I might not wake up, after all."

The dryad smiled slightly. "I fear that I can't talk any longer. I'm the one who must fall asleep and never wake now."

They sat in silence for a while as the Knight pondered that. The sun still beat down upon their heads. The Knight seemed to be struggling with some quandary, the dryad noted. She wilted into a position that brought her face down next to the ground. If she twisted her face and kept her eyes open, she could still watch him, though.

Finally, he turned to her. "Dryad," he called out as loud as he was able. Her eyes were shut. "Dryad? I will give you some more water!" he called out.

Too late, she thought before lapsing into unconsciousness.

Then, a little time later, she felt an infusion of strength. She lifted her head. The sky was darkening into twilight.

"Knight? How much time has passed?" she called out. She received no answer. She looked to where the Knight rested. His head was down, his arm was outstretched. His hand gripped an empty waterskin. Strangely enough, the vultures were no longer around.

She looked over to her tree and saw that it was strug-gling to revive, and succeeding somewhat. "This man died with honor," she whispered as she rose to her feet. Her tree's empathic response mixed sorrow with hope.

Songsayer
Giles Custer and Todd Fahnestock

Dayn Songsayer reined in his horse at the side of the road and took a deep breath. The road was busy, and the villagers looked at him warily as they passed. Not many friendly faces on the road these days, he thought. Dayn was determined to lend them a smile before long. Everyone was headed up the hill for the festival. Dayn had never been around these parts before, but he had heard rumors of a harvest celebration at a small temple to Paladine. The crowd appeared poor, but not as bad off as some he had seen. The people carried buckets of water or baskets of foodstuffs and blankets. They were not the type to have many spare coppers, but Dayn hoped he could make enough to spend the next few nights in an inn and possibly get some oats for the mare.

Dayn leaned over and patted his horse's neck as he stretched his own back. A groan escaped him. His horse snorted, as if to agree. She stamped her hoof and nodded her head in the direction of a shady copse of trees. It was hot. The sun was merciless. It had been so ever since the Chaos War. Would things ever go back to normal? Dayn squinted at the sky. Would it always be so hot? Were the rumors true, that the gods had forsaken Krynn yet again?

Dayn didn't want to believe the ugly tale, though many did. He'd grown up with the tales his father told of similar times long ago. The world had suffered so much when the gods were absent. No healers. Charlatans in robes walked the land, taking money from those unwise enough to believe in their gibberish about new gods. The voice of Paladine was seldom heard.

All of Krynn had almost fallen to the Dark Queen Takhisis. But whenever his father's tales were at their blackest, a shining star would always appear. Someone would always rise up with the courage and conviction to make things right again. But nowadays . . .

By the Abyss, if the heat didn't let up soon, Dayn might prefer to serve the Dark Queen. Dayn frowned and made the sign of Paladine, murmured an apology.

Anyway, the gods certainly were fickle, Dayn thought, as he jumped down from the mare and looped the reins over her head. Then again so were people.

Dayn waited for the next villager. A sandy-haired woman made her way up the dry and dusty road. Three young boys buzzed around her like hornets. They all carried empty buckets and seemed to be intent on beating each other to death with them. The woman was oblivious to it all, the calm in the middle of a storm. She was not old yet, but the years of hard work had made her tough and lean. Unlike most of the others, this woman didn't glance away. She looked him directly in the eye and nodded. Dayn would bet anything she had a sharp tongue hidden behind her cynical grin.

"Excuse me, good lady," Dayn accosted her. "I was wondering if you could tell me what all the empty buckets are for." Dayn's deep, rich voice often put people immediately at ease. He was told it had a soothing quality. It was an asset in his line of work. This woman was no different than most. She looked at the lute strapped across Dayn's back, and her expression softened a bit.

"G'day, stranger," she said. "You must be wanting something if yer callin' me a lady."

Dayn smiled. He was right about her sharp tongue. "I'm not looking for anything more than a kind word from a friendly face. I'm not from these parts. I have heard there is a festival going on, but I don't know what for."

"Aye, stranger. 'Tis in honor of Paladine." She said the word as if it left a sour taste in her mouth. "Every year after spring planting we gather at the temple for the god's blessing."

"We get to stay up all night," the oldest boy piped in.

"And build a big fire," the middle one added.

The youngest hid behind his mother's skirts. Dayn noticed the boy had his hand wrapped in a dirty bandage. The dark stains from old blood were still showing through it.

"The temple grounds are filled with berry bushes," the woman continued. "Everyone stays up the night, and at dawn we get to pick as many berries as we can eat."

"And the buckets?"

"Some fools expect to bring a bucket home, but most berries never get past their mouths."

"Indeed," Dayn said, then turned on his most charming smile. "I don't suppose you know where an honest man might sing for his supper?"

"A storyteller, are ya?" She eyed the lute. "I figured as much. No one's got much to give away around here, lad, but I imagine someone would put up a fine bowl o' stew if yer singing were as good as yer speaking."

"That's all I ask. Food for my belly and a song in my heart."

"Yer young yet, you'll soon find you need more than that to get by in this world. Come with me. I'll show you the way."

"Indeed." Dayn said, and followed his new friend up the hill.

* * * * *

The woman, Jayna by name, led Dayn into the temple grounds. The temple was small but beautiful. The white stone was flawlessly smooth and looked very old. It was built on the top of a hill with a wonderful view of the pastures and farmlands below. The temple had a small monastery for the clerics in the back. Their freshly plowed gardens were slowly being overwhelmed by the hordes of berry bushes all around.

The people had gathered around a fountain in front of the temple. There were perhaps forty families, more women than men. The Chaos War had seen to that. Everyone was chatting softly among themselves, and even the children were playing quietly. The mood was rather dark for a festival. Perhaps Dayn could do something about that.

Dayn headed for a berry bush. A little fruit seemed just the thing to cut this beastly heat. The bushes seemed to thrive in this oven. They were brimming with dark green berries. He grabbed a berry and was about to eat it, when he heard a lovely voice.

"You're not going to eat that?"

Dayn turned around and was smitten immediately. The voice came from a girl of eighteen or nineteen. She had long, raven black hair bound up in a beautiful bun, fixed with a wooden comb. A few long strands had come free, mischievously hanging in front of her deep, dark eyes. She brushed one strand away and hooked it behind her ear. She was pushing a steaming cart. Dayn could smell the soup simmering inside.

"We can't eat the berries until dawn. It's Paladine's way of reminding us that good things will come to those who wait."

"Really?" Dayn said with a smile. He carefully balanced the berry back on the leaves of the bush.

"Actually," the girl said, "it's mostly a way the clerics can keep the people from eating all the berries before they get enough for themselves."

"I understand perfectly. Is there any way you could spare a bowl of soup for a starving artist?" Dayn asked.

The young woman leaned back on her heels and crossed her arms. Her expression told Dayn that this was a small community. She knew him for a stranger; she probably knew each of the people around the temple by name. Her delicate black eyebrows raised, and her warm smile became a bit more distant.

"I give a free bowl of soup to everyone who gives me two free coppers," she said.

Dayn smiled. "I could sing for you," he offered.

The girl leaned forward and put her hands on the edge of the cart. One of those errant strands of black hair came loose and sloped along the side of her smooth chin. Dayn felt he could write a ballad on those provocative, rebellious hairs alone.

"If I gave soup for a song, I'd have everyone in town caterwauling at my cart and no money to take home to my father."

Dayn laughed. "I wasn't thinking of caterwauling at you." His voice worked its special charm. The girl leaned back from her aggressive stance and regarded him with new interest, although she was by no means convinced.

"The gods forbid I should ever be caught caterwauling," Dayn said. He unslung his lute and stroked the neck lovingly. With a sidelong glance at the girl, he said, "I suppose I may have caterwauled once or twice, but I assure you it was only late at night after too much ale."

The girl raised one eyebrow, as if to say, "You may continue."

"Perhaps we can come to an agreement. I will sing you a song, and if you think it worthy of a bowl of that fine stew I smell, then I will eat this night. If not, I shall move along and never bother you again." Dayn extended his hand.

She paused a moment longer, then spoke. "Very well, bard." She took his hand. "You seem very sure of yourself. Sing as you may."

Dayn knew that showmanship was all part of singing professionally. Many things made a successful bard, so said Dayn's father. A good voice was important. A long, solid memory was invaluable. Deft fingers were a must. Empathy for the audience could mean the difference between being the local hero or being run out of town. But timing . . . ah, Dayn's father said, it all came down to timing. Timing was a skill no bard could live without. A singer could have the most ragged whiskey-voice and the most fumbling of fingers, he could sing the most banal and boring song, but if he sang it at the right moment, the audience would cheer.

So Dayn took his time tuning his instrument. The girl, who said her name was Shani, set up her cart and stirred her soup, but so far there weren't any customers. Dayn smiled at the girl between plucks and asked about the soup business as he turned the pegs. By the time Dayn finished tuning his lute, a few villagers with nothing better to do had clustered around the cart.

"What would you like to hear, Shani?" the young bard asked.

"Something to make people hungry."

"My songs usually work better on the heart than on the belly, but I will give this one a try."

There were many songs Dayn could have chosen. It had crossed his mind to sing a wooing song of romance for young Shani. He was fairly certain she would have enjoyed that, but Dayn needed more than an audience of one if he were to make money in this town. He decided to stick with a song of spring.

Dayn began the song by simply humming. He caught Shani's eye and smiled before he turned to face the few others who had gathered. Once he was certain they were paying attention, he began strumming. His voice soon rose to meet the lute. The song told of the hard cold days of winter. Dayn's voice was quietly passionate. The few villagers grinned and looked at one another, pleased. A group of kids ran screaming past. Dayn smiled and let the uproar pass. He sang of the dark, lonely winter, and the people nodded. Life had been hard lately, leaving most of them sad and weary.

Then the song shifted. He sang of warmth spreading through the earth, thawing the stillness and bringing on a new season of life. The long cage of winter opened. The long preparation of early spring began. The birds sang and there was the promise of harvest.

Dayn prolonged the end, giving them a chance to hear the upper range of his voice. It never hurt to show off a little in the first song. The point was to get them interested enough to be hungry for more.

He ended with a little flourish on his lute. He paused, his eyes closed, feeling the music in his heart. That was it, the entire reason for being a bard. Each song brought a moment of grace, and every hard night on the road, every time he slept without dinner in his belly, every day he rode sweating in the sun, was worth that one moment. Dayn smiled his secret smile and slowly opened his eyes. His audience of four had turned into a dozen. Not a word was spoken as Dayn came slowly out of his trance. When he blinked and let the lute hang on its strap, they whistled and clapped. Some stomped their feet. One short, over-eager man even came up and thumped him on the back.

"Now that's talent, boy! You should be working that voice in Palanthas!"

Dayn smiled and nodded his thanks. He sought out Shani's face and caught her slight smile.

"You're staying for the festival, aren't you?" the man continued.

Dayn assured him he would be staying around Gotstown as long as he could afford, as it easily surpassed Palanthas in beauty. A few of those who gathered to listen bought some of Shani's soup while they praised him. They smiled and chatted before slowly drifting away to spread the news of the new bard.

When most of them had gone, Dayn turned to see a very different expression on young Shani's face. Admiration sparkled in those dark eyes. A shy smile had replaced her challenging look. She whisked one of those errant, black strands of hair away behind her ear and tipped her chin at a bowl that was already set out for him.

Dayn decided it was going to be a fine night.

* * * * *

As it always did, the afternoon brought more and more people over to the cart, begging him for another song. Dayn assured them he would sing when he was finished with his supper. He encouraged them, in the meantime, to eat some of Shani's amazing soup.

Shani's sales increased with each song request.

For his part, Dayn took a very long time nursing his soup. The price of a song grew in proportion to its demand, and Dayn was hoping to get the best price possible out of Gotstown.

As the shadows got longer, the people began lighting fires. It was nearing the point where the people's impatience would turn to annoyance, and Dayn began to tune his lute. He tried to get the old strings just right but was distracted by a commotion across the way. Dayn walked over toward the fountain just in front of the temple steps to see what was going on.

A old cleric of Paladine had latched onto two young boys. The two children were screaming and yelling. It was all the slight old man could do to hang onto them. The boys' faces were stained green. Obviously, they had begun the ceremony a little early. Dayn started to smirk but sobered immediately as he saw the grim looks in the crowd.

"Somebody help me here," the old priest said. He handed one of the boys to a farmer, but the man did not hold on tight enough and the boy ran away. The cleric turned his attention upon the other boy. Dayn recognized him as Jayna's son, the little boy with the hurt arm.

"Who is this boy's father?" the gray haired priest shouted to the crowd. "Who here hasn't taught their children proper respect?"

Jayna pushed her way through the small crowd, anger plainly written on her face. "He's my boy."

"He has committed a crime against Paladine! Against all the gods that created this world! Everyone knows the elderberries are sacred this night," the cleric said, his expression stern. The old priest turned his wrath on the scared little boy. "What do you have to say for yourself?"

The little boy cringed under the angry man's gaze. "You're hurting me."

Jayna stepped forward and grabbed the cleric by his white robes.

"Let him go, old man."

The thin, old cleric's face went white. "This is a temple of Paladine. If you can not—"

"I said let him go!"

"It is forbidden to eat the elderberries before sunrise!" the cleric reiterated.

"Look at his arm," the boy's mother practically shouted. "You're hurting him."

The priest noticed the boy's wound for the first time and let him go. The boy ran away and hid behind his mother's skirts, hugging her leg.

"I'm sorry," the priest mumbled.

"He's just a boy. He burned his hand two weeks ago, and I still can't stop the bleeding."

The old man looked truly sorry. "I apologize. I wish I could help you."

"That's right, you wish you could, but you can't, can you? At this festival you priests used to heal anyone in need. You used to help people. Now you don't do anything."

The woman's words stung the frail cleric, but he had nothing to say.

"Your god is dead!" Jayna shouted.

"No! No, he's not! He will return," the priest said.

"Just like the boy's father will return? He left years ago to fight your god's war. When will he return?"

The dead silence of the crowd became a low murmur. Other widows nodded in agreement.

"We must be patient, that is all."

"We don't need patience, we need help. How many veterans of that war are here? How many of them can't walk, can't work? What are you going to do about them?" Jayna said.

Someone yelled agreement. The cry was followed by several others, and a few men broke from the crowd to join the mother in accosting the cleric, who was backing away slowly, wide-eyed.

Dayn was only twenty-three years old, but he recognized the makings of a mob. Something had to be done, and quickly. He looked around for ideas, but nothing came. He only had one weapon, anyway, only one talent.

Snatching his lute, Dayn pushed his way through the crowd.

"People, people, good people. I know how you have suffered. I, too, lost many friends in the war. But we must keep faith."

Dayn jumped up on the fountain. The shouts quieted as people turned their attention to him.

"Paladine will return. He has done so before. The healers will return. So will the heroes. Remember the Second Cataclysm. Remember the heroes of the War of the Lance!"

Dayn glanced at the angry faces. He had their attention, but it was a tenuous hold. He had just the song. He lifted his lute and started to sing. He started with a fast-paced, rousing tune to match the temper of the crowd. He sang of Tanis's wisdom, of Caramon's strength, and of Sturm's sacrifice for all things good.

At first, it seemed to work. The crowd quieted. The shaken cleric slunk quickly away to the safety of the temple. But Dayn's illusion burst a moment later when someone threw a berry.

It hit Dayn on the forehead. It didn't hurt, but it shattered his confidence. A good performer knew when he had his crowd, and when it was slipping away. When the berry splatted against Dayn's forehead, he realized that this crowd was not his, not by a long shot. His strumming faltered. His voice dipped.

Another berry hit his tunic. A barrage of berries assailed him. Dayn winced under the assault and gasped as one struck him painfully in the eye. Shielding his face, he jumped down from the fountain and backed away from the crowd.

"Take yer songs elsewhere, bard!" a huge red-faced man yelled. "We don't want to hear about your old heroes!"

"We're sick of the old heroes! Where are they now when we need 'em?" another man joined in. "What are they going to do for us?"

"Ain't no heroes anymore!" A woman added her shrill voice to the throng.

"Never were heroes in the first place!"

Frightened, Dayn searched for a friendly face. Shani was there, but she was caught up with the crowd, shouting and laughing. He offered a silent prayer to Paladine as he stumbled backward. Never before had a crowd turned on him so badly. The berries didn't really hurt. But each small pelting was like a hammer to his heart. He had failed to reach them.

"Wait!" he said, but they weren't listening. They gathered closer around him. In a moment, he would be surrounded. What then? Would the berries turn into a stoning?

Dayn backed into someone. A strong hand grabbed his arm. Too late!

"No!" Dayn shouted, as he turned to see his attacker.

The man was well over six feet tall. His broad shoulders were draped in chain mail shirt and shoulder plates. A thick mass of wavy brown hair framed a sturdy, square jaw and penetrating brown eyes. The man smiled gently as Dayn tried to recover his wits. It was the kind of smile that instilled confidence, that could send young soldiers charging into battle. Dayn's terror fled in an instant under the spell of that smile.

"Easy lad." The man said, pulling Dayn quickly away from the crowd toward Dayn's mare. The barrage of berries followed them. "You've got 'em riled up. Things could get ugly."

Dayn agreed completely. They rushed to their horses. The stranger mounted a tall black stallion as Dayn leaped astride his mare. They kicked their heels into the horses' flanks and raced away.

* * * * *

They rode hard for a good half an hour before the strapping stranger chose to slow the pace. "We should be safe enough now." He turned in his saddle to face Dayn and grinned. "Your sense of timing could use some work, son. I would think you'd know better than to jump into the middle of an angry mob!"

"But they were going to hurt that priest!" Dayn countered.

The man's eyes narrowed. He paused a moment, then spoke, "Indeed, lad. It was brave, what you did. Brave, but stupid. No one belongs in a battle they can't win. I don't want to see a bard fight any more than I want to hear a soldier sing."

Dayn thought about that for a moment. He grudgingly had to agree that the stranger was right. "Anyway," Dayn said, "I want to thank you for helping me back there."

"Comes with the job," the stranger said.

"What job?"

"You think the only heroes are in your songs?"

"You're a hero?" Dayn wasn't sure about a man who called himself a hero, like he was talking about being a miller or a smith.

"I try to help those in need, lad. It's tough to match up to those songs of yours, but I do what I can."

Dayn looked up into the man's broad smiling face. He felt bad for doubting the man.

"You certainly saved my skin. Did you fight in the Chaos War?"

"Indeed," the man said. His voice was deep and steady. "Kresean Myrk Saxus at your service, lad." Kresean extended his hand, and Dayn leaned over and took it. The man had an iron grip. "I know more than I care to about that war."

"Dayn Songsayer. I'm pleased to meet you."

"It's a shame what happened back there, lad. I really liked your singing."

"Thanks." Dayn felt embarrassed by the praise. The big man's words felt better than he expected.

"Your voice is grand. Your problem is the song you were singing."

"My song?"

"You saw how those folks reacted to heroes from a past age. Maybe if they could hear about a hero from this day and age it might lighten their lives a great deal more."

The second Dayn heard Kresean's words his mind began to see the possibilities. Kresean was right. People didn't need long-dead heroes from a half-forgotten war. They needed today's heroes, someone they could see and touch.

"Of course!" Dayn exclaimed. "There must have been countless displays of valor during the Chaos War. What stories can you tell me?"

The huge man chuckled.

"Stick to me, lad. I'll do you one better." Kresean winked.

"How is that?"

"You want to write a true ballad of a hero?"

"Yes." Dayn's eyes sparkled with interest.

"The kind of ballad that pulls at the heart? The kind that everyone in this village will thank you for singing, will cry at the outcome?"

"Yes!" Dayn nodded. "That's exactly what I want to do."

"Then you've got to live it," Kresean said with finality.

Dayn's brow wrinkled. "Live it? What do you mean? The Chaos War is over, and—"

"Forget the Chaos War, lad. We got our faces kicked in on that one. Everybody knows it. It's a losing proposition to dredge up memories of that loss, and it's a fool's errand to try and make people believe we won."

"We did win. If we hadn't driven back the Chaos hordes, we'd all be dead."

"Ah," Kresean said, "there's a difference between winning and surviving. Look around you. Do people in this land look like they're reveling in the spoils of a war well won? No! These are people who were beat up and left for dead! Don't remind them. Give them something—someone—new to believe in. Piece by piece, we can build things back up."

Dayn nodded as Kresean talked. The bard was mesmerized by the deep voice, by the earnestness in Kresean's dark eyes. Dayn began to see things in an entirely new light. "How? All by ourselves?" he asked.

"Of course. When better to start? Who better to accomplish it?"

Dayn's eyes looked past Kresean, into a world of snapping pennants and trumpeting horns. He saw Kresean at the head of a great army, sun sparkling off the perfectly polished armor of legions of Knights, a sea of people standing on either side of the procession, clapping. Later that night, in the great hall, he saw himself singing a song of bravery, self-sacrifice, and victory as the Knights looked on. At the end, everyone assembled would be stomping their feet and yelling.

Kresean clapped Dayn on the shoulder, jolting him from his reverie.

"I'll do it!" Dayn said.

"That's a good lad. If I'd had a dozen men as stouthearted as you, I could've brought the Knights of Takhisis to heel at the High Clerist's Tower."

"You were at the battle for the High Clerist's Tower?"

"Indeed." Kresean nodded.

Dayn reached for his satchel, in which he kept all his writing materials. "You must let me get everything down on—"

"Lad." Kresean put a hand on Dayn's shoulder. "How many times do I have to tell you? If you want to write songs about defeat, go to Palanthas. I hear there are types there that love to hear such things all day long. Tragedies, they call them. But not in the countryside. Not here."

"Right." Dayn nodded. "Of course. So what do we do next, then?"

"Next?" Kresean said, and that infectious smile curved his lips. "Next we kill ourselves a dragon."

* * * * *

The morning was quiet. Only the sound of the horses' hooves on the road accompanied Dayn and Kresean westward. Dayn remembered when the birds would sing at this time just before sunrise. No more. Perhaps it was too hot for them to bother.

Dayn had been up most of the night listening to Kresean's stories of the Chaos War. His friend was not a Knight, merely a man-at-arms, but he had risen quickly through the ranks as those ranks had died around him. The bloodiest battle, so said Kresean, was the battle for the High Clerist's Tower against the Knights of Takhisis, but that was nothing compared to the terror of the Chaos army. Those abominations could kill a man without shedding a single drop of his blood. Some howling horrors could suck the wind from a man's lungs, make him die from suffocation. Others, inky black, could pass over an entire troop of soldiers and swallow them whole. The shadow creatures covered them and they disappeared. No screams. No remains. Nothing.

"What did you do? How did you survive?" Dayn had asked, thunderstruck by the terrifying nature of the Chaos hordes.

Kresean shrugged. "I fought and fought. Those that could not be harmed by weapons, we left to the mages. Those that could bleed, we attacked. I owe a lot to the men around me. They saved my life more than once. I wanted to do the same for them, but there is only so much one man can do. Most of us who made it to the end were just plain lucky. I barely remember the point at which I looked up and noticed that no one else was fighting. No Chaos fiends, no friendly faces. It was only later I heard that the leader of the Chaos hordes had been killed, and that was why the rest lost heart. Otherwise, I believe we would all have died. You simply cannot imagine—"

"Even faced with that, you still fought on," Dayn whispered, more to himself than to Kresean. But Kresean heard him.

"What else could I do? My friends all died fighting. I was just waiting for my turn, but my turn never came," Kresean said. He shook his head, as if warding off a bad dream. "That's why I want to help these folks with the dragon. Somehow my life was spared. I ought to do something worthwhile with it."

Now they were heading to a small town called Feergu, so small that Dayne had never heard of it. It was up in the mountains, and Kresean had got word of a young dragon in the vicinity killing off livestock. Then, a week ago, a young child had turned up missing.

"How are you going to kill the dragon?" Dayn asked his newfound friend as they rode along. "Won't you need a dragonlance or something?"

"Aye, I wish I had one. If it was full grown, there would be no hope without one, but if it is young, I should be able to take it."

"You're really going to fight a dragon?"

"That's right, lad, and you're going to write about it." Kresean twisted in his saddle, winked at Dayn.

"That's beautiful."

"Do you think that'll be something others would want to hear?" Kresean asked, smiling. "Do you think that will raise their spirits?"

"Definitely." Dayn felt he would explode from excitement. Kresean was right. This was the only way to write a ballad. Dayn would walk side by side with Kresean. Dayn would be there when the blood was spilled, when the danger ran high, when the victory was gained.

For the rest of the day, Kresean recounted tales from the Chaos War. By that night Dayn's admiration for Kresean had grown a hundredfold.

* * * * *

Two days later Dayn and Kresean rode over the crest of a hill and looked down at their destination. Feergu was a misty little hamlet nestled in a valley. Behind the town, the mountains rose tall, disappearing into the ever-present fog. Dayn felt trapped, hemmed in by those rocky giants. He wondered why the villagers had decided to settle here in the first place.

The town was a small place by the side of a swiftly flowing mountain river. It didn't even have a central square. There was just a smattering of stone and wood houses.

"Let me do the talking," Kresean said. "I've already spoken to the man they sent out looking for help. His name's Chandael. He was the first to tell me about the reward."

"Reward?" Dayn's brows furrowed. "What reward?"

"They've promised a reward to whoever kills the dragon," Kresean said.

"You didn't tell me we came to collect a reward."

Kresean clapped a hand on Dayn's back. "You're a crusader, all right, lad. Look at it this way. I know how much you love to sing. You'd do it for free, wouldn't you?"

"Yes."

"You don't, do you?"

"No," the bard had to admit.

"You don't have to feel like a thief, just because you earn your living. These people want to give us something. It's rude to turn it down. If you did someone a favor and they wanted you to stay for dinner, you would-n't refuse just because you'd have done it for free, would you? No. You accept their hospitality. Besides, we've got expenses to pay for. A little reward never hurts."

"Well, I guess. I just thought—"

"There are practical sides to everything, lad," Kresean said. "If I make a name for myself, someday I'd like to get a job as a captain of the watch or a councilman in a small city. I like to help people out, but I've got to take care of myself as well."

Dayn relaxed. "You're right. Of course. Sorry." He fiddled with his reins.

"Think nothing of it, lad. Your heart's in the right place. No mistake about that. That's all that really matters."

The two riders were noticed quickly as they road into the tiny town. The first few people they saw were quick to duck back into their houses, but soon the bolder citizens stood watching them from doorways. The glum-faced citizens watched the two men as they rode along the main trail that meandered through the cluster of houses.

"Excuse me!" a man shouted from a distance. "What's your business here?"

Kresean turned in his saddle to face the middle-aged villager who spoke to them.

"Good, sir." Kresean delivered one of his magnanimous smiles and gracefully slid from his horse. "I spoke with a friend of yours, Chandael. He said you are in need of a swordsman."

A short, nervous smile grew on the big man's face. "You've come to help then?"

"Aye, that I have."

The man sighed in relief. Soon twenty people gathered around, patting Kresean on the back and shaking his hand.

"Chandael's still gone looking for help," the big man said. "We didn't know if he had found anyone."

"Well, he found me. Sir Kresean Myrk Saxus at your service."

Dayn blinked. Sir Kresean? He wasn't a Knight.

Kresean's smile faded into a serious look. "The dragon—has anyone seen it again?"

"No, sir," the man admitted. "No one has seen it yet, but we've followed its tracks, and the way it takes apart a sheep is a terrible thing to see."

The villagers nodded their heads.

"We've gone out looking for it but only in large groups. It hasn't shown its face. We thought one man might succeed where many would fail. I would try it myself, of course, but I haven't even got a sword."

"Of course," Kresean said, careful not to hurt the man's feelings. "No one expects you to slay a dragon anymore than you'd expect a soldier to know how to plant a field."

The man nodded and seemed to feel better.

"More animals were lost again this week. Soon we shall all be forced to seek our livelihoods elsewhere. Our poor village barely has enough trade to survive as it is.

And with poor Kindy's loss . . . We fear more for the safety of our children with every day that passes." The man's gaze drifted to the ground.

"Do you think you can help us?" A woman broke from the throng and headed for Kresean. He turned to her and took her hand in his.

"What is your name, good woman?" he asked.

"Cessa. I have two daughters. I'm afraid to send them to herd the sheep. Yet if no one is there to watch them, we might lose the entire flock."

Kresean patted her hand. "Cessa, tomorrow at first light my comrade and I will find this rascal and liberate him of his head. I shall bring it back as proof, and you can do with it as you see fit."

A flicker of a smile crossed the woman's face, and a murmur went through the crowd.

"Thank you, kind sir. Thank you. The gods must have sent you."

* * * * *

They were given a room that night in Chandael's loft, which doubled as an inn for what travelers managed to find themselves in Feergu. Dayn couldn't sleep, but Kresean's light snores assured him that everything was going to be all right. He meant to ask the warrior about calling himself a Knight. Probably that was another practical necessity. The man was everything Dayn could've asked for in a hero. The bard finally drifted off to sleep, dreaming of shining armies and huge banquet halls in which to sing his ballad.

The next day Dayn and Kresean bade goodby to the villagers and rode west toward the dragon's lair. Heavy mist rode alongside them. Moisture clung to Dayn's skin like wet fingers. The mountain's bulk was a palpable presence before them. Everything seemed unreal to Dayn.

At the beginning of the ride, Kresean had been strangely pensive. If ever there was a time to talk of past war stories or to delineate a plan to fight the dragon, now was that time, but as they left the town, Kresean said nothing.

He's mentally preparing himself, Dayn thought. Best to leave him alone.

The entire ride passed in silence. Finally they came to the river ford where the people had lost the beast's tracks. Farther upstream the valley narrowed into a steep canyon with many caves along the water's edge, where the people suspected the dragon kept its lair.

"If this is the ford, then we're almost there." Dayn smiled at his companion. Kresean grinned back.

"We'll have this rascal's head stuffed in a sack before lunch."

The two crossed the river and crept up the rocky hill on the far side. The ground sloped down gently until it neared the water and dropped off into a sheer cliff. Dayn started to walk along the edge of the cliff. Below was a series of caves. There were half a dozen small openings, their mouths near the water. Among the rocks below, Dayn spotted some scattered bones. The remains were covered with tufts of bloody wool.

"Ah ha!" Kresean whispered and pulled back from the edge. Dayn did the same.

"Looks like this is it, lad."

"We found his lair," Dayn whispered excitedly. He could barely contain his excitement. "Do you think it's in there?"

Kresean nodded. "I do. Let's think a moment."

"Yes," Dayn said. "So, do we go in after it right away? Or lure it out?"

"Easy, lad. Not so fast. We wait."

"Wait?"

"Best to be prudent to start. Let's see the size of the thing first, then we can make our plan."

"Oh," Dayn said. "Okay."

They settled in to watch the cave's opening.

When half the day had passed, Dayn thought he was going to die of boredom. He had long ago given up lying next to Kresean and staring at the cave. Instead, he paced back and forth. A short while after Dayn had become bored, so had Kresean. Instead of keeping vigil on the cave, he had unpocketed some game stones and was tossing them in a patch of dirt he had smoothed. He seemed completely unconcerned. He'd invited Dayn to join a few times, but the bard wanted to get on with the adventure. This wasn't what Dayn had in mind when he thought of dragon hunting. Shouldn't the whole process move a little faster? Perhaps he was being impractical again. Certainly Kresean knew what he was doing. Still . . .

Dayn didn't want to follow that thought, but happily he was interrupted by Kresean.

"It's finally moving," the warrior said calmly. Dayn turned around and could hear the scraping sound. Kresean pocketed his stones and moved quietly over to the edge of the cliff.

Dayn flopped on his belly and stared down at the empty cave mouth. At first, he didn't see anything, but soon he heard a scraping below. It was coming closer.

"What now?" Dayn whispered tensely. "Do we ambush it? Don't you need to be closer? Are you going to stab it as soon as it comes out?"

"Just wait, lad."

Clamping down on his excitement, Dayn waited. He envisioned the beast bursting from its lair, unfurling its wings, and leaping for the sky. A reptilian battle cry would wail forth. Excess moisture would spray from its wing tips like deadly diamonds. It would turn its burning eyes upon the pair of heroes on the top of the cliff and—

The dreaded dragon lumbered out of the cave.

Dayn's excitement melted like a chunk of butter thrown on a fire. He let out his pent-up breath.

"That's the dragon?" he exclaimed.

Kresean was smiling. "Dragon enough for me, lad."

Dayn whipped his head about. "What?" He looked back down at the creature. He wasn't an expert on dragons, to be sure. He would be the first to admit it. However, he had heard tales of the fearsome beasts. He knew about dragonfear scattering entire armies. He knew that dragon fire could destroy a stone tower with one blast, that dragon lightning could blow the tops off of mountains. One shriek from a dragon could freeze a person's blood. Dragons were filled with magical might and fierce intelligence. Dragons were green, black, red, blue, copper, and gold and so on. This one was the color of mud.

It was no bigger than his mare. It looked like nothing more than a lizard—a very big lizard, true, but a lizard nonetheless. Whatever that thing was, it was not a dragon.

The reptile was moving with the lethargy of a cow. It was close to seven feet long, counting the tail, but never a dragon!

"Are you kidding?" Dayn asked.

"No," Kresean replied.

"But that's not a dragon!"

"It is to them, lad. That's all that matters. We're here to take care of *their* dragon. That's their dragon. Let's take care of it."

Dayn sighed and crouched next to the ledge. He looked disconsolately down at the giant lizard. How was he going to make a ballad out of this? Why hadn't some villager come and poked a spear into that hapless thing long before?

Dayn cleared his throat, lightly. "Well, go lop its head off, and let's get back."

"Not so fast. I've got a special plan."

Dayn looked at him. "You need a plan?"

"Always have a plan," Kresean said. "C'mon."

Dayn watched as the warrior backed slowly away from the ledge, then rose and started down the hill. It took a moment for Dayn to gather his wits, then he took off after Kresean.

"What are you going to do?" Dayn asked as he drew up alongside, matching strides with the taller man.

"A little something I prepared," Kresean said as they reached the horses.

"How could you prepare something?"

"I scouted out this job out ahead of time."

"I thought this was your first trip to Feergu!"

"It is, lad, it is. I'd never been to the village before, just to these caves after I heard about the commotion. Do you think I would have risked our lives coming out here for a *real* dragon? Be serious." He unstrapped the flap on one of his saddlebags, removed a large bundle, and set it on the ground. It was a young pig Kresean must have bought in the town. It had been cleaned and dressed and was ready for the spit.

"But I thought . . ." Dayn said. "Why not just go poke your sword into the damn thing?"

Kresean handed Dayn the pig and smiled. "I don't relish the thought of being bitten."

"What? You faced worst horrors in the Chaos War."

Kresean drew his sword and presented it hilt first to Dayn. "If you're in such a hurry, why don't you kill it?"

Dayn gazed at the thing over the belly of the dead pig. "I've never used a sword in my life!"

"Well I have, and I assure you that my method is much safer. Brains over brawn, lad. That's my motto. Now, here's what I need you to do . . ."

* * * * *

Half an hour later, Dayn and Kresean climbed the hill again. Dayn frowned the entire way. Kresean carried the pig, which was now stuffed with poisonous Frissa leaves.

They regained their perch and the huge lizard was still there, nibbling at the last remains of one of the sheep carcasses. Kresean wasted no time. He pitched the pig over the ledge. It landed with a thud a few feet from the reptile. The lizard whipped about and hissed. When the pig did not respond, the lizard hissed again, still oblivious to Kresean and Dayn. Slowly, the creature lumbered over. It prodded the thing with its nose a few times and touched it all over with the tip of its forked tongue. Finally, it began feasting.

The lizard devoured the pig, and the two men settled in to wait again. Dayn was miserable. An hour passed, and the lizard began retching. It vomited for an hour, then it wheezed for an hour. Finally, it flopped onto its stomach and lay there, breathing laboriously.

Dayn had his hands wrapped around his shins, his head on his knees. He looked at Kresean. "Now what?"

"Merely the end of phase one, lad."

Dayn growled to himself.

"Come help me with this." Kresean moved over to a boulder that sat near the cliff. He began pushing it toward the edge. With a sigh, Dayn went to help him.

Straining and grunting, the two of them pushed the boulder over the edge. The huge rock missed the lizard, but it started a mini landslide. Dozens of stones rained down on the beast, bouncing off its back and legs. The poor creature, lacking the strength to crawl away, was clobbered.

Dayn look at Kresean expectantly, but the warrior shook his head.

"Just a few more," he said, and headed for another stone.

With a series of three more minor landslides, they managed to completely bury the hapless creature. Kresean climbed down a more gradual part of the cliff and made his approach. Dayn watched as the warrior walked gingerly on top of the pile of rocks and stuck his sword into it. After a few tries, he hit something. He smiled and pushed harder. Kresean stabbed the spot repeatedly until the dirt flowed red. He raised his sword triumphantly and winked at Dayn.

"How's that for a tidy bit of dragon slaying?"

Dayn said nothing.

"Come on, lad. Help me dig this up, and we'll get the head."

* * * * *

"That certainly was a harrowing experience, wasn't it, lad?" Kresean winked, patting the dusty, battered lizard's head that rested on the rump of his horse. The left half of the head had been caved in by the landslides.

Dayn said nothing.

"So, have you given any thought to how you're going to compose our epic ballad?" Kresean asked. "I've got some titles I've been playing around with, if you want to hear. I was thinking maybe *Kresean and the Cave of Doom*. Or maybe *Flashing Swords and Dragon's Teeth*. How about—"

"How about *Cowardly Kresean and the Poisoned Piglet!*" Dayn yelled at the warrior. "How about *He Won by a Landslide!* You're a fraud! You lied to me!"

"I never lied to you," Kresean said, holding up his hand. "You're a bard. You have an active imagination. That's good. That's fine. That's what you're supposed to have. That's what will make the ballad something to cheer for. I came here to help these villagers, and I have. They were afraid of that dragon. The dragon's dead now. We did what they asked us to do."

"Stop calling it a dragon. It's not a real dragon! You told me we were going to fight a dragon!"

"You can make it as big as you want in your ballad, the bigger, the better. Don't go diminishing people's fears. They'll hate you for it. I thought you wanted to bring light into people's lives. You don't make people feel better by calling them cowards."

"I bet you weren't even in the Chaos War," Dayn said.

"Yes, I was!"

Kresean whirled his horse around and grabbed Dayn by the shirtfront.

"Don't you judge me! You have no idea what it was like. No idea what we went through! You would have run, too. Do you know what it's like to hold your best friend in your arms as the life seeps out of him? Have you ever seen a dozen of your comrades cut down all at once? Blood flying through the air? No! You've never even handled a sword! Don't propose to tell *me* how to be a hero!"

Dayn was shocked. He'd never seen this side of the man before. He looked at his horse's mane. "You're right. I haven't seen those things."

"We each have our specialty, Dayn," Kresean said, gentle again. "Yours is singing. Use it for something good. People need something to believe in."

"But—"

"After all, their dragon is dead—"

Dayn shot him a sharp look.

Kresean chuckled. "Okay, I mean the big lizard is dead. I'm just asking you to embellish the deed a little, for their sake and ours. Let them think they were saved by a hero. It's better that way for everybody."

Dayn frowned, and said nothing else on the ride back. He thought about what Kresean said. He had to admit that the warrior had a point. Songwriting was about embellishing. It was about delivering the most magical moments from real life to those who had very little magic in their own lives. Perhaps real life never matched up to the tales of bravery found in songs and stories.

* * * * *

As his voice slowly lowered on the last word of his new ballad, Dayn looked around at the villagers of Feergu. They were packed into every possible space in Chandael's tavern, and each person's face glowed. Dayn had sung his song masterfully, with just enough detail to make it realistic. There wasn't a dry eye in the entire tavern. After Dayn stopped, there was a long, reverent pause. Applause exploded in the room. The entire floor shook with stomping feet. A few people got up, hooked arms and began dancing in circles. More beer was called for.

Kresean rose from where he sat and came over to Dayn. "How do you feel, my lad?"

Dayn was surprised to hear himself say, "Not bad. Not bad at all."

Kresean tossed a bag of coins on the table in front of Dayn. "Fifty-fifty."

"A little reward never hurts," Dayn grinned, pocketing the coins.

The big man clapped him on the shoulder.

"I say we keep this up. Take it on the road, town to town. Your voice, my looks. There's no telling where it will end. We could milk this partnership until we're swimming in cream, until I'm a councilman in Palanthas and you're singing for a king. Until—"

"Until a real dragon comes along?" Dayn offered.

"What?" Kresean raised an eyebrow warily, then realized Dayne was kidding. Kresean bellowed with laughter, and the young bard joined in. The celebrating villagers surrounded them with cheers, and they laughed until the tears ran down their faces.

Gnomebody
Jeff Grubb

"This is a gnome story, right?" asked Augie, staring over the rim of his tankard. There was derision in both his glare and his voice—they had traded a number of tales that evening, each more implausible than the last.

"Not exactly," replied Brack, the older and more slender of the two sellswords.

The pair had met by chance in the tavern. They were veterans of separate units from the same side in the War of the Lance, now reduced to mere mercenary work in these years of chaos. As a youth, Augie had served in the personal guard of Verminaard himself, and Brack had been a lieutenant in the Green Dragonarmy. Now older, and presumably wiser, they chose their battles and their employers more carefully.

After a few moments of sizing each other up and determining that they had both fought for the same masters at one time, they slid into an easy conversation. They spoke of what regions would need their services, which wars and rumors of war would pan out, and the chaos they'd seen brought on the backs of the great dragons. The gnome wait staff brought the drinks quickly, and the dwarf at the bar kept a running tab.

Of course, over time, the conversation drifted to how the world in general had gone into the midden and that nothing was as good as it once was. This line of discussion quickly gave way (after a few more tankards) to stories of how things were in the old days.

Which of course brought Brack to mention of his last battle in the Green Dragonarmy, a disaster brought about in the pursuit of one man—or, to be more specific, one gnome and that gnome's invention.

Which brought Augie's question and Brack's answer and Augie's reply, "Whadayah mean, not exactly?"

Brack shifted in his chair, noted that his mug was more half-empty than half-full, and signaled to the serving gnome. He paused as the diminutive being brought him a full, foaming tankard, then continued, "I mean yes, it's a gnome story, in that it's about a gnome, but no, it's not a gnome story because it's not about a gnome at all."

The big man's bushy brows hovered over bleary eyes stained by many a drink that evening. "How can it be about a gnome and not about a gnome?"

"When the gnome does not exist," said Brack, "but his greatest invention survives to this day. Let me explain."

* * * * *

The patrol of hobgoblins, scouts in the service of the Green Dragonarmy, were having a bad time of it. Scouts were at their best in clear terrain and moderate climate, but ever since their invasion force had landed, they had been deluged by heavy rain and forced to reconnoiter through thick, bramble-filled overgrowth. Little to see, less to smell (other than wet hobgoblin), and nothing to report. They had been gone four days from the main encampment and were soaked to the skin. After a brief, heated discussion (the only heat the dozen creatures had experienced in three days), they decided to ascend one of the hills for a better view of the rain-damp fog.

"We shudda stayed in camp," said one particularly large hobgoblin.

"And what?" growled another. "It's just as marshy there. There's a swamp where our bivvie should be."

"At least then we don't hafta march around in wet boots," said the big one.

"At least yah have boots," returned the sergeant, a scarred hobgoblin with one good eye. "When I first signs up, we had to do this barefoot."

The big complainer bared his lower fangs, and the other hobgoblins assumed that a fight was coming and drifted into normal positions, a circle surrounding the sergeant and the big one. But the sergeant stared at the hobgoblin with an icy ferocity, and the big one closed his mouth and at last shook his head in agreement.

"Where we go?" said the big one, finally.

"Up," replied the sergeant.

The ground grew no drier as they climbed the small tor. Indeed, it now had the added difficulty of being steep as well as damp. The hill was completely saturated, and the hobgoblins began to slip as they climbed. Their trail became a broad swath of mud-stained grass, and their armor was soon decorated with clumps of hanging sod.

"Where we going?" asked the big one again.

"Up," said the sergeant.

"Down is easier," said one of the smaller hobgoblins, which earned another icy glare from the one-eyed sergeant.

The fog-shrouded hilltop loomed above them, and a great granite cliff suddenly reared from the tor, blocking their path. "Up," said the sergeant a third time, pointing at the small complainer.

"It's wet and slippery," protested the small hobgoblin.

"Stone is harder than mud," said the sergeant. "Therefore it's less slippery than mud." The other hobgoblins in the group looked around for anyone to gainsay this bit of wisdom. There was no one.

The small hobgoblin was soon scrabbling up the granite cliff, a rope tied around his waist. He started strong, but tired halfway up, and the sergeant had to bellow threats to get him to finish the climb. The sergeant made it clear it was safer to climb up than to climb down, so up the small hobgoblin went.

He disappeared at the cliff's edge and was gone, finding some tree or rock to secure the line. A moment later he appeared over the edge again and gave a thumbs-up to the patrol below.

The sergeant hooked a thumb at the rope. "Up you go," he said.

The big complainer looked at the thin strand of hemp. "Don't look safe," he said. He looked more afraid than challenging.

"Neither am I," snapped the sergeant, but the big complainer still stared at the rope. The sergeant sighed, "I go first, but when I get to the top, you follow, unnerstand?"

The big one (and most of the others) nodded in agreement as the sergeant began the climb. He found the stone was more slippery than the mud after all, and he had to clutch the rope tightly in order to keep from falling. At last he arrived at the top. The view was less than spectacular. There was slightly less rain up this high, but the hilltop was still wrapped in clouds. The surrounding whiteness parted slightly, allowing a brief glimpse of the neighboring hills before wrapping the hobgoblins in another gray, wool blanket.

They were on a gray promontory of bare rock, broken only by a single twisted tree, its thick and ancient roots shattering the surrounding stone. The small hobgoblin had tied the rope to one of the more prominent, arching roots.

"Not much to see," said the small hobgoblin. "We go down now?"

The sergeant scowled. He'd had to scrabble up here. He'd be damned if the rest of the patrol got off scot-free. Instead he leaned over the edge and let out an assault of obscenities, promising all manner of torture for the last hobgoblin up.

The rest of the patrol sprang into action, fighting among themselves for the opportunity to clamber up the rope. The big one, the complainer, was the first up the rope, but the others followed closely, not waiting for him to get more than a quarter of the way up before following. Soon most of the patrol was hanging on the rope up the cliffside, their twisted paws clutching the rope and the surrounding rocks. Some lost their grips and slid down, bashing into others, who in turn lost their hold and slid a few feet into the rest of the patrol.

The sergeant watched their attempts and muttered a curse, thinking of the (relative) warmth and the (relative) dryness of their base camp. His ruminations were broken off by a sharp snapping noise directly behind him.

It sounded like the noise a crossbow made when sprung. He wheeled but saw nothing else on the tor except the small hobgoblin and the gnarl-rooted tree. The small hobgoblin was looking at the tree, his eyes round like platters.

The sergeant scowled. Was the tree breaking under the weight of the hobgoblins on the rope? There was another sharp snap, and he realized he was close but not fully on the mark. The tree was holding. However, the added weight of the patrol on the rope was enough to start uprooting it. Large cracks began to spider through the stone as the hobgoblins' collective weight drove the tree's roots deeper into the hilltop.

It threatened to bring the cliff down on top of the hobgoblin patrol. A human leader might have called down to his men to tell them to abandon the rope or even to jump. The sergeant was a hobgoblin, and his first worry was his own skin. Already the smaller hobgoblin was bounding for the far side of the tree, and the sergeant was ready to follow.

The ground shifted as the sergeant began to run, the spidering cracks quickly becoming large chasms, and then larger chasms, and the ground beneath his feet started to disintegrate beneath the soles of his feet. He heard cursing screams below him from the patrol, soon lost in a torrent of sliding rock. Then something large passed him—the ancient tree itself, still tethered to the hobgoblin-strung rope.

The sergeant leapt forward as the last part of the cliffside vaporized beneath him, dragged down by the trailing roots of the tree. He landed on something solid and dug his claws into the earth in hopes that it would hold and not cascade back down the cliffside.

His prayers were answered. He felt the world sway for a moment, then right itself, while the rest of the hillside, except the tree, held firm.

Slowly the sergeant opened his eyes. The avalanche had pushed the rainy clouds back for the moment, and he had a clear view of the devastation below. The entire north half of the hill had fallen in on itself, forming a wide fan as it gained speed as it surged into the valley. He saw a few bits of armor and what might either be tree trunks or goblin torsos, but the patrol, big complainer and all, was gone.

The small hobgoblin sat down beside the sergeant. "Cor, whatta mess!" he breathed.

The sergeant considered for a moment adding the small hobgoblin to the body count, but decided against it. He shook his head.

"Bloody mess," was all he said.

The small hobgoblin nodded, and said, "Whaddaya gonna tell the Louey?"

The sergeant winced. The commanding lieutenant was *not* going to like his report. "Lemme think," he managed. "Lemme think."

The small hobgoblin shook his head and said, "Looks like a battle. Whatta mess."

The sergeant stroked his chin, then said, "Yeah, a battle. We got ambushed."

"Won't work," said the small hobgoblin. "No other bodies. You gonna tell them our boys got smoked without taking any enemies with 'em?"

The sergeant stroked his chin, then said, "Dragons. We got attacked by dragons?"

"We got dragons," said the small one. "They don't."

"Right." The sergeant scowled again. "Gnomes, then. Gnomes are always blowing things up! Yeah, dat's it! We got caught by some gnomish secret weapon!"

The smaller hobgoblin rocked back on his heels. "Dat's it! Who would ever want to go looking for a gnome?"

* * * * *

Augie took a long pull on his tankard and wiped the ale from his beard. "So this is really a hobgoblin story?" he said.

Brack drained the last of his own drink, and another appeared almost instantaneously by his side. "I like to think it was a gnome story, since the hobgoblins blamed their misfortunes on the gnomes."

"I take it you were the Louey they reported back to?"

Brack gave a shrug and said, "Of course. And of course since their story had more holes in it than Soth's soul, the Dark Lady blast him, I soon coerced the truth of the matter out of them."

"So that was the end of it, right?" said Augie.

"Not by half," replied Brack. "You see, I still had to report to *my* superiors what had happened, and I had to admit to them that the hobgoblins under my command— hobgoblins they recruited—were below average, even as hobgoblins go."

"Hmph," said Augie, draining his own mug, holding it out at arm's length to the side, then letting it go. Brack noted that a very fast gnome grabbed the heavy clay tankard before it had shattered and smoothly placed a new one, dripping foam, on the table.

"So you might have lost your command if you told them they had incompetent hobgoblins," said the larger man.

"Worse," said Brack, "I might have been forced to accompany them into the field the next time."

"You let the report stand," said Augie.

"With some minor clarifications," said Brack. "I made it one gnome leader, in particular, made it an accident as opposed to an ambush, and named the gnome. Rumtuggle. It sounded like a gnomish name."

"Your leaders bought it?" snarled Augie. "Old Verminaard would have seen through that in a moment if I laid it on him."

"Ah, but old Verminaard is no longer around, is he?" countered Brack. "No, my superiors bought it, because they assumed there would be some resistance anyway, which up to that point had been pretty nonexistent. Gnomes were considered the least dangerous of the lot. Kender, for example, would rob you blind and then come back for your seeing-eye lizard."

"So you used this Rumtuggle to explain a patrol's decimation," said Augie. "What's the problem?"

"Well, the saying is that once something is created, it has to be used. You make a plow, you have to farm. You make a sail, you have to explore."

"You make a sword," put in Augie, "you have to lop off a few heads."

"Exactly," said Brack, "and Rumtuggle proved to be a very capable excuse. A few head of cattle went missing and were blamed on Rumtuggle. A patrol got lost: Rumtuggle. The cash box was a few hundred steel light: Rumtuggle."

"Your superiors never saw through it?" spat Augie, astounded.

"The rear echelons had other, more important matters to worry about," said Brack. "I was careful never to put too much blame on Rumtuggle at a time. One or two of my fellow lieutenants caught wind of it, and a captain as well, eventually. They saw the value of Rumtuggle, and soon most of the mischances of our unit were blamed on a single gnome."

"Your superiors, the dragonlords themselves, must have caught wise at last," guessed Augie. "Did you admit your deceit?"

"I wish it were that easy," said Brack. "Actually it was much, much worse."

* * * * *

The gnomish delegation arrived at dawn. There were fifteen of them, all looking about as threatening as a pack of rabbits. Some were dressed in leather work-aprons, and others in farmer's shirts and slacks. One or two looked as if they had been rousted from their beds and dragged along by the mob.

They were led by a short gnomish woman with fire-red hair braided down her back and a stern look plastered across her face. The gnomes presented themselves to one of the guards by the outer paddocks, demanding to see someone in charge.

In another part of Ansalon, a band of gnomes suddenly appearing at an oupost would be cause for alarm, but this part of the front had been pacified, and this outpost was little more than a garrison with a few scout units. The guard, amused by the small delegation, demanded the gnomes' business.

"We are here to see about release of one of our people, unfairly held," said the flame-haired gnome.

The guard raised an eyebrow. He was unaware that the army had even taken "good faith" hostages. He asked what hostage the short woman was talking about.

She told him, and the guard fought the urge to laugh. He thought about it a moment, and asked the gnomes to wait. Then the guard beetled his way quickly to Lieutenant Brack's quarters.

"Rumtuggle?" said Lieutenant Brack, commanding officer of this particular outpost in the Green Dragonarmy. "They want us to release Rumtuggle?"

The guard nodded, snorting a laugh in the process. "They say they heard that we were holding him captive, and they have demanded his release."

"You told them he doesn't exist?" Brack asked, wide-eyed.

"I thought about doing exactly that," said the guard, "but then I thought they might not understand and might go somewhere else and ask someone else about it. The people they ask might not think to come to you about it."

"Hmmm . . ." Brack ran a thumb along his jawline. "I see your point. They might ask questions, which may cause others to ask questions." Brack sighed. "Send them to my tent."

The guard nodded, and within five minutes the delegation was in Brack's command tent. Several of the gnomes became immediately distracted and started sketching the design of the tent supports for future application. The red-haired gnomish woman would not be turned from her purpose and zeroed in on Brack with a sniper's precision.

"We understand you have one of our numbers here as a prisoner," she said curtly.

Brack managed his widest, sternest smile. "You have been misinformed. We hold no prisoners at this camp, not even good-faith hostages."

"We understand you have had problems with a gnome named Rumtuggle," said the woman.

Brack paused for a moment, then nodded slowly. There was no telling who else the gnomes would be talking to. "There have been reports of small accidents involving someone of that name." He chose his words carefully, telling the truth only as far as it served him.

"We"—she motioned to her motley crew—"represent the various small gnomish communities in our area. Rumtuggle is not among any of our communities. *Therefore*," she growled, screwing up her face and glowering at the lieutenant, "he must be your prisoner. You should release him at once."

Brack looked at the guard, who stood at the doorway. The guard shrugged. To the gnome the lieutenant said, "I assure you we don't have your Rumtuggle at this camp."

"You have him at another camp?" asked the woman.

Brack sighed. "No. We don't have him at any camp."

"We don't have him in any of our communities!" said the gnome woman. "No one has seen him for months!"

"Had anyone seen him before?" said Brack.

The gnome bridled and said, "I don't think you're taking this matter with the proper seriousness."

Brack took a deep breath and regarded the group. A small, heated discussion had broken out in the back of the party about how the lantern wicks in the tent could be better cut. These were not rebels, Brack decided. These were barely targets. Gently he said, "Your Rumtuggle was probably a wanderer. He wandered into our lives, caused some havoc among our occupying forces, and now will wander out. I doubt," Brack added with a hard look at the guard, "that we will ever hear about him again."

The gnome woman was not mollified. "Your answers are evasive, human. You have three days to release Rumtuggle. After that we will have to take action." She stomped her foot for effect. "Three days, human!" She spun on her heel and left the tent, her gaggle of gnomes in tow. One took a lantern with him, peering at the wick.

The guard waited behind, looking at Brack. The lieutenant sighed deeply and said, "I think we may have a small problem."

"Emphasis on the small," said the guard, breaking into a smile.

Brack smiled as well. "Very small, but for the next while, Rumtuggle should vanish from the reports. No point in stirring up the locals."

"And when she demands his release?" asked the guard.

Brack shrugged. "She's a gnome," he said. "In three days she'll have found something else to worry about."

Of course the gnome leader did not. Each day, for the next three days, a gnomish messenger arrived at the edge of the camp, demanding Rumtuggle's release. Each day Brack explained that they did not have Rumtuggle in their keeping.

On the morning of the fourth day, the cattle disappeared.

Brack never figured out how they did it. One night the cows were in the pasturage, the guards keeping an eye on them between games of dice. Then the sun came up on empty fields. Several hundred head of cattle, the provisions for most of the outpost, had vanished.

A messenger arrived, declaring that the cattle would be returned when Rumtuggle was released.

Brack looked at the messenger. He counted to five, then to ten. He explained that he could not release what he did not have and unless the gnomes gave back the cattle pretty damned fast he would unleash the entire fury of his unit on the surrounding area. A hungry army was an angry army. The gnome said he would be back the next day.

Privately, Brack worried. A hungry army *was* an angry army, but most of that anger would be directed at those responsible for feeding them—like their officers. Brack sent out scouts in all directions, both the hapless hobgoblins and real horsemen, in the hopes of finding whatever secluded valley the cattle had been squirreled away in.

They found nothing. The next day the gnome messenger returned. Brack counted to five, then to ten, and then to fifteen, then told him that they did not have Rumtuggle. The gnome said that he would return the next day.

Brack doubled the patrols, calling in favors from other commanders who knew about his fictitious gnome. Already the troops were restricted to salted meat, and would have to get by on hardtack if the cows were not returned. Brack sent word back up the line for additional supplies.

The patrols found nothing: no secluded vales, no herds of cattle in secret hiding places. All they found was increased evidence of lumbering in the area. Going into the gnomish towns was considered hazardous, since several gnomish inventions had gotten loose in the past and harmed some hobgoblins, and none of the nonhuman troops wanted to go anywhere near the gnomes, particularly now that Rumtuggle was apparently helping them.

The troops were getting hungry. And angry.

A query came from HQ asking what Brack had done about the cattle problem and notifying him that the rear echelon would be sending the provisioner-general to find out what happened to the missing cattle. The official would arrive the next day.

Hot on the heels of that message, the gnomish messenger returned, repeating the demand that Rumtuggle be released.

Brack counted to twenty but finally gave up trying to hold his temper. "I can't give you Rumtuggle!" he shouted at last. "There is no Rumtuggle! Rumtuggle isn't alive!"

The gnome's eyes grew wide, and he practically squealed, "You mean, you *killed* him?"

Brack stared down at the little figure. "What are you going to do about it?" he shouted.

The gnome seemed to quail for a moment, then said, "I guess we'll have to give back your cows, then." He departed, leaving Brack speechless.

The cows did not reappear immediately, not for the rest of that day, nor with dawn of the next day. The provisioner-general did appear at dawn, and Brack found him inspecting the vacant paddocks.

"You had four hundred and fifty-three head of cattle," said the provisioner-general, an officious skeleton of a man, regarding Brack over the top of his glasses. "They seem to be missing."

"Well, yes," started Brack, "we have had a problem with gnomes taking the cattle."

The provisioner-general looked dubious. "Gnomes? Raiding cattle? Unlikely."

"Ah," said the guard at Brack's side, "Well, these gnomes have had, uh, exceptional leadership." He was trying to help, but Brack shot him a venomous look.

"Yes." The provisioner-general flipped through a sheaf of papers attached to his clipboard. "This would be the 'Rumtuggle' mentioned in your earlier reports."

Brack looked at the guard again, then sighed. "Yes, that would be correct, but we have ordered the gnomes to return the cattle, and they have said they will do so."

"Hmmm," said the provisioner-general. "Did they give you any idea *when* they would be returning said cattle?"

Brack opened his mouth to respond, but instead there was only the noise of a distant twanging, followed by the approaching sound of a lowing, panic-stricken cow. From overhead.

The gnomes were returning the cattle—by catapult. The first of the four hundred and fifty-three head of cattle smashed into the ground between Brack and the provisioner-general, knocking both off their feet. Brack immediately started scrabbling away as the provisioner-general held his clipboard over his head in hopes that paperwork would stop the rain of cows over the dragonarmy camp.

* * * * *

Augie slapped the table with the fleshy part of his palm. "So it's a *cow* story, then!" he said laughing.

Brack managed a thin, patient smile. "It's a gnome story, one of those where you underestimate the gnomes and they turn out to be more intelligent, inventive, and dangerous than you thought. They found a way to hide the cattle, then built catapults. . . ."

"Cattle-pults," snorted Augie, almost spitting beer out his nose.

Brack sipped at his tankard, and Augie waved for another round. Another gnome appeared with more ales. Augie pulled himself slowly back together and rubbed the tears from his eyes.

"So the jig was up," he said at last. "Your little imaginary friend was revealed at last, and you were cashiered."

Brack shook his head. "Not yet. The cow-shot attack was only the beginning. We sent out forces, of course, but the gnome towns were abandoned."

"They fled before your victorious armies?"

"They had abandoned them earlier," said Brack. "They were keeping the cows inside the buildings. Of course none of our hobgoblins wanted to go find out because . . ."

"These gnomes were dangerous!" shouted Augie, almost losing his composure again. "They were followers of Rumtuggle!"

"Rumtuggle the Rebel," said Brack. "Who was supposedly dead, but now was being sighted everywhere, rallying the gnomes and the kender and whatever other races they could find against us. That just brought out the worst elements of all."

"Oh no, not . . ."

"Adventurers," said Brack, staring into his mug. "Any tinpenny warrior with a dream and a sword. They started rallying the gnomes into a real organized force. And if we caught and killed any of them, then *more* showed up."

"So what did your highlords do when all this activity suddenly showed up in your comfortable backwater?" asked Augie, smiling.

Brack sighed. "The worst thing they could possibly do."

"You mean?"

"Yes." Brack set down his empty tankard and picked up the refilled one, "They sent more troops in. To help us put down the imaginary gnome."

* * * * *

The dragonlord's armor was a shiny jet-black, and he rode an emerald-colored mount, its reptilian scales shimmering greenly in the wet morning fog. What Lieutenant Brack remembered most of all was his nose. It was a thin, aquiline nose with a great distance from tip to bridge, and the dragonlord looked down the entire length of said nose to regard Brack.

"You have rebel troubles," said the dragonlord icily, in the tone of a man who had far more important things to do. Brack wished the dragonlord was doing them.

"In a manner of speaking," said Brack, as calmly as possible. "There were some thefts—"

"Cows," said the dragonlord. "You lost some cows."

"But we got them back," put in Brack.

"Not in the same shape as you lost them," said the dragonlord. He struck a pose. "Rebellion must be crushed wherever it raises its head!"

Brack wondered if the pose was supposed to be heroic or just uncomfortable. "It has been a very peaceful area."

"Until now," said the dragonlord in a voice as serious as the grave. "Until this . . . Rumtuggle chose to challenge the might of our armies. He will live to regret it."

The dragon snorted in agreement. Lieutenant Brack looked at the dragonlord, wondering if he should laugh or scream.

By the end of the first week, he would have opted for screaming. More forces arrived, and with them a plethora of lieutenants, captains, and colonels. All answered to the dragonlord, and Brack was reduced to little more than a concierge, rushing about and making sure that all their needs were met. Most of these units had served together and had rivalries ranging from friendly and competitive to bitter and dangerous. Most of Brack's forces were now kept busy keeping the other encampments from raiding each other over slights, real and imagined.

The dragonlord was oblivious to such problems within the ranks, as was usual with those in charge. The various commanders jumped when he shouted orders, and they scuttled away to enact them. Usually that involved some new demand upon outpost commander Brack.

While overseeing a crew to clear still more land for the encampment of a newly arrived unit, Brack realized what was bothering him—he had suddenly rejoined the army, and he did not like it one bit.

The weather did nothing to help. The fogs that had helped created Rumtuggle in the first place had continued and, if anything, had gotten worse. They were combined with continual rains that drenched the area. Given the large number of troops now contained in the immediate vicinity of the outpost, the entire region was now a foot-sloshing bog.

Each day the dragonlord flew through the grayish fog atop his mount and spent the day reconnoitering the area. However, with the exception of more fog, broken by the occasional shattered, rocky hilltop, there was nothing to be seen, and each day the dragonlord returned in a fouler mood, resulting in more orders for the subordinates and ultimately more irritation for Brack.

Finally the dragonlord drew up a plan. Since the weather was against them (undoubtedly influenced by foul rebel wizards), they would press outward, putting any settlements discovered to the torch until the combined forces of the enemy were forced to either flee or engage them on the field of honorable battle.

Only Brack, unused to blind obedience, asked the question, "What if the enemy has already fled?"

The dragonlord chortled and said, "These rebels are fanatics, and this Rumtuggle is the worst of all. No, they want to fight, and we will triumph!"

The other subordinates glared harshly at Brack for lengthening the briefing by asking stupid questions. The dragonlord laid out his plans for which units would be where, how to form a huge, sweeping formation that would course over the land like a wave, sweeping everything in its path. They would ride forth on the morrow morn, rain or shine. He looked at Brack with piercing eyes and asked if there were any questions.

Brack kept his thoughts to himself, and the sub-commanders were left to their units. Brack noted at the time that at least the dragonlord had showed the good sense to keep the most quarrelsome units on opposite flanks of the force, where they would not be able to taunt each other.

The next day was rain, not shine, but that did not slow the juggernaut of the dragonarmy. The dragonlord was at its head, astride his mount, and Brack's forces were slightly to the left, just outside the vanguard. Most of the hobgoblins scouted, and his few cavalry forces were to act as skirmishers. The rain grew heavier, and struck with such force that the soft earth spattered on the assembled soldiers.

Brack considered telling the dragonlord the truth but felt that after a few days' march and finding no official resistance, the dragonlord would fly away and things would get back to normal.

In truth, they barely got out of camp. As the dragonlord raised his hand to give the order to move out, a hobgoblin scout came staggering up, covered with mud.

"Gnomes!" shouted the hobgoblin. "Rumtuggle is waiting with his army!"

Upon reflection, Brack was to decide that the muddy scout, survivor of some other mishap while on patrol, had decided that Rumtuggle would be a suitable target to blame. Upon reflection, Brack was to decide this, but there was no time for reflection.

The entire army was electrified by the news and sloshed forward over the muddy parade fields and into the even muddier hills of the surrounding areas. The hillocks broke up the lines of units into packets of swordsmen and archers, of hobgoblins and cavalry. The rain grew worse, which Brack had thought was not possible, and the fog closed in so that an entire unit could walk into a river without seeing it—not that the dragonlord would notice if a unit completely vanished.

Actually Brack did notice something as the ground dropped away at his feet. He found himself half-falling, half-sliding down an embankment. Other swordsmen and archers nearby cursed as they were similarly caught unawares. Mud caked on his armor and greaves as Brack and his unit fought to clear the far side of this particular gully.

That was when he and the others saw them—tall shadows among the fog, along the upper ridge of the embankment. Some had swords, some had bows and arrows. They were waiting for the dragonarmy.

Someone to Brack's right gave a shout and let loose an arrow. Five arrows returned out of the rain and caught the original archer in the chest and belly. He went down, but five of his companions unleashed their arrows, and several of the shadows fell away. There were shouts now, as the sword-wielders above half-ran, half-slid down the embankment to meet Brack's unit.

Behind Brack a horn sounded charge. Ahead of him, beyond the enemy line, a similar horn responded. Brack was heartened for the moment. They had the enemy surrounded!

A shape loomed up in the fog, no more than silhouette. It was large and man-sized, and Brack lashed out with his blade. As he struck, he wondered if this was some human ally of the gnomes, some adventurer who was helping the small rebels.

Brack's thoughts were interrupted as his blade pierced the man's armor and the soldier he fought collapsed. The blade had skittered over armor of a type similar to that found in the dragonarmies. No, not similar. Exactly like it.

Brack wiped the rain from his eyes and stared down at the wounded soldier clutching his side. He had not recognized his foe in the mud and fog. The man was a soldier in dragonarmy armor.

They were fighting themselves. Some group had gotten turned around and they were attacking each other.

Brack shouted for his men to stop fighting, but there was no stopping the juggernaut once it had begun collapsing on itself. Other horns were sounding now as various flanks swept forward to enclose an enemy that was not there. They collided with each other and locked themselves in battle. Most did not recognize their own forces. Some fought only because they were themselves being attacked. A few recognized their foes but blamed sorcery. A few, particularly the last to arrive from the outer flanks, saw it as a chance to settle old scores.

Brack saw only carnage, as his troops ceased to be anything more than a bloodied and bloodthirsty mob. He tried to retreat and ended up almost skewered on a brace of pikemen charging at full tilt into the muddle. He ran forward and danced as arrows stuck in the soft earth at his feet. At last he found a tributary of the muddy river and followed it upward, away from the battle.

The fog was clearing only slightly as he poked his head up out of the dell. He saw a huge, immobile form laying in the grass. Carefully he approached it and saw that it was the green dragon, its emerald scales now striped with blood, its wings and torso peppered with dragonarmy arrows.

Beside the great beast's head was the dragonlord, his helmet off, his long face buried in grief in his hands. Brack walked up, put a hand on the dragonlord's shoulder. The warrior looked up, and Brack was unsure if the dragonlord was crying or if it was only rain washing down his face.

"Our own troops," the dragonlord said at last, looking at his dead mount. "The gnomes turned our own troops against us. What mysterious power could turn our mighty forces against each other?"

Brack did not say what his first thought was. Instead, he knelt down next to the dragonlord, and said, "Let me tell you about gnomes. . . ."

* * * * *

"And that's *my* story," said Brack, setting the empty mug down on the table. A serving gnome made to remove it, but Brack held up his hand—no more for him.

"What did you tell the dragonlord?" asked Brack.

"I told him that Rumtuggle the Rebel Gnome had come up with his greatest invention, a device so powerful that even the dragonarmy could not find him and defeat him. Any attempt would end in frustration if the enemy was lucky, and disaster if he was not." Brack rose unsteadily to his feet.

"Did he believe it?" wondered Augie, still seated. "Did the dragonlord believe you?"

Brack shrugged. "I don't know. I tendered my resignation then and there and walked away. Been fighting small-unit engagements ever since, for whoever can pay. Fighting against real opponents, for real reasons."

"What about the dragonlord?" asked Augie.

"He might have done the same," said Brack, fishing a sack of coins from his belt, "or he might still be out there, trying to hunt down a gnome that isn't there, sacrificing more armies to the altar of his own stupidity."

"What of the gnome's invention?" said Augie, "the cattle-pult? Where were the gnomes hiding? What was it that spooked the hobgoblin scout?"

Brack shook his head, and said, "You don't understand." He handed the sack of coins to the gnome waiter and asked, "Gnome, do you know of one of your race named Rumtuggle?"

The gnome, who had been bringing the drinks all evening, brightened visibly. "Yes! I have a great uncle named Rumtuggle. He was a mighty warrior and gifted inventor and fought in the war! Everyone knows about Rumtuggle!"

Brack smiled, fished out a few more coins, and handed them to the gnome, who scuttled off. "Every family has at least *one* Rumtuggle in it, nowadays," said Brack. "That's the greatest gnomish invention. Rumtuggle—the gnome so powerful that he invented himself! Think about that the next time you fight gnomes."

Brack disappeared, leaving Augie at the table. The old warrior looked deep into his near-empty mug and began chuckling. The chuckling became laughter, and the laughter became a roaring bellow.

The gnome waiter brought Augie another ale, while the dwarven barkeep counted Brack's coins.

The Road Home
Nancy Varian Berberick

Listen, I don't care how many people you ask—you're not going to get the truth of the matter of Griff Rees from anyone but me. Griff Raven Friend, some call him; others say Griff Red Hand. In the army of the Dark Queen, in the days before the Second Cataclysm, he was known simply as Killer Griff. Those are the names others gave him. He himself took the name Unsouled, but it was a private name, and I only heard him speak it once, a time ago when we were down around Tarsis, when he was very drunk and thought himself alone.

A wild night at the end of the Falling starts this story. On that night Griff was right here in the Swan and Dagger. Long legs stretched out, he sat picking his teeth with a bone-handled dirk, listening to the wind outside and the roar of the tavern around him, maybe to the dark ebb and flow of voices only he could hear. A newly filled jug of ale sat frothing at his elbow. The remains of his supper lay all over the table, the greasy carcass of a whole duck and all the good things that go with it.

The Swan and Dagger was thunderous that night, howling back at the wind. The air hung thick with the smoke of poorly trimmed candles and fumes from the fireplace. Filled to the walls it was, with the usual clientele Baird Taverner gets in the Swan—ne'er-do-wells of all stripes, goblins, humans, hill dwarfs, and even a few mountain dwarfs like me. Everyone there came of the same dangerous tribe: narrow-eyed vengeance-seekers, quick-fingered thieves, and reckless ramblers who'd hire their swords for a good weight of steel coin, no matter whether they were hired for a border skirmish, a private raid, or a swift assassination.

I'm one of those hirelings, only it's not a sword I let out. It's Reaper, my hard-headed warhammer. Griff was one, too, and none better in this part of Abanasinia than Killer Griff.

It was wind that blew me into the Swan and Dagger, wind and the breath of winter coming. Griff was looking right at me when I came in. His eyes narrowed a bit and his lip curled in the sneer that was his smile. When he lifted his hand, a lazy wave, I went to join him.

"Sit," he said as easily as if it had been five days since he'd seen me last and not five months.

I took the warhammer off my hip and set it on the table. When I sat, Griff poured out some ale from the jug and shoved the tankard my way. I drank long and slow, then looked around to see whether anything remaining from his meal seemed worth picking over. Nothing did; Griff had done that duck to the bone.

"Hungry, are you, Broc?"

"Not so much," I said, looking past him to the bar where Baird Taverner stood listening to a whip-thin goblin whine and wheeze over his woes. He was a shabby thing, that goblin, his clothing naught but patches and rags, and he'd lately been in a fight with someone or something mean enough to rip off half the flesh of his pointy left ear.

"Sniveling about the price of dwarf spirits," Griff said, squinting into the thick air and looking where I did. "It's gone up some since last you were here. Baird's getting twenty-five coppers for it now."

Twenty-five. You could drown yourself in ale for twenty-five coppers, and I had nothing like that much in my pocket. Still, I might have figured the cost would rise. You don't get dwarf spirits easily these days, what with Thorbardin shut up tight against the world and my dear mountain kin hoarding most of it for themselves. What

Baird got he paid hard for, so he charged a steep price to tap a keg.

"I'll stand you a drink," Griff said, leaning back and gesturing to the taverner.

I stopped him. "Don't. I can't afford to be in your debt."

He shrugged, as if to say I must please myself. "Where have you been, Broc? Someone told me you were dead, killed out there in the hills of Darken Wood."

I'd heard the same tale told of me in several versions. "Did you mourn me, Griff?"

In the uneasy light of candle and hearth the scars on his face shone like cruel silver as he leaned back in his chair and yawned.

"My heart broke," said the man whose heart sat like a stone in his chest, beating but never moved. "Good to see you again," he added roughly as he lifted the jug and filled the tankard for me again.

I drank his health with a silent gesture, drained the tankard, and filled it a third time as he leaned across the table. That close to him, most people look away, from the scars and from his eyes. I never looked away, though sometimes when I met his eyes I saw ghosts there, peering out at me. That night, as on other nights, I thought Griff's eyes held the ghosts of all the people he'd killed.

"Listen," he said, the word falling heavily between us to let me know he had something to say worth hearing. He tapped Reaper's head. "Broc, are you looking for work?"

"I'm here," I said simply. "Me and the season. It's not a good place when the snow falls, that wild wood yon. I'd rather be under roof."

He took a long pull of ale and banged the tankard onto the table. "So says the Dwarf of Darken Wood. Well, I can give you work to make sure you can buy yourself the finest house in Long Ridge and stock it with dwarf spirits all the year through."

I leaned forward, wiping ale foam from my mouth. If I had any money, I'd not be wasting it on a fine and fancy house. A room over the Swan and Dagger was enough for me, with some coin left over to buy enough dwarf spirits to warm away the winter.

"It's a sweet job," Griff said, hitching his chair closer to the table. He glanced right and left, then dropped his voice low. "We'll be in and out before anyone knows what happened."

The job was a vengeance killing down in Elm High, one of the big towns on the Whiterage River. The details were not unusual: a ruined daughter, a son murdered trying to defend his sister, and a father too old to do what needed to be done and rich enough to offer Griff one hundred in steel coin to fund the expedition, two hundred more when we came back with the proof of our success.

"That proof," I said, "what would it be?"

Griff slashed his thumb across his neck. A head. Well, that's easy enough.

"How much for me?"

"The usual."

One-third. Over at the bar, the goblin whined some more and shoved enough coins at Baird to see his cup refilled. One-third of three hundred—a fine payday.

"Done," I said.

In the moment I said it, Baird Taverner pointed across the smoky room to us. Griff cocked his head as the crowd at the bar shifted, then parted. A young woman stood revealed, gray eyes wide and slender hands clasped modestly before her.

Dove among the wolves, I thought.

She took a timid step forward, then clasped her hands tighter and made her step firmer. She had a gauntlet to pass of gropers and grabbers, but she managed that well enough. She had a sharp elbow, that one, and she looked as if she knew how to use her knee if she had to. Right to us she came and stood at the table. This close to her, I saw it wasn't her hands she clasped but a small green velvet pouch kept close. By the look of it, a good deal of coin nestled in there. By the look of her, lips pressed tight and eyes anxious, that was all the coin she had.

"I've come to find Griff Rees," she said, "and they tell me he is here."

Griff said nothing, only eyed her, cool and quiet, so that she must look at one or the other of us. She did that but once, then stood in silence until at last I said, "It's not me you're wanting, girl. It's that lout across the table from me."

Her glance thanked me, and she turned to Griff. She flinched a little to see his scars, and she could not hold his eye; no shame to her for it.

"I've come," she said, "to hire you, Griff Rees, for a job of work."

"Have you now?" Griff said, drawling lazy and low. "Well, you've come late, mistress. I've just taken"—he smiled to mock—"a job of work." He leaned back in his chair, shouted to Baird for more ale, and seemed surprised to find the young woman still there. "Did you not hear me?"

She stood tall and straight, her black hair glinting in the firelight. She said she had heard him, and she said she hoped he would give her as good a hearing. "For I've got the steel to pay you well."

Griff's dark eyes lighted. He wasn't one for sentiment, and so the sad tale of the ruined daughter and the murdered son wouldn't move him to dismiss this young woman if her purse proved deeper than that of the old man who couldn't take his own revenge. He threw out his leg and hooked a chair with his foot, dragging it over to the table. She sat, looking around her uneasily, her pouch and her hands in her lap.

"I am Olwynn Haugh," she said, "and I am a widow. My husband—" Her voice faltered. "My husband was a farmer, below in the valley. He is lately dead. I have a child, Cae, she's but a month old, and I want to take her and go home to my father. I want to be with him before winter sets in and—"

Griff laughed, the sound like a bear shouting in the hills. "Mistress Haugh, someone has misinformed you. I don't hire out to escort young ladies home to their fathers." He leaned across the table, giving her full sight of his scarred face, his dark and dangerous eyes. "I travel harder roads than that."

"And crueler," she said, her eyes on the table, on me, on anything but his face. "I know who you are. That's why I want to hire you to protect me on my way. My father lives in Haven, and the best road to there passes around Darken Wood."

Well, Olwynn Haugh was no fool, that much we now knew. We've a long history around here in Abanasinia, one full of dark threads and some bright. In these afterdays many of the doings are grim, and much of that grim work goes on in Darken Wood, home to cutthroats and thieves and people like me who aren't so delicate about whom they kill or why as long as the pay is good.

Olwynn lifted her pouch and put it on the table. It didn't seem as fat as it would need to be to tempt Griff away from a job promising one hundred steel to start and two hundred to finish.

"Look," Griff said, wearying of this conversation, "take your money and go hire a half-dozen strong men to guide you home. Say some prayers to gods along the way, if you still believe in them. I've other work to do, and it's time for me to be at it."

He turned from her. In his mind, the matter was finished. Olwynn took up her green velvet pouch and opened it.

"See," she said, presenting all her wealth, "I do have the steel to pay you. Here is a ring my father gave me, as well as a necklace of emeralds and rubies that belonged to my mother and my grandmother before her."

The ring was of good enough make. You might get a few steel for it from a generous man. The necklace, though—that looked like something out of Thorbardin, and a lot older than this girl's grandmother. Each jewel was perfectly cut and enchained. It was worth a good deal more than a few steel if you showed it to the right person.

Across the room the skinny goblin leaned his back against the bar and made sure he had a clear view of us. I drew Reaper closer to me. Griff saw that, but he never moved. A look had come on him, white and terrible. I swear by Reorx himself or whichever of the vanished gods you'd like me to name, I swear his hand trembled and the ale slopped over the brim of his tankard.

Firelight glinted off the little heap of steel coins, a pile much too small to outweigh the three hundred promised Griff for that simple killing down in Elm High, but he wasn't doing that kind of reckoning. He wasn't doing any reckoning at all. He stared, like a man come suddenly upon an adder, and what held his eye was that ring sitting atop the little pile of steel, a long narrow oval of gold upon which was embossed a double eagle, a fierce raptor with two heads, each in opposition to the other.

The farmer's pretty widow smiled and grew easy, believing she'd shown just what was needed to hire her man: good coin and, if the sum weren't enough, a golden ring and some jewelry to make up the difference.

"Will you do it, then?" she asked, gathering up the pouch and cinching it tight.

"Done," Griff said. From the sound, his mouth must have been drier than ash. He reached for his ale and drank the tankard down. "Be ready for us in the morning."

"So soon? But—"

"Tomorrow, or not at all," he growled. "Meet me outside of here at first light."

She made no other protest and left us. Me, though, I had a thing or two to say. I poured myself some ale, then said it.

"Have you lost your mind? You just passed up the best job I've heard of in months. For what? Maybe a third of what that old man in Elm High is promising to pay?"

Griff looked at me long, all the ghosts in his eyes staring out at me. "What's it to you?"

"One hundred steel," I said, and never mind that his look raised the hair on the back of my neck. It was money we were talking, ghosts be damned.

"One hundred steel . . . " He traced the figure in the ale-slop on the table. "So what? You can have all we make on this little trip to Haven. I don't care."

Out the corner of my eye I saw the rag-eared goblin was gone from the bar. That could mean something, or it could mean nothing. I wasn't of a mind to chew it over now. "And you? What will you make? Are you doing it for free?" I snorted derisively. "Can't say I've ever heard of Killer Griff giving it away."

"So what?" He said it just as if he didn't care. He leaned forward again, elbows on the table, spilled ale wetting his shirt where his arms rested. He didn't look at me. He kept his eyes on the table and said, "Broc, did I ever tell you how I joined the Dark Queen's army?"

I frowned, not knowing where this offer of history came from and not much wanting to hear it. "No, and—"

"Well, listen."

I listened, but he said nothing, while all around us in the tavern the smoke hung and voices rose in shouts and dropped low in growls.

"Listen," he said again, finally lifting up his eyes, those deep wells all full of ghosts. "I'll tell you about a boy, skinny brat, living on his father's farm, away up on the plains of Estwilde. He wasn't nearly grown, that boy, and not a day older than he had to be to take what was handed him. . . ."

* * * * *

The boy, said Griff to me on that windy, wild night in the Swan and Dagger, the boy stood at the well, winding the crank to pull up the bucket from the dark deeps. Water, in those days just before the Second Cataclysm, was scarce. Rain never fell anymore. The well stream, which had always run swift under the ground, had months before choked to a trickle. The boy became used to letting that bucket of his tumble far down and cranking it back up again, turn and turn, until his arms ached with the work.

As he stood cranking, the boy looked out across the brown and dying fields, at the crops burned to ruin, the dust swirling in the ever-blowing wind. He cocked his head, listening to the sounds of the farm, his mother murmuring to his sister, his baby brother cooing in the cradle under the shade of the roof, his father talking to someone behind the barn. He looked up high, the back of his neck prickling. It seemed to him that he heard thunder or felt it rumbling, but the sky was hard and empty.

Like some great beast waking, the ground beneath his feet shuddered faintly. Dark, a cloud rose, up over the hill, past which lay the town. The wind turned, and the thick smell of burning came to him.

"Fire!" the boy shouted, abandoning the well. "Ma! Da! Fire! Fire in the town!"

Halfway to the house, he saw his mother pointing toward the hill, her eyes wide, her mouth open. The boy stopped to look where his mother pointed. All the blood in him went cold. It was smoke, aye, rising over the hill, but there was more—a great cloud of golden dust roiled and rolled before the darkness of smoke.

"Gods preserve us!" his mother cried. "Paladine save us!"

The boy's belly cramped with fear as that golden cloud became an army, dark and solid and gleaming in the sun. Swords and war axes shone, and the sunlight glinted like bright little spears from the black armor of a troop of Dark Knights riding at the head.

Knights of Takhisis!

The boy didn't think that. Well, he hadn't the wit for thinking, had he? Terror ran in him, sweeping away all thought. No matter, that. He knew who came riding. Who hadn't heard tales of what those merciless Knights had done in Kalaman? Everyone knew how they'd swept south from there into Estwilde on a bloody tide of rapine and killing.

The dark troop moved fast, horses' hooves chewing up the road. Their voices came like the sound of a river at flood. The Knights kept to their course, thinking the little farm unworthy of their notice. Some of the foot soldiers didn't hold so true a line. Roaring, they plunged across the field between the road and the farmyard. The boy saw faces contorted with the blood-chilling rage of men who'd lately been at a killing and lusted for more. He bolted to the house for his mother, and he ran right into the arms of his father.

"Cellar!" his father shouted, his infant son in his arms. He thrust the boy into the house, herding his wife and weeping daughter before him. Down under the center room lay a root cellar, cool and dark, a place to hide and pray these rampagers would satisfy themselves with looting. "Hurry, boy! Hurry!"

They had the hatch up from the floor. The boy tumbled in, shoved by his father. The infant wailed. Outside pigs squealed, cows bawled, and the army's thunder shook the little house to the walls. The boy reached up to take the shrieking infant. Reaching, he heard his father cry out. His sister's horrified scream echoed in his bones. The hatch crashed down, hitting the boy in the head and plunging him into stifling darkness.

There he crouched, half-conscious and bleeding. Just like in your worst nightmare, he heard his mother wail, he heard his father plead for mercy—not for himself, but for his wife and children. He heard the weeping and the sobbing and then the sudden silences like gaping holes never to be mended, unhealing wounds. All the while he shoved his thin shoulders up against the hatch, furious, raging, and trying to get out.

What did he think he'd do if he got out? Well, well, he was a boy, you remember, and full of mind-clouding fury. He thought he'd kill them, every one of those raiders.

When all the silences had fallen above, when all the deaths were died, the boy's cursing was the loudest thing in the world to hear. He fell still, heart racing, terrified and knowing his own silence came too late. The hatch opened, and a hand reached down and grabbed his arm, dragging him up into the day. Light glinted off a deeply embossed golden ring, bitterly bright and stabbing the boy's eyes.

Ach! It was a slaughter-field the boy found up there, red-running with blood. Bodies lay around the floor of the front room, his fair sister's, his father's twisted and broken, his mother's covered in blood. The infant lay dead upon her breast. Shivering, belly-sick and cramping, the boy vomited, falling to his knees, and got kicked hard for doing that. A big man—that one with the big hand and the booted foot—yanked him to his feet. Fire crackled outside, smoke curled all around inside the house. The big man pulled the boy close so they were eye to eye. He stank of blood and sweat and murder.

"Mine," he growled in Common Speech. "Mine!" He dragged the boy outside, where Griff's wrists were bound, then tied on a long lead to the saddle horn of a pale horse.

That simply did the boy become a slave. The big man mounted his horse and rode away at the head of his murdering mob. The boy followed—well, he had to, didn't he?—and he went in stunned silence until, atop a rise, his master stopped to look for sign of the army he'd left and must catch up again. The man looked ahead, but the boy looked behind him and saw his home, the little farmhouse, the barns and outbuildings. They sat like ashes on the land, and in the sky ravens circled, lowering for a meal.

In that moment the boy screamed his rage for the deaths of his family. Thus flew his first, fledgling war cry.

* * * * *

"That's how I joined the army of Takhisis," Griff Rees told me, still leaning on his elbows, soaking up the spilled ale.

I said nothing, because I had nothing to say. I've been told sad tales and sorrowful in my time, and this was one, but I've never known it to help a man to hear me say, ah, the shame of it; oh, the pity.

I looked long at him through the haze of low-hanging smoke from Baird Taverner's badly drafting hearth, thinking about how he'd joined the Dark Queen's army with a war cry in his throat and his heart turning to stone.

He said to me, there in the Swan and Dagger, that he would like to have killed the big man who enslaved him, but though he plotted and planned, he had no chance.

"Instead, I survived, fighting with the army, becoming as strong and ruthless as any soldier."

I poured out the last of the ale, sharing it between us, all the while thinking that the killing you do in war is hard work for a man, worse work for a boy. He did it, though, that skinny boy who saw his family die on the plains of Estwilde, for among the slave's duties was the obligation to defend his master in battle. He did that war-work well, learning the art of killing in hopes he'd get to use it in a better cause, to kill the man who'd murdered his family. He was an apt student. Soon they began to name him Killer Griff. Maybe it was then he thought he'd lost his soul, killed it in the killing, all the while yearning to work a particular murder. His yearning was never sated. In time he and his master parted, swept away from each other by the terrible tide of war that overwhelmed the High Clerist's Tower in those rending days at the end of the Summer of Chaos.

"Ash Guth was his name," Griff said. "He must have changed it, after. I've searched hard and never heard so much as a word about him since the war ended. Not from that day till this have I seen sign of him." He looked down at the table, then up at me. "Not outside of nightmare."

There must have been a lot of those, I thought as he turned his dark eyes on me and I heard his ghosts howling. Ah, not the ghosts of all those he'd killed in his time. Never them. I knew it now, I saw it: These were *his* ghosts, his phantom kin peering out from his eyes.

"I've got him now," Griff said, tracing death runes in the spilled ale. "Got him sweet and sure, and there's no way I'll lose him again."

Like a cold finger at the back of my neck came the memory of the nickname I'd heard only once: Griff Unsouled. He looked like that, sitting there, his arms in the ale-slop, like something animate but with no spirit.

I thought, once, for only a moment, that it was too bad for Mistress Haugh to be leading her father's death right to him, but then I decided that was no matter to concern me. There isn't a killing I do or help at that isn't worked for gain. This one would serve that end just fine. Besides, would you deny that Griff Rees had this killing coming to him?

* * * * *

If anyone had asked me, I'd have picked a different horse for Olwynn to ride than her dancy little red mare. For that matter, I'd have advised she ride no horse at all but that she and Griff take the Haven Road walking, as I did. It's a good road in good seasons, broad enough for three riders to go abreast, but lately storm rains had washed away the sides, leaving it narrow and soft at the edges. The red mare hated those soft sides, and she always found herself slopping around there. Olwynn, riding with Cae in a sling and close to her breast, did her best to keep the mare going straight down the firm middle, but the mare was contrary-minded as any mule, veering right and left and shying each time she felt the yielding edge of the road. Two hours out of Long Ridge, the mare had slipped three times and twice threatened to throw her rider— infant and all—into the road. Whatever hopeful idea we'd had of how far we'd get that day lay in ruins.

"Slit the damned horse's throat," Griff growled the fourth time the mare went slipping off the road. It was the first thing he'd said since we took to the Haven Road, and he didn't say more than that. He rode ahead, dark and quiet. Me, I was left with the mare and the girl, trying to get them back onto the road again, dodging hooves and teeth all the way while Cae set up a long, howling wail.

The Dwarf of Darken Wood, that's what Griff names me, and maybe you wonder why I spend so much time in that place. There are many reasons. One is the silence.

Olwynn held the child close, whispering soft sounds that were not words, when the mare ducked her head to start kicking. I moved fast and punched the beast hard between the eyes just as her head came down. I did some harm to my fist and none to the mare, but I got her attention. She let me lead her up out of the mud and onto the road again.

"Thank you," Olwynn said, her voice low and shaking as she took the reins from me. "I—I'm not so good with horses. My husband, though . . ." She let the thought go, rocking her baby. "Well, thank your for your help, Broc." She said it sweetly, no smile upon her lips but the light of one in her quiet eyes.

"Come on!" Griff called, his pied gelding restless. "We'd like to get at least a mile up the road before nightfall, eh?"

We made good time after that. The mare seemed be weary of contrariness now and enjoyed the chance to trot in the brisk morning. I ran ahead of the riders, jogging along the road, checking right and left, my pack a comfortable weight on my back, Reaper on my hip, near to hand.

It's not a good place to be, Darken Wood on the Haven Road. All the pretty stories you hear of dryads singing in the glades, the tragic tales of the ghosts in Spirit Forest, even the brave legends of centaurs over in the western part of the wood—these are true. When you're going into Darken Wood from the Haven Road round near Solace and Long Ridge, though, you'd be a fool to worry about specters and dryads and centaurs. What you find there are bandits and outlaws hiding in the aspen woods, men exiled from home and kin by law or, like me, by choice. You'd be a witling to go in there without weapons and the skill to use them.

Behind me, Olwynn's little daughter cooed and sighed, the tiny sound drifting on the wind. Birds flitted over Solace Stream, kingfishers dived for a meal, finches and warblers came out from the wood to drink. A doe, wide-eyed and startled, leaped across the road and plunged into the darkness of trees. I stopped, listening to her run, and to the following silence as smaller creatures, fearing predators, swiftly ducked for cover. I waited until I heard the wood return to normal, heard the song of birds and the sigh of cold wind from the north, then went on.

The road no longer ran straight, for it had been cut out of the wood to parallel the wandering stream, and it became more narrow. I glanced back, then signaled to Griff that I was heading out of his sight, around the bend to see the way ahead. He gestured assent, and Olwynn spoke to him, her voice low. If she had asked after something, he gave no answer.

A dove among wolves, so I'd thought her the night before in the Swan and Dagger. Well, she was that, wasn't she? A little dove homing with a deadly message for her father, aye. He could make a neat plan, Griff could.

I rounded the bend where, off to the east Solace Stream runs chattering and laughing out of Crystalmir Lake, and there I stopped, cursing to see a tangle of aspens fallen across the road. The rains of days before had filled up the lake so that the runoff swelled the racing stream past its banks. We'd have to leave the road and thread the verge of the wood where trees grew close together, their roots weaving snares for our feet. That red mare was going to enjoy this. I went closer to the pile, still cursing, trying to think how best to get the mare off the road and into the wood. The crisp sound of hooves at jog fell upon the silence. As if to protest, a jay cried in the wood, another echoed, and a third joined the racket. Some small creature rustled within the tangle of fallen trees, drawing my eye.

My heart lurched hard against my ribs as I saw a thing hidden from the casual glance. Every one of those trees had been taken with a wood axe, and every one of those raw new wounds told me the trees had been cut down in the night.

"Griff!" I shouted, running back, "heads up!"

The jays fell silent. The wind turned, carrying the near scent of sweat and horses. I rounded the bend and saw them, two riders abreast. Griff had his sword out, the steel shining in a fall of sunlight. Behind him, like a trap closing, came ten ragged figures, some human, some goblin. They made a half-circle across the road, catching us between them and the fallen trees.

"Back!" I shouted. "Behind you!"

An arrow hissed past my ear, and a second flashed past the eye of the red mare. The beast bolted. Olwynn screamed, flung over the mare's back, Cae clutched to her breast as she fell onto the road. She lay there, helpless, the breath blasted from her as her child shrieked. Griff was off his horse and over her at once. To see him, you'd have thought he was protecting his own dear daughter, so fierce and fiery were his eyes now. He was protecting, all right. Not Olwynn, no, but something more—his road to revenge.

I leaped past Griff, swinging Reaper hard, and took out the knees of a tall, thin goblin who fell screaming. He struggled, trying to gain his feet, and I saw that here was the rag-eared fellow who'd gone suddenly missing from the Swan. Reaper harvested, smashing that goblin's skull to bloody bits.

Olwynn shouted, "Broc! Behind!"

I turned on my heel, Reaper already swinging. Bone crunched, someone howled in agony, and a stocky human fell to the ground.

Olwynn cried out again in wordless terror, and I jerked around in time to see her hunched over her wailing child, trying desperately to protect herself and her baby as two goblins rushed her. With her, they must be certain, lay the pouch full of steel coins their fellow had seen in the tavern.

With his wild, terrible war cry—ah, that cry the same as the first one he ever shouted—Griff leaped over Olwynn's huddled body. His sword glinted as he plunged it into the gut of a goblin, the gleam quenched in red, red blood. Yet seven remained, five humans and two goblins, all of them certain of their skills, certain of the treasure they had come for.

I grabbed the mare's reins as she dashed past and grabbed Olwynn's pack from the saddle horn. Griff snatched his pied gelding and his own pack. One swift glance passed between us. With slaps and cries we sent the horses plunging into the knot of ambushers.

"Run!" I shouted, flinging Olwynn's pack at her as Griff grabbed her wrist and yanked her to her feet. "No! Not ahead! The way is blocked! Into the wood!"

We scrambled off the side of the road, into Darken Wood, and none of us wasted time looking over our shoulders.

* * * * *

We ran, but not for long. The wood was sparse along the verge, but we soon found that beyond there it grew thick and close. Trees leaned together, brush clogged what clear spaces might have been, while roots reached up from the ground to trip us. Olwynn's breathing came in gasps and sobs, ragged with effort and fear. Cae wailed constantly, her cries muffled against her mother's breast but still loud enough to be followed. Shouts and curses echoed behind us as the bandits untangled themselves from the horses and plunged into the wood. One long keening cry rose up, someone discovering his dead.

"Faster," I said to Griff as I ducked past him, looking for the slender trails I knew.

He grabbed Olwynn's wrist again, dragging her stumbling behind. The girl and her screaming child in tow, we splashed across a swollen stream. Once up the other side Griff stopped, still gripping Olwynn by the arm.

"Shut the brat up!" he growled, head up, ears keen for sound of pursuit.

We heard enough of that. Behind us, bodies crashed heavily through the brush, harsh voices shouting oaths and threats. All round us, though, lay silence. No creature of the wood made a sound. In that silence Olwynn shrugged from under Griff's hand, drawing herself away from him. Sweating in the cold air, her arms trembling as she held the infant to her, she said, "Cae is hungry and cold and frightened. Find me a quiet place, and I will quiet her."

Cae wailed louder. Griff put his hand on the grip of his sword, a slow, considered motion. The pulse leaped in Olwynn's throat. She didn't back away, though, and softly she said, "I have hired you, Griff Rees, to protect me. Surely you don't threaten me now because my child is hungry and tired?"

She held her ground. Griff smiled the way you'd think Winter itself would smile, heartless and icy. "Am I not keeping your father's precious treasure well enough, Mistress Haugh? You're still here and standing, aren't you?"

Back behind us a rough voice raised up, and another answered. In silence, I cursed. I'd taken this job for easy money, and it seemed to me the money was getting harder all the time.

"Griff," I said, "let's get going."

Snarling, he said, "Broc, take us to some place quiet so Mistress Haugh can tend her child."

Well enough, I knew where to go—who better than the Dwarf of Darken Wood?—and so I went, thrusting through the low growth, leaving Griff to shoulder through the tall with Olwynn, her child in full voice, behind.

Closer now, the rough voice shouted, "Hear 'em? Up ahead!" The bandits came crashing along our trail, led by Cae's wails. We heard one of them howl with glee in the very moment I found the two crossing trails I sought, one broad and clear, the other narrow and twisting. I smelled the stink of goblin on the wind. Maybe Olwynn did, too, for she closed her eyes and breathed softly, as if she were praying.

"All right, then," I said, pointing to the narrow trail winding out like a snake. "That's our path, Griff. At the end the ground rises. You'll find three caves. You want the middle one. It's deepest, and a spring wells up in the back. Go there, and don't leave the path, or you'll be lost before I miss you."

Behind us a deer leaped, crashing through the brush. Pursuit came closer.

"And you?" Griff said.

I gave him my pack, then pointed to the ground. "Covering the marks of your big boots."

He laughed grimly and got Olwynn moving again. They took the winding path, Griff ducking low, once or twice holding a whipping branch back for Olwynn when he thought to. I waited until they were gone up the path, then swiftly covered the marks of their passing. That done, I made a trail for the pursuit, my own clear boot prints, indeterminate marks off to the side, and some scuffing that looked as if someone had fallen a time or two and scrabbled up again. A spring bubbled up on the left of the trail not far ahead. I crossed it and left wet prints on the stony ground beyond.

Standing still off the path, I listened. A gravelly voice drifted to me on the wind, a goblin speaking in his own coarse language. Satisfied, I ducked into cover, making myself invisible in thickets as the bandits came closer, my rusty clothing fading into the rusty bracken. Eyes on the trail, ears straining for the sound of wailing Cae, I waited, breath held. Breath held, and Reaper held, just in case.

One goblin came, then another, and several humans followed.

"I'll wear their skins for breeches," the first goblin said. He had a look about him that reminded me of the rag-eared fellow I'd killed on the road. Kin, doubtless.

To the west, a crow cried again. Something fainter, smaller, seemed to answer. Cae! The goblin who was looking for new breeches stopped, obliging the others to do the same. He cocked his head, his pointed ears swiveling, just like a cat's.

"Ar, it's nothin'" growled a tall human. "Just a rabbit caught outside its hole."

The goblin hung on his heel, listening. No other cry sounded. He took his companion's word and went on. One by one, they passed me, all of them looking as if they'd had a hard time with thorny thickets. Smiling, I watched them. They kept their eyes on the trail and their noses to the wind. I heard them splash in the spring, heard them go on, and congratulated myself on work well done.

With luck, they'd follow the stony trail right back to the road again, though they wouldn't know that till they'd come in sight of Gardar's Tower five miles or more away.

By then, I thought, slipping silently into the wood, that goblin would be minded to find himself a new pair of breeches somewhere else.

* * * * *

They aren't long days, those of the Falling, and we'd wasted much of the first day of our journey to Haven on the dancy red mare and the bandits. By the time I reached the three caves, light lay old on the ground, and shadows were long. We'd be going nowhere until morning. Griff knew it as well as I. The middle cave had a settled look about it when I came walking up, packs against the wall inside, Olwynn sitting in the thin sunlight outside, her babe asleep in her arms. She huddled close in her cloak. The wind blew colder up here than down below, and stronger. Few trees grew to break it.

They greeted me variously, Griff with a curt nod and Olwynn with a smile and a glad word.

"I worried for you," she said, settling Cae more comfortably. "You were a long time gone."

"As long as it took," I said. I scooped up a newly filled water bottle and drained it dry.

"Will we have a fire?" Olwynn asked, looking from one to the other of us.

I snorted. "Sure. I'll build it while you go stand on the hill and shout to every bandit and outlaw in Darken Wood that we're here." I reached into my pack and pulled out some jerked venison. "Eat that," I said, tossing it to her.

The little dove didn't flinch from that growl of mine. She only tucked her child closer to her body and moved inside the cave, out of the reach of the waking wind. I turned to walk away, thinking I'd take the first watch and thereby gain a night's uninterrupted sleep. Turning, I saw Griff shrug out of his own cloak, the thick green wool, and pass it over to Olwynn.

Softly she murmured her thanks.

"Never mind that," he said roughly. "Get some sleep now. We'll be early up."

Never mind that, eh? Perhaps she didn't, but I took it up the hill with me, laughing. What a tender guide he was! Or so she might think. Me, I recalled words of Griff's spoken harshly in the wood: Am I not keeping your father's precious treasure well enough, Mistress Haugh? Precious treasure, all right, and more like Griff's than her father's, for she was his way into his enemy's house.

I forgot all that when Griff came up the hill much too soon to relieve my watch. He came walking in the light of the red and silver moons, and something about the look on him, bone-white and skullish, sent a spider-footed chill up my neck.

He said, "What?" when I looked hard at him, and he scowled and spat.

"You," I said. "You look like . . ."

"Like what?"

I shrugged. It was hard to explain. He looked like Death walking, hollow-eyed and unstoppable, and no surprise there. For Olwynn Haugh's father, Death is what he was. But he looked like one caught by Death, too; like a man gnawed and chewed over and not much left on the bone. Wind cut across the top of the hill, whining a little. It had grown colder since the sun's setting. Griff put his back to it, hunching his shoulders. Eyes on the cave, that yawning dark mouth, he nodded, almost absently.

"Go on down," he said, " and see if you can get a fire going."

"What?" I almost laughed. "Are you crazy? Every bandit—"

He rounded on me, snarling, "Do it! You hide out in these hills all the time, and no one knows you're here till you walk up on 'em. Are you going to tell me you never build a fire?"

I wasn't going to tell him that. No one makes a quicker or cleaner fire than I do. Still, it seemed too risky now. As quickly as he'd roused to snarl, however, that easily did Griff calm again.

"Those bandits are long gone," he said. "We won't see them again. The girl's my passage into her father's house. I've got to keep her and her child safe and well till we get where we're going."

Well, she was my passport too, to a fine fat fee, one that would keep me warm and fed and in dwarf spirits all the winter through. I thought about where the bandits would be now and reckoned they were either back in Long Ridge or cursing me up one side of Gardar Tower and down the other. The wind ran from the direction of that old pile of stone, and nothing in the sky or the scent of the chill air spoke of a storm to change the sky's mind.

"All right, then," I said, shaking my head. "A fire it is."

Griff said nothing, only sat down in the lee of the hill where the wind wouldn't bite and took out his bone-handled dirk and a small whetstone. Plying one against the other, he watched the blade bleed small sparks while I scuffed around a bit to see if we had more to say to each other. We didn't, and so I left him to watch.

When I returned to the cave, Olwynn smiled to see my arms full of wood and tinder. She set her child upon the ground, snug among the packs, and rose to help me at the fire-building. One breath she drew to speak, that small smile still on her lips, when all the silent night ripped apart, torn by Griff's wild war cry.

* * * * *

Seven men fell upon us with howling and steel, seven bandits who didn't know when the game was over. Moonlight ran like spilling silver along the keen edges of swords. Olwynn cried out, "Broc!" and Cae woke shrieking and screaming.

"Into the cave!" I shouted. "All the way back!"

She didn't wait to argue or ask a question. She ran with her child wailing, hunched over and seeking the safety of deeper darkness. The bandits laughed, thinking they'd have no trouble getting past me. Well, there were seven of them, and maybe they'd have been right. We never learned about that, though. No sooner did I smash the knees out from under one of the goblins than the other one died screaming. Griff's blade slipped between his ribs from behind. The thick coppery stink of blood filled the air as I finished my man, relieving his skull of his brains, and spun on my heel, Reaper's weight carrying me, to shatter the ribs, then the whole chest, of another.

We were good, Griff and I, workmanlike at our killing. It took less time than the telling to dispatch two more with sword and hammer, and now there were but two bandits left. One was a tall, thick-shouldered fellow, the other thin with a poxy face. Each had a fine bright blade. The tall bandit lunged for Griff, the other feinted toward me, sword tip circling tightly, taunting just beyond Reaper's range. Griff's man lunged again, then side-stepped Griff's return. In that stepping, he moved toward the cave's mouth. Cae's bawling echoed far back in the darkness. Laughing, the bandit vanished, swallowed into the darkness, trusting Cae's howling to lead him.

"Damn!" Griff shouted, leaping too late to stop him. "Damn and damn!" and he flung himself into the cave, leaving me standing, eyes locked with the pox-faced bandit.

He grinned, that bandit, a baleful light in his eyes. Just a little light flickered, and I spied his intent. I stepped back and to the side just as he lunged. Stumbling, he turned to find me. Reaper, whistling in the air, took him in the back of the neck and shattered his spine. With his own sword I put him out of his pain.

Steel clanged on stone inside the cave, then one blade belled against another. Closer than I'd thought to hear, those sounds, and closer still Olwynn's sudden cry of dread. In the instant, one sword fell clattering to the stony ground, and then the other. Olwynn bolted past me, child in arms. Like demons, two men followed, the last bandit weaponless, Griff on his heels.

Blood dripped from the bandit's sword arm, and his other hand clenched tight. I leaped over the corpse at my feet, Reaper ready, but I moved too late. The bandit turned, hitting me hard between the shoulders.

I fell, the breath blasted from my lungs, gasping like a drowning man. The stone-fisted man snatched a sword from the ground, laughing and lunging for Griff. Olwynn screamed again, but not in terror or pain. Here was rage, tearing up the night, tearing up the inside of my skull. In one smooth motion she set down her child among the packs near the wall and grabbed the stone the bandit let fall.

I heard it, then, that sound I'm used to hearing, the cracking of bone, as Olwynn's stone smashed down on the man's shoulder. I laughed—I actually did as the breath came rushing back to me. The laughter died on my lips as the bandit turned. He shifted his sword to his left hand. Silver and red moonlight ran down the length of the blade, gleaming on honed steel edges. Then there was no light, there was only blood, black in the moonlight, as Olwynn fell to her knees.

She turned up her face to the sky and the stars, just as if she were praying. Cae's wailing fell to whimpering where she lay shoved among the packs, then to silence. In the first moment of that silence, Olwynn closed her hands round the blade. Her blood poured over her hands, pulsing with the same rhythm of her breath. She opened her lips. Some word trembled there as her eyes met Griff's. The word fell away unspoken as she collapsed.

The little dove lay dead among the wolves, killed upon the road home.

* * * * *

"Son of a *bitch!*" Griff shouted.

He kicked the body of the tall, thick-shouldered bandit, tumbling it down the hill to lie with the others. Wolves and ravens would feed well here. We'd picked over the corpses of all the bandits, rummaging for what seemed worth taking, flints and strikers, a small leather pouch of coin, and two good dirks. We'd have taken their swords, too, but those needed carrying, and we didn't want the burden. I hid them deep inside the cave, a weapons cache.

Only one other body remained, that of Olwynn Haugh. She lay inside the cave, and I'd wrapped her in her cloak and folded her hands upon her cold breast. Now I stood with her green velvet pouch, tossing it gently from one hand to the other.

"Son of a bitch," Griff whispered, looking at dead Olwynn.

I've said it—you could look into the eyes of Killer Griff and see the flames of a long-ago burning. You could see the very place a boy once crouched, bleeding and stunned, a dark and suffocating hold where smoke and terror and grief made knotty fingers to tear the soul from the body. You could hear the voices of that nightmare, a father's desperate plea for the lives of his family, a mother screaming as her baby died. He was in that place, that dark place of his nightmares, even as the new sun rose behind him and threw his dark shadow over the body of Olwynn Haugh, over her child.

He stood looking down at the child, eyes cold and narrow. She'd wailed the last hours of the night through while we rolled corpses down the hill, hungry and frightened, until at last exhaustion took and stilled her. She stirred now, as if she knew he was looking at her. One little fist waving in sleep, she sighed. Griff looked past her to Olwynn dead, then reached out and scooped up Cae. So small was she that her head fit into one of his big scarred hands. With the other he could have snuffed the life from her, smothering. For a moment I thought he would do that and leave her dead here with her mother. We'd hie us back to Long Ridge, and maybe he'd have the satisfaction of knowing he'd seen his foeman's kin dead.

But that wouldn't get me paid.

"Griff," I said, "we'd better get going if we're going to make Haven tomorrow."

He looked at me from those nightmare eyes of his, and he laughed bitterly. "Then what? How do I find the bastard now? I don't even know what name he's using."

I shrugged as if the problem was nothing to worry about, steering him back to where I wanted him to be—in that place where I'd get my money.

"We know he's somewhere in Haven. You still want to find him, so we'll find him." I cocked a thumb at Olwynn's child. "When we do, she'll get us into his house just like her mother would. How happy will they be to let in the man who saved the grandchild from murder?"

He grunted, thinking.

"Could work," I said, still tossing the green velvet pouch from hand to hand. The coins made lovely music clinking together, the sound of my warm winter. "We don't know his name, but we know his daughter's. We can find him."

Griff, he still had his eyes on the child, and a coldness stole over his face, ice creeping on a still pond. Yet when he looked up at me again it seemed to me that the coldness wasn't there anymore, that it had been my imagination painting the expression.

He grabbed the pouch in midtoss and bent to pick up the baby. "Broc, what's the best way to Haven from here without going back to the road?"

Well and good, I thought.

Cae sighed, and her lips moved in one of those unwitting smiles of babies, sleeping in the arms of the man who planned her kinsman's death.

"The best way is down through the Centaur Reaches," I said, easy again and ready to finish what we'd started. "The centaurs and I, though, we don't get along. I can take you across the wood and around the Reaches to where the Elfstream runs. We can follow it right to Haven."

All his ghosts peering out at me from his eyes, Griff said that route was good enough for him, and so we left the cave, Olwynn Haugh's cold tomb, and went away again into Darken Wood.

* * * * *

Ah, my feet like the old stamping grounds! They find their way almost without my eyes, knowing the game trails and the clear runs beside little streams the way townfolk know their streets and roads. So my feet and I led Griff west and south through the golden wood while wind blew chill through the shimmering aspens and bracken rustled under foot. High in the sky, geese went winging in spearhead formation, their calls sounding year's end. All the world smelled sweet and sad in its last glory. It wouldn't have been such a bad walk south in the gold and the quiet, but we weren't long gone from the hill before Cae awoke in full voice and hungry.

Squalling, she writhed in Griff's arms, waving her fists. Jays flew up from the trees, fleeing her storm. The child's wailing echoed all around us, and nothing Griff did to calm her made a difference. He walked for a while with her in his arms, then for a while holding her against his shoulder. Nothing stilled her, though her cries, at first piercing, eventually became weaker, more piteous than those first demanding yells.

"We're going to have to feed her soon, Griff."

"Feed her what?" He said that the way most men do when a child is on hand and the mother isn't, surprised to have to bustle around looking for food. He shifted the child from his right shoulder to his left, scowling. "I don't see any goats or cows around here."

"Water, maybe." I took the leather bottle from my belt. "It'll fill her belly anyway."

We tried to trickle some into her mouth. That didn't work. Griff wet his finger for her to suck. That didn't work either. Then I soaked a twist of cloth, and she took it with a gleeful cry. The wind picked up a little, blowing chill. Griff hunched over the child, lending body warmth. His scarred face close to hers, he whispered, "Ah, now, ah, now, there, that's all right. Take some more. That's right. . . ."

It was strange to see him at that work, to watch those hands I'd known only as killer's hands holding Cae so tenderly. As I watched, ghosts stared out at me from his dark eyes. One of those ghosts in life, I remembered, had been a young brother, a boy still in the cradle that day the Dark Queen's army fell upon a lone little farmhouse out there in Estwilde. They say in Thorbardin that lessons learned early linger long. Well, perhaps that's true, and the boy Griff must have learned one or two gentle lessons before the hard schooling came rampaging.

"Come on," I said when it seemed Cae had taken all she would. "We have some ground to cover before night."

We made good time after that, but a darker silence attended us now as we went down through the aspen wood. The sky grew heavy overhead, and clouds moved in from the east, changing the sun's gold disk to dull silver. The trees, the earth, the strengthening wind itself smelled of rain. All this I saw, and none of it, it seemed, did Griff note. Up hill and down, across streams and on trails thin as shadows, he listened to ghosts whose rest was a long time coming. His gentle mother, his father, his sister, and his baby brother—all these cried their deaths to Griff as he went walking with the grandchild of their murderer in his arms.

They did something to him, those voices, and they had more power over him now than they used to have. Through the darkening day I saw it: They changed him, they hollowed him, and it seemed to me, as I led him along the secret paths of Darken Wood, that Griff was actually losing flesh, growing white and stark and starved. Griff Unsouled, spirit-killed and animate, he went like Death, walking down to Haven with ghosts shouting in his head and an infant resting trustfully in his arms.

Trustfully, aye, and she grew quieter by degrees, sleeping sometimes, more often simply lying still, exhausted. When she did rouse, her hungry cries were but whimpers. By the middle of the afternoon the whimpering turned to silence. For the first time I wondered, would the child survive the trip to Haven? Griff wondered, too. I saw him check on her often. No gentle word did he speak now, no soft, whispered comfort remembered from another time. He looked at her with hard eyes and cold, assuring himself that his little passport to vengeance still lived.

Wind picked up, whirling leaves down from the trees, rattling in the brush. Leaden clouds hung lower till you could see them clinging round the hills like ragged shawls on the shoulders of old ladies.

"Keep going," Griff said, shifting Cae in his arms, tucking her warmly beneath his cloak.

He said that as the first fat drops of rain pattered on fragile leaves.

"No." I made my voice hard enough to tell him I wouldn't be gainsaid. "Now we stop. Haven isn't going anywhere before tomorrow."

I led him and the baby and all the ghosts aside from the trail, across a small stream, and round the back of a small hill. There the wind broke, whining around the rising ground, and there I found an overhang of stone, lone outrider of the hills we'd left behind. Griff put the infant down on a clear patch beneath the overhang. She stirred a little, but there wasn't much strength in her for crying.

I peered out into the darkening day. "I'm going to find us some supper. See if you can find enough dry wood to get a fire started."

I had a pocketful of snares and the notion that a warm broth of whatever I caught and killed might go down Cae's throat easier than water. When I looked behind me, I saw Griff standing over her, the child a little bit of life at his feet. His eyes were almost gone in blackness, the planes of his face carved away by shadows.

He was sitting before a hot, high fire when I returned, Cae in his arms. He had nothing to say when I showed him the rabbits I'd snared, and he didn't eat what I skinned and cooked. Not until we had a good broth of the leavings did he unbend and rouse himself. The child must be fed, and he went at that work as he had before, soaking a twist of cloth and tempting her to take it.

For all he tried, Cae didn't take the food. She'd been a day and a night without her mother, without the rich milk she needed. I knew it looking at her: Nothing we'd concoct would help her. I knew it, but Griff didn't, or he wouldn't admit it. He kept at her, teasing the cloth to her lips. No word did he speak, though, and not the smallest bit of tenderness did I see from him. All that, it seemed, he'd spent in the afternoon. He had only the single-minded need to see her fed, and she wouldn't feed.

I believed, as I rolled myself in my cloak to sleep, that Olwynn Haugh's little daughter would soon join her mother in whatever land of the dead folk travel to when all the warring and striving is done. She'd go and leave Griff with no way to his revenge and me no path to those steel coins that would keep me warm and in dwarf spirit through winter.

Damn, I thought, falling asleep. Damn me if easy money isn't the hardest to earn.

Cae didn't go to join anyone, though; she held tight to her little strand of life. I saw it was so when the night had flown and gray morning hung low in mist. Griff stood just beneath the stony overhang, and he turned when he heard me up. Cae lay in his arms, covered in folds of his green wool cloak. Killer Griff, Griff Unsouled, looked around at me, empty-eyed, his scarred pale face written in lines of hatred sharp as knives.

"How's the child?"

He shifted the baby in his arms, and if I didn't know better I'd have thought it was a sack of rags he held, so limp was the child now. Coldly, he said, "I'll have my vengeance. Let's go."

We went, and no other word did he say all the way down to Haven.

* * * * *

You find a man in a city the same way you find a man in the wood. You track him. In Haven, Olwynn Haugh's father wasn't so hard to track. We found his trail all over the city, that double-eagle stamped on ale kegs and wine barrels and on the flanks of barges. He was a rich man, a well-known importer, and only one question, dropped in the right tavern at the right moment, found him for us. His name was Egil Adare, and he lived on the hill, his house overlooking the city and the harbor where his barges brought in goods from all over Abanasinia, even from beyond. Sight of his ring opened the door of that fine house for us. Sight of his grandchild sent the servant scurrying, an old woman looking over her shoulder and clucking like a hen as she led us through the grand house, up winding stairs and down breezy corridors.

They live well, the merchants of Haven, and I saw in every room I glimpsed that this one, this Egil Adare, lived like a king. Griff saw it too, his eye alighting on golden statuary, silken hangings, rich velvet draperies. He saw, and he said nothing, only followed the servant, Cae in his arms. Like grim Death he went stalking, and like Death, white and hollow, he stood outside the door of his enemy, waiting as the servant knocked, then entered.

"Griff," I said, "I'll wait—"

—outside to guard the door, to find a way out of this mazy mansion once the killing was done. He gave me no chance to say so.

"Come with me," he said. To me, but looking at Cae all the while.

The door, shut by the servant, opened again. Griff lifted Cae to his shoulder. Her little head lolled, her thumb fell from her mouth. She whimpered faintly, then stilled.

Griff stepped before me into the chamber, a counting room where the largest piece of furniture was a broad desk upon which ink wells gleamed like jewels and quills marched in perfect alignment, the merchant's little soldiers. No sign of the merchant himself did we see, but his double-eagle, those two heads in opposition, glared at us from every panel, from the hanging behind his desk, even from the thick blue and gold carpet underfoot. Griff's shoulders twitched, just a little, to see those sigils, but he never lost his stride. Boots tracking mud across the richly woven carpet, he made a little thing of the distance between him and the desk.

I shut the door, paneled oak and heavy, firmly behind us and stood with my back to it. Cradled in Griff's arms lay Cae, unseen beneath the green cloak, hidden. Cradled in mine lay Reaper, not hidden. The tapestry behind the desk stirred. A hand pushed it aside, and Egil Adare stepped into his counting room.

He looked more like a vulture than an eagle, that merchant, his hooked nose a beak, his ropy neck long, and his hooded eyes restless and watching everything, judging whether he saw predator or prey. I could see that he had been a big man, that his hands, now gnarled and swollen in the joints of every finger, had once been broad and strong. Where I come from they'd say those hands had been hammer-fisted.

Griff kept still as a breathless night, head up, eyes cold. Thus he stood, straight and proud before the man who had murdered his kin. In him his ghosts howled, keening their death agonies, then falling—suddenly!— silent. So it had been in every nightmare that owned him, waking and sleeping. Now he stood before the shaper of those nightmares, waiting to be recognized. He wanted to see shock in those muddy, brown eyes, surprise and then fear. The old man gave him nothing.

"I am Egil Adare," the merchant said, shifting his glance so he looked at neither Griff or me, but at some point in the distance between us. He put a hand beneath his desk, sliding open a drawer. A small leather pouch sat in there, fat and full. We were meant to see it, as beggars are meant to see a hand reach into a pocket, withdrawing the few coppers that will send them on their way. "I am told you have news of my daughter."

Griff's heart must have pounded like drums in him, but no one could know it by looking at him. He stepped forward, letting his cloak fall open. Cae never moved, not when the green wool, sliding, brushed her pale cheek, not when Griff set her gently upon the broad desk and placed her exactly between Egil and himself. She whimpered a little then, moving her hands, turning her head. She was looking for Griff, the source of all the warmth and care she'd known these two days past, but he wasn't paying any attention to her now.

"Here is the news," he said to Egil Adare, his voice rough and hard. "Your daughter is dead. This," he indicated Cae, "this is all that is left of her."

The merchant's face went ashen. He stepped to the desk, eyes on the child lying so still and silent.

In the instant, Griff's sword flashed out. "Hold," he said. "Ash Guth, you hold right there."

Ash Guth, Griff said, speaking the name he'd known so long ago. Like a man turned to stone, the merchant held. His thin lips parted. In his eyes sprang a light, recognition. Soft, unbelieving, he said, "You? Is it you?" His eyes narrowed, and he drew himself up, all his thin bones. "How did you find me? I thought you were—"

Griff's laughter rang like blades, one against another. "You thought I was dead? Did you think you were the only one to survive the Dark Queen's assault on the High Clerist's Tower? Well, you see you're not the only one, and if you have forgotten me, I haven't forgotten you." He lifted his sword so the light coming in through the window glinted all along the edges. "Or the debt you owe me."

The old man shuddered, understanding at once what I had yet a moment to grasp. "You—you killed my Olwynn?" He looked at me, then swiftly back to Griff. "You killed her?"

Griff smiled, as a wolf smiles. He said neither yes or no, but he knew which conclusion the old man would draw.

Tears sprang in the merchant's eyes. "Olwynn," he whispered, imagining every horror. "Oh, my child. . . ."

Upon the desk Cae stirred again. Her lips parted, trembling with hunger and great weariness. She saw Griff standing above her, and she knew him. She lifted her hand, just a little, and touched the edge of the blade. Blood sprang, one drop, from her finger. In Griff's eyes a wan light gleamed, pale like the phosphorous you see over swamps where dead things lie rotting.

My blood ran cold in me as I understood how deep was the vengeance he planned, a deeper one than I'd reckoned on. He was going to make Egil pay his debt with more than his own death. *Your father's precious treasure,* so he'd named Olwynn and her child. In bloody coin would he extract his debt, doing to Egil what had been done to him, for if others had killed Olwynn before he could, still he had her child. This dark a deed even he hadn't done in all his long years of killing. Still, it wasn't my vengeance, and not my place to trim it. I do what I'm paid to do.

Outside in the hallway voices murmured, one servant to another. I tightened my grip on Reaper's haft. Any moment a servant could knock at the door, the old man could cry out.

"Griff, if you're going to do this—"

He turned, snarling, "Shut up!"

Just as he moved, the merchant reached for the child on the desk. He stopped still in his tracks as the tip of Griff's sword touched his breast, then traveled higher to his throat, the drop of Cae's blood glittering on the steel like a tiny ruby. Swiftly, the tip dropped again, resting at the infant's throat.

"You killed my mother," Griff said to Ash Guth who'd renamed himself Egil Adare. He leaped, like a panther pouncing, and snatched the old man by the shirtfront, dragging him around to the front of the desk. "Her name was Murran. You killed my sister, and her name was Bezel. My father's name was Calan, and you killed him even as he kneeled to beg for the life of his infant son. That infant's name was Jareth, and he screamed all the killings through until at last—" his eyes never leaving the old man's, Griff lifted his sword, the tip dancing over Cae's throat "—until at last there was only silence."

Egil Adare fell to his knees, cowering. "My grandchild," he sobbed. He reached a trembling hand to Griff, then let it fall. "Oh, Olwynn's daughter . . ."

Cae whimpered, and then she wailed, crying with more strength than I thought she had in her hungry little body. Her eyes, blue as springtime skies, turned to Griff, widening as she recognized him.

Him, though, he stood there, his steel like silver in the failing light of the day. He looked down at the child, she his weapon of vengeance, her death to be put against those of his kin in a dark healing. He smiled like rictus.

"Please," the old man sobbed, as surely Calan Rees must once have begged. Tears poured down, and it looked as if his face were melting. "Please, oh, gods, please don't kill the child. . . ." He bent down, he did, and pressed his forehead to Griff's dusty boots, wetting them with weeping. "My grandchild. Oh, my grandchild . . ."

"My brother," Griff snarled. Rage ran like fire now burning everywhere through him. "My mother, and my sister, and my father—my *soul!* You stole them all from me, you bastard!"

My soul, he said, catching all his dead in those two words, all his grief, all the years of nightmare, and all the killing he had himself done, one death after another, each in some way meant to echo those first deaths or to still the echoes of them.

Griff's hand tightened on the sword grip. His knuckles whitened as Cae smiled up at him. She lifted her hand, touching the steel again. She found her voice, and she made that cooing sound babies make. I hadn't heard it from her since last she lay against her mother's breast.

"Spare the child," Egil moaned.

Griff kicked him away. Like a beaten dog, he came crawling back. Whispering, wheedling, the most powerful merchant in Haven abased himself like a beggar. "You want to kill me. I know it. I see it. Do it! Do it, but spare the child!"

He rose to his knees, he tore the shirt from his breast, baring himself to the sword, pale skin tight over protruding ribs.

Griff stood still as stone, barely breathing. The old man's sobbing sounded like the pulse of a faraway sea.

Then it too fell still. Once again I heard footsteps pass the door, voices murmuring. Whispered one woman to another, "He'll be wanting his supper soon. D'ye think those two'll be staying?"

"Griff," I said, warning. "Are you going to do this, or aren't you?"

Like fire, his eyes, and he spat, "Take it easy. You'll get your pay."

Egil Adare, cringing on the blue and gold carpet, looked up at me, his eyes overflowing with tears. Ah, but he'd heard something, that canny merchant, he'd heard talk of pay.

"Listen," he said, only to me. "I can pay you anything you want. Stop him!"

I laughed, and I turned from him. I didn't get to be this old by double-dealing. All I wanted was for this dark work to be done. It seemed to me I could hear every voice in the house now, all of them creeping closer.

In the light from the window Griff's sword shone, bright and clear. He lifted it high, glinting over the tiny body of the child he'd carried out of Darken Wood. Were the ghosts howling? Oh, aye, they were screaming in him.

The old man flung himself forward, clinging to Griff's legs, his forehead pressed to the knees of the man whose family he'd destroyed. "Don't, please. I'll give you every-thing I have!" He pulled back, his arms flung wide. "Take anything you see here!"

The sword hung, unmoving, over the silent child.

"Take anything!" Egil Adare cried, the wheedling whine back in his voice. "I'm a rich man! Spare my grandchild and I'll give you jewels, I'll give you all the steel you want!"

So he said, but the dearest thing Griff wanted this old man had long ago destroyed.

Griff's hands tightened on the sword grip. His eyes grew strange and still when he saw his own scarred reflection in the polished blade. All his ghosts stared back at him, howling, the mother, the father, the sister. Ah, the infant brother screaming all the deaths.

"Anything," Egil sobbed, his face white and dirty, running at the nose. "Anything, take everything. . . ."

In the instant he said it, moaning his last plea, Griff did just that. He looked Egil Adare straight in the eye, and he took everything.

* * * * *

Now you have heard the truth of Griff Rees, who was stolen from his home in the days before the Second Cataclysm. He'd been a long time gone, on hard roads and cruel, by the time Olwynn Haugh came into the Swan and Dagger to open her little green velvet pouch and show him how much she could pay him for the safety of his company on her road home.

If Olwynn's road didn't bring her all the way home, it did lead Griff there. Soon after winter he took the north-running ways to Estwilde. I haven't heard that he's farming there, but they do say he's settled near where his father's farm used to be. That was a time ago, maybe eight years, or nine.

I haven't seen him a day since then, but news travels, and the word that comes to me is good. Some of it says Killer Griff has found himself some peace, maybe even his soul.

Well, it's always "maybe" when you're talking about that kind of thing, peace and souls, but true enough it is they say that the little girl he's raising up as his own, that one with the springtime blue eyes, is the smile on his lips and the light in his heart.

Noblesse Oblige
Paul B. Thompson

Mile after mile the winding trail ran, closed off from the sky by a dense arch of leafy branches. The first exuberant growth of spring had transformed the forest from a hall of barren trunks to a living cavern of green. Sunlight scarcely penetrated to the forest floor, leaving the horse and rider in perpetual shade.

Roder nodded in the saddle. The old charger, named Berry because of his red coat, had a gentle swaying gait that lulled his rider as surely as a summer hammock. Roder had been on the road since before dawn, and the excitement of his hasty departure had worn off after many miles of calm woodland.

He'd ridden out from Castle Camlargo, an outpost on the western edge of the great forest. On a scant hour's notice Roder had been given an important dispatch by the commandant of the castle, Burnond Everride, to deliver to the neighboring stronghold at Fangoth. In between the two castles lay the vast forest, home of wild animals and even wilder outlaws.

Roder's slack hand dropped the reins. Without a hand to guide him, Berry at once fell to cropping tender leaves from the branches encroaching on the narrow track. The sudden cessation of motion roused Roder like reveille.

"What? Huh?" His hands went to his head and found the heavy helmet perched there. His memory returned when he touched cold steel. His mission—the dispatch.

He checked the waxed leather case hanging from his shoulder. Lord Burnond's seal was intact.

Since Berry was having a snack, Roder decided to get down and stretch his legs. He stooped to touch his toes, then arched his back, leaning against the weight of the sword strapped to his left hip. The sword was a potent reminder of the cause of his journey.

Outlaws. Half a dozen robber bands used the forest as their hideout, and their depredations were giving Lord Burnond fits. Most of the tiny Camlargo garrison was out chasing one gang or another, and when the time came to find a courier to take the commandant's message to Fangoth, Roder was the only man left to carry out the delicate mission.

"The forest bandits refuse to acknowledge our sovereignty. Our last three messengers vanished in the wilderness without trace," Burnond solemnly warned him. "Are you still willing to carry this dispatch to Lord Laobert?"

"I am, my lord," Roder declared. "I shall not fail!"

What was that?

Somewhere ahead, screened by ferns and bracken, someone was shouting. Above the voice in distress came a more ominous sound—the clang of metal on metal. Even Berry noticed and stopped stripping the bushes. The old warhorse's instincts were still strong. At the sounds of fighting he snorted, nodded his head, and began pawing the ground with a single heavy hoof.

"I hear it," Roder said breathlessly. He tugged his brigandine jacket into place and tightened the strap on his helmet. "Bandits!"

Berry was very tall, and it took some effort for Roder to get his foot in the stirrup and hoist himself onto the animal's broad back. He wrapped the reins tightly around his left hand and thumped Berry's flanks with his spurless heels. "Giddup!" The old warhorse couldn't manage a gallop, but he stirred himself to a stately canter, straight down the path toward the sounds.

Once the horse was in motion, Roder wondered if he'd ever stop. Berry plowed on, paying no heed to low branches that threatened to sweep Roder out of the saddle. Leaves swatted his face, and limbs rang against the comb of his helmet. He shouted, "Whoa, Berry! Whoa!" but the warhorse would not stop until he'd delivered his Knight to the fray.

The trail wound right, then left, descending a sandy slope tangled with tree roots exposed by heavy rains. Somehow Berry managed to avoid tripping on this hazard. Roder lifted his head and saw a two-wheeled cart overturned in a small brook that cut across the trail at the bottom of the hill. Four men, mounted on short, sturdy ponies, were milling around. Two of the men carried crude spears, saplings really, the tips hacked to points and hardened by fire. The other pair brandished blazing torches, with which they were trying to ignite the turned-over cart.

"You there, stop!" Roder cried. He dragged at his sword hilt. The blade was longer than he thought, and it took him two pulls to free it. The marauders looked up from their work and pointed. Above the brook the trees parted enough to admit sun and sky, and the light flashed off Roder's polished helmet and sword. The men with brands hurled them into the cart. The canvas canopy burst into flame, and two people leaped from the wreck to escape the fire. One slender figure in a long brown dress staggered ashore and was caught by a spear-armed brigand. He dragged the girl over his saddle, and with a whoop, galloped away. The other person from the cart, his clothes ablaze, threw himself in the water.

Horrified to see a young girl carried off before his eyes, Roder let out a yell and steered Berry after the fleeing bandits. The heavy charger built up speed thundering down the hill, and for a moment it seemed he might overtake the robbers on their nimble ponies. But just as his rear hooves got wet, Berry snagged his front legs on a snarl of floating rope. The lines were firmly tied to the cart, and the horse twisted sideways and fell heavily into the brook.

Roder went flying. He landed hard enough on the muddy bank to drive the wind from his chest and see stars in daylight. Berry stepped free of the ropes and trotted riderless up the hill after the bandits.

The sun stopped spinning, and Roder felt cold water seeping into his boots. A shadow fell across his face, and he looked up to see a young man gazing down at him.

"Are you all right?"

Roder bolted from the mud. Somehow, in all the running, flying, and falling, he had managed to keep his grip on his sword. He presented the muddy blade to the stranger. The pale-faced young man backed away.

"No, wait! I'm not one of tbe robbers!" he said, waving Roder's sword aside. "That's my cart there. My name's Teffen—Teffen the carter."

Roder lowered his weapon warily. "What happened here?"

"I'm a tradesman, on my way from Kyre to Fangoth," said Teffen. He was little more than a boy, with a pale, pleasant face, spoiled by a rather long nose and sharp chin. Teffen was dressed like a townsman—trews, broadcloth tunic, and a leather vest. The sides of the vest were scorched. "My cart got mired in the creek, and before Renny and I could get out, the outlaws attacked."

"Renny?"

"My sister." Teffen's eyes widened. "They got her! They got Renny!" He turned to pursue the long-departed brigands. Roder caught his arm and spun him around. Under the broadcloth the boy's arm was slender but hard.

"Wait," said Roder. "You can't catch four men on horseback by yourself."

"Let me go!"

Roder released him. "You'd better listen to me. I know about bandits. They're ruthless killers. The woods are full of them."

Teffen planted his hands on his hips. "Who are you?"

He drew himself up to full height. "I am Roder, of Castle Camlargo."

"You're one of the Dark Knights?" Roder nodded gravely. "We paid tithe to you to traverse your lands. We were supposed to be protected! You must help me save my sister!"

"Under other circumstances, I would, but I have an important mission—I must deliver a dispatch to Fangoth as soon as possible."

Teffen looked as though he might cry. "You know what they'll do to her, don't you?"

Roder tried not to think about it. Lord Burnond's message, seal intact, still hung from his shoulder. The sheaf of parchment was a tremendous burden, far heavier than its true weight.

"In the end, they'll kill her," Teffen was saying. "Of course, by then she may be better off dead."

"Don't say that!"

"Who am I fooling if I pretend otherwise?" the boy shouted. The following silence was lightened only by the gurgling of the stream.

Roder looked from the sword in his muddy hand to Teffen's plaintive face. "I'll save your sister," he said at last.

Teffen fervently clasped his hands. "May the gods who still live bless you!"

Embarrassed, Roder pulled his hands free on the pretext of washing them in the brook. As he splashed water on his face and rinsed the gray muck from his sword, he said, "Do you have a weapon, Teffen?"

"Just this knife." He held up a milliner's blade, no more than three inches long. "I had a short sword, but a bandit knocked it from my hand. It fell in the water somewhere."

"Never mind." Roder didn't plan to fight the bandits anyway. He had some idea he and the boy could sneak into the robbers' camp by night and free Renny. Swordplay was something he wanted to avoid.

He took off his helmet, scooped up a double handful of cold water, and let it pour through his long, blond hair. When Roder stood up, he found Teffen watching him in a curiously attentive way. Teffen, aware his attention was noticed, turned away, slogging through the knee-deep water to the wrecked cart. Smoke from the burning cart made him cough.

"What were you carrying?" asked Roder.

"Dry goods, mostly. Bolts of yard cloth, wool yarn, a cask of buttons." What hadn't burned was hopelessly sodden. "It's all gone, looks like."

"Worldly goods can be replaced," Roder replied, tucking his helmet under his arm. "What matters most is saving your sister's life and honor."

Teffen kicked the charred underside of the cart. "You're right, my lord. I'm glad you came along when you did, or I'd have no hope at all." He looked around suddenly. "My cart horse ran off when the bandits cut the traces. Where's your steed, Sir Roder?"

Good question. Roder shaded his eyes and gazed up the trail where Berry and the robbers had disappeared. He put on a good front. "Silly, brave old horse! When Berry hears the clash of steel, he has to gallop into the thick of things. Once he realizes he's lost me, he'll come back."

"Time is fleeting, my lord. Poor Renny—"

"Yes, of course." Roder sheathed his sword and walked onto the east bank of the stream. Teffen poked around in the ruined cart for a few seconds and soon joined Roder carrying a small canvas pack.

"My things," said the boy in response to Roder's inquiring look. "Shall we go?"

Roder led the way. He carried his helmet, letting the late day sun dry his loose, flowing hair. He was the very image of a Knight, with his broad shoulders, black brigandine, helmet, and sword. His wet boots squished loudly as he walked, spoiling the effect, and by the time the sun set, his feet still weren't dry.

The brigands' trail—and Berry's—was easy to follow. The robbers rode two abreast down the narrow path, and Berry's iron-shod hooves left substantial dents in the dirt. At intervals the bandits' horses pulled up in a group and milled about, then set off again. Roder imagined they could hear Berry and thought the Knight they saw at the brook was bearing down on them. Strangely, they didn't try to leave the path, though their smaller mounts could easily have done so, leaving Roder's big warhorse to flounder in the underbrush and closely growing trees.

He remarked on this to Teffen, who shrugged and said, "Who knows what bandits think?"

"They want your sister for ransom," Roder speculated. He was sweating under the weight of his equipment. "You don't dress as if you have much money, though your manners are refined for a tradesman."

Teffen kicked a rock off the path. "Our family had money once. Our fortunes failed after the great war, and we've been working folk ever since."

"There's no shame in that."

"I'm not ashamed of anything I do."

Roder cast a sideways glance at the boy. Something in Teffen's manner—his stride, the determined set of his jaw—convinced Roder there was truth in his statement. Teffen, noticing Roder's scrutiny, changed the subject.

"How long have you been a Dark Knight?" the boy asked.

"I've been at Camlargo all my life."

"That's a curious way to put it." Teffen smiled in an obscure way.

"I was abandoned at the castle gate as a baby. Lord Burnond became my guardian and raised me."

They were walking close enough together that their shoulders bumped. Teffen said, "I'm sure it was more interesting than growing up in a milliner's shop."

"I can't complain. I get to spend a lot of time with horses. I like horses."

Darkness came early in the deep forest. The setting sun's oblique rays could not penetrate the thick curtain of leaves, causing twilight to fall much sooner than it did on the plain. Roder and Teffen had marched for hours without closing the gap. Teffen was deeply worried about his sister; Roder could tell by the fact the boy said less and less as their hike progressed. The trail remained fresh; the robbers seemed just beyond reach, over the next hill, around the next turn. . . .

Roder was tired. His feet were blistered where his wet stockings rubbed, and he was ravenously hungry. He diplomatically suggested pausing for quick meal. To his surprise, Teffen readily agreed to rest. They found a fallen ash tree a few steps off the trail. Roder sat astride the wide trunk and spread his kerchief on the moss-encrusted wood. Teffen perched on the other side of the tree, hands clasping a knee to his chest. He sighed.

"We'll find her," Roder said. "They can't have done anything with her yet. They're still moving—they must know we're pressing them."

"I just wish we were fifty strong instead of two," Teffen said.

"There aren't fifty Knights at Castle Camlargo."

Teffen gazed off into the darkening wood. "Really? I thought there'd be more than that."

"There's never more than thirty Knights at the castle. There's a hundred men-at-arms, you know, but the whole garrison is out right now, hunting outlaws."

"I heard the forest was dangerous before I left home, but I had no idea how bad it was. Which band do you think attacked Renny and me?"

Roder whittled slivers of hard, white cheese off the block he carried in his pouch. He offered a chunk to Teffen. "There's any number of gangs roaming the forest, but Lord Burnond says two bands in particular are a menace. One's run by a villain named Gottrus—'Bloody Gottrus' the foresters call him. He was once a retainer of Lord Laobert's, but he was branded for theft and driven out of Fangoth. They say he's killed a hundred people, men and women alike, and robbed over a thousand."

Teffen bit off a piece of smoky cheese. "Who's the other outlaw chief?"

"A mysterious fellow known as 'Lord' Sandys." Roder rummaged in his pouch and found the bunch of grapes he'd tossed in before his hasty departure from the castle. Unfortunately, his fall on the creek bank had pulped the sweet fruit. He withdrew his sticky fingers and shook his head.

"What so mysterious about him?"

"No one can say what he really looks like," Roder said, wiping his fingers on the kerchief. "He's a clever rogue. Last year he robbed a merchant caravan of fifteen hundred steel pieces, even though the wagons were guarded by fifty mercenaries."

"Has this Sandys killed a lot of people?"

"His share, I'm sure. He's an outlaw, but they say he's cut from different cloth than Bloody Gottrus. Gottrus is a killer and plunderer. Sandys, they say, has some kind of personal vendetta against the Knights—"

Teffen bolted from the tree. His movement was so swift and sudden Roder missed his mouth and poked a sliver of cheese into his cheek.

"What is it?"

"I heard something. A horse."

Roder stood up, hand on his sword hilt. "Where?"

"It came from that direction." Teffen pointed down the gloomy trail from whence they'd come. He stiffened. "There!" he hissed. "Did you hear that?"

Roder wasn't about to admit he heard nothing. With no pretense of stealth he dragged his leg over the fallen tree and walked past Teffen to the middle of the path. His nonchalance evaporated when he spotted a dark gray figure far down the trail, silhouetted against the near-black tapestry of trees. It was a man on horseback, waiting there.

Roder pulled at his sword hilt, but it didn't seem to want to come out the scabbard. Red-faced, he shouted, "Hey!" at the phantom. Like a ghost, the man turned his horse away, and vanished silently into the trees.

"Teffen! Did you see—?" Roder realized he was addressing empty air. The boy was gone, too. Poor lad, he's probably frightened and hiding, Roder thought.

"Teffen? Teffen, where are you? It was just one man, I'm sure. He turned tail when he saw me." He stood absolutely still and listened. Tree frogs and crickets were beginning to wake up for the night. Beyond them he could hear nothing. He decided Teffen must have run off.

"Idiot," he said good-naturedly. Teffen would return once he realized there was no danger. No sense blundering after him in the dark woods. Roder scratched up some tinder and twigs and used his flint to start a small campfire. If Teffen had any sense at all, he'd home in on the light or the smoke.

Roder sat down with his back against the fallen ash tree. The little fire crackled just beyond his feet. He laid his sword and scabbard across his lap and resolved to remain awake until Teffen returned. His resolve failed him. By the time the fire had burned down to a heap of glowing coals, Roder was well asleep.

Something brushed his cheek. In his torpor, Roder scratched his face to shoo the fly. It came back and nudged him a little more firmly. Not a fly, then. Berry.

"Go 'way," he mumbled, rolling away from the annoying horse.

Something tickled his nose. In his sleep-addled mind, Roder thought he was at home, at Camlargo. His small room was plagued with spiders during the warm months. He hated them. He once knew a boy who died of a spider bite. When the insistent tickling returned to his ear, he knew it couldn't be Berry bothering him. It must be—a spider!

He rocketed upright, kicking his feet and slapping his own face with both hands. His backward progress was stopped when he ran into the ash tree trunk.

"Eh?" he said. A lantern flared. Roder looked up into a cold, grim face.

Leaning against the fallen tree was Teffen, a hooded lantern in his hand. With him were five rough-looking men clad in deerskins, their faces smeared with soot.

"What's this?" asked Roder, unsure of what he was seeing.

"The charade is over," Teffen said. "Good night, good Knight." He nodded. Before Roder could protest, the hard-looking man nearest him raised a mallet and brought it down on Roder's tousled head.

Lord Burnond was not going to like this turn of events.

* * * * *

Roder opened his eyes with effort. It felt as if someone had poured sealing wax on them.

"Ow," he groaned. "I'm sorry, my lord. I didn't mean to oversleep—" He blinked and tried to wipe away the haze and discovered his hands were tied to his ankles. It was an extraordinarily cramped position, made all the more unpleasant by the dull throb of pain in his head.

A bucketful of cold water hit him. "Good morning," said a calm voice. Roder shook off the water and inner cobwebs and saw a slim pair of legs in front of him, clad in soft suede boots and black leather trews.

"Ugh, who is it?"

The legs bent, and Teffen squatted down nose to nose with Roder. "Did you sleep well?" he asked genially.

Roder strained against his bonds. "No, damn you! Let me go! Ow! What's this mean, Teffen?"

"I thought the situation was clear. You're my prisoner."

"But I'm a Knight of Takhisis!"

"Are you? The quality of captives around here is going up."

Another, stockier pair of legs entered his view. "This is all he had on 'im," said the newcomer. "Some kinda seal on it."

"That's an official dispatch!" Roder protested. "Put it back! Don't touch it—" Fragments of the red wax seal fell on his shoes.

"Let's see what the commandant of Camlargo has on his mind, eh?" Teffen perused the scroll sent by Commandant Burnond. "Hmm, interesting."

"What's it say?" Two more pairs of legs crowded around, peering over their leader's shoulder.

"You know none of you know how to read," said Teffen. His cronies merely grunted. "How about you, Roder? Can you read this?" He held the unrolled parchment in front of Roder. Neat lines of script filled the page from top to bottom.

"Of course I can read it," he snapped. "That's a very important dispatch from my lord Burnond Everride to Lord Laobert, commander of the garrison at Fangoth!"

The outlaw chief scrutinized the document again.

"Remarkable," he said dryly. "I had no idea Burnond was so literate."

"You know Lord Burnond?"

He stood up. "We're competitors, you might say." He rolled the scroll into a tight tube and stuck it in his boot top. "So, Roder, my lad. Now we've got you. The question is, what are we going to do with you?"

"You'd best let me go."

"And waste a good hostage?" asked Teffen. The brigands laughed.

Roder was starting to sweat, his heart pounded in his ears. The bruise behind his left ear ached, and he felt as if he might throw up if they didn't release him from this painful hogtie. "What is this all about? What about rescuing your sister?"

More laughter. Teffen knelt and displayed his short knife under Roder's nose. Roder closed his eyes and steeled himself for the strike, but instead of plunging the blade in his back, the youth slit his rough bonds. Roder shivered with relief until four strong hands seized him by the arms and hauled him to his feet.

"Time for a genuine introduction. My name is Sandys," he said. "As I am of noble lineage, I am called 'Lord' Sandys."

All the blood drained from Roder's head, and his knees folded like a pair of dry cornstalks. The outlaws dragged him his feet again, snickering.

"I see you've heard of me," the former Teffen said.

"It was all a trap," Roder gasped. "The robbery, the cart, your sister—"

"You can meet my 'sister,' if you like." He indicated the fifth man present, a rangy fellow with a face as tan as an old boot. His long reddish hair was pulled back in a thick hank. The outlaw grinned and held a tattered brown gown to his shoulders. Roder closed his eyes and cursed his own stupidity.

"You make a fine sister, Renny," Sandys said. The rawboned bandit laughed and tossed the old dress on the ground.

"We usually work the carter-and-his-sister routine on wealthy travelers," the bandit chief said. "Once we saw you were by yourself, it seemed a good idea to land you and see what you were up to."

"You make me sound like a trout," said Roder.

"You took the bait like one."

Roder swallowed and darted his eyes from side to side. He was somewhere deep in the forest. A smoky campfire smoldered in the center of the small clearing. Crude tents of deerskin and bark lined the edge of the clearing. He counted just five men with Lord Sandys.

Sandys handed him a hollowed gourd. "Drink," he said. "No doubt you've got a headache."

Roder took the gourd gratefully and gulped the liquid inside without sampling it first. It wasn't water but some raw, fiery liquor, which scalded his throat all the way down to his stomach. His popeyed expression made the bandits roar.

"What kind of tenderfeet are the Knights sending after us these days?" said one. "Is this all they have left?"

"My job was to deliver a dispatch, not chase bandits," Roder croaked.

"So I've seen, but Gerthan's point is well made. How old are you, Roder?" Sandys asked.

"Twenty-five."

Sandys narrowed his eyes. "How old?"

A chill ran down Roder's spine. "Twenty."

The outlaws laughed at him again. Sandys smiled. "That's all right, Roder. I'm but twenty-four myself. It's not how old you are that counts, it's what you've done with your life."

Stung by their laughter, Roder said, "I see what you've done with yours!"

"Your order made me into an outlaw," Sandys shot back. "Lord Burnond confiscated my ancestral estate and drove my family into poverty."

"Did he make you steal?"

Sandys drained what liquor remained from the gourd. Wiping his mouth with the back of his hand, he said, "I know two great thieves, Roder. One lives in a castle and is deemed noble. The other lives in the forest and owns nothing but the clothes you see."

The outlaws, laughing some more, turned and went about their morning chores. Roder stood where they left him, paralyzed. He could see they'd brought his gear along, including his sword, which was leaning against a tree scant feet away. Berry was there, too, tied to a picket line with the brigands' horses. Could he reach his horse before the bandits could react?

"Forget escape," Sandys said, still standing there. "You won't last a day in the woods. If a beast doesn't get you, other outlaws will—and not all the bandits in this forest are as tolerant as I am."

"What's to become of me?"

"I don't know. Would your commandant pay to have you back?" The look on Roder's face answered that question. "Too bad. He should prize his spies more."

"Spies?"

Sandys suddenly backhanded Roder across the face. Though slight of build, the bandit chief had an iron hand. Roder's aching head rang from the blow. He balled both fists, then stopped himself when he remembered Sandys was armed and he was not.

"Stop playing the fool!" Sandys said fiercely. "I see through Burnond's stratagem!"

He massaged his throbbing jaw. "What are you talking about?"

"You came to the forest to spy on us, didn't you? Why deny it when I have the proof before me?"

"You're mad! I told you, I was sent by Lord Burnond to deliver—"

"To deliver this?" Sandys snatched the scroll from his boot and flung it in Roder's face. "Don't make me laugh! It's gibberish—just random scribbles. Did you think I wouldn't be able to read it?"

Roder picked up the dispatch. He unrolled it and look it over, puzzled. The parchment was cut square, and he couldn't tell the top from the bottom. He turned it this way and that.

Sandys pulled the scroll from Roder's unresisting grip. "Why do you persist in this stupid game? Next thing, you'll ask me to believe a Dark Knight can't read."

He flushed. "It's true, I cannot read."

"Can't read?" Sandys muttered, color draining from his face. "That's what I thought. . . ." He backed away, and shouted to his men: "Gerthan! Renny! Rothgen! Wall! Urlee!"

Only four men answered their chief's call. "Where's Rothgen?" Sandys said sharply.

"He took two pails down to the spring," his "sister" replied. Renny squinted in that direction. "He is taking a long time—"

"Get to your horses. We're getting out of here!"

The robbers stared. Sandys roared some choice profanity, and they bolted into action. Roder looked on, absolutely thunderstruck. Gerthan ran past a moment later, a horse blanket draped over his shoulder. He pointed to Roder and said, "What about him, Sandys?"

"We don't have time for fools. Leave him."

Gerthan spat and shook his head. "He knows our faces," he said. "We can't let him live."

Sandys was already across the clearing when the sound of Gerthan's dagger leaving its sheath galvanized Roder to action. He sprang for his sword, still leaning against a tree a few steps away. Gerthan's footfalls were close behind. Roder grabbed the sword hilt and swung around. The tip of the scabbard clipped the bandit's nose. Leaping back, Gerthan shifted his grip on the dagger from thrust to throw. Roder frantically tried to free the sword from its casing, but it was stuck tight. An inch or two of blade emerged, coated with rust. His heart stopped. After falling in the stream, he'd shoved the sword in the scabbard without drying it.

With nothing else to do, he presented the sword, scabbard and all. The covered blade was a clumsy defense, but it was all Roder had. The bandit feinted a throw, and

Roder waved his sheathed blade wildly. His grip was poor, and the heavy weapon flew from his grasp, tumbling through the air to land six feet behind his attacker. Gerthan grinned and took aim.

Somewhere in the dense greenery a horn blasted. A black arrow, fletched with gray goose feathers, sprouted from Gerthan's ribs. He groaned loudly and dropped the dagger, following it to the ground a half-second later. Shouts followed, and the sound of men and horses crashing through the foliage. The horn blew again, closer. Roder spun around, trying to spot the source of his unexpected salvation. He saw Sandys vault onto a pony. Armed men on horseback and on foot were flooding the little clearing, dozens of them. More arrows flickered into the turf around him. Who was attacking? Another outlaw band, warring on Sandys's gang?

Heart hammering, he knew he should do something. Picking up Gerthan's dagger, Roder tore after Sandys, leaping over stones and tree roots. The bandit's pony scrambled ahead, opening the gap between them until a trio of horsemen appeared directly in Sandys's path. Sandys wrenched his horse around and found Roder blocking his way, dagger in hand.

Shouting, the bandit slapped the reins on either side of the pony's neck and galloped at Roder. Whatever rush of courage Roder felt a moment before left him when he saw Sandys bearing down on him. He reversed his grip on the dagger as he'd seen Gerthan do, and flung it at the onrushing bandit. The next thing Roder knew he was flying through the air. He hit the ground hard and cut his chin. He didn't see the thrown dagger land on the nose of Sandys's horse, rapping the animal smartly. The dappled brown-and-white pony reared.

Roder clambered past the pony's churning legs and threw himself on Sandys. The bandit was a seasoned fighter, but he'd fallen across some rocks, struck his head, and lay there partly stunned. Roder landed his hundred seventy-five pounds on top of him.

"Get off, damn you!" Sandys shouted, trying to shift the bigger man aside. Roder got his hands on Sandys's wrists and pinned them to the ground. Sandys had an impressive cursing vocabulary and exercised it freely. While they struggled, men and horses surged around them.

The shouting and neighing subsided. Roder glanced away for only a second and saw the mounted men around them wore the tabard of the Fangoth garrison. Knights! He straightened his elbows, pushing himself up for a better look. Sandys took advantage of his distraction to plant a boot on Roder's chest and heave him off. He rolled to his feet and found himself staring at the somber faces of twenty Dark Knights.

Roder grabbed Sandys and turned him around. Face streaked with dirt and blood (most of it from Roder's chin cut), Sandys's shirt was torn halfway to the waist. Beneath his jerkin, Sandys's chest was tightly wound with a long linen bandage. It took a moment for Roder to understand why—"Lord" Sandys was a woman.

As he stared at the female outlaw, Sandys lashed out and punched him hard in the face. The Knights roared with laughter as Roder staggered back. He spat blood and found an eyetooth was loose.

"I've had enough of you!" he said in a rush of new-found rage. But he found his way to Sandys blocked by an imposing gray charger. Roder was about to take the rider to task when he realized who'd stopped him. There was no mistaking that iron gray beard and leonine head.

"Lord Burnond!" In a paroxysm of relief he clasped the old commandant's leg. "My lord, you came after me!"

"Get away, boy," Burnond said crossly. "We're here to settle these outlaws, not save you." He looked to the other side, where Sandys stood with her two surviving men. "Put them in chains," Burnond said. "Add them to the ones we've already bagged."

Foot soldiers prodded Sandys forward. She glared at Roder. He couldn't fathom her expression—it was more than anger. Hatred? Or something like grudging respect?

Burnond ordered the herald to blow his cornet, and more men emerged from the trees. Some were in the livery of the Fangoth garrison, others Roder recognized from Castle Camlargo. If both knightly contingents were present, then there were some two hundred Knights and men-at-arms in the clearing.

"Bring the prisoners along!" Burnond shouted.

Lines of captured brigands, chained together in long strings, filed past Burnond Everride. Roder was astonished at their number. Carefully, diffidently, he asked where the other outlaws came from.

Burnond cleared his throat. "We took Bloody Gottrus's camp last night," he said. "Gottrus himself died fighting, but we captured most of his gang."

Sandys and her two surviving comrades were thrown in with the rest. Roder stood quietly beside the commandant until a shackled Sandys staggered past. The sight of her in chains affected him strangely.

"Sandys—" he said, stepping toward her.

Burnond ordered the prisoners to halt. "Is this the bandit known as Lord Sandys?"

She looked at the ferns, trodden into pulp by the Knights. "That's her," Roder said quietly.

"Her? There've been rumors to that effect, but I didn't believe them. Very well, let her be so marked." A squire hung a wooden tag around Sandys's neck with her name painted on it. Burnond was about the dismiss her when Roder remembered the dispatch.

"Wait!" he said, darting out to snatch the parchment from Sandys's boot. "Your dispatch, my lord!"

"My what? Oh, that." Burnond took the scroll from Roder and crumpled it in his fist. "It's nothing."

"What? It's a vital message for Lord Laobert!"

"Still playing your part, I see," Sandys said wearily. "Give it up! It was all a ruse, wasn't it?" She nodded at Roder. "You sent this mercenary into the forest posing as a Knight, to find us out, didn't you?"

Burnond arched an iron-gray brow. "Roder's no Knight, and he's no mercenary, either."

"You sent out this clever spy with a fake dispatch," she said, "knowing the forest brotherhood couldn't resist waylaying him. All the while you were on his trail with your troops, waiting to pounce on us."

"In a manner of speaking, my 'lord.' Roder's mission was a diversion, to distract your kind from our forces moving into the woods from east and west. I never dreamed this trap of mine would catch such big game as you and Bloody Gottrus. You're wrong about the boy, though—he's no spy, no fighting man at all. He's the stableboy at Castle Camlargo, that's all."

A silence ensued as Sandys glanced from Roder to Burnond and back to Roder.

"The boy's a fool," Burnond said. "He has no aptitude for the manly arts."

Sandys managed to smile through her swollen lips. "I'm the fool, Burnond. Roder had me convinced—up to the point I discovered he couldn't read. After that I had him pegged as a bounty hunter. Stableboy? Your stableboy attacked me on foot while I was mounted, and only his quick thinking kept me from getting away. If all your Knights were as manly as Roder, the bandits would have been cleared from this forest long ago."

He stared at them both, speechless. Lord Burnond had tricked him and now exposed him as an utter dunce—and now it seemed that Lord Sandys the outlaw was sticking up for him.

"Your eloquence is misplaced," Burnond replied loftily. "Those who resist the forces of order will inevitably fall. That is their destiny. Roder's destiny is in the stable at Camlargo. In two days he'll be back there, and you'll be in the dungeon for your many crimes. Move them out, sergeant!"

The line of prisoners lurched onward. His face burning, Roder watched Sandys go. In fact, he found he couldn't keep his eyes off her.

* * * * *

The capture of Lord Sandys and a large portion of Bloody Gottrus's feared outlaw band created a sensation in the countryside. People flocked to Castle Camlargo from as far away as Lemish to see the infamous brigands brought to justice. Burnond Everride compounded matters by issuing a proclamation that anyone with evidence against Gottrus's or Sandys's gangs should come to Camlargo and confront the villains at their trial. People came by the hundreds to do just that.

All of this passed with Roder back in the stable, diligently forking hay into the byres and mucking out the many stalls. Berry was back, having been recovered from Sandys's camp by Burnond's men. In his own stoic way, the old horse seemed glad to see Roder again. He demonstrated his feelings by stepping on Roder's toes with a heavy iron-shod hoof.

A scaffold was erected in the castle courtyard. Here the outlaws were paraded before the angry crowd one by one, to receive their howls for vengeance. Roder waited for Sandys to appear, but Burnond was saving for last the rare spectacle of hanging a female outlaw. Roder tried once to visit her in her cell, but the Knights on duty would not allow him in.

"Go back to your dunghill, boy," one of them told him. "Leave justice to real Knights."

The second day of the trial went much the same as the first. Chained prisoners were led out of the dungeon to the wooden platform, to await their turn before their accusers. It was midafternoon before Roder spotted Sandys at the end of the line. Her cuts and bruises looked improved, and she'd been put in clothes suitable for her gender. In a simple homespun shift, she looked more like a farmer's wife and less like an infamous outlaw.

Things went slowly. Some of Gottrus's worst men were ahead of her, and the accusations against them were lengthy and many. Some of the tales of murder, theft, and rape were lurid and horrible. The outlaws were all crowded together on the raised platform. Between chores Roder returned to the stable door to check on Sandys and monitor her progress to the scaffold.

It was late morning. Soon the proceedings would have to break for lunch. Guards were thinking about their meal, and the crowd was howling at a particularly venomous outlaw. While the courtyard was distracted, Sandys made a furtive moment that Roder spotted. The outlaw had produced a short length of wire hidden in her hair and was trying to use it to open her manacles. Roder opened his mouth to cry out, but said nothing. He bit his lip as the heavy chains fell from her wrists. She caught them with her knees, preventing them from noisily striking the ground. Even the brigand in front of her didn't realize that she was free.

Sandys took a small step backward while facing ahead, then another. Roder was fascinated. He stuck a piece of wheatstraw in his teeth and leaned against the door frame, chewing. In one swift movement the outlaw dropped off the platform, turned and dashed to the castle wall some yards away. Her timing was excellent. Amazingly, no one had noticed.

Roder watched intently as she tore the sleeves from her shift and used one to make a scarf for her head. She squatted close to the wall, tore a doublespan of cloth from the hem of her shift, and used it as a sash for her waist. She used smut from the wall stones to dirty her face. In moments the notorious outlaw had taken on the appearance of an unwashed peasant woman. There were several score like her in the courtyard that very moment.

Sandys sidled around the edge of the crowd. Her disguise was perfect, and the men-at-arms paid no attention to her. She worked her way closer to the gate. Commandant Burnond was observing the trials from a balcony on the second floor of the keep, and Sandys passed directly below him. His impassive gaze betrayed no surprise, no alarm, only arrogance.

Roder spat out his straw and shouldered his pitchfork. This was his chance.

Sandys walked right out the open gate, against the stream of local folk filing in to see the brigands meet justice. The guards ignored her. A dozen paces from the castle, she began to walk faster. Down the hill were open fields of grass, and beyond that, the forest. Once out of sight of the gate, Sandys struck out across the meadow. Distant shouts from the courtyard crowd could still be heard. Her escape was still unnoticed, but the vengeful roar put haste in Sandys's step.

"Hold!"

Roder, pitchfork in hand, appeared on her right. She gauged the distance between him and the edge of the woods. Too far; he could easily catch her if she tried to run. She angled a bit to improve her lead, then said, "Well, stable boy. How did you know where I was?"

"I watched you," he said. "I saw everything you did. You were wonderfully clever."

"How did you get here ahead of me?"

"Postern gate. I ran."

She inched a few more steps through the knee-high grass. "You think you can stop me?"

"If I brought you back now, it'd show Lord Burnond I'm no fool."

She palmed the sweat from her eyes. "Is that what you want? The approval of the Knights? You'll never get it, not even by recapturing me. You'll never be anything but a stablehand to them."

He slowly lowered the pitchfork. "I know."

"You do?"

"I thought about what you and Lord Burnond said the day you were captured. He's known me all my life, and he thinks I'm a worthless shoveler of manure. You knew me for two days and thought I was a clever spy. That's why I'm going to let you go."

She folded her arms. "Roder, you *are* a fool. How do you know I didn't say those things just to flatter you?"

He shrugged. "Doesn't matter."

Frowning, Sandys strode over to him and eyed him up and down. Without warning, she took his face in her hands and kissed him fiercely.

He gaped. "What was that for?"

"You'll figure it out."

She lifted her skirt and started running for the woods. "I'll see you again, Roder. Count on it!"

He leaned on the pitchfork and watched Sandys race through the still grass. Burnond would be apoplectic over her escape, no doubt. Roder would enjoy that. He touched his lips, where the taste of the infamous bandit "Lord" Sandys lingered. He enjoyed that, too.

See her again? Why not?

Sandys reached the thick green line of trees and plunged in. She never looked back.

Much Ado About Magic
Kevin James Kage

"Hello!" shouted the kender.

Laudus started. His hand flew to the side, tipping an inkwell and soaking a manuscript with rich black ink. Rising from his seat, the old man thundered across the study and thrust his head out the window.

Fifty feet below him, the little man stood at the gates of the tower, peering about and shouting "Hello!" every few moments.

"Be quiet!" the archmage said.

"Hello!" the kender said as he spotted the man. He waved his arms in greeting. "I say! Could you open the door, please? It seems to be stuck!"

"Absolutely not! Leave at once!"

"I can't leave! I have some very important information to relate!"

"Absolutely out of the question! Go away!"

"But it's very important!"

Mustering his patience, the archmage said, "Well, what is it?"

The kender looked taken aback. "I couldn't tell you! You might be a spy!"

The old man scowled and threw the now-empty inkwell. It struck the ground to the right of the kender, bounced a foot more, and landed with a dusty thud. The kender looked astonished beyond measure.

"Thank you!" he said cheerfully. "But all I really need is the door opened!"

Laudus looked about for something else to throw, but he found nothing disposable. He opted for the next-best solution.

"Cedwick!"

Moments later, a lanky young man stumbled into the room. Though merely an apprentice, he stood a full head taller than Laudus and possessed a good deal more hair. "Almost done, Master," he said. "Your fine robes have been packed as you requested, and I've taken the liberty of packing—"

"Enough, enough," Laudus said. "I'll finish the packing. There's something else I want you to do. There's a kender outside."

"A kender? Why?"

"How should I know? Go deal with him!"

"Maybe he wants to give you information for the Conclave meeting."

"Foolish boy! The Conclave doesn't inform outsiders of its meetings. Least of all, kender." He waved a bony finger at his apprentice. "Don't you fill the kender's head with any ideas. If you so much as mention the Tower of High Sorcery, we'll never be rid of him!"

"Of course, sir," Cedwick bowed. "What if he has some important information, though?"

"No kender in the history of Krynn has ever had important information." After a moment, Laudus added, "Unless, of course, he stole it."

From beyond the window, the kender began to sing a bawdy drinking song in an off-key tenor voice.

"Go get rid of him!"

"Yes, Master!"

Quite suddenly the kender changed keys, becoming considerably more shrill and, amazingly enough, more off-key. The old man felt a headache coming on.

* * * * *

"I've come to speak to Master Laudus about the Conclave meeting," the kender said brightly.

A little voice inside Cedwick's head told him he had heard incorrectly. The kender couldn't have said, "I've come to speak to Master Laudus about the Conclave meeting."

"Excuse me?" the young man asked.

"I've come to speak to Master Laudus about the Conclave meeting," the kender repeated.

Cedwick stood there dumbly. It still sounded like "the Conclave meeting."

"You've come to speak to Master Laudus about the Conclave meeting?"

"Yes!"

"No, you haven't."

The kender nodded. "I have! I heard the Conclave was holding a very important meeting about the disappearance of magic, and I have information on the subject."

"Well, then, why are you here at my master's tower? Why didn't you go to the Tower of High Sorcery?"

Cedwick suddenly remembered he wasn't supposed to mention the Tower of High Sorcery. This could mean trouble.

The kender, however, seemed unsurprised.

"Because!" he said. "Everyone knows the great Master Laudus is attending the Conclave meeting, and I thought he could best relay my information, being a higher wizard than me."

"You are a wizard?" the apprentice asked.

In truth, the kender did look like a wizard—or perhaps a satire of one. He wore a voluminous gray robe. Silvery symbols covered every available inch of the cloth. Clutched in one hand, the little man held an intricately carved staff. From its look, it had probably been a hoopak at some stage of its life, but the sling had been replaced by a beautiful shard of blue crystal. The kender's other hand could not be seen, for it lay buried beneath a mass of rings, bracelets, and assorted bangles. No less numerous were the necklaces and pendants about the kender's neck. Earrings dangled from his pointed ears. The apprentice wondered how this fellow managed to stand with the weight of that jewelry.

"Well, I'm not exactly a wizard," the kender admitted.

"Not exactly?"

"I'm more of a wizard slayer."

"A wizard slayer?"

"Why do you repeat everything I say?"

"Why do I—" Cedwick began before thinking better of it. He stared at the kender incredulously. "What do you mean you are a wizard slayer?"

"That's my name! Halivar Wizardslayer. What's your name?"

"Cedwick," the apprentice mage said hastily. "So you don't actually kill wizards?"

"Of course I do! I wouldn't be deserving of my name if I didn't, now would I?"

"Have you killed many of them?"

"Every one I have ever met," said Halivar. "That makes—" he glanced at the sky, thinking noisily, "Eight— well, seven. The eighth was an alchemist, not a wizard, but he had a magic ring and—"

"Why do you kill wizards?"

"Oh, it's not that I mean to kill them or anything! I really have nothing against them at all! It's just that when I come into contact with a wizard, sooner or later, he dies."

"Are you telling me I'm about to die?"

"No, no! You're standing in the protective circle. You're completely safe."

Cedwick looked down. To his surprise, he found himself standing in a crudely drawn circle in the dirt.

"You did this?" he asked the kender.

"Before you arrived," Halivar said, nodding. "Just coincidental that you stood in it. Lucky for you!"

"Now, look," Cedwick said, stepping forward.

"No, please! Don't leave the circle! It would be just awful if I killed you!"

The young man shook his head. "I don't believe you have a curse."

"Oh, yes, I do! I'm sure of it. That's why I've been studying magic! I want to end the curse."

Cedwick glanced at the kender sharply, "You say you've been studying magic? How?"

"I have these books!" the kender said, smiling. From beneath the folds of his robes he drew forth a set of four mismatched tomes tied together with a length of cord.

Cedwick's eyes grew wide. "Please let me see those!"

Halivar thought for a moment before he said, "Okay, but don't step outside the confines of the protective circle!" The kender set the books down along the edge of the circle and stepped back a dozen feet.

Cedwick knelt and carefully picked up the books. Even without a close inspection he could tell they were genuine spell books. Furthermore, they appeared to be spell books of four different mages. The spines of all but one book bore sigils of protection. He guessed that a little of their original magic remained, just as certain artifacts within Master Laudus's tower held some of their powers.

"Where did you get these?"

"I found them!"

"Found them?"

"Well," Halivar said, "it seemed to me that the wizards would not be needing them anymore, being dead and all. So I thought I could use them to help understand what was happening."

Cedwick rose to his feet. "You understand that studying magic without the approval of the High Council is a serious offense?"

"Is it really?" the kender said inquisitively. "I've never committed a serious offense before. Not on purpose at least!" His eyes hardened, his brow furrowed, and he stood straight and resolute. "What is the penalty for such a crime?"

The young man couldn't help but chuckle at the kender's sudden resolve. "This is your punishment. You must go home. Leave these books and any other items you have acquired from mages here with me, and don't try to learn magic again."

Halivar hesitated. "I can't do that."

"Why not?"

"Because I have very important information for the Conclave! I must deliver it to Master Laudus."

"Oh, yes, I forgot. Well, you're in luck! I am in charge of deciding who will see Master Laudus."

"Really?"

"Of course," Cedwick lied. "Why do you think he sent me out to greet you?"

"Well, may I see the him now?"

"Not yet. First, I must hear your story."

"Oh, of course." The kender bowed, but he stood there a long moment without saying anything.

"Go on! Speak up!"

The kender looked as if he were having a difficult time of it. Finally he looked levelly at Cedwick and stood straight as an arrow, as if he were a man facing his death without fear.

"Master Cedwick, I have destroyed magic . . ."

* * * * *

". . . And so as I was picking up the broken bits of mandolin and offering an apology to the minstrel, the alchemist's carriage collided with the vendor's cart, and the sausage flew into the magic circle," Halivar finished.

"So the sausage disrupted the spell?" Cedwick yawned.

"No, the sausage attracted the stray dogs."

"So the dogs disrupted the spell?"

"No, no, no! It was the crate of apples the dwarf was carrying! Haven't you been listening?"

Cedwick thought he had been listening. Of course, he thought he'd been listening the first two times the kender told the story as well.

"So if I were to sum the story up into a single sentence," he said, "I might say that due to a string of accidental mishaps—"

"That were by no means my fault!" the kender added hastily.

"That were by no means your fault, the spell you tried to cast was altered in such a way as to destroy magic."

"Just so!" the kender beamed.

Cedwick gave a longing glance toward the tower and wished he were packing again.

"You do realize that the rest of the world believes magic is gone because the gods have departed, don't you?"

"Of course!" the kender said. "Uncle Tasslehoff defeated Chaos and the gods departed, and so it's only natural for everyone to assume that's why magic is gone!"

"I want you to understand," Cedwick said, "because of that, the Conclave isn't likely to believe your story."

"No?" Halivar pouted. He looked at the apprentice mage. "You believe me, though, don't you, Master Cedwick?"

"What I believe doesn't matter, Halivar. Master Laudus and the Conclave must believe."

"Oh! I'll go explain it Master Laudus then!"

"No!" Cedwick said quickly. "If you approach him with this story, he is likely to find the idea preposterous. In the end, he may dismiss the idea simply because it came from—" He paused. "Well, from a kender, Halivar."

The wizard slayer pursed his lips. "He would?"

"Just because Master Laudus is part of the Conclave," the young man explained, "doesn't mean he is infallible. Perhaps because of his training, he can't believe anything less than a god could take away magic. Do you understand?"

"I think so."

"Good."

"So you mean to say," the kender's eyes widened, "that I'm a god?"

"That's not what I—" Cedwick began, when suddenly, the tree line exploded in a clap of thunder.

Cedwick fell to the ground, and Halivar clamped his hands over his ears. Green foliage flew in every direction, and behind it billowed a thick black cloud of smoke and debris. Something struck the tower behind Cedwick with a deafening thud.

Cedwick spun his head around to glance at the tower, expecting part of the wall to be missing. To his astonishment, it appeared entirely undamaged. However, a large lump of metal sat smoldering on the ground where it had landed after deflecting off the wall.

"Good thing there's some magic left in the walls," Cedwick thought aloud, but he realized he couldn't hear his own voice because the warning siren was wailing too loudly.

Warning siren?

Cedwick turned back toward the source of the explosion. A long, cylindrical metal snout emerged from the cloud of smoke. It rode forward unsteadily on a pair of mismatched wheels. Behind it appeared a horde of tiny sputtering men and women. They coughed and gagged and seemed very relieved when they finally cleared the smoke.

Gnomes.

They pushed the cannon forward a few more feet, and then a few of the little creatures began to reload their cannon. Cedwick quickly rose to his feet and began running toward them.

"Stop!" he shouted, his arms flailing.

Much to his dismay, no one heard him. This mainly stemmed from the fact that the gnomes could not figure out how to shut off their warning siren. In fact, they looked rather perplexed that the cannon even had a warning siren.

Several gnomes worked diligently on disengaging the warning siren, while another group occupied themselves with a debate as to why there was a warning siren, and half a dozen more targeted the tower for another blast. Behind the cannon, a delegation of four gnomes busied themselves with looking important and impressive.

Not one of them, in fact, paid any heed to the advancing young man. Nor did it occur to them that someone might be standing directly in the path of their cannon.

That person happened to be Cedwick.

"Stop!" Cedwick cried again, throwing himself to the ground, shutting his eyes, and covering his ears.

A long moment passed, and Cedwick felt quite certain he was about to be the recipient of a cannon blast. Quite suddenly, the siren ended. At last, when he decided that he might be still alive, he opened his eyes.

A dozen gnomes stood around him, looking down at him expectantly. The apprentice mage stood up, brushing off his white robes and trying to look as if falling in the dirt was a normal thing to do.

The lead gnome, dressed in his finest workman's leather, bowed deeply.

"Howdoyoudo?" the gnome said, then remembering himself, he slowed his speech. "I am Jobin, the executive vice-director of the Subcommittee of Accidents and Mishaps pertaining to the Guild of Magic Analysis and Prestidigital Improvements."

"I am Cedwick."

"Are you a wizard?" Jobin asked.

"Of course."

"Cedwick!" came a bellowing voice from above.

Cedwick turned to see a graven face leaning out of the study window.

"Master!"

"What is that confounded racket? Have you gotten rid of that kender?"

"No, I'm here!" said the kender happily.

"What are these gnomes doing here? Cedwick! If I have to come down there—"

"You won't, Master Laudus! I assure you. I'll handle the situation."

"See that you do!" said the archmage and ducked back into the tower.

Instantly the air filled with a fugue of gnomish chatter. With a shrill toot from a bright silver whistle, Jobin silenced the party.

"We are honored, Master Cedwick, to meet one who knows Master Laudus. We have journeyed long and far to speak with him."

"Then why were you attacking his tower?"

The gnomes shot each other baffled glances.

"We were doing no such thing!" Jobin asserted.

"You fired a cannon at the tower!" Cedwick cried.

"Yes," the gnome nodded. "That is our signal cannon."

"Signal cannon?"

"Indeed! We use it to announce our arrival and to request an audience with whomever we are visiting. It is quite ingenious really! A measured amount of explosive powder is stuffed into—"

"But why fire it at the tower?" Cedwick said, "Couldn't you have fired it into an open area?"

The gnomes pondered this idea excitedly for a moment. Several of them broke away from the group to examine and modify the cannon.

"Truly you are a wise man, Master Cedwick," said Jobin solemnly.

"He is! He truly is!" came a voice from behind the apprentice mage. Halivar bounded forward, one hand still clamped over an ear. Apparently, his rings had become tangled with his earrings and the whole mess was proving difficult to separate.

"Who might you be?" the gnome inquired.

"I'm Halivar Wizardslayer," the kender said, "the god!"

Cedwick interjected, addressing Jobin politely. "May I ask what business you have here?"

"Certainly! As I said, we are here to see Master Laudus!"

"Regarding what?"

"We have very important information that will be relevant to the upcoming Conclave meeting."

"Conclave meeting?"

"Yes. That's why we are here, you see—because Master Laudus is going to the Conclave meeting."

"If you don't mind me asking—?" the apprentice began.

"Yes?" said the gnome.

"How is it that everyone in the world knows about the Conclave meeting?"

The gnomes looked at each other uncomfortably.

"Is it a secret?" Jobin asked.

"Yes," replied Cedwick.

"We probably shouldn't discuss it near the kender then."

"It's okay!" Halivar said. "I already know."

"How did you find out, Halivar?" asked Cedwick.

"My Aunt Fern told me," said the kender, "only she's not my aunt. She's really a second cousin once removed. Or is it a first cousin twice removed?"

"Please, Halivar. Just the explanation."

"Anyway, she heard it from Glider Snapdragon, who got it from Miriam Redrash, who overheard a drunken wizard talking about it in jail."

"How coincidental!" said Jobin. "We too heard of the Conclave meeting from a drunken wizard. Only he wasn't in jail. He was sitting on a fence."

"Really? I wonder if it was the same wizard."

"It doesn't matter! I understand now, thank you," said Cedwick with irritation.

"Don't be alarmed," the kender whispered loudly. "He gets a little cranky."

Cedwick turned to the kender to argue that he was not even a little cranky when a sharp wailing—similar, but distinctly different from the warning siren—erupted a few meters away. Spinning to face the new noise, the young man noticed a bulky gnomish contraption bearing down on him at a frightening pace. Just when he thought the thing would crush him and continue straight on into the tower, the loud wail sounded again, and the front of the beast suddenly belched a cloud of white steam. The lumbering thing came to a sudden stop.

Cedwick stared at the gnomish aberration. In most respects, it resembled a wooden cart. The front of it, however, supported what might have been an old iron stove. From the front of the stove jutted a large metal cylinder out of which steam was pouring. Connected to the bottom of the cylinder were two smaller cylinders. These, in turn, connected via a metal shaft to the wheels. They were called spitspins, Jobin announced proudly, presumably because they spun the wheels around, all the while spitting hot steam.

"You may not know it, Master Cedwick," the gnome added confidentially, "but the Guild of Safely and Efficiently Getting from Point A to Point B is not the most reliable of guilds. The Veryveryhot broke down three times this morning," he added in despair. "I honestly wouldn't use it, but my second cousin Smidge designed it, and she's very enthusiastic about the thing."

As if on cue, a female gnome popped her soot-stained head out from behind one of the Spitspins, smiling and waving a well-bandaged hand. She very nearly fell off the cart. Balance restored, she went back to tinkering with the machine. There came a sound like bacon sizzling, and the little gnome gave out a yelp of pain.

Cedwick had a sudden inkling as to why they called it the Veryveryhot.

"Of course," the gnome said, "without it, we never would have been able to bring the signal cannon, much less the God Trap."

"Excuse me?" was all the young man could think to say.

Halivar, however, thought of quite a lot to say.

"Really? A God Trap?" he said. "Can I see? How does it work? Will it really trap a god? I doubt if it could trap me!"

"We based it on the Graygem," Jobin said proudly, "and we were going to use it on Chaos, except we had a slight problem with a new weapon we were testing. It delayed our arrival." He paused, as if unsure how to go on. "I really should be explaining this to Master Laudus."

"You're in luck!" cried the kender as he climbed on top of the God Trap. "Master Cedwick is the man in charge of deciding who speaks to Master Laudus."

Cedwick sighed. What *had* he gotten himself into?

The gnome perked up considerably. "In that case . . ." he straightened his workman's leather and cleared his throat. "Master Cedwick, it is my sad duty to inform you that the Guild of Magic Analysis and Prestidigital Improvements has accidentally trapped magic."

Something inside the young man made a noise not unlike gears popping loose. He assumed it was his sanity becoming unhinged.

The gnome droned on. "The Subcommittee for Accidents and Mishaps has further determined that the magic of Krynn is located inside the complex and wonderful device inadequately named the God Trap Machine. We are therefore here with said machine in order to assist the wizards in the Tower of High Sorcery at Wayreth in removing the magic from the God Trap Machine and restoring it to Krynn proper."

"That can't be true!" said the kender. "I myself personally destroyed magic!"

"I'm afraid you're wrong," replied Jobin. "In actuality, we gnomes trapped magic in our machine."

"Impossible," said the kender. "Even gnomes couldn't build something that traps magic."

"Well, magic certainly wasn't destroyed by a kender!" Jobin said, his face flushing, and his speech steadily increasing in speed. "Akendercouldn'tdestroymagicifhetried. Ithadtobegnomishingenuity."

"Ridiculous," the kender retorted. "Kender ingenuity can destroy anything! It's vastly superior to gnome ingenuity!"

At this, Jobin did a very un-executive-vice-director-like thing and punched Halivar in the stomach. The kender tumbled over in a jangling mass of jewelry, but not before swinging his staff, tripping the gnome. Jobin also went down, and upon impact, nuts, bolts, and screws flew everywhere.

In reaction to this assault on their leader, half a dozen gnomes in Jobin's party hefted wrenches and hammers and glared hostile gnomish glares at the winded kender. The small group of gnomes who had been so diligently modifying the signal cannon to point in a harmless direction suddenly resolved to point it directly at Halivar. Several other gnomes quickly ran to assist Jobin, who flailed miserably under the weight of his workman's leather.

A moment later—just when both the kender and the gnome had risen to their feet and decided to hit each other again—Cedwick stood between them.

"Stop!" he shouted, a strange fire burning in his eyes.

"But—" both the gnome and the kender began.

"You will not have a fist fight on the Tower grounds!"

Both the kender and the gnome shrank away from him, and Cedwick suddenly realized he must be more intimidating than he thought. He kept up his vicious stare, wondering idly if it might work just as well against other people. The gnomes and kender continued to back away, holding their noses as they went and shifting farther and farther upwind. Cedwick thought about this idly as well, until he realized that intimidated people don't generally travel upwind as they back away.

Suddenly he smelled it.

For a moment he thought the gnomes might have been using more than wood to power the Veryveryhot. Then, quite unexpectedly, something tugged meaningfully at his robe. Glancing down, he discovered a large clod of dirt smiling up at him.

Two beady, piglike black eyes squinted at him. Meaty, filth-encrusted hands soiled his robe. Something that resembled hair grew out of the top of the clod of dirt and spilled out across the rest of it.

"Hello!" it said through rotting teeth.

Cedwick drew in a sharp breath of surprise, then rather wished he hadn't.

"Does Master Laudus always allow gully dwarves to come to his Tower?" the kender asked, still holding his nose tightly.

"Never," Cedwick answered, although today apparently everyone was allowed on the Tower grounds.

"Helg come for High Robe. Looking for High Robe," the grimy little creature said. "You High Robe?"

The Conclave was not doing a very good job of keeping its plans a secret.

"I—" began the apprentice mage.

"High Robe!" the female gully dwarf said delightedly. "Me come far! Bring message from great gully dwarf shaman."

"If this has anything to do with lost magic—"

Helg stared at him a moment in awe. "You smart High Robe!" she said. "You know secret shaman message!"

"Little One," Cedwick said, "you did not steal, destroy, or in any way take magic."

The gully dwarf made a sour face.

"You not smart after all," she said. "You sure you High Robe?"

The apprentice mage's expression transformed from one of weary calm to one of sheer bewilderment.

"Course gully dwarves not steal magic!" Helg said. "Big men lose magic. Stupid. How lose magic? Magic everywhere!"

Cedwick began to wonder what sort of nightmare he was in, where kender and gnomes picked fights on his front lawn and gully dwarves lectured him on the nature of magic.

"That why I come to Tower. Helg show Robes where is magic!"

"Do you know where magic is? Can you show me?"

"Helg show!"

Very slowly and deliberately, the gully dwarf reached into her bundles of rags. Carefully she removed an object from its resting place and dropped it in the young man's outstretched hand.

Cedwick peered at it, suddenly realizing that the source of Helg's magic resembled a small, very desiccated frog.

"Frog magic," said Helg. "Very powerful!"

The apprentice mage began to turn green, a color the frog had not been for some time.

"Frog magic, indeed," he heard Jobin remark to Halivar. Halivar snorted in derision.

Helg, however, heard them as well, and she reacted much less tolerantly. Faster than a desiccated frog could hop, she was across the courtyard. Two pudgy fists gave both the gnome and the kender a clout in the head.

This time, the scene erupted into an all-out war. The gnomes responded to the gully dwarf's temper by scampering for suitable weapons. The kender smacked the gully dwarf with his staff; then, for good measure, he struck Jobin as well.

Jobin, not at all pleased at being clouted and struck, decided to retreat to the safety of the Veryveryhot. Helg followed quickly. Halivar, beset momentarily by several angry gnomes, swung his staff about as if it were a sword. Fortunately, it was not.

"Stop!" Cedwick cried amid the confusion. However, at that exact moment, someone set off the signal cannon, which in turn sent the warning siren blaring.

The whole spectacle became a massive brawl. The gnomes, outnumbering the gully dwarf and kender twelve to two, fought each other, "just to be fair." Guild fought guild, and committee fought committee. Cedwick caught sight of Jobin and his cousin, wrenches locked. Somewhere above the screaming of the siren, someone was shrieking to be let out of the signal cannon.

The young apprentice mage waded into the fray, struggling to restore order, but every time he pulled a pair of fighters apart, another pair took their place. Just as he settled the second argument, a third fight ensued. By the time he finished with those two, the first two were at it again.

Standing atop the God Trap Machine, Helg held aloft the mummified frog, preaching, "This! This what happen when man lose sight of magic!"

Cedwick felt it was the most profound statement he had heard all day.

Quite suddenly, Halivar brought his staff down on part of the God Trap Machine. Something swiveled sharply, and with a loud crack the top of the God Trap flew off at tremendous speed. The unsuspecting gully dwarf rocketed off the machine with a startled cry. Even the gnomes stopped their sparring to take notice.

With a thud, Helg flew directly into Cedwick. The apprentice mage collapsed in the dirt. As his head connected with the ground, something within the young man mentioned that this might be a dandy moment to lose consciousness.

But he didn't.

"Cedwick!"

The apprentice mage's eyes snapped open. Dread clutched his heart. He crawled to his feet.

"Thank goodness!" Halivar said. "I thought I killed you!"

Cedwick paid him no mind. In the doorway of the Tower stood Master Laudus. Shadows played about his gaunt, narrow features, and his eyes burned with electric intensity. His arms moved in precise, rehearsed motions, and his robes flowed about him in billowing ripples.

Something sizzled through the air, landed amid the brawling mob, and exploded in a cloud of smoke. Instantly, the gnomes, kender, and gully dwarf began to gag and choke on the fumes. Cedwick's eyes watered from the stench.

Blinking away tears, the apprentice caught sight of the archmage. The old man motioned to him. His glare told Cedwick everything the young man needed to know.

Cedwick stepped out of the cloud and prepared for a lecture.

* * * * *

As the smoke cleared, Cedwick returned to the group. None of them were fighting anymore. Without exception, they all sat on the ground and gasped hard for air. They watched each other with wide-eyed stares.

When they worked up enough energy to speak, the babble began.

"Hey, was that magic?"

"I thought magic was gone!"

"Robes have strong magic for not-have magic!"

Cedwick silenced them by raising his hand.

"I have just, uh, spoken to Master Laudus," he said smoothly. "The demonstration you just received is an example of how great a wizard he is even without magic."

The others nodded solemnly.

"What did he say?" asked Jobin.

"I gave him your information. He has asked us to carry on research in his absence."

"Then our mission was successful?" Halivar asked.

"It would seem so."

The group cheered. Cedwick silenced them.

"Since we cannot be sure what exactly happened to magic," the apprentice mage explained, "Halivar will be placed in charge of 'The reacquisition of magic in the event that it has been destroyed.' The gnomes will be in charge of 'The reacquisition of magic in the event that it is merely trapped.' In the meantime, Helg will teach me the arts of frog magic. I will act as a personal liaison between the three groups."

The audience applauded, and several gnomes commented at the profoundly gnomish ingenuity of the plan.

"Let me add that I am honored to work with each of you," Cedwick continued. "You have proven yourselves dedicated to the search for magic. Such dedication is hard to find."

All the little faces beamed at this point. Cedwick smiled in return.

"Furthermore," the young man said, "each of you brings a personal insight to this dilemma. Such varied experiences will make it easier for us to find magic together."

The gnomes applauded this, and the kender shouted "Bravo!" The gully dwarf merely grinned a huge gully dwarf grin.

Cedwick grinned back. "So I would like to thank you, in advance, for the personal sacrifices you are making . . . "

Suddenly, the expressions of the group turned to blank stares. The gnomes looked at each other, searching for some meaning to the statement. Halivar glanced down at the floor.

"I say sacrifices, because that is clearly what is required," the apprentice mage said. "Even with all of us working together, it may take years, even decades, before we complete our research. During that time, we will work tirelessly. Wanderlust shall never affect us, nor shall we permit the rigors of travel to interfere with our schedule. Instead, we will sit in musty rooms devoid of sunlight. We will read book after book, until we can no longer remember what trees and birds and flowers look like. We may forget all the joys of the outside world. It will be grueling—even boring—but we make this commitment, not for ourselves, but for the future of magic."

He paused again, as many eyes stared back at him. A few of the gnomes applauded again. However, one pair of eyes—the kender's—refused to meet his gaze.

Cedwick went on, "Nor shall we despair for our friends and our families. We may never again see those we love. We may never again find the life we knew. Little Helg," he motioned to the gully dwarf, "may never again taste the stew of her homeland. She will never affectionately whomp another gully dwarf. Instead, she will live here among strangers, where whomping is not allowed. Here, in this Tower, she must break from every gully dwarf tradition. She must even bathe daily. Is that not sacrifice?"

The gnomes nodded in assent, although a few commented quietly that regular bathing didn't seem such an awful sacrifice. Helg, however, wore a mask of abject terror. From the other side of the room, Halivar sniffled softly.

"Yes, we must all make sacrifices," Cedwick said nobly, "but perhaps the greatest sacrifice shall come from the gnomes."

At this, the gnomes glanced at him in bewilderment.

"Yes," the apprentice mage continued, "already, they have sacrificed so much simply to be here. In the coming years, their life quests will go unfinished. Their committees back at Mount Nevermind will scorn them. It is quite possible that they may live their remaining years in exile. These brave souls choose to sacrifice their entire lives for magic. What greater sacrifice can there be?"

The gnomes looked about in disdain. A low murmur passed through the crowd.

Prodded by his fellow gnomes, Jobin rose to his feet. Gradually, all the gnomes joined him where he stood.

"Master Cedwick," Jobin said, slowly and carefully, "upon consideration of the circumstances involved in this daunting task, the gnomes of Mount Nevermind must regretfully decline the honor of working with you and your esteemed comrades.

"Furthermore," he went on, "we now have cause to believe that the God Trap Machine is not responsible for the disappearance of magic on Krynn. We believe that the data received from the Guild of Magic Analysis and Prestidigital Improvements may be erroneous. Thus, we have resolved to return to Mount Nevermind and begin a formal inquiry into the matter."

Cedwick listened to the news gravely.

"We will truly miss your wealth of knowledge and ideas here in the Tower, but what you propose is quite important. Have a safe journey, Executive Vice-Director."

The gnomes gave a loud cheer. Jobin assured Cedwick that it was an expression of profound disappointment.

As Cedwick watched them gather their materials onto the Veryveryhot, he felt a familiar tug on his robes. The young man knelt down to speak with the gully dwarf.

"High Robe," Helg said, holding out the frog, "you take frog? Not need Helg?"

"Helg, must you leave?"

"Must," Helg nodded fervently. "Have to tell shaman. Tell him you very smart High Robe. Tell him you have frog."

"Thank you, Little One," Cedwick said. "You can go home."

The gully dwarf carefully placed the frog at his feet and scampered away into the forest.

"Master Cedwick?" came a timid voice from behind him. The apprentice turned and smiled at Halivar Wizardslayer.

"Yes, Halivar?" he said. "Are you ready to begin the sacrifice?"

Halivar blanched. "Actually," the kender said, "I was wondering if—you know, if you really needed me."

The apprentice mage put his hand on the kender's shoulder.

"Halivar," Cedwick asked, "are you having doubts?"

Halivar nodded, too ashamed to speak.

"But Halivar," Cedwick said, "you were the one who started this. Without you, I never would have considered such an undertaking."

"I know," said the kender, "but I was thinking. Maybe I should keep wandering around for a little while longer. Maybe when I destroyed magic, I didn't destroy all of it. I could keep looking while you study the issue here at the Tower."

Cedwick smiled. "That's an excellent idea, Halivar."

Halivar looked up and grinned. "Is it? I mean, it is, isn't it?"

"Of course," said the apprentice mage, grinning in return. "I would never keep a god against his will."

The kender's face filled with joy, "Thank you, Master Cedwick! You are truly a great wizard!" He added, "I'm really very glad I didn't kill you earlier!"

"I'm rather glad you didn't also," the young man confided.

"Maybe my curse is over!"

"Just so," smiled Cedwick. "Just so."

The kender gave a jingling bow, which Cedwick returned. He smiled a very god-like smile and wandered away, blowing on a newly found whistle and admiring an empty inkwell.

Cedwick watched in silence as the kender disappeared into the forest. After a while, even the whistle faded away.

"Well?" came Master Laudus's stern voice.

"It worked," said Cedwick.

"Of course it worked. It was my idea."

The archmage appeared from around the corner leading his horse and the pack mule.

"Master Laudus, I'm truly sorry—"

"What's done is done, Cedwick."

Cedwick sighed in relief and went to help his master into the saddle.

"No, no, Cedwick," said Laudus, stopping him. "You get to ride this time."

"I do?"

"Yes. You have a very important responsibility."

To Cedwick's surprise, the old man lifted him off his feet and set him on the horse, backwards. The old mage knelt down, picked something up off the ground, and placed it in the apprentice's hands. He swung himself onto the horse.

"You get to mind the frog."

A Pinch of This,
a Dash of That
Nick O'Donohoe

Act 1, Scene 1: A Road to Solanestri
Sharmaen: If I by praying could but raise his eyes
High as his scholar's face has raised my heart,
Then would I give as much to absent gods
As my most-present love endows to me.
Amandor (reading): "Granite and basalt, flint, chalcedony—"
Hard reading this. Gods, take this adamant
To other scholars; grant me something soft
And palpable.
> *(He looks up and sees Sharmaen)*
> > *Most thoughtful, prescient gods!*
You grant all I may wish, and proffer more.
—The Book of Love, act 1, scene 1.

"Religion," Daev said firmly, "should be kept safely away from ordinary folks." He slapped the reins to make the horses go faster.

Kela laughed. "You're just saying that because you nearly got burned as a heretic."

"You're on the run with me."

She touched his sleeve playfully. "We're not on the run. We're a touring company. Besides, I want to be with you." She waited for a reply, then sighed and peered at the road ahead, heat shimmers and all.

After a moment she said, "Is that a man by the roadside?"

Daev squinted, shading his hand. "Maybe. Yes."

A kender's head popped up between them from the wagon back. "Young or old? I can't tell."

"Old, maybe." The man was robed head to foot and trudging along slowly, pulling a cart. "Not a casual traveler." There was a flash of sunlight off something at the stranger's waist. Daev finished tensely, "Armed."

Kela put a hand on his arm in concern. "You think it's—"

"I think our reputation has caught up with us. Frenni?"

The kender said excitedly, "A fight!"

"Not yet. Hide in the back." Daev transferred the reins to his left hand and felt behind the buckboard until he found his sword hilt.

"You're not leaving me out!"

"You'll be our element of surprise," Daev said soothingly, and added from bitter experience, "A kender is always an element of surprise."

Kela touched the dagger at her side. "We outnumber him."

"Yes," Daev said dryly, "and you and I have at least ten months' experience with swords. That ought to frighten any seasoned warrior."

Frenni, muffled by the wagon curtains, sighed contentedly. "Finally, something exciting."

"Something exciting," Daev echoed unhappily and hefted the sword again.

* * * * *

They pulled alongside the figure, who looked neither to the left nor the right as they stopped their wagon. "Not afraid of anything, is he?" Kela murmured.

"That must be nice," Daev muttered back. Aloud he said, "Do you wish some water?"

The man gestured to his cart without exposing his face. "Thanks, I have some." Whatever had flashed at his waist was now hidden. He said, "Where are the two of you going?"

"Xak Faoleen," Kela said before Daev could reply. "We're—" she caught herself and finished lamely, "—hoping to work there."

"To work." The man sounded amused. "With a covered wagon painted many colors and pictures of warriors and lovers and dragons painted on it?" He laughed, and Daev tensed. It wasn't a particularly sane laugh. "What sort of work?" the man asked, and waited.

"We're players," Daev said finally, and added, "I think you knew."

The man nodded. "I think you also make and sell books."

In the back of the wagon, Frenni shifted. Daev took his hand off his sword to wave him back, then grabbed it again quickly. "We're not scribes. Wouldn't making books require scribes?"

"I hear you have a new machine, better than any scribe."

Kela clutched her dagger handle and said tightly, "Have you been looking for us?"

The stranger said, "I've been following you. I'm surprised I was ahead of you. I must have passed you in the night, but I've finally found you."

Daev, giving up, stood and drew his sword. "Who are you, and what do you want?"

"My name is Samael." He threw back his cloak and drew something with a single swift motion.

Daev braced to parry, then realized that he was fending off a metal scroll case.

Samael laughed his crazy laugh again. "I want you to print my book."

* * * * *

They rode along together, Samael sitting on Kela's left and Daev on her right. Once Samael threw his hood back, they were both surprised to see that he was only in his late twenties, older than they but hardly the seasoned warrior they'd feared he was. Samael said anxiously, "Will my cart be all right back there?"

Kela unscrewed the scroll case. "The hitch I made should keep it balanced, and we'll tow it." She slid the scroll out carefully and unrolled it. "Are these recipes?"

"Sort of." He smiled at her. He had very light blue eyes and a pleasant smile that contrasted sharply with his tanned face. He pointed to the headings:

To be loved.

To fall in love.

For confidence.

To be nigh-invincible in battle.

To be brave.

To produce fear.

To be attractive.

Daev, reading over her shoulder, said dubiously, "All these work without magic?"

Samael shrugged. "Some of them simply change people's attitudes. Others . . ." He pulled a powder from one of his many vest pockets. "Watch."

He tossed the powder against the wagon wheel. There was a loud *bang* and a flash of flame.

Daev quieted the horses as Frenni poked his head out and said admiringly, "Can you give me some of that?"

Daev said courteously and hastily, "Samael, this is Frenni, and we'd really rather you didn't give him any."

Kela, immersed in the scroll, said in fascination, "Do these powders work the same every time?"

"If you mix them exactly right." For the first time Samael sounded anxious as he said, "Will you print my book?"

Before Kela could say anything, Daev drawled, "I'm not sure. It's a great expense to print and sell even short books such as yours."

"I don't have much money." Samael gestured behind them to his cart. "If you sell the book, I can sell the powders from the recipes, and then I could pay you—"

Kela said suddenly, "We thought you were older when you were walking."

Samael grinned at her. "I try to look older on the road. Keeps people away."

"We saw the scroll at your belt," Daev said thoughtfully. "It looked like a scabbard. I thought you were a veteran of campaigns."

Kela went on quickly, "Daev, could he act in your new play? You said we needed one more person—"

"You wouldn't have to pay me," Samael broke in. "I'd do it in barter for your printing the book—"

"And he could help with the sets, and you know he could turn that flash powder into a stage effect—"

"All right. As long as he can learn to act."

Kela looked admiringly at Samael. "He can play the lover. I'm sure he'd be perfect."

"Ah," Daev said, startled. He dropped the subject and stared ahead, brooding.

"Is something wrong?" Samael asked politely.

"Mmm? No, everything's fine for now." Daev played with the reins restlessly. "But if you found us by tracking the books we've sold, who else could?"

Scene 2: A Conference in Shadows
*Old Staffling: Don't laugh at me, young cream-faced fools.
I've fought a dragon with this stick, and jammed the screaming
gears of gnomes' machines, and stood as tall as any Solamnian
Knight on the fields of war. When I smile, you should scream.
When I blink, you should look for danger.*
—The Book of Love, *act 1, scene 2.*

Palak tucked his cape around himself and his bundle as he descended the dark, stained stairs. Why, he thought petulantly, does he do these things underground?

It was a real concern for him. As leader of the Joyous Faithful Guard, he would have preferred that every penitent confess as publicly as possible, not in chains somewhere far from the people who would be encouraged by repentance.

He knew the answer to his question, though. This man was underground because he liked to do his business underground. No one had ordered him to come up because they were all more than a little afraid of him.

Even Palak, fanatical as he was, hesitated at the iron door before rapping on it and calling out, "Tulaen."

A voice said calmly, "I'm with a penitent. Wait."

Palak, sitting on the bottom step, wrapped part of his cape around his head, put his hands over his ears, and waited for the screaming to stop. It took longer than he thought strictly necessary, but he wasn't about to interrupt.

The calm voice said, "All right." The door opened, and Palak faced a large, bald man with a drooping mustache. "I'll be right with you," the man said.

Palak came in. Tulaen had washed his hands in a bowl and was drying them, looking thoughtfully at the dead woman. Palak glanced at all four corners of the room rather than looking at the woman.

Palak said, "What is it that is attractive about this work? Is it the joyous moment when, in tears, they confess?"

"Not really. I can postpone that indefinitely."

"Ah." Palak considered. "What did you do before you came here?"

Tulaen's face clouded over. "I lived with a family. I think it was my family." He shook his head. "Well, there's no bringing them back."

Palak swallowed and changed the subject tactfully. "Tulaen, I've come to offer you an opportunity to advance the Faith." He waited for a nod or a meaningful look. When none came he went on nervously, "There was a young cleric named Daev . . ."

"I heard," Tulaen said neutrally. "Wrote books, didn't he? Heresies. He should have been burned alive at the stake, but he's disappeared." He shook his head. "Very sad."

"Well," Palak went on hurriedly, looking into the empty, patient eyes of the torturer, "we have evidence that he's alive."

"Evidence?"

Palak raised the bundle he had been carrying and slapped it on the table, tugging the cord undone. He lifted the books one at a time, reading the titles angrily. "*The*

Dangers of Fanaticism. Medicine: Is it More Effective than Prayer? Oh, here's a nice one: *Is Truth Absolute?"*

Tulaen picked up the bottom book and leafed through it. *"Follies of the Faithful, Illustrated.* Nice drawings." He held it open for Palak. "Tell me, how can that look like you and like a swine at the same time?"

"I want you to find him and kill him, quickly," Palak snapped.

Tulaen gestured to the dead woman. "I don't kill quickly."

Palak looked automatically, then looked away in spite of himself. "Granted. Just be certain you kill him. An entire faith falls if you fail."

"More importantly, I fail." Tulaen regarded Palak. "I promise you, I won't." He stuck out a huge palm. "Pay up front."

"Shouldn't you come back and prove to me you've done it?"

"My word is good. No one has doubted me before." He smiled gently at the dead woman, then back at Palak. "Do you really want me coming back?"

Palak handed him all the money.

Scene 3: The Village of Xak Faoleen
Love is a book, and every single page
And line and metaphor and simile
Means less and less, unless you read in me
And read me more and more. And so engage
In reading romance, promises and sighs:
I read them raptly in your reading eyes.
—The Book of Love, act 2, scene 1.

Samael passed the notebook to Kela, who stared at him open-mouthed.

"Nicely read," Daev conceded. "Clear, loud enough— didn't drop the ends of your lines—and very passionate." Somehow he had hoped Samael would need more coaching at love lines.

"Perfect," Kela breathed. She shook her head hastily. "Oops, I'm sorry. Now you want me to do my lines?"

Daev murmured, "That would be nice."

She glanced down, closed the book and held it out to Samael as Sharmaen was to hold the prop book. "No, sir, I beg you, read more carefully,

But you have skimmed the matter here, and missed
The subject I have worshipfully kissed
Whenever I discerned him—"

The scene went on until they kissed passionately over the book, then let the book slide to the stage floor. Samael, being taller, practically wrapped himself around Kela.

Daev, as the jealous father Stormtower, rushed in and pulled the lovers apart. Samael staggered as Daev read his angry lines with surprising force.

Getting into the action, Frenni, as Old Staffling the grandfather, burst in and verbally abused Daev/Stormtower, thwacking him with a hoopak/staff. The first blow knocked the wind out of Daev; the second, on his shin, set him dancing.

Frenni leaned on his staff and said critically, "You could dance funnier, but that's not bad."

When he finally found his tongue, Daev said with a tremor in his voice, "How would you like to have your entire throat ripped out and pulped with a rock?"

"No idea," Frenni said. "Does it hurt?"

"Excruciatingly."

"Have you had it done?"

Daev looked disconcerted. "Well, no—"

"Then how do you know?"

"Never threaten a kender," Samael said. "It only encourages them."

"All right," Daev said through clenched teeth. "No more improvising. No more making up lines and movements, and *no more real hitting*, or you can't be in the play. Do you understand?"

It was an empty threat, since they needed Frenni badly, but the kender went along. "All right," he said sullenly. "We'll do it the same boring way every time."

"That," Samael said with great satisfaction, "is how my potions work."

After the rehearsal he produced a small balance scale and a system of weights from his cart. "Precise amounts of ingredients—salts, herbs, dried animal parts—produce the same results every time," he said.

Frenni said indignantly, "Who wants that?"

Samael put a small amount of salt on the scale and checked it, grain by grain, against the weight on the other tray. "People who want the same thing to happen every time."

"Do you want the same meal every night?" Frenni argued. "Of course not. Variety is adventure. Why, when I cook, even though it's the same dish, it's different every time. A dash of this, a pinch of that, and it's completely different."

Daev shuddered. "It's true. Some of his meals are excellent. Some taste like badly sautéed rocks."

Frenni, still smarting from the "no improvising" rule, put his hands on his chin. "Plays should be like that: different every time. In fact, you should write a new play that makes sure it's different for the audience every time."

"What kind of play, O great kender director?"

Frenni missed the sarcasm. "I think we should do a play with explosions, and dragons, and a village burning, and a battle, and magic."

"I see," Daev said caustically. "A play about a dragon that explodes over a village and sets it on fire, killing the wizard he was battling."

Frenni looked at him in awe. "Is that what it's like to be a real writer?"

"Of course. Do you want anything else?"

"Well, I think it should be funny."

Daev threw up his hands. "Can't we do the play we've got?"

"It's awfully good," Samael said.

Kela, looking at him, said, "It's perfect."

Daev watched her staring at the alchemist. Nettled, he said, "Perfect."

"All the love lines."

"They just came to me," he said dryly.

She clapped her hands. "The romance is so tender."

Daev was beginning to be unhappy with the play, though he had written it to feature Kela. "Can we just go over the set and effects design?"

Kela passed her notebook to Daev, pointing to some sketches of which she was particularly proud.

Daev reviewed Kela's set designs, choked, and explained briefly about minimalism, imagination, and money. All in all she took criticism much better than Frenni had. She sat back down and sketched quickly. "Don't worry. I'll be done tomorrow morning."

"Wonderful. That leaves us one whole day to build and sew everything." Daev ran his hands through his hair, wondering how soon it would turn gray. He added irritably, "Are you going to keep that beast?" Kela had adopted a stray dog, rangy and brown, which clearly adored her.

"I'll name him Tasslehoff."

"Everybody names dogs Tasslehoff." But Daev scratched the dog under the chin. "Maybe we can work him into the play."

The dog grinned. So did Samael. "Why not?" said the youth. "She worked me in."

"Very true," Daev conceded, but it didn't help his mood.

* * * * *

That afternoon, as he had for the past four days, Samael carefully weighed out ingredients and folded them into paper packets for his customers. An attractive but pinched-looking young woman watched him carefully.

"Thank you for buying this—um, Elayna," Samael said mechanically. "You'll receive your copy of the book the night before the play performance."

Elayna clutched the package as though it contained jewels. "This will make me attractive?"

"You will be attractive," he assured her. "Mix the ingredients as described in the book and drink them with water. Avoid leading military skirmishes while on this prescription." He looked up to see that she understood that was a joke, saw that she didn't, and looked down indifferently.

Kela, completing a sketch with a flourish, offered it to Elayna. She stared at it, pleased. "I don't really look like this."

"You do," Kela said earnestly. "You just need the potion."

Elayna, vastly pleased, bought the sketch as well as the ingredients and the book.

Daev stopped by, drenched in sweat. Without looking up, Kela ladled him a dipper of water. He drank half of it and poured the rest over his head. "The stage is finished." He added heavily, "Thanks so much for helping."

"I helped," Frenni pointed out and poured water all over himself from the bucket. Kela and Samael shielded the items on the table protectively.

"You were a great help," Daev rumbled, "as my bruises testify. As for you other two . . ."

Kela held up a purse. "Doesn't this help?"

Daev weighed it on his palm, impressed but trying to hide it.

Samael, tired though he was, grinned. "We sold some ingredients to a fat man named Mikel who wants to get thinner. We sold two doses of powders to thin women who want to get fatter. We sold powders and a portrait to a short man named Vaencent who wants to feel tall and powerful. We sold five or six packets with partial ingredients for love potions. The customers'll use home ingredients to finish them out." He laughed his demented laugh. "That's a surprise, right? Oh—we sold four potions to make the drinkers fall out of love. There are a few broken hearts in this town."

"They all bought books," said Kela, "and tickets to the play."

Daev rubbed his palms together. "I hope they like the play."

"They're dying for the play," Kela said frankly. "The way people talk, you'd swear that nothing new has happened in this town since the Cataclysm. Anyway, it's a wonderful play, your best so far." She added, starry-eyed, "Amandor's lines—"

"—should do the trick, and Samael delivers them fairly well," Daev finished.

"Perfectly."

"Not perfectly, but very well." Daev had been hearing far too much about the perfect Samael lately. "It won't matter if we don't finish the set paintings, the costumes, and the effects, will it? Samael, how is the proofing coming?" It seemed to be taking forever, and Daev had agreed to let the alchemist alone until it was done.

Samael pointed to a stack of trays, each filled with blocks of carved letters. "I ran the test copy this morning, then changed it and ran another copy. I changed it again—"

"You all think *I* change things too much," Frenni muttered.

"It's a wonderful book," Kela chimed.

"I assumed it was perfect," Daev said shortly. "It's a good combination. The potions advertise the play, we presell the book, and happy customers tell all their friends about the next performance. Now all we have to do is get the book proofed and bound for tonight." He emphasized "tonight."

Samael looked up, shocked. "I want to proof it one more time."

"How many times have you proofed it already?"

The young man looked down again, scanning the pages. "This next one will be the fifth."

"The *fifth?*" Daev looked at the others in disbelief. They were all staring at him. "Listen, all of you. We have to complete the sets, finish the costumes, set up Samael's special effects, print the book, bind the book, distribute all fifty copies as promised, and we have to do it all in *one night.*" He rubbed his eyes. "Gods, I can't believe we open tomorrow."

Now even Tasslehoff looked worried.

Daev pointed at the bare stage. "Kela, paint the backdrop. Samael, help me with the sets and the costumes. We'll do the effects last. Frenni, your job is to print the book, bind it, and run it from house to house."

Samael shook his head, frowning. "But I want to help print—"

"Frenni's a specialist," Daev assured Samael. "No more proofing," he added firmly.

"He can do the book," said Frenni. "I could work on the special effects!"

"Finish the book, Frenni, and you can help with the special effects. Now go." Daev tugged on Samael's sleeve, dragging him off to work.

The alchemist resisted. "Can't I just proof it one more time?"

"Name of the gods, let it go. It will be fine." Daev said with only a hint of bitterness, "I'm sure that, like everything you do, it will be wonderful and perfect." He called back to Frenni with more asperity than was necessary, "Set up the print trays on the table and start running copies. Double time."

"All right," Frenni said sulkily. He watched the humans leave to work on the scenery.

"They don't appreciate my hidden talents," he muttered as he moved the trays of print and stacked them on the table. "I may not write, but I can sure improvise. You want a dragon? I can do a dragon." He spun around, ducking and weaving from an invisible dragon, and set another tray down.

"You want magic? I can do magic—which is in very short supply nowadays." He set one of the trays on the end of his hoopak and spun the tray, walking with it to the table. As the tray spun and wobbled, he slid it dexterously on top of the others.

Carrying the last tray, he kept up the griping. "Double time he wants, double time he'll get. All the more time for special effects later on." He wasn't watching where he was going, tripped on a tree root and fell sprawling against the table. All eight trays of set pages slid down, letters and words raining down like stones in an avalanche.

Frenni dusted himself off and looked in dismay at the mess. The set pages had gaps interspersed throughout, ingredients and instructions and sometimes titles missing.

He thought of what the others would say when he told them what happened and sighed. Some days working with humans just wasn't as much fun as he'd thought.

Scene 4. A Road at Night

Sharmaen: I fear my father's thunder.
Amandor: *Gentle sweet,*
his love is tropical, his anger chill,
Such men mix hot and cold; their troubled air
will cloud and draw their lightning. Fear them not,
Saving your terror for the icy men
Loveless, unsummered with a wintry heart.
—The Book of Love, *act 2, scene 2.*

A hand crawled desperately on the road dust, as though trying to escape the body attached to it. The pulse throbbed visibly in the wrist.

The crawling slowed—became intermittent—and the hand twisted upside down, fingers quivering in the air like the legs of a dying spider.

Tulaen regarded the hand with as close to regret as he would ever show. "If only you had known more," he said to the corpse. "You could have said so much more. You might have lasted till morning."

He stood, the cold night wind stirring his beard. Tulaen slept very little.

"You traded a haying wagon to a man, a kender, and a girl on the road. They gave you a stack of books. You said the girl sketched you." He tugged at his beard, thinking. "I wonder, now—does she sketch the pictures for the books?"

He looked at the blood trail behind the corpse. It was three times the length of the body and could have been so much more. "Well, there's no use asking you. At least you knew where they were going."

While waiting until morning, he tied a log to a rope and slung it from a low hanging limb. He set it spinning in the faint light and chopped it with his broadsword, ducking with practiced ease. For the next log he put a patch over one eye and led with his left. For the last he tied his feet together, and still the spinning log never hit him.

By dawn he had an impressive pile of splintery tinder and kindling. He cooked a quick breakfast and began his walk toward Xak Faoleen.

Scene 5. A Stage, in Xak Faoleen
Sharmaen: Crisis pursues, and crisis we pursue
Mid-scene in madness, endings overdue.
—The Book of Love, *act 3*

The stage was nothing but boards on sawhorses, with stairs at either side and a second level to stand in for hills and balcony scenes. The theater was row on row of planks on upright logs. The backdrop was painted cloth—beautifully painted by Kela, a neighborhood scene, but only cloth and paint nonetheless. The few pieces of scenery—suitably minimalist—were some upright crenellated boards for a castle, three torches in stands for a hallway by night, and two standing branches for a wood.

The whole effect, Daev reflected, was much like magic must have been. Already they felt the distance, like an invisible wall, between the world of the actors and that of the audience.

Daev, Samael, and Kela had toiled until nearly dawn, when the kender stumbled up, panting, and announced that he had delivered the last of the books to the prepaid customers. His face showed disappointment that most of the work was done, the special effects all prepared. But after a day and a night of steady work, they had finished and were ready to face a waiting audience.

Frenni stepped onstage. Actually he shuffled, hampered by wearing a bass drum, a light drum, cymbals, a hunting horn, and a hand-cranked bullroarer, which made a noise like a spinning hoopak. Daev had been quick to see the comic possibilities of strapping every available musical instrument to a kender and watching him try to play them all at the same time.

After Frenni performed the overture, to great applause, the rest of the cast marched on and bowed.

Daev kept his expression but frowned inwardly. Something was off about the applause. The rhythms were sporadic, and some audience members were tapping lightly while others were pounding their fists on the benches.

The kender stepped back. Daev moved forward, arms raised, and spoke the prologue.

He made eye contact with the audience and faltered. They looked entirely normal until Daev looked closely at their eyes.

Some of them did look fascinated. Some of them were leering at everything, including the dog and the kender. Some of them looked furiously angry, deeply insulted by a play that hadn't been performed yet. Some were quite clearly already in love, and one person was in tears for a tragedy that wasn't on the bill.

Elayna, dead center in the front row, looked gorgeous but also strangely imperious. When approached by admirers—and far too many of the men who had purchased love potions felt free to approach her while the performance was on—she came dangerously close to striking them.

Daev finished the prologue, stepping back before bowing, and led the others backstage. Kela saw his face and said, "Is something wrong?"

"Your book, Samael," he said quietly. "Perhaps I should have let you proof it a fifth time."

Frenni clanked up, shrugging out of the band gear noisily. "It's a best-seller. I only have one copy left," he said proudly.

Samael opened it and froze. "Wrong font?" Frenni asked worriedly.

"No, no—but . . ." Samael thumbed back and forth frantically. "These aren't my recipes."

"They are too," Frenni said self-righteously. "Every word you wrote is in that book."

Samael loomed over the kender. "Not in the order I wrote it."

"Mostly in the order."

Daev looked on interestedly. "What are the differences?"

Samael stabbed at the recipes. "This was supposed to make people attractive. Now it makes them attractive and invincible in battle. This one was to induce melancholy. Now it induces melancholy, anger, and a desire to dance. The sneezing powder . . ." He peered at it with genuine horror. "Paladine alone knows what else it does now."

"They're basically the same," Frenni pointed out defensively. "It's just that I needed to fill in some places when the letters fell out before printing."

Samael lifted the kender off the ground with one hand. "The letters *what?*"

"Fell out. Don't worry. I got them all back in, every letter, before I printed the book."

Samael dropped Frenni. The three humans looked at each other in silence.

Daev spoke first. "Frenni, what did you add to these recipes?"

"The usual thing," the kender said indifferently. "A dash of this, a pinch of that."

Daev turned to Samael. "How long until they recover?"

He shrugged. "Assuming they all only took one dose, just before the play, they'll peak during act five."

Daev closed his eyes, contemplating the potential for disaster. "The perfect audience. Well, don't get too close to the front edge of the stage."

Frenni said, "Because we'll fall off?"

"Because not a god from past times or future could guess what's going to happen if the audience gets its hands on you. They're all a few dwarves shy of a mine, if you catch my drift."

Frenni said, hurt, "My best scenes are in act five."

Samael said, sadly, "My book is a disaster."

Daev said, "I think maybe we should pack up between scenes."

Kela looked starry-eyed as she watched Samael tweak the last hair of his false beard into place. "C'mon everybody," she said. "The show must go on, and all that. They'll like the play. How could they not, if they have any heart at all?"

Dave said coldly to her, "You're right. The audience is waiting. So get out there and kiss." He pushed her and Samael onstage hand in hand, and he wished he had never in his life tried to write about love.

* * * * *

The action of the play went well, as it should have. The father threatened the lovers, the grandfather took their part and fought the father physically, and the lovers met and kissed in spite of obstacles. Tasslehoff, with a pair of absurdly small wings and his spine and wagging tail tricked out with a sawtooth ridge, made a passable rogue dragon. With a helmet to block his vision and a ridiculously short lance under his arm, Daev charged the "dragon" but struck Frenni, knocking the kender's hat over his eyes and starting a blind sword fight. A sheet of metal and exploding flare powder made an excellent storm.

Daev, the stilts and absurdly long arms making him even taller, got laughs just by standing next to the kender in long beard and floppy clothes.

The audience interrupted occasionally, calling out, "Kiss her more!"

"No! No! Hit him."

"Louder and funnier!"

"Sweeter!"

"Give us a fight!"

By the last scene of the second act, the father had forbidden the lovers to meet, the grandfather had threatened more destructive but well-meaning help, and the dispirited lover Samael/Amandor had retreated to his books again. Kela/Sharmaen, real tears flowing down her cheeks, vowed to make everything right in a single night.

A man and a woman leaped up cheering. Three other audience members leaped up and knocked them down, and it was time for intermission.

* * * * *

Backstage, Daev clapped his hands for their attention. "All right. Let's hold it together and finish fast." He glared at the kender. "Remember, fake blows and *no improvising*. Keep the curtain call short and make a bee-line for the wagon." It was already packed except for the fifth-act costumes and props.

Samael nodded and left. Frenni, sulking, stomped off to change costumes. Daev gently wiped the tears from Kela's cheeks. "Do you love him so much?" he said softly.

She blinked at him mutely and said through her tears, "I just want it to work out for them. Lovers ought to be together forever." She dashed away, drying her face and looking for her props.

Daev stared emptily after her. "I always thought they should be. I thought . . ." What he thought he left unfinished.

* * * * *

Tulaen walked into Xak Faoleen, looking quizzically at the empty homes and deserted streets. Clearly something important was going on or some disaster had caused the townsfolk to flee.

Tulaen disliked missing disasters. He quickened his pace, moving to the central square. Once there he barely glanced at the stage and actors, moving slowly through the audience and checking their faces. He was non-plussed by the strangeness of people's postures and expressions, but he was indifferent to them: none of them was Daev or the young woman who sketched.

He tapped one of the audience members on the shoulder, lightly. "Excuse me."

The man emitted a high-pitched shriek and ran off. Tulaen shrugged and continued searching the crowd. Bored and frustrated, he glanced at the cast onstage for the end of the second act. The father was too tall to be the one he looked for; the grandfather was too short. The woman had the wrong color hair, and the lover was nothing like . . .

Tulaen looked at the backdrop more closely, saw the magnificence of the painting that went into it, and smiled for the first time in quite a while. "Actors who print books," he said, shaking his head at his own folly.

He moved slowly to one side of the stage. There was no hurry now. He tested the edge of his sword on his thumb, feeling only satisfaction when his thumb began to bleed.

* * * * *

"Last act," Daev hissed backstage. "The wagon's ready. Keep them laughing, move the action along, and don't waste time on the curtain call."

He called out loudly, "The final scene. A woods, outside town," and half-pushed Tasslehoff onstage.

The dog, grinning happily, entered and sat at stage center. Pieces of brush were strapped to him, and a sprig of leaves was tied to his wagging tail.

Kela waltzed on stage, patted the "woods" and announced Sharmaen's plans to trick Amandor into marrying her with the unwitting help of her clumsy grandfather and angry father.

Samael/Amandor strode on and promised, at her request, that he would do whatever she asked.

Frenni/Old Staffling, disguised in a sorcerer's costume, entered pretending his staff was a magic wand. He produced flashes from it with powders supplied by Samael, and he laid out four fire-fountain pots the size of ale kegs. Frenni/Old Staffling's hat fell off each time he set down a fountain; each time, without seeming to notice, he caught it on the end of his staff and flipped it back onto his head.

Daev took a deep breath, tested the wooden stilts to be sure he could keep his balance, prayed that the fire fountains would all work as Samael had said, and strode out, waving an outsize gauntlet and threatening one and all with death and destruction.

There was the sound of soft clapping. The actors turned.

Tulaen entered stage right, still applauding. He stopped and raised his sword.

Daev knew exactly what the big, evil-looking man had come for. He stepped back, raising his prop sword in as threatening a manner as possible.

Tulaen slid forward effortlessly and swung his sword. Daev stumbled back, wondering why he wasn't dead.

"No blood?" Tulaen asked. From the stage he picked up the chunk of wood, sandal still attached. "Ah. Not your real foot." He moved forward again. "Yet."

Some of the audience thought that screamingly funny. One of them did in fact scream. Daev retreated upstage, confused by still being alive.

Tulaen swung again, deftly circling over Daev's prop sword, and sliced all the fingers off Daev's empty left gauntlet.

Tulaen kicked at the empty glove fingers, scratched his head, then brightened. "You must be in there somewhere," he said mildly.

Daev backpedaled, bumping into Frenni and sending him sprawling. Kela and Samael were watching with befuddled expressions. Frenni bounced up in a handspring and said jealously to Daev, "Who is that guy? You'd never let me improvise like that."

"He's a real assassin," Daev gasped, pulling back before Tulaen sliced off his left hand. "Do something. Whatever you want."

The kender brightened. "You mean it?" He spun his staff over his head, leaped over a sword slash, and brought the staff down full on the assassin's bald head.

Tulaen blinked, feeling nothing more than a tap.

Frenni, encouraged, vaulted back out of range, planted himself and swung on Tulaen from behind, striking the assassin in the midsection with a resounding *smack*.

"*No more fake fighting*," shouted a desperate Daev. "Hit him as hard as you can!"

Someone near the stage shouted, "Hit him harder than you can!"

Frenni spat on his hands and aimed his best blow at Tulaen. Tulaen speared Frenni's beard, lifted it up and tucked it over Frenni's face and kicked the kender. Frenni rolled into a ball inside the beard, wobbled to the far edge of the stage, and dropped off.

Daev said desperately to the dog, "Tasslehoff! Kill!"

Tas wagged his tail and, barking, bounced around Tulaen. The assassin was quite fond of dogs, having slain several in his childhood. He merely raised a lip and growled. Tas tucked his tail between his legs, lowered his head, and slunk off stage right.

The audience howled—some with laughter, some with bloodlust, some attempting to sing. They were on their feet now, excited by the violence on stage.

Kela and Samael stood frozen. Kela, with anxious glances at Daev and at the audience, said in a stage whisper to Samael, "Amandor, this man means to harm Da— my father Stormtower. If you save my father's life, perhaps he'll let us marry."

A voice from the audience called, "I already told you, kill him!"

Another voice called, "Kiss him, then kill him!"

A frightened voice quavered, "Run for your life."

Samael looked uncertainly at Tulaen, set his jaw, and dashed off stage right. A woman called out, "Coward!" and a piece of fruit smashed on the edge of the stage.

Tulaen looked back at Daev impassively. "We'd better give them a show." He closed in on Daev and sliced off some of the costume padding from Daev's midsection.

In desperation, Daev kicked over one of the fire fountains, aiming it toward the assassin, and pulled the priming string. Instead of emitting a shower of sparks, the fountain exploded with a deafening roar and a soaring fireball lit up every enthusiastic, deranged face in the audience. An immense puff of smoke enveloped half the stage.

Daev stepped out of it, coughing, and said conversationally to Frenni, "Changed the mix on the fire fountain, did you?"

The kender, still tangled in the beard and struggling on stage, said, "A little."

"Interesting." Daev leaned on his sword. "What did you put in?"

Frenni said airily, "Oh, you know, a dash of this, a pinch of that."

In Daev's opinion the line didn't deserve it, but it got the best laugh of the day.

When the smoke finally cleared, Tulaen stood there, dazedly blinking at the audience. His clothes were smoldering, his beard was a charred crisp that left a burned-feather smell, and his eyebrows were gone. He was almost enjoying things.

So was the audience, one member of which was sneezing hysterically. A man who was sobbing and snarling at the same time struck the sneezer.

The woman now hopelessly in love with the sneezing man giggled but struck the sobbing man with a piece of bench anyway.

Daev watched, appalled, as a ripple, as from a stone cast in a pool, spread from the small group. The entire audience began jostling and muttering.

Samael ran in from stage right, sword at guard position. He shouted, "Daev!" and with his free hand lobbed a small pouch over Tulaen's head.

Dazed though he was, Tulaen turned without any seeming effort and warded off Samael's lunge, raising a boot and kicking Samael offstage again.

One audience member laughed until he sobbed. The man next to him sobbed until he laughed. They punched each other enthusiastically, occasionally landing blows on bystanders who became participants.

Daev managed to catch the pouch and undo the drawstring as Tulaen turned and charged, swinging his sword in an unstoppable, brute-force slash. Daev stumbled backward, the last of his costume padding undone.

Seemingly without haste, Tulaen closed in for his first truly bloodletting cut.

Holding his breath, Daev threw the entire powdery

contents of the pouch straight into the face of the assassin.

Tulaen crumpled, sneezing. Daev, sword held shakily at the ready, retreated stage left.

Tulaen rose, facing the audience, and stared into Elayna's furious eyes.

He dropped back to his knees, overcome by wheezing and adoration. For the first time in his bloody and indifferent life he felt joyous, hopeless love. He dropped his sword, held his empty hands straight out to her in pleading, and announced, "I love you more than anyone I have ever killed!" He sneezed again.

Elayna, gorgeous and invincible, climbed on stage. Tulaen raised his watering eyes hopefully and saw three things:

Elayna's perfect but hate-filled face looking down at him.

Beyond her, the actor who played Amandor, as he brought the haying cart around and the other players leaped on it in the midst of a townwide fistfight.

Elayna's fist, which seemed small at first, but which in the last moment before it reached his eyes seemed beautiful, gracious, and absolutely enormous.

Epilogue. A Road Out of Xak Faoleen

Sharmaen: If peace has triumphed by my plans,
The fault is woman's and is man's,
Since once the wars of hearts begin,
True wars must lose, and love must win.
Come, give your hands now. Let us all agree:
Books are but letters; love is alchemy.
—The Book of Love, *epilogue.*

They were well out of town before slowing the horses to a trot. Samael peered behind them. "Do you think he'll follow us?"

"Not for a while," Daev answered. "When he wakes up, I don't think he'll find any reliable witnesses. We've got some time." He considered. "We've got more than that."

"We still have the printing press," Samael said cheerfully.

"We still have half of our props," Frenni said.

"We have my notebooks," Kela said.

Daev felt the purse at his belt. "We have a fair amount of gold."

Kela hugged him suddenly. "We still have our play and all your wonderful words. I haven't been able to think of anything else since we started rehearsal." She held him tight.

Samael glanced sideways at Frenni, who was watching with interest while he sat with an arm around the panting, happy Tasslehoff. "I have some work to do inside." He lifted the canvas flap. " Tasslehoff, come. Frenni, you too."

"But—"

"I'll need the help." He pushed the kender backward into the wagon bed. Tasslehoff followed happily, and Samael closed the flap behind them.

"So the thing you loved was the play," Daev said wonderingly.

"Of course. You wrote such beautiful things about love—you're so wonderful, Daev. There's no one like you in the whole world."

"But I thought—" He shook his head. "Never mind what I thought."

Kela looked up at him, her eyes shining. "What are you thinking now?"

Daev was thinking that perhaps he'd been exposed to too much of the love potion. He stopped thinking and kissed her.

Much later he had a disturbing thought. "Kela?"

"Yes, love." She was nestled in his arm, but she was sketching the view ahead in a notebook. She frowned, trying to get the sunset shadows right.

"I've been reviewing our recent past."

In seven lines she added a tree, which was not in the panorama ahead but which balanced the distant mountains nicely. "It's been exciting."

"Now I understand how much I love you—mostly because you—"

"Accidentally, of course—"

"—made me jealous." He paused. "*Was* it accidental?"

She laughed and kissed him.

That was no answer at all, he realized as he kissed her back.

"Frenni's right," he muttered to himself as he kissed Kela again. "In some things, thinking is less fun than improvising."

The kender's head popped out from under the canvas wagon back. "I heard my name."

"I expected you to interrupt earlier."

"I wanted to, but Samael sat on me."

Samael gave one of his demented-sounding laughs. "You two needed privacy, and I needed something to sit on while I corrected the revised version of the *Alchemist's Handbook*." He looked disapprovingly at Frenni while he showed them the corrections.

Daev was thinking aloud. "There's a play in this somewhere. . . ."

The Perfect Plan
By Linda P. Baker

Demial kept the door of the hut latched tight. She kept the heavy curtains drawn, edges overlapping, shutting out the light, the stars, and prying eyes.

No one else in the tiny village of Toral barred their doors and covered their windows. They went about their lives as they had before Ariakan's army had come, over a year before, almost as they had before the war. It was as if they were denying that anything dark and hurtful would ever come into the small mountain village again.

Demial knew that wasn't so. After all, she had fought in the war, hadn't she? It wasn't really darkness or the memories that she thought to keep out, though. It was nosy neighbors.

She kept the curtains closed all the time, and she dropped the wooden bar securely into place every night, even before she sat down alone to her meal. She checked the door and the windows again every morning before she picked up the staff that stood beside her fireplace. She checked them before she cast a spell with the staff that had belonged to a Nightlord, the gray-robed mage who had been her war leader, mentor, and teacher, who had taken Demial under her wing and out of this village.

As she did each morning, she cleared a space before the cold fireplace and knelt there, with the plain, wooden staff in her hands. No words for the spell came into her mind, as they once had, memorized perfectly. Magic didn't work the way it had before the gods departed at the end of the Chaos War. The magic should not have worked at all, not without the power of Takhisis, the dark goddess who had ruled the Gray Wizards. It did work, however, and for that Demial was grateful. She didn't question. She merely accepted the gift that had been left to her.

She asked only what she needed of the staff: warmth and food and sometimes some inconsequential, frivolous thing. Not too often a frivolous thing, because she feared that the staff's power was limited, that it would not answer her requests indefinitely.

This morning, as every morning since she'd joined Quinn's quest to reopen the mine, she asked only for a small amount of strength, enough to make her day go well. Asking to be just a little bit stronger than her tall, thin frame allowed was not a frivolous thing.

She clasped the staff across her body, her fingers finding a comfortable grip on it. The thick top was carved in the rough image of a dragon claw and was sharp edged with its hint of rough dragon scales. The roughness smoothed out, however, as the carved whorls began their graceful corkscrew down the staff, narrowing, growing farther apart until there was only smooth wood leading down to the brass-clad tip.

There were no words for the magic now, no memorized spells, no books of ancient runes. There were only her thoughts, her wish for what she wanted the staff to do. The magic did not feel the way it had during the war, when casting a spell had made her hot and electric, and she had basked in the approbation of the Nightlord. At that time she had felt something grow within herself, swell and build and burn until it could no longer be contained. It exploded outward, and the magic was cast into the air.

Now the magic came from without. It was no longer something to which she gave birth. It was something that happened outside her, over which she had no control, though it still made her nerves sing. It was wild and unschooled, and it left her feeling elated and invincible but also terribly sad for that which was gone forever.

This magic, the response to her wish, skittered along her arms and down over her skin. It probed at her muscles and slipped inside, leaving her shivering and shocked as ragged bursts of pain arced along her nerves. For a moment, she slumped over the staff, actually feeling weaker instead of stronger, but the sensation and the pain only lasted a moment. Then warmth coursed through her muscles, melting the weakness like hot water poured into her veins.

She knelt there a moment longer, enjoying the tingle of pleasure the spell left in its wake. Energized, she bounced to her feet, ready for the day. She put the staff back in its place, leaning against the fireplace.

Demial tidied the small room quickly. There wasn't much work involved. Brush up the crumbs from her breakfast, wash out the plate and leave it to dry on the table, straighten the light blankets on her bed. She flipped the heavy wooden bar up, laughing softly at how easily it moved for her slender, strong fingers.

She was running a little late today. The edge of the morning sun was already visible over the trees, and the village street was empty, except for Lyrae, balancing her baby on one hip and a water bucket on the other.

"Lyrae, good morning!" Demial hurried to catch up, being careful to come up on Lyrae's right, next to the bucket. Otherwise, she'd find herself with an armful of mewling infant. Lyrae had lost two babies during the war and had never expected to have another. Since this one had been born, she had not been parted from it, not even long enough to walk to the village well and draw water. While the woman couldn't stand to be out of sight of the baby, she didn't mind allowing someone else to hold it, a fact that Demial had discovered by unpleasant accident the first time she offered the woman some help with the morning burdens. It was part of Demial's plan to appear sweet and helpful, but she was only willing to go so far. The slobbering, grasping child was too far.

"Let me help you with that." Deftly, before the young woman could protest, Demial slipped the leather bucket from her grasp.

As Lyrae thanked her, a blush staining her soft features, Demial smiled. She forced the corners of her mouth to stretch into a smile. She'd practiced at home until she could do it perfectly, so that it looked nowhere near as brittle as it felt.

Lyrae shifted the baby into both arms, nuzzled its round face, and smiled her thanks. "It's so sweet of you to help." The baby looked just like her, brown haired and brown eyed. Demial's own hair was brown and straight as a stick, but her eyes were yellow. A cat's eyes, her father had always said, with a sneer in his voice. A demon cat's eyes.

Demial followed the younger woman through the little gate into the yard of her hut. She set the bucket into its frame and, with a wave of her hand, started up the path again toward the mine.

"Demial, wait!" Lyrae dashed into her hut and returned with something wrapped in a cloth. "A piece of cake, for your lunch."

Giving a quick thanks for the cake and another wave, Demial walked briskly away. Smiling to herself, she tucked the cake into the pocket of her tunic. On through the village she went, up along the path that wound through the gardens, waving to the workers there. At the top of the slope, where the path leveled off, she took the steeper, rockier shortcut up the mountainside, to the mine. As she approached the entrance, she saw none of the bustling activity she'd expected. Most of the work crew was standing on the worn slope that led up to the clogged hole into the mountain, and their expressions ran the gamut from disgusted to dejected.

Before the Summer of Chaos and the war, Toral had been a small but prospering mining village. From the mine that snaked back into the mountain, the villagers had brought out crystals, a hard, gray flint, and a lovely blue-veined marble that was much in demand by the nearby plains cities for use as building ornamentation. Occasionally, they found something more valuable as well, a rough bloodstone or garnet that could be polished and sold to a jeweler. Ariakan's army, however, had collapsed the entrance to the mine and crushed the soul of the village. Now the villagers eked out a living from scrubby gardens and what game they could trap.

As she strolled up the slope, Demial's gaze flitted from face to face, searching for Quinn. Her pulse quickened as she saw him, standing tall and strong and sure, among a group of workers.

Her gaze was fixed on him, so she didn't notice the mine until one of the women said, "Just look at it." Her voice was as tired and dispirited as if it was day's end instead of beginning.

Demial followed her pointing finger. No further explanation was needed for the long faces and the slumped shoulders.

It had been Quinn's idea to clear the rubble from the entrance and reopen the mine. He saw it as a way to rejuvenate the village. Because it was his goal, part of his ambition, Demial had made it hers, too. When he reopened the mine and the grateful villagers handed him the mantle of leadership for his role, she planned to be right there at his side. She had worked harder than any of them, had pushed herself unstintingly, and all the while had kept the cheerful expression plastered on her face.

The week before, they had rapidly reached a point where there were no more loose rocks to be hauled away. What was left was packed tight inside the hole into the mountain.

So yesterday they had rigged ropes around the biggest boulders blocking the entrance and worked them down the hill a safe distance. The roar when they all pulled together and jerked the boulders loose had been exhilarating, but now that the dust cloud had cleared there was a new pile of rocks and debris clogging the mouth of the cave. It looked as if they'd done no work at all, as if the last backbreaking weeks of dragging rocks away from the entrance had been for naught.

Looking at the mine, she swallowed hard, but what she was feeling was elation, and she swallowed again, before it could show upon her face. How perfect! Everyone was standing around looking as if someone had just kicked a favored pet, but she wanted to break into a smile. It was all coming together, her perfect plan. All the pieces were falling into place as if guided by the hands of the gods. Holding back her smile, Demial squared her shoulders, assumed an air of dogged determination, and marched up the remainder of the slope to Quinn.

He turned toward her. His expression brightened, his eyes lit up. She could see the strain and disappointment around his mouth—that pretty, pouty, boyish mouth, which was going to be hers soon. She'd wipe the lines of fatigue and disappointment from it, soothe the frown that painted a **V** of wrinkles into his forehead.

"It looks as if we have to start all over again," he said, gesturing toward the mine.

The corners of Demial's mouth quivered. She ducked her head to keep from grinning up at him like a cat that had trapped a fat, juicy bird. Slyly, but loudly enough for her words to be heard by those around him, she said, "When do we get started?"

He was still for a moment, then he laughed aloud. He swung toward the mine, gesturing for the others to follow. "Demial's right. Let's go to work!"

As he attacked the rock pile, the others joined in. They picked up the sleds they used to cart the loads of rock and debris away and formed a ragged half circle around the pile.

Demial lifted her first rock of the day. It was just large enough that she could carry it comfortably. She cradled the sharp-edged rock in her arms as she carried it to her sled. She sneezed as dust puffed into her face, then went back for another rock. Her magic-enhanced muscles shifted smoothly under her skin. She was capable of lifting much more, but she had to be careful. She carried just enough, loaded just enough into the sled, to be impressive, not enough to arouse suspicions of magic.

Her morning passed slowly, as had all the other mornings since she'd joined the mine project. Take a load of rubble to the crevasse, push it over the edge, drag the empty sled back to the mine, then begin again. As the sun rose higher and the dust became grime that caked her face and her neck, she worked automatically, lifting and dragging.

She thought of her perfect plan to use magic at an opportune time to finish clearing the mine. The staff would make quick work of this job. Another few weeks of backbreaking work like this, and the villagers would be ready for a little magic. They'd be so weary, so grateful.

The trouble was, she couldn't just waltz up to the mine with the staff and wish the mine opened. She had to come up with an explanation that made sense, some way of explaining how she had such a powerful artifact in her possession and why she knew how to use it. So far the answer had eluded her, but she had no doubt that she would think of something. She was good with words, good with explanations—like the clever story she'd made up to tell the villagers how she'd escaped Ariakan's army and spent the hot, hot summer and war in the port city of Palanthas, working in a tavern.

Her lip curled slightly as she started back up the path. That story had been easily accepted. It was no stretch for the villagers to believe that Demial, troublemaker and daughter of the village drunkard, spent her days waiting tables in a seedy waterfront bar.

Quinn fell into step with her. "You should take a break," he said. "You haven't stopped all morning."

She curbed the smoldering anger that was always so close to the surface, adopting the guise of cheer and determination that she wore like a colorful shirt. "Neither have you."

"Then we'll rest together," he said, as if he'd been waiting for the chance. He stopped her sled, caught her arm, and steered her into sparse shade.

The cooler air smelled of dried evergreen needles and new growth, reminding her that spring was not far away. She hoped all her plans would fall into place by Spring Fest, when the village would spend a week in celebration of the coming season.

As she sank down on the grass, a breeze ruffled the strands of hair that clung to her forehead, lifting them and cooling her skin. She must look a sight, long hair escaping the tight braid, dirt smeared through the sweat on her face, but Quinn smiled at her as if she wore linen and jewels.

He sat down at an angle to her, aping her cross-legged posture, and his knee brushed against hers. He turned his face into the breeze, giving her the chance to study him. The frown lines were gone from his mouth and forehead. His wheat-colored hair was plastered to his head with sweat. His face was as dirty as hers and tired, but tired was good. Tired only meant they'd been working hard, accomplishing something together.

Her stomach rumbled as she brushed at the dirt on her hands, and she remembered the cake Lyrae had given her early that morning. "I have a treat. Lyrae gave it to me this morning," she exclaimed, reaching into her pocket for the cloth. It came out much flatter than when she'd put it in, the white cloth spotted with moisture.

She opened the soiled cloth, exposing smashed and crumbled bits of yellow cake.

Quinn laughed aloud at her dismay.

It was a good, hearty sound, and she tasted it, the way she could taste rain in the air or a bird's song in the morning. She smiled, rueful and amused. "I guess I remembered it too late."

"Nonsense." Quinn plucked one of the bigger bits with his dirty fingers, threw back his head and dribbled it into his mouth.

Demial watched the movement of his throat, the rise and fall of the muscles under his beard-stubbled skin. He was a handsome man. Even dirt couldn't spoil the effect of his angular cheekbones and his long, elegant nose. She looked away, flushed, as he reached for another piece of cake.

"It's not so bad, even flattened." He gave her hand a little nudge, indicating she should try it.

She shook her head and pushed the cake toward him. Her mouth was suddenly much drier than from mere thirst and the teasing laughter was gone from her throat.

He shot a quick glance from beneath his brows. "Everyone knows what you have been doing for Lyrae. Even Rory. It's the only reason he comes to the mine every morning, because he thinks it's good for her to be on her own, and because he knows you check on her when you pass by."

The praise was so unexpected that she didn't know what to say. She gaped at him, feeling a flush of warmth, a twinge of guilt for her real motivations. "I don't . . . I haven't . . . I don't . . ." The words tumbled across her tongue, conflicting emotions swelling in her breast. She leaped to her feet, annoyed by the inner conflict she was feeling. A deep breath dislodged a frantic rush of words, intended as much to convince herself as him. "I don't do anything. I just carry her water. She always has the baby with her, and I'm stronger than she is, so I carry the water. It's nothing."

"It's more than you know." He caught her wrist to stop her from turning away.

Her breath seized in her throat, choking her worse than words ever could. His touch was the closest thing left in the world that felt like magic, the sizzle of skin on skin, and it was the first time he'd been so bold in his touching, the first time he'd broken through his reticence.

She knew the reason why he was so reticent. Again and again she'd heard him say, sadly, quietly, "My heart is in the grave." He still grieved for the woman who was gone, the one who was dead. Demial was determined to make him forget that woman. She shivered, and he noticed. He even liked it, because he teased the jagged lifeline down her palm and smiled at her, the same boyish smile with which she'd fallen in love when she was a little girl of five.

"Don't be embarrassed. It's wonderful, what you do for her—what you do for us all." His finger made another sweep of her palm and wrist.

Abruptly she was five again, on a day when her father had drunk too much. He was supposed to be working in the fields, but he passed out, leaving her to find her way home in the growing dusk. It was seven-year-old Quinn who had come from the river, out onto the path, leading his family's milk cow, scaring her out of her wits. She hadn't squealed in fear as most girls her age would have, but he'd taken one look at her, known she was frightened, known she was never going to admit it, and reached out to touch her wrist. "Help me lead this cantankerous beast back to the village, will you?" he'd said. "Stupid cow doesn't even know that I'm trying to take it home."

She smiled down at him now, remembering the placid cow and a seven-year-old boy's smile. "I don't do anything for you, though, do I?"

He met her gaze squarely, all banter gone from his voice. "Yes, you do. You can't begin to know how much happiness your smile brings to us all."

It was more of an opening than she could have ever wrangled on her own. "Perhaps I should do more," she said softly. She placed just enough emphasis on the last word to be mildly suggestive, not enough that he would be frightened away if it was something he didn't want to hear.

He shrugged, the smile going a little tight.

Demial nodded and turned away quickly before overeagerness could turn her face bright and brittle. "I think I'll just go get a drink of water before I start back to work."

As she topped the little rise that would take her out of sight, she turned back to him. He was sitting where she had left him, watching her. "Maybe I could cook supper for you sometime, to make up for the smashed cake?" she said.

For a moment he looked at her, and she thought for sure he was going to refuse. He was going to say sadly, with that annoying dignity, "My heart is elsewhere. I couldn't possibly." But to her delight, he nodded, showing white, white teeth in his tanned face.

Demial walked briskly away, allowing a smile, a real smile, to split her face. Cunning and hunger had aided her plan. She could go back to work now and toil without feeling the complaints of her body at the physical exertion, or of her mind at the boredom of carrying rocks.

On her way home that evening, she didn't mingle with the other villagers as she normally would have, joining in their tired laughter, stopping to greet the old people who sat near the well waiting to hear the news of the mine project.

Instead she hurried home to eat and to clean up before everyone gathered in the common area around the square to talk of the day's work and of the coming festival days.

Her hut was as nice as any in the village. It had a fireplace that worked and windows with real glass and a big, comfortable, clean mattress stuffed with fresh straw that crinkled when she moved in the night. The table and bench bore a golden sheen from years and years of use. Demial hurriedly polished with a rag, wiping away any hint of dust. She smoothed the blankets on the bed and fluffed the closed curtains with her fingers before putting the stew on to warm.

Marta had left a loaf of sweet, fragrant bread on the stoop, and Demial sliced it and set it on the table. She carried wood for the old lady from the communal pile every other day and in return always found some little something—a jar of jelly or a loaf of bread or a piece of pie—

left beside the door. The old lady firmly denied that it was her doing. No matter; such little kindnesses were all part of the plan.

After she had eaten, Demial checked that the bar holding the door was fastened securely, slipped out of her dirty work clothes, and closed her fingers around her staff. It was smooth and warm and welcoming, as if it was as lonely for the touch of a mage as she was lonely for the touch of magic.

She stroked it, the smooth grain of the wood and the gently curving whorls, as she took her place in front of the fire. Soon she would have to apply herself to the very real task of finding an explanation for the staff, of how she had come to discover its power so that she could use it at the mine. She smiled as she thought of Quinn's face, when she wished for the magical spell that would restore the mine.

Quinn would be outside soon, joining in the villager's evening gossip. She didn't have time tonight for wool-gathering. She caressed the staff and stoked its magic, and wished a wordless wish for cleansing, for soft sweetness. The spell danced around her, lifting her hair and tracing on her skin.

When it was done, the staff safely back in its place, she went to the back window and drew the curtains. Using the greenish glass for a mirror, she checked her appearance. Perfect. Her hair shone as if it had been oiled. She was as silky soft and sweet smelling as some pampered city lady.

With a grin that was as shiny as her hair, she wheeled away from the window, leaving the curtains pulled wide. She drew on her best tunic, belt, and slippers and threw open the curtains on the other window, then the door.

A darkness covered her as the door flew open. She jumped to find Quinn, lazing in the doorway, blocking out the waning sun. He wore his best trousers and vest, and he smelled of river water and soap. His hair had been slicked down except for the unruly curls in front, which stood up in wet tufts. The cool shadow of his body crawled up her body as he drew closer.

"I was hoping you would be joining us tonight," he said huskily, offering his arm to escort her.

* * * * *

Demial woke early as sunlight poured in the tiny back window and slithered its way across the floor. "How does anyone sleep like this?" she wondered, rolling up to a sitting position.

Her head was heavy, weighted down by her hair and the ale she had drank the night before. She groaned softly and threw an arm over her eyes to shut out the light. She had never had a head for drinking. After the way she'd been raised, she'd never bothered to develop one. Blurring her brain with drink didn't make any sense to her, but Quinn had offered her a tankard, so she'd taken it. He'd been in such high spirits that she'd wanted to join him.

It had worked, because he'd sat by her all evening, laughing at her jokes and listening to her thoughts on the mine as if her words were wisdom. A fuzzy head was a small price to pay for taking her plan one more step toward completion. Now all she had to do was come up with an explanation for the staff and to use it. After that Quinn would be hers, because . . . well, between the smiles she bestowed upon him and the magic she would perform on the mine, how could he not?

She was standing in the middle of the room, staring at the staff, when a commotion woke her from her reverie. She turned her head to the side. The noise sounded as if most of the village had gathered just past the well and were all talking at once. The only remaining dog was barking at the excitement. Strangely, though, she couldn't hear any of the children. Normally, they were right in the middle of any excitement, their shrill little voices cutting through conversation.

"It sounds as if half the village has decided to start May Fest early," she said to herself as she jerked on her robe and shoes and hurried outside.

Most of the adult population of the village was gathered in the common area near the well, grouped in a knot near the bench where the elders sat in the afternoon enjoying the sun, waiting to hear the gossip of the day. Their voices were more subdued now, but still excited. Lyrae, baby on hip, went past Demial's hut at a quick trot as a young man ran to the well to draw water, while someone else came past carrying a blanket.

Across the way, Quinn was just coming out of his hut. His shirt was thrown carelessly over one bare shoulder, and he had his boots in his hand.

Demial detoured down the path toward him. She ignored the growing cacophony, admiring the play of muscle under his skin as he bent to set his boots on a stump at the edge of his yard.

"What's all the noise?" he asked.

"I'm not sure."

His easy grin was hidden, his voice muffled, as he tugged his shirt on over his head. His abdominal muscles rippled as he yanked at the shirt. He stomped his feet into his boots, pulling them on and up. He started walking, and she slipped into step with him, as if walking together were the most natural thing in the world.

The crowd near the well was clustered around someone or something. What could have happened? Had one of the old ones taken sick and died, sitting in the morning sun? The bright golden light seemed absurdly cheerful for someone to have died in it.

"What's happened?" Quinn demanded.

The crowd parted, allowing him into its center. His steps slowed. A sudden, eerie silence fell as he stepped forward.

Apprehension washed over Demial. Not caring what they thought of her, whether they thought it was her place or not, Demial followed him, holding on to his shirt, pushing against the press of bodies that closed about him.

She felt his gasp through her fingers, pressed against his back, heard the rumble of his "Oh, gods." She knew somehow, with that same prescience that had told her Quinn would soon be hers, that this something was worse than death.

Quinn went to his knees, giving her a view of what was at the center of the crowd.

All her carefully laid plans, her perfect world, her vision, went as bright and washed out as if she'd stared too long into the sun. For seconds, minutes, she couldn't even see anything, and then when the swirling white light cleared from her vision, she wished it was gone again.

Taya.

Quinn was on his knees, small nonsensical sounds that were nearly whimpers coming from his throat. With a grip so tight it threatened to break her small fingers, he held the hands of a woman . . . what was left of a woman.

Taya . . . childhood rival . . . girlhood nemesis. Taya the good.

Quinn leaned even closer, wrapping his long arms around the woman's shoulders.

Taya, who had supposedly taken Quinn's heart into the grave. Taya the blessed. Light to Demial's dark.

Even now, she was stealing the light, stealing what was Demial's. As if to confirm what her mind was repeating, to make her believe it, the woman standing on Demial's right murmured the name.

"Taya."

The one small murmur was like the rocks caving in on the mine. Words tumbled, spilling and roiling around Demial, drowning out whatever Quinn was saying to the woman as he held her.

"It's Taya."

"Where's she been all this time?"

"She left during the war, to serve with the forces of Kalaman."

"What's happened to her?"

"Look at her hair."

"What's wrong with her?"

Demial had been straining to hear what Quinn was saying. Only now did she look, really look at the figure he was holding. She could see only a portion of the woman's too pale face, one thin shoulder, and one emaciated arm.

Taya was sitting, barely supporting herself. She was speaking in a voice that creaked like an old wagon wheel, but the words didn't make any sense. They were words like "mountains," "battle," "river." "Number," maybe. The words did not flow together into any semblance of meaning.

Quinn rose, and Demial gasped. As carefully schooled as she was in never showing her true feelings, she couldn't hide her horror. Quinn's expression was dull, shocked, the expression of a man who had just awakened to a nightmare.

There was not even a hint of the strong, blonde beauty Taya had been. It was as if someone had starved her, beaten her, broken her bones, allowed her to heal not quite right, then started over again. Her body was shrunken and trembling. Her hair was ragged, dull as straw.

Quinn helped her to her feet, grasping her arms and pulling her up gently.

Taya managed to stand but only with Quinn's support. She turned her head. Her quirky, not quite focused gaze landed on Demial, and Demial realized there was something of the old Taya still there—her eyes. Her bright, bluer-than-the-sky eyes. She looked at Demial, gaze sharpening. Taya stared right at her, and the mumbling stopped.

Demial took a step back and felt her heel come down on someone's foot. Did Taya recognize her? If she did, she gave no indication. The young woman leaned against Quinn's broad chest and allowed herself to be lifted up. She looked like a child in Quinn's arms, a limp, lifeless child.

"Put her in my hut," said one of the young men, pointing. The building he indicated was small but frequently used for the sick or injured due to its proximity to the well and because it had a real bed instead of a mattress on the floor.

As Quinn turned toward the hut, the villagers started to close Demial off, trailing after him, and she pushed forward again to walk at his side. She had never thought to see Taya again. She had never thought to see another woman in Quinn's arms again. Seeing her now, seeing him with Taya, made Demial sick to her stomach, but she had to stay close.

It was no different than when she was child. She'd hated them together then, and yet she'd been part of the circle, the bad girl everyone tolerated because Quinn and Taya tolerated her. Yet Taya was always ready to tease, to torment, when Quinn wasn't looking, always smiling sweetly when he was.

Quinn twisted awkwardly to get his small bundle through the door and laid her gently on the narrow bed.

Demial's stomach lurched violently when he stroked Taya's hair back from her face.

Lyrae appeared at her side, pitcher of water in one hand and a stack of cloths in the other.

Demial gaped at her, Quinn forgotten. It was the first time she'd seen Lyrae without her baby nearby. Demial's first response was to grin with delight. Rory would be happy. All it had taken to separate her from the child had been Taya.

A frown erased the joy. Quinn was reaching for the water and towels in Lyrae's hands, refusing to relinquish his place beside Taya.

Lyrae said, "You have to let us take care of her."

He tried again to take the towels.

"Quinn!" Lyrae said sharply. "Move away." Much more gently, she nudged Quinn with her knee. "Go on. Outside. You can come back in when we're finished."

Touching Taya once more as if to assure himself she was there, Quinn rose.

Demial went with him quickly, before she could be drafted into helping. The thought of touching that soiled, skeletal body was more than she could bear. But . . . Taya had looked at her as if she knew her. What if she started to talk?

Demial glanced back, hesitating. Maybe she should stay, make sure Taya didn't say anything. . . . Lyrae had pulled away a layer of dirt-encrusted cloth and was peeling back another. The bare flesh beneath was a mass of scars, swirls of raised, puckered welts that left the skin between unblemished. Burns: the kind that could only be left by magic.

Demial shuddered and turned away, closing the door behind her.

Outside, most of the villagers had drifted away. Those few who remained shuffled away, moving on to start their day, as Demial closed the door.

Quinn was sitting on the ground, his back against the wall of the hut. He braced his arms on his knees, hands dangling limply between.

Demial eased down beside him, shifting carefully to sit on a patch of grass.

Quinn drew a ragged breath and said, "Gods, Dem, what could have happened to her?" His voice was so broken, so . . . lost.

She bit her lip against the urge to leap up and run away or to screech at him. No one called her that. No one! With a force of will, she remained where she was. She put on her best comforting face.

"Where's she been all this time? What—?" His voice finally cracked. He hung his head, unable to go on.

Demial was saved from having to answer by the opening of the door. Lyrae came out into the yard. She was carrying the bowl. It was filled with soiled towels now. "She's asleep," she said, mainly to Quinn. When he said nothing, she said, "Are you going to sit with her now?"

"No!" Demial quickly leaped into the breach. "I will. Quinn can go on to the mine."

"No." His voice was flat, final. "I will. You go on to the mine." When Demial tried to protest, he took a deep breath and let it out. His voice softened, and his fingers twitched. "You can . . . you can sit with her tonight."

Demial nodded and walked away quickly before she said something, did something, to show how little she cared for the idea of Quinn being alone with Taya—and how little she herself cared for the idea of sitting with her.

Her thoughts were occupied as she walked the path up the mountainside. She really didn't want to be in the room with Taya, but . . . wouldn't it be the best thing to do? Wouldn't Quinn appreciate her just that much more?

At the mine, work was already proceeding as usual. It was a little slower, maybe, as everyone paused here and there to speculate about the reappearance of Taya. Everyone stopped to hear more about Taya from Demial. They sighed when she could only tell them that the woman was sleeping, then went back to work.

With no magical spell to power her and with her own lack of enthusiasm, Demial had to cut back on the amount of rock she carried. It made her self-conscious, and she kept looking over her shoulder, sure the others were suspicious, but they all seemed preoccupied with their own thoughts and tasks.

Her shoulders and elbows started to ache. Her forearms felt as if the muscles were being stretched. She suffered each rough place in the path, but it was all a dull pain, compared to thinking of Quinn's face as he stroked Taya's hair back from her face. Compared to wondering what he was doing now.

As she had the day before, after work Demial went first to her own hut, wanting to change her robe. She needed a few moments of solitude to ready herself, to calm herself. Then she went up the walk to the hut.

Taya was awake, but not quite conscious, mumbling something, under her breath, something repetitive and singsongy. Instead of hovering near Taya's bed, as Demial had expected, Quinn was sitting near the one tiny window. His face was pale and harrowed and tired.

She went to him and knelt at his side.

"It's all she's done all day." He waved in the direction of Taya. "I listened. I listened for a very long time, but none of it makes any sense. It's all about a mountain and a battle, or something. I didn't even know—" His voice broke, and he looked away from the small room and from the woman on the bed. "I thought she was dead. I was sure she was dead. Where has she been all this time?"

"Does it matter so much?" Demial gritted her teeth, forced the words out through lips clenched tight. "She's home now." She laid her hand upon his forearm. The muscles were taut and knotted.

Demial smoothed his clenched fingers open, rubbing his hand until the muscles relaxed. "Have you had anything to eat? Why don't you go and rest for a while? I'll stay here with Taya." She almost choked on saying the name but managed to keep her voice easy and natural.

He shook his head. "No, I shouldn't leave her."

Demial ground her teeth to keep from showing her true feelings. "Quinn . . . you can't stay with her every moment. Even you have to sleep and eat. What about the mine?"

"Do you think I care about the mine?"

Anger flared in her, cold and sharp, but she managed to squelch it. It surprised her how much it mattered to hear him say it, how it hurt to know that all the work they'd done didn't count. Why had she expected anything else, though, now that he had Taya back? "Of course you care about the mine. You know you do. You're just tired and hurt right now. Please . . . take a break. Rest. I'll stay here."

He looked at her, misinterpreting the anguish in her face. He relented, covering her hand with his and squeezed. "Thank you," he said. His smile was tired, but genuine. He touched her, finally, turning his hand over, enclosing her fingers. Instead of cheering him, though, touching her only seemed to sadden him more. He stood quickly, murmuring, "Thank you," again as he left.

Demial stayed on the floor a moment longer, scrutinizing her surroundings. This hut was much smaller than hers, almost claustrophobic with its low ceiling and one tiny window. The fireplace was huge in comparison and had only banked coals glowing in it now. There was a small table, scarred from much use, and two chairs: the one that Quinn had been sitting in and an even smaller one beside the bed. Finally she had to look at that bed, at what lay upon it. Once she'd looked, she couldn't look away.

There was barely enough body underneath the blanket to make a shape in it. As if aware of her scrutiny, Taya moaned and moved restlessly, tossing her head on the pillow, showing more energy than Demial would have thought she possessed. She writhed against the blanket, pinned by its weight, fighting to get out from under it.

Demial shuddered. It was a feeling she knew, being pinned down and helpless, and she would not watch even her worst enemy suffer it. She was across the tiny room in two steps and peeled the blanket away.

Lyrae had dressed Taya in a cotton nightdress. One of the sleeves was pushed up, and Demial could see that Taya's left arm had been broken between shoulder and elbow but never set properly. The flesh was flawless, though sickly white, and showed an unnatural, lumpy curve where the line of her arm should have been straight and clean. Where the sleeve was bunched, the skin showed the beginnings of the scars Demial had seen earlier.

Taya's face was scarred, too. Not so noticeably as her body, but there was a long, white line that started beneath her jaw and traced the outline of her face in front of her ear. There was a pebbling of tiny craters on the same side, as if someone had thrown droplets of acid on her temple. Whatever had happened to her, she had barely missed losing an eye.

The overall effect of white marks mingled with blue veins on the pale skin was strangely exotic, in a macabre sort of way. More repellent was the dull, life-less dry straw that had once been Taya's glorious hair. Once, it had poured through Quinn's fingers like water, like shining silk. She could see him still, reaching out to catch up a strand of it, holding it up high over Taya's head and letting it cascade back into place. She could see Taya's laughing face as she turned and mock-reprimanded Quinn.

Taya's hands flew up, writhing in the air. Her eyes opened, and she stared straight at Demial. She went absolutely still, rigid. "Demial?" she whispered in her ruined voice.

Demial gaped. Before she could respond, before she could even decide how to respond, Taya's eyes glazed over and she began to mumble again.

"Mountain. Mountain. I found the mountain. Hide here. Mountain." Then her voice trailed off, growing shrill and unintelligible but for the occasional word, and even then making no sense. The flow of words caused a prolonged, racking cough, and droplets of blood sprayed the front of the white nightdress, the corner of the pillow, and Taya's face.

Grimacing, Demial dipped a cloth in the bucket of water and attempted to wipe up the mess without actual-ly touching her patient. Taya made it difficult by having another twisting and turning spell, striking out with fin-gers so gaunt they would surely break if they struck anything.

Looking at the broken body was nauseating. Actually having to touch it . . . the thought made her skin crawl, but there was no other way. As Taya arched, Demial slipped her hand between the bed and Taya's shoulders, turning her hand to grasp her neck and hold tight.

Taya went lax across her hand, head lolling back the way a young child's would if it wasn't supported. Her hair felt like straw, brushing against Demial's fingers, but the body was not what she'd expected. Though she showed no flush, Taya's skin was burning up, fever hot, as if the magical fire that had scarred it was still burning inside.

Demial had expected her to feel like a husk, dried and dessicated, but she was actually very heavy, quite substantial for someone so tiny. She felt . . . real. Real and alive. She was so still across Demial's arm, but she was alive, breathing, heart beating. Demial could feel the beat pulsing against her arm, the uneven edges of scar tissue beneath her fingers where she touched bare flesh, the push of one sharp shoulder where it seemed to protrude.

Demial shuddered again, moving her head so that she could feel her own thick braid against her even, strong, smooth back. She watched her own fingers flex as she wiped the blood and spittle from Taya's face. Taya didn't struggle against her. She lay limp and trusting in Demial's hand.

The marks on Taya's face would have been exotic had they been decoration, painted on for Festival. However, this was from a battle so horrible that few would have crawled away with their lives. Perhaps the wounds were from that last horrible battle.

Demial had walked away from that battle. In fact, she had only one scar from the whole war, from early on before good had joined evil against a common foe. One tiny scar was not even as long as her hand, a thin, curving line of white along her ribs where she had allowed a Solamnic Knight's sword to come too close. The Knight had paid for her mistake with his life.

What if she had to wear that mark, and more, on her face? On her arms and back? As Demial eased Taya back down to the bed, the woman's eyes opened, slowly, this time. If she was surprised to find Demial touching her, she didn't show it. In fact, she looked grateful. She breathed, "Demial." She was sure this time, though before it had been a question. "Help me."

She rolled away from Demial's hand and began to mumble again, of mountains and battles and numbers.

Her voice, cracked and tired in the beginning, gained strength until she was shrill, frightened, and frightening. Demial sat by the bed and wished she could cover her ears, but all she could do was wait. Long minutes became hours while the sounds grated on her nerves. Loud to quiet to loud again.

When Marta came in later, carrying a steaming bowl of soup and fresh towels, Taya had almost worn herself down to quiet again.

The old lady left the soup and an oversized spoon on the table by the bed. "How's she doing?" she asked. She set the cloths on the table beneath the window, then bustled about, lighting the candles in the room while Demial mumbled a reply to her question.

Demial was only aware of how dark the room was after it grew bright with flickering candlelight. She stood and stretched her tired muscles. She was stiff from sitting so long, yet her back and shoulders were as tired as if she'd arched and twisted every time Taya had done so. Her throat was dry as if each of Taya's cries had been her own.

Marta filled a cup and brought it to the edge of the bed. Demial took it and drank the cool water herself before refilling it for Taya. She stopped the old lady from taking her place at the bedside.

"I'll do it." So far Taya had said nothing other than her name and inexplicable mad ravings, but who knew what she might say?

She eased Taya up. Taya roused and opened her eyes. She touched the cup to Taya's lips. The young woman opened her mouth and gulped hungrily at the water, making Demial feel guilty that she had not thought to offer it before. She grasped at Demial's forearm as the cup was withdrawn and said clearly, "What number do you believe in?"

Demial shook her head and eased Taya back against the pillows. The fingers gripping her arm flexed. Taya didn't have enough strength to hurt her, just enough to communicate her agitation.

"What number do you believe in?" she repeated.

Demial knew what was coming now.

"What number do you believe in? What number do you believe in?"

Taya's voice would grow more and more shrill; the words would tumble out faster and faster, until her poor voice would wear out. There was no answer that was right. Choosing a number made her more frantic. Telling her to hush made her louder. Saying that she didn't understand made her change to another equally nonsensical question. There was no touch, rough or gentle, that could soothe her. Demial had already tried everything.

Almost everything save the clear broth that was steaming the air near her elbow. Demial dipped the spoon in it and brought soup to Taya's lips.

"What num—?" Taya's wild gaze danced around the room, sliding past walls and furniture and Marta, stopping at Demial.

"There," Demial said, the way she'd heard mothers and fathers soothe their children. "There now." She scooped up another spoonful of the broth, blew on it to cool it, and fed it to the pale pink mouth that suddenly resembled a baby bird's gaping beak.

"Hmphh."

Demial looked up from the feeding. The quick glance up at Marta jarred the spoon, and she spilled soup across Taya's chin. She used her fingers to wipe it away.

"Hmphh!" There was more emphasis this time, a combination of disbelief and amazement and maybe just a little respect. Marta pierced Demial with a gaze that seemed to see beneath the artifice of her practiced smiles and cheerful demeanor.

A flush warmed her cheeks. "What?" she asked, only keeping the sharpness out of her voice with effort.

"Who'd have thought it?" the old one said softly.

"Thought what?" Demial returned to her task, dipping, blowing, dribbling broth into the baby bird's beak.

Marta thrust a cloth into her hand to use for wiping Taya's chin. She continued to watch a moment longer. "Who'd have ever thought you'd watch over this one like she was your own sister?"

Demial didn't dare look up. That piercing gaze would see right through her, would see her for the fraud she was. It wasn't the first time that she'd realized not everyone was taken in by her sunny smiles and her small good deeds, but it was the first time the thought bothered her. "We were friends once," she said simply.

"Hm-m-m," Marta agreed in a tone that didn't really agree. "You were thick all right. I remember that, but for all that, I never thought you liked her much."

"I like her fine," Demial snapped. Taya started nervously at the harshness in her voice, and she lowered it carefully. "I told Quinn I'd take care of her. I always do what I say I will."

"Hm-m-m."

Demial clenched the spoon handle tightly. If that old fox said "hm-m-m" once more . . .

Marta shifted into motion, quick steps that belied her ancient, thin-looking bones. "I'd better leave you to it then."

Before Demial could react, the old lady was out the door, saying over her shoulder, "Someone'll be in with your supper soon."

The door closed behind her, and Demial sat, spoon dangling, dripping broth into her lap. Why hadn't she watched her tongue? She'd been so disconcerted to hear the truth, but now she had to stay with Taya until someone else came. She'd been sure Marta would relieve her.

Taya shifted, her fingers beginning their dance in the air. "I believe in Mishakal, goddess of light," she said. "I believe in—"

Demial turned back to her and cut off her litany with more broth. "Yes, I know," she said. "So did we all, at one point or another. Look where it got us."

* * * * *

It was Quinn who brought her meal. He came quietly through the door with a bowl of stew in one hand and a board with bread and cheese in the other.

He startled her, and she came up quickly, fists clenching, feet spread for the best balance, before she realized who it was. She smiled at him sheepishly. "I must have dozed off."

She had leaned her arm on the table and rested her head upon it, just to ease the muscles in her neck for a moment. Taya's voice must have lulled her to sleep.

She could tell Quinn had slept, too, but it had done him no good. His eyes were tired, drooping, bloodshot as if he'd been out in a windstorm. She wanted him to come to her, to touch her wrist, but he only stood in the doorway, looking at her as if he didn't know what to say, as if he were loath to come in.

His gaze slid past her to Taya, and his expression softened. His eyes blinked rapidly. "I've brought you something to eat," he said, advancing into the room.

Demial looked down at Taya. She'd been asleep until he spoke. Now she moved and worked her mouth as if she was about to start talking again.

Demial would have liked to hate her, for the words that would soon pour out, for the wounded way Quinn looked at Taya, but she didn't have the strength.

"I'll stay with her now," he said, coming up behind Demial, "if you want to eat. If you want to rest."

Demial nodded and moved away. She wasn't hungry, but she was tired, so tired. She paused in the doorway and looked back at Quinn.

He was perched on the edge of the small chair, leaning over Taya, smoothing back her hair.

"I'll come back in the morning," Demial said, "so you can go to the mine."

"That's all right," he said. "I don't care about going to the mine. You go."

He didn't even look back, but Taya's eyes were open, and she was looking right at Demial.

Demial wrenched herself away, not even bothering to take a candle to light her way. She stumbled home and fell across her bed in darkness.

She was still tired when the sun woke her. She rolled over, confused for a moment that the curtains were open, allowing bright cheerful sunlight to cut across the corner of the bed. In an instant she remembered everything, and reality slammed into her. She blinked away the sudden tears and rolled out of bed. She dressed slowly and walked up the path to Taya's hut. Quinn sat in almost the same position as when she'd left the night before, his big hands dangling uselessly between his knees. Taya was sleeping restlessly, moving beneath the blankets.

Demial went to the bed and folded the blankets back to her waist. "She doesn't like the weight," she told him.

He glanced up at her and tried to smile, but it only looked as if his mouth was too tired or too frozen as if he were too numb with grief.

"I'm going to check on the mine. Maybe work for a while."

He nodded, lowering his head.

She knew there was no point in trying to convince him to go. Taya had robbed him of his dreams for the village. The girl had robbed Demial of her dreams, too.

The mine was even more depressing and lonely than it had been the day before. There were fewer workers, and among those who had bothered to come there was less energy, less life. Quinn was the heart, the lifeblood, of the project, and his heart was elsewhere now.

Demial stood watching the listless movements of the workers and felt something angry swell up inside her. She had worked hard. The magic had not stopped the tiredness at the end of the day, the aching muscles, or the blistered hands. She had given of herself to the mine, and she refused to have it all go to waste now.

She plastered a smile onto her face and strode up to the entrance to the mine. With energy and cheer she didn't feel, she grabbed a sled and took her place in line. "Rory," she called, "you're going to have to move faster than that to keep up with me!"

The big man looked back over his shoulder, meeting her gaze with tired, dispirited eyes. After a moment, though, he grinned. "No skinny woman can best me in carrying rocks," he laughed and set off at a cheerful pace with his sled.

When she laughed with him, the others laughed with her.

"What do you think?" one of them asked, pointing to the far side of the entrance where the end of a heavy, wooden beam lay beneath a pile of stone, then to the other side where another pile of stone loomed formidably. "Which side should we try to clear first?"

She looked back and forth, considering carefully. "I think we should work to free the beam first. If it's still whole, we can use it to shore up the arch as we go farther in."

She glanced around at the small group who had waited for her answer, holding her breath to see if anyone would challenge her choice. It was the kind of advice for which they would have looked to Quinn only a day ago, and she waited to see if someone would say they should ask him.

No one even mentioned him. They all nodded in agreement, then stepped up behind her to fill their sleds.

Demial had neglected, again, to enhance her strength with the staff, so her day was painful, but she was so filled with determination that the time seemed to pass quickly.

As she trudged back through the village that evening, Lyrae stopped her and said, "I told Quinn that all of us would take turns sitting with Taya, but he won't hear of it. He said you and he would handle the responsibility. Please, Demial, you know that any of us will help. You have only to ask."

Demial nodded and walked on, knowing that she had to change clothes quickly, force herself to eat, and

Linda P. Baker

take Quinn's place at Taya's side. So now Quinn wouldn't allow any of the others to sit with Taya. Well, it was no comfort to her at all to know that he had such faith in her.

No comfort to her at all as she learned this new cadence of her days . . . work at the mine, wash and eat quickly, go and sit at Taya's bedside until Quinn came to relieve her. Sleep until morning sunlight and begin again.

Sometimes she thought she would go mad with the routine of it—with the numbness of lifting one foot after another, always knowing what the next step would bring. When she looked at the progress of the mine, however, and the workers who looked now to her for inspiration and motivation, the surprising pride of that washed away the pain of seeing Quinn with Taya, with his bowed back and his old man's face.

The hours became days, and the days became weeks. The time for May Fest had come and gone with hardly a mention by anyone of celebration. Taya's return had cast as much of a pall upon the small village as it had upon Quinn.

The only time Demial ever saw Quinn was at Taya's side. Occasionally, they stepped into the yard together for a moment, but it was always painful, seeing him, stooped with sadness and mute with anguish.

She knew that something had to happen, eventually. She could not go on indefinitely. When it came, she was not prepared for it.

She turned one day from putting the bundle of soiled bedclothes outside the door to find Taya's gaze upon her. The blue eyes were open, unblinking and clear.

"Demial," she croaked, "I knew it was you."

She was sane. Totally lucid, as she had not been in weeks, not since that first night. After weeks of babbling nonsense, Taya was looking at her, clear-eyed and sane. What would Taya say now? The words that Demial had feared all these weeks: Revelation. Condemnation. She had thought herself beyond caring, but she found she was breathing rapidly.

Taya tried to lift her hand to reach for Demial.

Demial drew back, just one tiny step. She flushed with shame. How many nights had she sat there, holding the crooked fingers, soothing a mad woman's ravings, and now when Taya reached for her, she backed away in horror? Just when she'd thought there was nothing more Taya could take away from her . . . Taya sapped her courage.

"Taya?" she whispered again, and she swallowed and forced herself to move forward, to sit on the edge of the chair and to slip her cold fingers into Taya's.

"Demial. I knew it was you."

The words were like sandpaper coming out, so dry they hurt to hear. Automatically, Demial caught up the cup of water she kept on the bedside table, lifted Taya's shoulders, and held the cup to her lips.

Taya sucked at the water hungrily. It eased the harshness of her voice. She held onto the cup, held onto Demial's arm with growing strength. "Demial. I knew it was you."

"Of course it's me." Demial extricated her arm and the cup from the thin fingers, and Taya made no attempt to draw her back. She lay on the pillow and stared up at the ceiling with her sharp, blue gaze.

"I saw you . . . on the path. The day I came . . . back." The voice, though stronger, was still ragged. Each breath was still an effort. "Mountains," she said, then stopped to gulp for air, and Demial thought she was slipping into madness again. Instead, Taya went on. "I wasn't sure. Didn't know. But I had to. I came home . . . to the mountains. Looked and looked . . . for the mountains. For a long time, I . . . couldn't find my way."

Demial could say nothing. She was amazed and just a little in awe at the image that came into her mind of the weak and half-mad Taya searching, determined to find her way home.

Taya turned her head, pinning Demial with the surety in her expression. "Then I found . . . mountains. I hid. Saw you. On the path. Saw you. I knew . . . I'd made the right decision."

Demial shifted under the weight of Taya's gaze, edging back in the chair. "I don't understand." But she was afraid she did. Taya was one of the few who knew who she was, what she'd done. Taya had come home to expose her.

Eerily echoing her thoughts, Taya said, "I know about you." For this statement, the ragged voice had strengthened, had gone silky and soft. "I know all about you. I saw you. With Ariakan's legions. With your gray wizards and your robes. You were . . . You were like . . . a storm. A fire. Lightning. Your leader fell, and you took up her staff. You carried on the battle. You were . . . magnificent. Even the troops in my company were inspired by you. They charged for you, dying. Dying."

Taya's voice, at last, faded.

Automatically Demial lifted the cup of water and the thin shoulders, supporting Taya so she could drink. Her fingers were so numb, she couldn't even feel the cotton nightdress or the burning flesh beneath.

The water strengthened Taya again. "They all died, didn't they? All except you. I should have known you wouldn't die. It's what you've always been best at, isn't it? Surviving."

Praise and condemnation all in one. Admiration for someone who had betrayed her own people. "I don't—"

She stopped, confused. Taya was the one person who knew, the only one who'd ever known that Demial had saved herself, had survived the raid on the village that fateful summer day, had secured herself a position in the Gray Wizards by betraying the location of the village and the valuable mine.

"I suppose you've come to tell everyone the truth."

Taya stared at her with something like pity. "No. No, I haven't. I wasn't sure until I saw you, but then I knew I'd made the right decision. I came home to die."

Demial jerked, dropping the cup. It clattered on the hard-packed floor, showering droplets of water in a shiny arc.

She jerked again as Taya reached out and grabbed her wrist. "I knew when I saw you. That you could do it, for me."

"Do it! Do what?" Demial snatched her arm away. She jumped up and back, sending the chair clattering to the floor, but she knew. Oh, gods, she knew! She wheeled to run away, but Taya's voice stopped her. It had gone soft and whispery again, low enough that the slither of Demial's robe on the floor was enough to drown it out.

She couldn't move away. "What?"

"You can do it, Dem. If not for me, for Quinn."

"Don't call me that," Demial snapped automatically. She forgot all the careful schooling she'd given her face. Smile. Smile softly. Smile brightly, and no one will ever know. "Nobody calls me that. I hate it when people call me that."

"Your father called you that," Taya said softly, with pity and understanding in her face. As well there was a hard-edged something that Demial had tried so hard to school out of her own: determination and malice.

Fire and nausea rose up in Demial's stomach. Her fingers clenched and unclenched. If Taya said it again, if she looked at her like that again, Demial could do it. She would do it and gladly. Except . . . except . . . Abruptly all the fire went out of her, all the anger and the hatred. She couldn't do it. No matter what, she couldn't do it. It was as much a shock to her, a revelation, as it would be to Taya. She really couldn't do it. "I can't," she whispered. "I can't."

Taya laughed, an ugly, disbelieving sound that turned into a hacking cough. Her shoulders shook. Her lungs sounded as if they were old, brittle paper being ripped in half. She turned her head on the pillow, wiping her own mouth, leaving the linen cover stained with phlegm and blood. "Yes, you can. You're the only one who can."

Demial righted the chair and set the cup gently in its place. It gave a soft tap of metal on wood.

Taya reached for her arm again.

The other woman's flesh burned, but she didn't know if it was because Taya's skin was so hot or because hers was so cold. Before she could shake her head again, Taya said, "You can do it, Demial. Kill me."

"I can't."

"Help me die."

"I can't."

Taya caressed the tender flesh on the inside of her wrist softly, like a lover. "It'll make you safe. After I'm gone, there won't be anyone, will there? There won't be anyone who'll know about you."

"It doesn't matter. I won't. I can't."

Taya turned her brittle nails inward and dug them into Demial's wrist. "You have to. Why does it matter? I'm dying anyway. You'll only be helping me. It's not like it's murder. You've never minded murder anyway, have you?"

Demial shook her head, aware that the movement might be interpreted to mean "No, I've never minded murder." Something inside her was breaking, tearing, with a sound like Taya's coughing. "You don't . . . I can't . . . I don't . . . You don't understand. Things are different now." She stared at Taya with mute appeal, wanting to beg.

Taya gave up. Her fingers went limp on Demial's skin. Tears welled up in her eyes. They seemed tinged blue, like a high mountain lake reflecting the sky, until they escaped her pale lashes. Then they looked like big drops of silver, sliding down the pale cheeks. "Oh, Demial, I'm sorry. I'm so sorry for all the things I said in the past. You must know. I don't think the others realize it, but you do. You know I'm never going to be better. You can't think I want to lie here like this. I see you watching Quinn. I see you watching him wasting away, day after day. I saw him on the path, too, that day I came back. The man who comes in here every morning . . . that's not the Quinn I saw. Neither one of us wants him to waste away."

Demial was tired—so tired. It was too much, too difficult to make her brain work. If she could just lie down for a while, just a little while. "I can't."

"You have to do it, if not for me, then for Quinn. I know there's no room in your heart for me, but surely you'll save Quinn."

That was the end of it. Taya fell back onto the pillow, and her eyes drifted shut. She was limp and waxy. Her chest barely moved with her breathing. She looked like a corpse already—except for the tears. Big, silvery, raindrop tears oozed from beneath her lids and ran down into her hair.

Demial didn't move for a very long time. Her legs and arms felt as dead as Taya looked.

How odd, she thought. How odd to realize how much she'd changed, to finally understand how much the mine and the village and Quinn and all of it meant to her. How odd to learn how much she hated herself for what she had been. . . .

She laughed softly to herself. If she hadn't felt the Vision fade, hadn't felt her goddess slipping away, the magic slipping away, she'd believe the gods were still present. She'd believe they were trickster gods, working a mean-spirited joke.

She stood as Taya stirred. The sick woman's eyes opened. They were tired now, and bloodshot, but still they had the power to stop Demial. "I'll be back," she told Taya. "It'll be all right. I'll be back."

Taya nodded, believing her. Trusting her.

The air was cool and refreshing after the closeness of the hut. There was a light breeze blowing, wafting the scent of someone's fire and meadow flowers and coming rain. The night was quiet except for the soft rustle of leaves in the breeze. The only indication that there was even anyone in the village was the flicker and glow of candlelight and firelight through the windows. It shone even from her own windows.

She stood in her doorway and looked about in surprise at the spotless room. A merry fire was blazing in the fireplace. The table was cleaned of her leftover meal. Her blankets were spread smooth over the mattress. The floor was swept.

With a sudden twinge of panic, her gaze flew to the fireplace, to the staff that was leaning there, exactly as she had left it. She felt ashamed for her momentary, uncharitable fear. Someone had come and looked after her home, looked after her, the way she was looking after Taya. That was all.

She wondered if it had been Quinn, but she knew it wasn't. She wished it could have been, but it was probably one of the people who worked with her at the mine.

Quickly, before she could change her mind, she snatched up the staff and hurried back to Taya's hut. As she approached the door, she saw that it was open. She rifled through her mind for an excuse to give to Quinn, for some reason that would explain why she'd left Taya unattended to go and get her walking staff, but there was no one inside except for the slight figure on the bed, and she realized she must have left the door open when she left.

The cool air had whisked into the room, setting the fire and the candles to dancing. It had also set Taya to shivering.

Demial closed the door quickly. "I'm sorry. I left the door open."

Taya smiled. "Yes. It was nice. The smell . . . so much nicer than the air in here. I love the smell just before the rain."

Demial swallowed. For how long had she hated this woman? How many times had she looked at Taya's pale, blonde beauty and longed to kill her? Now . . .

"You have to, Demial," Taya husked, staring up at her. The woman was reading her mind. Her hands moved under the light sheet that covered her. "For Quinn. You have to let me give him this."

Demial nodded, not trusting herself to speak. She wasn't sure what she'd say, whether she would cry or scream or just mumble nonsense of the sort she'd heard out of Taya's own mouth.

"How will you . . .?" Taya let her gaze wander to the ceiling, to the wall, back to Demial. "How will you do it?"

Demial brought the staff into Taya's range of vision, holding it to her breast, wrapping both hands around it.

Taya looked at it, looked back at her, eyes wide. "Your leader's staff? The one I saw at the battle."

Demial nodded again. "It has . . . it still has some magical powers. I don't know how. I don't . . ." She stopped, realizing that the staff did not have much power left, that this might be its last spell. She wondered if she could go through with it.

"You'll tell Quinn that I was awake for a while? Tell him . . . I love him. I'd give him to you, but . . . he was always yours anyway, wasn't he? He always loved you best anyway."

Demial's mouth dropped open. "You're crazy!" she said without thinking, then regretted the words immediately. She felt flushed with shame.

Taya only smiled. "Maybe," she said softly. She looked at Demial and said, "I'm ready."

Demial wanted to scream at her, "I'm not!" but she didn't. She went to the door and threw it wide open. Crossing to the tiny window, she opened it, too. Fresh air, even heavier with the coming of rain, flooded the small room.

Taya's smile widened, and she whispered, "Thank you."

Demial couldn't watch her, couldn't watch what she was going to do. She knelt near the fireplace, turned so that she could see the fire on one side and the bed on the other. She turned so that she didn't have to watch Taya die.

She waited long moments for her hands to stop shaking, for her heart to calm. Then she closed her eyes, and she wished for death for Taya. She wished for peace and an end to pain. The spell was slow in coming, so gradual she feared that she had miscalculated, that the staff hadn't enough power left in it. It began to sing to her, to hum with power. The spell grew in the staff for a long time, the power building until the staff was vibrating in her hands, shivering as if it would break free. She clutched it tighter, thinking to control it, but there was no controlling the magic now.

The staff leaped in her hands, jerking her shoulders painfully. It cracked apart, breaking under her grip, sounding extraordinarily loud, like a tree falling or like the crash of lightning. She cried out and fell away from the exploding wood. Fragments flew up toward her face. A sharp pain stabbed as a splinter gashed her temple, and the magic spilled out over the room, washing across the broken pieces that lay across her lap and on the floor. The sensation wasn't malignant or horrid, as she expected it to be. Instead it was cold, so cold. The magic smelled of shadows and molting leaves. Blood trickled down her face. She shivered and whimpered softly and slapped at her own body, frantically brushing the pieces of broken wood off her.

The spell burst away, leaving her alone and bereft, and it touched Taya. It was beautiful. It was blue, like her eyes, and swirling, like a summer sky filled with clouds. It formed into a strange crescent that traveled up the length of Taya's body and down again and up again. Taya smiled and held her hands up, fingers spread, as if she was feeling the touch of a light spring breeze. With each pass, the magic was less substantial, until it was nothing but a shimmering movement, a something in the air that was there but not visible.

The next instant it wasn't there at all, and neither was Taya. Only her body remained. Demial could tell, without even rising up to look at her. Even in her frailest moments, Taya had never been so still.

Demial climbed to her feet, looking down at the shattered remains of the staff about her feet. The staff was intended to be her salvation, fixing the mine and binding Quinn to her.

She gathered the pieces, light as dried corn husks. There was no life in the wood now, no beauty. It was as dead as the body on the bed, as lifeless as her dreams. She threw the pieces into the fireplace and watched the glowing embers there catch at dried wood. She watched the tiny blue flame that leaped up and consumed the remains of the staff. None but a wizard would ever understand the emptiness that came over her when she saw the staff become ash.

Demial forced herself to approach the bed. She'd seen hundreds of dead bodies, torn apart with bloody wounds and with eyes gaping. She'd killed scores herself, in battle, with her magic, with weapons, even with her own bare hands, when the battle lust took her. It took all the courage she had to approach this one, but she was glad she'd forced herself to look.

Taya's face was even paler, but she was so peaceful. The thin, pink mouth was soft and relaxed, still hinting at the smile that had brightened her face as the spell embraced her.

Demial started to pull the blanket up over her, to cover her face. Even in death, though, she couldn't bear to weigh the fragile body down.

When she left the hut for the last time, Demial closed the door behind her gently, leaving the window open to let in the cool air. She walked back through the night, noting that most of the huts were dark now. Had it been that long, since she'd gone to her hut for the staff? Her own fire was still burning, low but bright and cheerful, in her fireplace.

She sat on the bench before the fire, and her mind went blank for a very long time. She was only roused when a voice cut through the numbness, and only then after it spoke her name twice. She roused only after she felt the warmth of an arm against her arm, a hip against her hip.

"Demial. Demial."

She found Quinn sitting beside her, hands dangling between his knees. She wiped the dried blood off her face, trying to disguise her movements, but Quinn was looking away. He wasn't paying attention to her.

It was very late. The fire was only a small fluttering of flames, a dying fire. Death. Dying. It wasn't morning yet though. Quinn had left the door open, as she had, and she could see that it was still dark outside. No stars were visible in the inkiness, just darkness. Shadows. Like death.

"She's gone," Quinn said. His voice was quiet but strange, as if he could just barely contain his sorrow, as if he might at any moment break down and sob.

"Yes," Demial agreed. "It was very peaceful." She roused herself, knowing she had to gather her strength. The one thought that was clear in her mind, despite her numbness, was that she ought to tell Quinn the truth. All of it. Everything. "She said to say 'I love you,' and then she said, 'I'm ready.' Then she died. It was what she wanted."

Quinn sighed and turned away from her, as if the pain was going to eat him in half and he didn't want her to witness it. "Oh, gods . . . " he breathed.

She swallowed. She tried to lift her hands and put them on him, to soothe him and console him. Her arms were heavy, but she managed to lift one. She could touch him, while he would still allow it. Before she told him.

She put her hand on his broad back, feeling the strength there, the muscles moving under the skin as he shook. She liked his back. She'd always liked his back. It was broad and strong, and since she was a child, she'd dreamed of laying her face on his back, of resting her weight on him. So she did now. After a lifetime of dreaming such a thing, she let herself lie against him, resting her weight and her sorrow and her fear on his good, broad, strong back.

He sighed, and she felt the movement beneath her face, a ripple of muscles against her cheek, a rush of air into lungs, and the thump of his heartbeat.

"I killed her," he said.

The words came to her as a shock. They were said so

calmly, so easily, that she must surely have misunderstood. Perhaps he was only expressing guilt, or . . . She drew in a quick, sharp breath. Surely he hadn't guessed what she'd done! Demial drew back, and hesitated.

He shifted back on the bench, moving farther away, and his face was strange. His mouth worked, eyes bright as the embers in the fireplace and as weirdly hot.

She braced herself for his grief, his accusation, and he shocked her even further by chuckling.

"I killed her," he repeated again, almost with glee, almost with pride. "I wished her dead, and it worked. Like magic. It worked!"

Demial shook her head, too confused to speak. Was it just that her mind was too tired, or was it that he wasn't making any sense? "Quinn, I'm sorry. I'm so tired. Please. I don't understand what you're saying." She reached out to touch him. "I know you always said your heart was with her, in the grave. . . . "

The chuckle gave way to outright laughter. "Demial, don't tease me. I know you weren't fooled by all that. You always saw right through me."

She gaped at him.

He covered her hand with his larger ones. "You're joking with me, but I suppose I deserve it." He brought her fingers up to his lips and kissed them lightly.

Her fingers were roughened from working in the mine. Just hours ago, she could have used the staff to make her skin soft and sweet again. Now all she did was stare dumbly as his lips moved on her scarred knuckles.

He sighed playfully. "All right, I can see you're going to force me. I'll say the words. I didn't love Taya. I never did. I only said those things about her to keep other women interested. When you came back, I began to say them especially for you. I knew that remembering her made you jealous, and it pleased me to see the fire in your eyes when I mentioned her. Now I know. It's always been you I loved."

Her heart would have leaped, would have tasted the joy of her triumph, but he said it with such callous lack of emotion. "I don't understand."

"I was just teasing you, before, saying all that about missing her and my heart being with her. In the end, I hated her, Demial," he said lightly. He released her hand and leaped to his feet. He quick stepped across the small space between her and the fireplace, jittering with unspent energy. He wiped his hand across his mouth. "She was my childhood friend, my perfect friend. That was long ago. I wish she'd been killed in the war. I wish I'd never had to see her like that. I wish I could have remembered her the way she was. I hate her for coming back, for making me see her that way. I wanted . . . I wanted her to die quickly so that my life could go on! Oh, I stayed with her. I played the part of the true and faithful lover, the way everybody expected me to, but I hated doing it, and I hated her.

"Gods! All those hours in that horrible, little room, listening to her ravings . . . I wished her dead, and now she is. I wished her dead, and it worked, and now we can be together."

He looked at her expectantly, but Demial sat, still and stunned. Numbness was nothing compared to this. This was like being dead. Except . . . her chest was still rising and falling with breath, and her back was cool from the breeze, and her shins were warm from the fire. Warmth and cold and air, did the dead feel those things?

He came to her. He went on one knee before her, leaned in, and laid his cheek against her shoulder. "So?" he asked, voice muffled against the robe that still smelled of Taya and death.

Demial didn't move away as his breath seeped through the cloth, as it moistened her skin, sliding across her shoulder and down towards her breast and up along her neck. "So . . . what?"

"I said 'Now we can be together,' and you're just sitting there as if you're paralyzed. Don't you realize what this means? I've almost done what I was supposed to do, done what the whole village expected of me. Soon the mine will be finished. It's what I've been waiting for, the perfect moment to cement my plan. Now they'll follow my leadership. We'll open the mine again and make this village better than it was before."

Demial stared at the fire and felt a little spark, hot and orange, flare up in her breast. It was the first hint that she was going to come back to life, that she was going to be able to feel something again. It wasn't joy that her perfect plan was within her grasp. It was laughter—cold, hard laughter.

All her diligent work at the mine had given her the acceptance she wanted. Everyone in the village respected her now. She could have the man she'd always wanted. All the pieces of her perfect plan had fallen into place, like the wooden shapes of a child's puzzle. And she *would* have the man she'd always wanted, because it wasn't going to be safe to do anything else. She was going to have to take him, just to keep an eye on him. Her perfect mate thought, after all her hard work at the mine, he was going to step back in and take over where he'd left off, that he'd become the leader, and she'd fall into place as his perfect follower.

She shifted, moving so that his forehead no longer had the support of her shoulder, forcing him to sit up. "I'm tired right now, Quinn," she said coolly. "I want to sleep for days and days. We'll talk about it then."

His surprise was plainly visible on his handsome face. "All right." He stood slowly, giving her time to change her mind, say something, to reach for him. When she didn't, he touched the top of her head, so lightly he barely stirred her hair. He kissed her just as lightly. "We'll talk about it later, Dem."

He was gone, long strides taking him away into the darkness, and she was alone again.

The dying fire was all red and orange and yellow, without even a hint of blue to the flame that would have

The Thief in the Mirror
Richard A. Knaak

He felt so cold, and she looked so warm. He wanted to reach out and touch her, just as he had always wanted to touch the others before her. However, Mendel did not permit him that; the cursed little bald man didn't want him to take any chances. Vandor Grizt was expected only to watch and wait, wait to obey his master. Wait and obey, that was all Vandor was permitted.

The gem-encrusted brooch she wore he once would have coveted for himself, but as Vandor could not keep it and Mendel would have no use for it, his interest in the jewelry swiftly faded. He had come here for something else, something more important.

She stared past him, amber eyes admiring her reflection. He knew her name, but only because Mendel had told it to him. That she had reason to be vain was obvious. But such mundane observations were beyond his purpose . . . at least so he told himself.

With a sweep of her long, silver hair, the noblewoman rose from her mirror and departed the chamber, no doubt on her way to visit the lover her much older and generally absent husband knew nothing about. Vandor watched her as she paused to admire a tiny sculpture, then look herself over one more time in another mirror.

He ducked away, shivering from the ever-present cold. Her chance glance at the second mirror had nearly put them eye to eye. She probably wouldn't have been able to see him, but one could never tell . . . and Vandor Grizt had no desire to taste Mendel's anger.

At last she stepped out of the chamber, closing the door behind her. Vandor eyed the prize he sought, the very sculpture the noblewoman had stopped to admire. It had been given to her not by her lover but by her husband, and she could not suspect that it contained latent magical forces. Probably even her husband had not known it when he had purchased the sculpture. Mendel, though . . . Mendel had learned of its existence only two days after the sculpture had arrived in Lauthen. Mendel always knew, Chemosh take him!

Vandor shifted position, knowing he would not have long to act. The ungodly chill made him feel stiff and clumsy, but he could no longer hesitate. He had to do it and do it now.

The mirror melted away from his hands as he reached out and seized his master's prize.

Fingers tingled as blessed warmth coursed over those parts of his arms that protruded from the mirror world. Without meaning to, he paused to savor that warmth, allowing it to spread even a little to the rest of his body. How delightful to be warm again, however briefly, to feel even some hint of the real world!

The warmth grew until the heat no longer pleased Vandor, but rather began to burn. Tendrils of smoke rose from his hands, and his sleeves began to shrivel and blacken. With a sudden sense of urgency, the thief picked up the statuette, an intricate figurine of a dryad and her tree, and drew it into the mirror.

As ever, it took some gentle forcing to make the object pass through the mirror. Once it was done, Vandor Grizt folded his arms, cradling his prize, and turned around to stare at the chamber from which he had stolen the statuette. Here, inside the mirror, everything lay bathed in cold, blue light. The statuette, which had been brightly colored, almost lifelike, now resembled some frost-covered miniature corpse.

Vandor shivered and, turning from the mirror surface that separated reality from reflection, returned to Mendel.

The journey took but a thought. Where, before, the dark-haired thief had stared into a room of rich furnishings and elegant appointments, he now looked into an old, decrepit chamber lined with row upon row of dusty bookshelves. Once those shelves had been lined with scrolls, tomes, and artifacts, the envy of almost any mage, whatever color his robes, but necessity had, over the past few decades, obliged its aging master to utilize much of the collection. What remained were only the vestiges of greatness, just as what remained of Mendel was only a shadow of the black-robed terror who had dominated this region for more than a lifetime.

Mendel's power might be dwindling, yet over Vandor it remained absolute, even some thirty years or so after the Chaos War.

Looking around, Vandor could see no sign of the cadaverous little man, the foul rodent who had kept him in absolute servitude since that fateful day some ten years after the War of the Lance. In the past, Mendel had precisely scheduled his every waking moment. He could be counted on to know how long Vandor's errands took and when he would return. Mendel was beginning to slip. Where was he now?

In his hands, the figurine grew colder, even colder than usual. Knowing what would happen if he waited much longer, the thief pushed the prize against the mirror before him. The mirror resisted at first, as it always did, but then both Vandor's hands and the statuette came through. He quickly stood the dryad on the small wooden table on the other side of the mirror, the one that Mendel had placed there years ago to ensure that his slave would never again have an excuse for losing one of the treasures.

As Vandor's hands pulled back into the pale, cold world behind the mirror, the once-great Mendel stalked into the room. He had lived more than two normal life spans, and it had been during the second half of that overly lengthy existence that so many changes in the man had occurred. Where once he had stood taller than

Vandor, who was six feet, Mendel had somehow shrunk to barely more than five. He moved hunched over, which accounted for some of that height loss, but Vandor often wondered if the man's deep ties to the old magic of the gods had had something to do with what had happened. Magic had all but vanished from Krynn, and Mendel was clearly shrinking.

The flowing brown hair, broad, sharp nose, and strong chin had given way to a vulturelike head with heavy brows, under which peered bitter black orbs. Mendel still wore the black robes of his office, but they were worn and not of the best quality. He could replace the robes readily enough, thanks to the precious objects Vandor stole for him, but never the power those robes had once represented.

"So, returned at last!" rasped the mage, leaning on his formerly magical staff. "You've kept me waiting too long, dandy!"

As Mendel's appearance had changed he had become increasingly prone to making disparaging remarks about the thief's time-frozen features. Vandor's handsome, patrician face, his piercing emerald eyes, coal-black, shoulder-length hair, elegant mustache, and expensive gentleman's garments had served him well during his life, garnering him entrance to both a superior class of maidens and an even more superior class of valuables. However, to be envious of Vandor's good looks hardly seemed fair. Vandor did not change because he could not change. He remained the reflection of what he had been that day when, fool of fools, greediness and, especially, vanity, had made him linger to inspect Mendel's intricate and bewitching mirror. Not until too late did he discover that the mirror had been set as a trap for just such a one as he.

"I came as quickly as I could. The Lady Elspeth remained far longer at her table than we'd thought, Mendel."

"A vain crone!" the black robe snapped, referring to a woman whose beauty any other man would have admired. "So in love with herself is she that she failed even to notice the rarity of such an artifact under her very nose!"

"I doubt she has any sense of magic, Mendel. To her, the figurine seemed only an exquisite work of—"

Mendel waved him to silence. "When I want your opinions, Grizt, I'll wring them from you!" The wizened man clutched a large, diabolical-looking medallion dangling on his chest. "Quit wasting my time with your prattle!"

Vandor clamped his mouth shut. One thing could affect him here in the world of mirrors, and Mendel held it in his hand now. Not only did the medallion keep Vandor under control, but the mage could use it to punish the thief. The cold, cold world Vandor inhabited would seem a blessing in comparison to that punishment, he knew.

Seeing that his slave had quieted, Mendel nodded. "All right, then, dandy! What of more important matters? What of the Arcyan Crest? Did you find it? Did Prester have it, as my stone indicated?"

Of the few artifacts the once-great wizard still possessed, the onyx scrying stone remained the most useful, if only because it aided Mendel in hunting down the magical items so desperately needed by mages these days. When the gods departed after the Chaos War, they took with them much of the magic of the world, but a little magic remained in once-powerful artifacts. If a mage could locate an artifact and channel its latent power, he could still cast spells of a potentially great magnitude. Inevitably, the magical object would be drained of power, but few spellcasters gave thought to that.

This was the course Mendel had dedicated himself to, soon after the departure of the gods. Over the years he had forced Vandor to scour many places in search of the artifacts whose existence was hinted at by his scrying stone. One such piece was legendary, and it had eluded the black robe's grasp. The Arcyan Crest was said to be the size of a medallion with the symbol of the House of Arcya set upon it. Its creator, Hanis Arcya, had used the crest to augment his formidable powers until his death. Unfortunately, as Vandor had heard too often from his master, the first great Cataclysm had ended the House of Arcya, and since then the crest had been a thing of rumors, glimpsed here, reported there, never proven to be anywhere.

Now Mendel's stone had indicated to him that the crest might be somewhere in the vicinity of the palatial abode of Thorin Prester, a former red robe who still seemed adept at having matters turn out to his benefit. The stone's murky directions plus his own driving envy had made Mendel adamant on this point—Prester had to have the artifact, and if Grizt could not find it that was because he was not searching hard enough.

Even knowing the possible fury his response might unleash, the thief in the mirror replied, "I have searched his place from top to bottom, Mendel, from side to side, corner to corner—wherever I can find a reflection from which to spy, even from puddles in the rain. I've haunted his entire sanctum again and again, and I can state categorically that he does not have—"

"Lies! Lies!" The vulture face blossomed crimson. Mendel's eyes fairly bulged out of their sockets. The mage raised his staff high and with surprising speed, considering his withered appearance, struck out at the jeweled and gilded frame of the mirror.

Vandor's world rocked, an earthquake of titanic proportions. Mendel had, in times past, told him that if the mage completely shattered the looking glass, his ungrateful wretch of a slave would cease to exist. As futile as his existence was, Grizt still clung to the hope that some day . . .

"Lies!" Mendel rasped again. "I think, my dandy thief, you've grown a tad too used to the chill in there! I think you should warm up a little!"

"Mendel!" Vandor Grizt gasped. The mirror had not shattered, but he was overcome by dizziness and fear. "Think what you're doing! If you lose me—"

Too late. The furious, bent figure clutched his medallion tight, glaring at the handsome reflection that did not belong to him. "Come out, Grizt!"

An inexorable force pulled Vandor toward Mendel's side of the mirror, toward the real world. Try as he might to fight it, the thief could not. First his hand went through the mirror. Then the rest of him was sucked through, all definition of form vanishing.

On the other side of the mirror, a yard from his master, Vandor Grizt reformed . . . yet not completely so. A haze surrounded him, a grayness, as if he had become part smoke. The mirror from which he had just been plucked could almost be seen through his writhing body.

"For the love of the gods, Mendel!"

"There are no more gods for you, Grizt, save for me."

Vandor had never been a violent man, always preferring stealth and the ladies to unnecessary adventure. Sometimes, though, he had been forced to take action, and if ever there was anyone he would gladly kill, it was his tormentor—now. He had no opportunity, though. Before Vandor could move even one step, his hands began to smoke. The sleeves of his shirt crinkled black from heat. Vandor felt his skin beginning to crackle as horrible pain wracked every fiber of his being.

"For pity's sake, Mendel! I'm burning up!"

"So you are." The mage watched without emotion, visibly gauging just how far he could go with his slave's suffering. When Vandor had almost given up, Mendel uttered, "Begone to the mirror, spectre!"

Instantly Vandor found himself sucked back into the mirror. Now was one of the rare instances when he appreciated the chill, foreboding surroundings to which he had been doomed. All signs of the inferno that had engulfed him disappeared. He shivered, grateful for the blessed cold, for the safety of his mirror prison.

"Let that be a lesson to you! No more lies! Prester has the crest, and you'll find it, won't you, my little mirror thief?"

Vandor could not look at him. "Yes . . . Mendel."

"This was only a taste of what I could do to you, Grizt." The horrific punishment through which he had just put Vandor brightened the mage's spirits.

"Remember . . . I also have your actual body under a continuing spell. I need new infusions of magic to keep that spell going, you know. Think what would happen if I were forced to allow the preserving forces to fade from your empty shell."

Vandor fell against the mirror, pleading with the madman on the other side. "No! Please! Mendel . . . Mendel, you would be taking away the one thing that means anything to me, and I would be of no use to you at all! Where will you find another thief so knowledgeable of the ways in which the rich and cunning hide their treasures? Where will you find another with the cleverness to see behind their facades? Where will you—"

". . . Find another as vain as you, Vandor Grizt? Certainly bold . . . at least you used to be. What other fool would dare steal from a wizard without any magic of his own to protect him? Who else would think he could enter my sanctum not once, but twice, to take away those things most precious to me?"

Vanity had indeed been Vandor's downfall. Another mage had promised him much for a token carried by his rival. That alone should not have been worth the risk, but the mage had played on Vandor's reputation, that no thief could compare to Grizt. Vandor had stolen that trinket and stolen it with ease, understanding that even the best wizards underestimate their security. The very fact that he had no magical powers himself encouraged him to find a different way inside the sanctum, one that no spellcaster would predict of a mortal man. Vandor would wait weeks before striking such places, planning his moves, but when he acted, he usually acted well.

Emboldened by his first success, Vandor took on a second such challenge, then a third. The fourth brought him to the then-impressive abode of the great black mage Mendel. Mendel's citadel was a slightly more time-consuming affair, but in the end Grizt made his way out undetected . . . so he supposed.

When but a few weeks later, a hooded black robe of more than attractive female features offered him a sizable ransom to steal from Mendel again, Vandor Grizt at first hesitated. The prime rule of any good thief is never to strike too soon again at the same place. However, he learned that Mendel intended to be away for two weeks. Unable to resist both the challenge and the feminine allure of the one offering to pay for the job, the daring thief took the assignment. He even chose a different mode of entry, knowing that the wizard might have discovered traces of the last trespass. Entering Mendel's inner sanctum proved to be a little more difficult the second time, but finding the artifact in question, now that caused inordinate trouble. It was small and rumored to be hidden in an unusual place, the female black robe had said. Vandor had cautiously searched everywhere in the sanctum, behind paintings and wall hangings, before finally coming to the covered mirror.

There he made his fatal mistake.

At first he remained wary of the mirror, studying its intricate framework but unwilling to approach. Then, curiosity got the better of him, and Vandor lifted the black curtain a bit. Seeing his own hand reflected in the mirror, the thief raised the curtain more.

At this point, vanity took over. Vandor paused too long to take an admiring glance at himself, a glance that became a lingering look at the handsome thief who had dared not once but twice to steal from a deadly black-robed wizard. How clever, how handsome he looked.

Before Vandor could realize what was happening . . . he was drawn into the mirror. Instead of looking into the mirror, he now found himself looking out . . . out at his own limp, sprawled body.

"Always think yourself so clever, dandy!" Mendel mocked now as he listened to Vandor plead from behind the mirror. "The very next day after you'd first had the audacity to steal from me, I brought the mirror into play!

I then searched around, and it wasn't too difficult to find some bauble that a petty thief as arrogant and foolish as yourself might be tempted to steal! I already knew your great weakness, your love for yourself! Ha! I knew that you would not be able to resist gazing at yourself in the covered mirror, and so with the willing aid of one of my own order, a most delectable associate, I set about preparing your doom!"

Mendel had not returned to his citadel for an entire day. In that time Vandor had grown frantic and very cold. He was trapped in the mirror and continued to stare at the body from which his—spirit?—had become separated. In every way he still looked like himself, even down to the clothes he was wearing before the mirror captured him, but his true corporeal form was abandoned on the other side, dying.

"For your crimes against me," the mage reminded him, "I commanded you to a lifetime of servitude. When—and only when—I'm satisfied that you've served your punishment, I'll return spirit to body and make you whole again—but not before you find me the Arcyan Crest!"

"My body!" Vandor gasped. "Is it still well? The spell you cast over it keeps it intact?" It was his only hope.

"You doubt me?" Mendel's hand rose to the medallion.

"No! No!" The thief sank back.

His gnarled master seemed mollified. "Better, then! All right, Grizt! You've failed me once, but you've brought back this other prize, so I cannot complain too much. Tonight, though, you will return to Prester's sanctum and search it again! This time you must not fail. I am losing patience!"

"But if he doesn't—"

"He has it! Do not doubt me!" Again the staff came up and rattled the frame of the mirror.

Grizt remained silent as his foul prison trembled. He knew he could not convince the damned mage otherwise. He feared the medallion's tortures. Even the medallion's worst could not compare with his fear that some day he might not have a body to which to return.

"I will find it," he promised.

"See that you do."

* * * * *

The great hall. A banquet room. The kitchen. Prester's bed in which Prester himself slept. The room in which his only child rested, a small girl not even ten years of age. The spell that bound Vandor to Mendel's special mirror allowed him to travel anywhere there was a reflection, be it glass, metal, or a bowl of purest water. The spell permitted the thief of mirrors to reach out as far as the length of his arms, sometimes even the upper half of his torso if he struggled.

Moonlight shining through a partially open window glittered on a polished breastplate once worn by Prester's grandfather, a Knight of Solamnia. Through the breastplate Vandor Grizt emerged, glancing about the room, Prester's personal library, counting the seconds before the growing heat would consume him. He had been in the library before and noticed nothing. However, libraries were often the location of wall vaults, hollowed-out books, and hidden drawers in desks.

Vandor sank back into the breastplate, only to emerge a moment later from the tiny, metallic surface of a desk drawer handle. Slim hands with tapering fingers reached into the real world and drew open another drawer. Grizt felt under the top, looking for a secret hiding place.

Nothing. He returned to the breastplate, which offered him a better view, and studied the chamber again. Assuming Prester had the Arcyan Crest, which Vandor doubted, he might not even realize its significance. Even some of the former wizards from whom Mendel had forced him to steal had not always recognized the prizes in their own possession. That had sometimes made his task more easy, but just as often it made things more frustrating, for victims with no idea as to the true worth of a treasure were wont to store it anywhere.

On a hunch—and hunches had, for the most part, served him well in the past—Vandor Grizt returned to the bedroom of Prester's daughter.

He had not searched the room as thoroughly as he should, feeling some guilt about rifling through the young child's belongings. The girl's mother had died when she was but five, the victim of some malady. Unlike her husband, the mother had had no taste for magic, but she did boast a noble lineage encompassing not one but several great houses through the centuries. Little money had come with that lineage, but her noble station had given her husband a status that aided his ambitions, going from red-robed mage to landowner.

Vandor studied the slumbering child, guessing that she would never wake from so deep a sleep. Slipping out of the small mirror in her chamber, he reached into a nearby chest and quietly but quickly searched the contents. Clothes, pins, toys . . . all the things of a well-born child. Vandor recalled his own early childhood, a kitchen brat in a lord's castle. He had gained a hunger for fine things from that existence, ever watchful as the nobles wasted what he so coveted.

Across the room he spotted a cabinet, but at first a useful reflective surface near it resisted his searching eyes. Vandor's gaze drifted to a small stand by the child's bed. On the stand stood a mug of water, only partially emptied. Enough of a reflective surface for his needs. With careful planning, it would enable him to search the cabinet.

He had to make this a most thorough search, even more so than the last. If the Arcyan Crest was hidden anywhere in this castle, Vandor had to find it. He had no doubt Mendel would keep his promise to punish him for failing.

Transferring to the mug took but the blink of an eye, but from there the thief moved with caution. Not only might the mug wobble, but the child just might wake because of his nearness.

Slowly Vandor Grizt rose from the water. Head and arms floated above, a misty layer below them. Concentrating on maintaining his partially solid form, Vandor stretched his left hand forward, seizing the nearest drawer handle.

With some difficulty, he searched the first two drawers, returning quickly to the safety of his chill realm whenever the burning grew hot enough to threaten him. Unfortunately, Vandor found nothing in either drawer, and the time he had wasted irritated him. Determined, the spectral thief reached for the third.

A high squeak from the drawer made him freeze.

In her bed, the young girl turned over, mumbling. Vandor vanished into the reflection, then, when he felt the water rock, jumped swiftly into the mirror on the other side of the room. From there he watched as the child sat up and drank from the mug. The thief silently cursed; if she finished the water, he would have no method by which to reach the cabinet again.

At that moment he noticed the brooch in her hair.

That a child would wear a brooch in bed seemed odd enough, but the piece looked valuable, making Vandor all the more curious. He waited in frustration as the girl finally put the mug down and lay back on the bed. He waited until she had fallen asleep, then, with one last look at her face, shifted back to the container.

The remaining water barely covered the bottom of the cup, but it served for one with no corporeal form. Pushing himself, Vandor managed to get as much as half his torso above the mug. Gently he leaned over and studied the brooch as closely as he could. Eyes accustomed to darkness had little trouble making out the various details of the jewelry. A ruby sat in the midst of two warring griffons of gold, their diamond eyes glaring at one another. A kingfisher flew above, sword and shield in its talons. Tiny encrusted points thrust out from every edge of the item, which resembled a miniature sunburst. The brooch was valuable purely in terms of coin; Vandor knew it was invaluable to him. He stared at the child's bauble with the eyes of one who has seen the culmination of a lifetime quest.

He had found the Arcyan Crest.

Why Prester would keep so valuable an object, even if he did not know its true nature, on the person of a small child, Vandor could not say. Sentiment, perhaps. Assuming that the former red robe did not know its magical history, he might have given it to the child as some heirloom from her mother. Had not Prester's wife come from royal lineage . . . possibly even descended from Arcya?

All that mattered to the thief of mirrors was that he now beheld the one object that might prompt Mendel to grant him his freedom. To walk again among men, to kiss a fair damsel, drink a little ale, and pick a pocket or two . . . But first he had to steal the brooch from the child.

Already his body sweltered from heat. Wisps of smoke rose from his fingers. However, Vandor Grizt did not return to the water in the mug. He could not wait any longer for his freedom. His tapering fingers gently lifted the brooch so he could undo the clasp. Another second or two and he had the Arcyan Crest free. Child's play! he thought to himself, admiring his own pun even as the pain, coursing through his body, began to overwhelm him.

Holding the crest close to him, he dove into the watery reflection, then from there to the mirror across the room. True mirrors gave him a swifter path back, and with a treasure of this nature Vandor desired the swiftest path possible. The longer the artifact remained with him in this chilling realm, the more peril there was. Real objects lasted only a little longer in the mirror realm than he could last outside the mirror, only they froze where he burned.

"Mama's jewel . . ."

Vandor Grizt stiffened in the mirror. The little girl, blonde hair half obscuring her features, stared back at him from across the room, an indecipherable expression on her delicate features. She pointed at him, at the crest he held, in a manner so accusing that the thief felt she could see him with strange clarity.

Flee, you fool! he told himself. No force held him here save astonishment, and he could not afford that now. Grizt thought of Mendel's cursed mirror, knowing full well that to think of it meant to take the first step in returning.

Yet, even more astonishingly, he remained in the child's room.

"Give me Mama's jewel!"

Suddenly the thief found himself dragged toward the mirror. The Arcyan Crest—the young girl's brooch—struggled to free itself from his grasp. Try as he might, Vandor could not keep his hands from passing through the glass.

The realization struck him. The little girl was a mage! Small wonder to him now that Prester had given her the crest. Prester must have seen his daughter's talent, a rarity since the Chaos War. The crest would only increase her abilities.

The child continued to glare accusingly at him, but Vandor fought back fiercely. If he forfeited the artifact then not only would he lose his one hope of gaining his freedom but Mendel would punish him horribly.

The war of wills continued. Grizt's arms were extended completely from the mirror but no farther. The battle might have gone on for the rest of the night if not for the inevitable. The thief's hands, then his arms, began to smoke. Before Vandor's very eyes, his fingers, his expert, thieving fingers, blackened. The skin peeled away, then the muscle began to burn, revealing darkening bone. Yet, despite the incredible agony, the horror, Vandor Grizt refused to yield.

He heard a minute gasp, then felt himself falling backward head over heels. He was unable to orient himself for a moment. Slowly it occurred to him what had happened: the child had noted his terrible fate. She couldn't help but allow her concentration to lapse, not only saving him but enabling him to escape.

Escape to where, though? Vandor blinked, seeing that now he stood on the inside of a mirror in a familiar chamber—Lady Elspeth's. He knew it to be hers for suddenly the noblewoman gasped, dropped a small hand mirror, and turned his way. However, Vandor had already disappeared, the power of Mendel's sinister look-ing glass pulling him away. He found it astonishing that he had been cast into a foreign mirror without his knowl-edge, or the wizard's permission. Or Lady Elspeth's . . . although Vandor might be condemned to be a phantom, still his thoughts sometimes turned to solid flesh. He had marked the beauty of Lady Elspeth. That desire must have been present when he had been cast loose by the startled girl.

To hold such a woman . . .

That dream might at last be within his reach, he real-ized. In his hands he still held the Arcyan Crest. All he had to do was bring it to Mendel, who would be so pleased with him that he would at last grant Vandor Grizt a return to his body. . . .

An intense cold radiated from his hands.

"By Shinare, no!" Vandor knew exactly what the bone-numbing cold preceded. He pictured Mendel's mirror, hoping he still had time.

Mendel's chamber came into view. Vandor reached out, trying to thrust the Arcyan Crest through the mirror.

The artifact faded in his hands, vanishing as if it had never existed.

Vandor Grizt felt like screaming. His vindictive master would let him burn long and hard for this, no doubt sav-ing the thief of mirrors only at the last moment, assigning him yet another impossible task. Vandor could suffer that torture gladly if he didn't fear that this time Mendel might destroy his mortal body. After being preserved magically for so many decades, Grizt's body would decay rapidly once Mendel released the spell.

To be so close to achieving freedom . . .

He shook his head, trying to think. Vandor could do only one thing, a desperate measure, but all that remained to try. He could tell his master that he had not yet found the artifact. It would buy Grizt some time, staving off the inevitable. If Mendel thought the Arcyan Crest still exist-ed, he would not punish his slave too severely. If he thought the crest was nearly within reach . . .

Vandor was still struggling with what to say when Mendel entered.

The avaricious gleam in the crooked figure's eyes immediately informed the thief that Mendel would have little patience today. His obsession with the crest had grown and grown.

"You have it? You have it?"

"No, Mendel, but—"

His master's fury shocked even him this time. Mendel roared, unable to even articulate. He raised the staff high and, to Vandor's horror, struck not at the frame, but this time at the mirror itself. He smashed hard and hard again, without holding back.

"Incompetent! Bungler!" Again the staff struck. "Fool!"

As he raised the wooden staff for a third strike, Mendel caught himself, for suddenly the mage lowered the staff, his eyes wide. Anger barely held in check, he leaned forward to inspect the magical mirror. Vandor, on the other side, was reeling from the blows. Mendel's foul visage filled his vision.

"No damage. Nuitari be praised," the old man muttered, apparently not recalling for the moment that his god, like all the others, no longer graced the heavens of Krynn.

Grizt spoke, seizing the moment and praying that his own cleverness would not defeat him. "Master, it is true I do not have the crest, but I think I'm close to its discovery!"

The anger in Mendel's eyes faded a bit, replaced by a wary interest. "How so?"

Now the lie must be convincing. "When I searched tonight, I came across Prester. He looked very furtive, as if he had just come from some place important, some place deep in his sanctum—"

"Could mean anything."

"Yes, but he carried with him an object similar to that one you had me steal for you but a month ago. Remember that tiny emerald spider?"

The emerald spider had been an old talisman Mendel had come across by accident. A merchant traveling through the region had been carrying it along with his other goods, gems, and jewelry befitting his noble clientele. Mendel had spotted it and had known it immediately for a magical artifact. With so few competent mages of the old school left, many items such as the spider had fallen into the hands of the unwary and then disappeared forever into their houses.

Two nights later, Vandor had reached out from the glittering reflections of the merchant's gem collection and taken the spider. Mendel, ecstatic, took only a few minutes to leech the power from the artifact, not great power, but it had enabled the vulturish man to cast modest spells for several days.

"Did the artifact he carried appear to mask an inner fire, buffoon? Did it evince life?"

"If it once did, Prester no longer cared. As I watched, he discarded it into a rubbish container."

Mendel rubbed his chin. "So he had already drained it of its magic, then."

"Yes, that is what I supposed, but the important thing is he brought it from another place of hiding, where there must be other magical artifacts. You see? You were right as usual, Mendel! Prester must have the Arcyan Crest! Now I know it's only a matter of time until I find it!"

"No." The crooked figure stared down the ghostly thief. "It is only a matter of one night. One night, Grizt! I'm tired of waiting! Bring me the Arcyan Crest tomorrow morning or you'll discover I've been merely gentle with you so far. . . ."

Vandor swallowed hard. "One night?"

"I tire of these delays . . . and your excuses!" Mendel shouted.

Vandor appeased him quickly. "I'll find it, Mendel. I promise!"

A calculating look formed in Mendel's dark eyes. "If you do, you might even get your body back. You'd like that, wouldn't you, dandy? To walk as a living, breathing bit of flesh again? I won't really have much need of you any more once you find me the crest. I could let you go this time. . . ."

Despite knowing that he could never bring Mendel the artifact in question, the thief could not help but feel hopeful. "Freedom? You'll grant me my freedom?"

"First find me the Arcyan Crest."

Mendel turned, dismissing both the mirror and the thief within. Vandor watched him go, knowing that the black-robed figure was already busy plotting uses for the legendary artifact. Mendel shut the door to the chamber, all but forgetting Vandor.

How could he give his master what no longer existed?

He had one desperate idea. Perhaps Vandor could find something, another precious object, that might fool the mage, that might fool him long enough for Mendel to bestow his reward, releasing Grizt's body and allowing him to regain life. Once human again, Vandor could conceivably escape before Mendel learned the truth. It was far-fetched. It was dangerous. It was the only hope he had.

* * * * *

The day passed unmercifully slowly, interrupted by only two brief appearances from his master. The night came at last. Vandor waited for Mendel, for only Mendel had the power to compel the mirror to send him on his tasks.

Finally the mage stalked in, left hand clutching the cursed medallion. "Well? Why aren't you off yet? You will go to the home of the red robe Prester, you will go only there, and you will search all night if need be! You will find the Arcyan Crest! Understood?"

"Yes, Mendel, I understand." Released by the medallion, Vandor wasted not a moment more, darting into the mirror realm. He had to find some object he could use to replace the one he had let be destroyed, something that might fool Mendel. Unfortunately, it would have to come from Thorin Prester's domain; Mendel had commanded he go only there, and thanks to the magic of the medallion, Vandor had to obey that command.

Within seconds, the thief of mirrors entered the former red robe's house. He darted from one reflective surface to the next, searching Prester's home from top to bottom . . . room after room . . . leaving the child's chamber to the last. Vandor feared to go there, feared that the young girl with magical gifts might catch him again.

What a fool he was! What a fool! Why had he ever lied to Mendel? Doing so would only make matters worse for Vandor in the end. The black robe would punish him not only for losing the legendary artifact but for trying to lie about it as well.

One possible place where there might be other valuables was Prester's own room. Vandor had searched it before, but now he knew he must search it again.

Prester still slept deeply as Vandor searched his bedchamber one more time, appearing and reappearing in one reflective surface after another. Reaching out of the large mirror overlooking the man's desk, Vandor hunted through the small wooden chest he had noticed on previous visits. Unfortunately, the chest contained nothing the thief needed. Time was running out. There were few places left to search. Vandor grew frantic.

He suddenly sensed eyes watching him. They belonged not to Prester, for that one still slept solidly, but rather to a smaller, unfortunately familiar presence.

"I knew you'd come back."

The sun could only be a few minutes away from rising. Vandor had no time for little girls with frightening abilities. He immediately dove back into the mirror.

That is to say, he attempted to do so. The thief of shadows struggled, head and arms trapped on the outside of the glass. He eyed the young wizard fearfully, not knowing any longer whether he feared her or Mendel's wrath more. "I don't have your brooch any more!" Vandor desperately explained. "Let me go, please!"

The child glanced at her father, who still slept soundly despite all the commotion. Her gaze returned to Vandor, and she said, "You'll burn again." When her prisoner said nothing, she frowned. "If you stay outside the mirror, will you burn again?"

"Yes! By blessed Shinare, yes!"

"I'm sorry."

A gust suddenly hurled Vandor completely into Prester's looking glass. He tried immediately to flee but could not move.

The girl came over to the mirror. She stared into it, giggling. "I can see myself standing next to you!"

Vandor stood in the mirror, watching her with growing apprehension. The thief of mirrors repeated his earlier words. "I don't have your brooch any more. It's . . . it's gone."

"Silly ghost . . ." the little girl giggled. "I've got it here!" She pointed to her hair, at the same time speaking so loudly that Vandor expected Prester to awake, but the father remained still. Whatever magic this girl wielded she wielded well. Mendel would have been very, very jealous.

The full impact of her words struck him. "You—" Vandor blinked. "You have it?"

At last he took notice of the elaborate brooch fastened to her hair. The ethereal thief stared in disbelief. True enough, a brooch identical to the one he had stolen clung there, griffons and kingfisher with jeweled eyes. Yet, it could not be the very same brooch, for that one had vanished before his eyes, a victim of the whims of the mirror realm—or so Grizt had thought.

"Is that . . . is that the same one?"

"It's the one Mama gave me."

"But I—but I took it."

An enigmatic expression crossed the child's features. "It always comes back to me. I forgot that before, but it always does."

"Indeed?" Grizt did not pay much attention to the girl's response, already breathing a sigh of relief. There was still a chance for him. Already he was calculating his chances of stealing the Arcyan Crest again. What did it matter if, after he put it into Mendel's hands, it disappeared again? Just so long as he would not be blamed for failing the damned black robe. . . .

"Are you really a ghost?"

"A ghost?" Her words made Vandor shudder, for he often felt like a ghost. Only the knowledge that his body remained preserved by Mendel's spells kept him sane. To be a ghost forever . . . Grizt could imagine no worse fate. "No, my spirit is trapped in a mirror," he answered, "but I'm very much alive. The man who makes me do this— steal things—possesses my body. If I don't do what he says, he'll destroy it."

She seemed to believe him immediately. His words were truthful, and what was more rare for him, sincere. Desperation had given Vandor Grizt sincerity.

"I'm sorry for you," the little girl finally said.

"If I don't return soon, I'll be punished." He glanced up. Already the darkness seemed to be waning. Predawn. He had scant minutes remaining. "I have to return by first light. It's nearly that now."

"I didn't tell Papa about you," she mentioned. "I thought I dreamed you." She leaned forward. "My name's Gabriella. What's your name?"

He was beginning to see light! Why had the black robe's mirror not forced him back yet?

"Vandor Grizt. Little mistress, you said you wouldn't like to see me burn. Much worse will happen if I don't leave now!" He held out his hands. "See? I've got nothing of yours this time!"

As dawn began filtering into the chamber, Prester stirred. The girl looked at her father. "He should sleep longer."

Grizt tried to avoid thinking about what her statement indicated: power but not the experience to wield it sensibly. She was able to keep her father sleeping but only for a time.

"Please, my fine young lady! Let me go! It'll be our little secret that I came here at all! Wouldn't that be a grand thing? You like secrets, don't you?"

"If you go without Mama's jewel will the bad man hurt you?"

Vandor sighed, too unnerved to lie. "Yes."

Her expression darkened. The thief felt a new twinge of unease. Never had he seen such an expression on so otherwise innocent-looking a child. "I don't like him," she said at last. "He's just like Garloff. Garloff's a nasty wizard in a story Mama used to tell me. Garloff was evil, not like Huma. Huma was the hero in Mama's story."

Grizt had lost the path of the conversation, his eyes straying to the growing daylight. How much longer could she hold him here? Certainly not forever, and when her hold slipped, Vandor would suffer worse than ever. "Gabriella, listen to me!"

She did not. Her eyes brightened, and she peered at him in a manner vaguely familiar. "Garloff is like your wizard, and you're just like Huma." Before the thief could absorb the obviously absurd comparison, the little girl added, "He won't hurt you if I give you Mama's jewel."

Vandor Grizt blinked, uncertain that he had heard correctly. "What?"

Gabriella carefully removed the brooch. She cupped it in her hands, covering it so tightly that Vandor could not see it. "He won't hurt you if I give this to you. Here."

Gratitude nearly overwhelmed Vandor Grizt. She wanted to give the Arcyan Crest to him in order to save him from Mendel. The little girl saw him as some tragic hero out of one of her late mother's stories. In the past, when he was alive in the real world, there had been many women who had fallen sway to his lies, believing him to be a great champion rather than merely a well-dressed thief. He had never dissuaded them, never felt guilty . . . until now.

"Gabriella," he managed, "thank you." It pained him that she would give up so valued a belonging to the black robe, who would use it simply to enhance his miserable existence, but by no means did Vandor intend to turn down her generous offer—not if it meant finally escaping the world of mirrors.

"Papa gave this to me after Mama died." She opened up her hands again, revealing the brooch in all its glory. It appeared to glow in the gathering daylight. "He told me all about it."

Not all, Vandor suspected. If the girl knew that the brooch contained magical powers, he doubted that Gabriella would part with it even to rescue her new storybook hero. That he dared not mention.

"Here, Sir Vandor." The little girl reached out with the artifact, nearly touching it to the face of the mirror.

Grizt took it with hands still unburning, hands that trembled in relief. He stared at the desired object, stared at the griffons and the kingfisher who seemed to mock his hopes. "Thank you, my lady."

She giggled again, and her expression darkened once more. "You have to give it to him, Sir Vandor. I don't want him hurting you again."

Did she really think that he would keep the bauble for himself? Magical artifacts were useless to him, all the more so in the shadow world. He started to assure her but held back, seeing something in her eyes that disturbed him. What sort of child stood before him? At times she frightened him more than Mendel. "I will, my lady," Vandor finally managed. "I will . . . and thank you again."

The slumbering form moved restlessly again. Gabriella calmly looked at her father, then returned her gaze to Grizt. Never had he seen so old a look in the face of a little girl. "Goodbye, Sir Vandor. Please come to play with me some time."

The thief found himself flung from the mirror, the stubborn pull of Mendel's own looking glass suddenly and at last triumphant.

Yet . . . as Vandor returned to his familiar prison, he noted with some surprise and relief that for once he felt no pain in the transition. Even the harsh cold did not bother him much this time. Grizt wondered that the little girl could be responsible, that she could be so powerful. The Arcyan Crest, on the other hand, held tremendous power and perhaps some of that transferred—

The Arcyan Crest! Vandor thrust the girl's brooch through the glass, placing it carefully on the table in

Mendel's chamber. Only then did he sigh in relief. His youthful admirer had given the precious artifact to him in order to save his life; but if he kept it too long in the mirror realm, surely it would be destroyed this time, and Vandor Grizt would only have had himself to blame for repeating his folly.

A moment later, the cadaverous form of his cursed master appeared in the doorway. "You have it? Give it to me, you stupid cur! I want it!"

After the calm manner in which Gabriella had spoken to him, Mendel sounded much like a spoiled child . . . a spoiled child who could dangle the thief's life before him. Nonetheless, Vandor was tempted to reach out and grab the artifact back. If not for the gnarled mage's hold on him, the thief would have let the chill realm destroy the Arcyan Crest. Mendel's aghast reaction would be well worth the loss. Vandor sorely wanted to leave the realm of mirrors; he wanted his body back, though, wanted it more than anything.

"It's there," he muttered. "All yours at last, Mendel."

"The Arcyan Crest!" The gleeful figure scooped up the brooch, cradling it in his hands. Mendel's eyes surveyed his prize, fingers stroking the fine craftsmanship.

Vandor Grizt studied the mage in disgust. Mendel did not deserve such a treasure. He himself had made no effort, had sacrificed nothing. Grizt, at least, had the credo of a thief; he worked to earn his prizes. Mendel could thank the little girl for the Arcyan Crest. Only because she had been willing to part with her mother's heirloom for Vandor's sake did the black robe now have more power with which to stoke his ego.

"So long . . ." cooed the aged spellcaster. "So long have I sought you . . . you are mine now . . . mine."

Mendel had his great desire, now Vandor would at long last have his. "Mendel . . . my body."

"Cease your prattling! I've more important things on my mind!" The archmage went back to stroking the artifact.

Grizt, this time, would not be silenced. "My body, Mendel! You said that if I stole this for you, I might—"

"Talk to me no more about your wants, dandy! You'll obey my every command or suffer the consequences for it! Don't think you have any choice!"

"But my body—"

"You have no body." Mendel glared at him. "Not for some thirty years, fool! Did you think I'd waste precious power on preserving that bit of tawdry meat? What does the husk of one paltry thief compare to my needs? Be satisfied with serving me, Vandor Grizt," he said, laughing, "for you'll be doing so for the rest of my life!"

A roar of agony escaped Vandor. He threw himself against his side of the mirror, trying to reach for the throat of the monstrous mage. All these years he had been tricked. What a fool he had been. Mendel had led him by the nose, making promises he never intended to fulfill. Gabriella had thought him a ghost; how accurate she had been. Vandor the ghost, dreaming of what never could be, must have amused his master.

To hold a woman again, drink fine ale, feel the warmth of day without fearing its searing heat . . .

A ghost. All these years he had been nothing but a ghost.

Vandor tried to force himself through the mirror. He felt something begin to give. He pushed harder, fury and bitterness fueling his strength.

Unfortunately, Mendel saw him and reacted accordingly. The Arcyan Crest in one hand, Mendel touched his medallion with a smile.

A shock of unprecedented pain coursed through Vandor. It was worse than ever, undoubtedly enhanced by the Arcyan Crest. Screaming, the thief fell back into the mirror, practically sobbing.

"I think . . . yes, I think I've had enough of you," the vulturish mage proclaimed. "This would be a most excellent time to test the limits of the Arcyan Crest. I will draw the magic from the mirror and from what little there is in the spell binding you as well and augment the potential of the crest. Let's see if the tales of its power are true."

Grizt fell against the other side of the mirror, gasping, still recovering. "Damn . . . damn you, Mendel."

"You should be happy, Vandor Grizt. I am putting you out of your suffering—and at least you won't have to suffer very long."

Holding the artifact high about his head, Mendel muttered a chant. The phantom thief braced himself, certain that his end was near. In a twisted way, Mendel had spoken the truth. At least Vandor was grateful that it would be swift.

The sinister spellcaster spouted a final word and waited. Vandor felt the edges of the mirror quiver.

Suddenly, Mendel stumbled and gasped. His hand shook uncontrollably, nearly dropping the Arcyan Crest. The dark mage struggled to keep his grip on the artifact, his face already covered in sweat from the effort. A red glow rose around the magical crest.

"How . . . dare . . . you?" Mendel hissed, staring not at Vandor but at the magical brooch. He looked suddenly smaller, drained.

Vandor blinked. Instead of absorbing magic from the mirror and channeling it into Mendel, the crest instead seemed to be sapping the power from him.

You have to give it to him, Sir Vandor. I don't want him hurting you again.

Gabriella had said that to the thief, her face so old, so unnerving. Had the strange child planned something sinister? Did she now reach out from her home to punish Grizt's captor? Could she have the power to do that?

Mendel's entire body began to shiver, and the gnarled spellcaster's skin, already so pale, grew parchment white. Nevertheless, Mendel fought back. He did not seem at all prepared to surrender.

"Insolence!" he snapped, clawing at the air. "You dare? You dare? I am Mendel! Mendel!"

The black-robed mage muttered something else and slowly but surely seemed to regain his footing. Vandor's hope turned to dread; now it seemed the Arcyan Crest no longer rebelled against its wielder, but rather Mendel's distant adversary, a young girl with much magical ability but, as Vandor knew, lacking the maturity to best manipulate her skills.

Now Mendel was gaining strength, and the young girl, back in her home, must be losing hers. Grizt knew his master well enough to realize that Mendel would continue to drain the girl until nothing remained. The thought that Prester's daughter would die horribly for his sake upset the thief more than he would have guessed.

The insidious wizard was standing straight now, laughing at his unseen foe. "How I've waited for this, Prester! How I've waited to remove your smug presence from Ansalon!"

Prester! Mendel did not even know that he threatened the life of Prester's child, a young girl, not that he would have cared. The mage believed that only his old rival could command the power to contest him thusly.

With all his strength Vandor reached out as best as he could, taking advantage of his master's distraction. Try as he might, though, even with half his torso free of the mirror, the ghost-thief could not reach the black mage.

The thief pulled back and tried something else. Desperately he threw himself against the mirror again, battering it from inside. It had to give, had to give!

Suddenly he saw it. Near the spot where Mendel had struck the mirror before, a tiny crack had developed. It was not much of a crack, but it was enough to somehow weaken the magical mirror. Desperately, Grizt struck at this spot again and again, knowing each second that passed pushed his young savior to the brink.

Suddenly, without warning, the crack gave and Vandor Grizt found himself falling through the mirror.

The thief rose from the floor, staring in disbelief. He saw he had some solidity, even though he could still see through himself from certain angles.

Solidity meant that he could put his hands around Mendel's throat.

However, his action had not gone unnoticed. Mendel, watching him with a smirk, waved the medallion in his clutch. "The knight-errant, Vandor Grizt? Or simply too much taste for revenge? A bad idea to leave the mirror. Don't forget I am still your master."

Pain wracked Vandor, forcing him down onto one knee. He looked up, watching in mounting horror as Mendel worked his spell. Heat began to overwhelm the thief. The longer he struggled futilely, the worse the heat was destined to become. Already his garments began to blacken, the process swifter than ever thanks to the Arcyan Crest.

Vandor forced himself to his feet, fighting impossibly against the power of Mendel's cursed medallion. He no longer feared for his existence, earthly or otherwise. He knew he would die. All he sought to do was reach the foul mage and find some way to prevent Mendel from ever torturing anyone else again.

"Lie down . . . and burn away," his master growled, perhaps just a bit hard-pressed. "You're nothing but vapor, anyway, dandy! Simply a puff of smoke."

Grizt's hand caught on fire. His arms began to flicker. He could feel the flames begin to eat at his flesh even though he had no true flesh to burn.

Mendel smiled, looking stronger. "Prester and you! I have enjoyed this day immensely, Vandor Grizt!"

Gritting his teeth, the ghost howled and flung himself forward.

The look of shock that blanketed Mendel's face pleased Vandor immensely. The black-robed mage released his hold on the medallion as he sought to cover his eyes from the flaming figure crashing upon him. Vandor managed to seize his tormentor by the throat—

—slipping through him an instant later.

Wracked with an agony he could no longer endure, Vandor sought out the nearest reflection, a silver goblet sitting on a table, reaching out to it with his mind. A moment later, the numbing cold of the mirror realm swept over him, blessed cold to help assuage his pain.

His moment of revenge had failed. Grizt had not maintained his solid form long enough to put an end to Mendel and now—

Mendel cried out. Vandor, still not recovered, managed to look up from his place of hiding. The foul wizard stood clutching the Arcyan Crest . . . or rather now it clutched him. The talons of the kingfisher seemed to have come alive, Mendel's hand and wrist were caught in them. Stranger yet, the black robe looked smaller again, smaller than ever, as if he had shrunk several inches.

"Nooo!" Mendel shouted to the air. "You cannot do this! I command it!"

Vandor watched in amazement as his tormentor shrank. The glow surrounding the artifact had changed. Now it glowed yellow and that yellow encompassed Mendel. Vandor's determined attack, however ill fated, had distracted Mendel just long enough for Prester's daughter to collect herself and seize the advantage.

With a last horrified shriek, the aged wizard collapsed to his knees. As he did, the glow washed over his twitching form. Vandor blinked as the glow at last faded, the Arcyan Crest clattering to the floor. The talons of the kingfisher returned to normal, and as for Mendel, he had vanished altogether.

Disbelieving his eyes, the thief emerged from the mirror, tentatively making his way toward the artifact. His mind raced with the thought of what had just transpired, what would happen to him, and, just as important, what he should do now with the ominous device. Knowing his time was limited, Vandor reached for the crest.

The ruby in the center glistened with movement, and Vandor Grizt the thief could not help but look at it.

A screaming face stared out at him.

Mendel's screaming face.

In horror Vandor pulled back, and as he did, the Arcyan Crest, Mendel still entombed, faded.

It always comes back to me, little Gabriella had told him.

Vandor thought of the brooch back in the delicate but

deadly hands of Prester's daughter. No longer did he harbor any fear for her; rather, oddly, he felt some for his old tormentor.

Vandor looked up, eyes fixing on Mendel's mirror. An urge came over him, and he seized the wizard's staff, which Mendel had dropped during the struggle. Raising it high, Vandor struck the mirror again and again, shattering the cursed artifact, his chill prison. He then waited for himself to fade away as the mirror's magic died, but surprisingly nothing happened. With almost gleeful abandon, the specter stamped on the shards that lay on the floor, crushing them until no large pieces remained intact. At last, his fury spent, Vandor began to laugh and laugh, stumbling back to admire his handiwork.

He was free. Free of Mendel, free of the mirror. A ghost, yes, he was now a ghost, but no longer a slave.

The heat of the real world once again began to tell on him, but this time more gradually and with less intensity. By now Vandor should have been burning up, and he realized that Mendel's disappearance meant he could pay longer visits to the real world.

Even so, Vandor Grizt was taking no chances. He returned to the goblet, staring out at the chamber and the broken mirror.

"Farewell, Mendel. Thank you, Gabriella," Grizt whispered. Whatever his ultimate fate, for now he would savor his freedom. A changed world lay open to him, and the ghostly thief intended to explore it.

There were, after all, so many, many mirrors. . . .

Reorx Steps Out
Jean Rabe

"Ah, by the bushy beard of Reorx, I certainly'll make an impression at the festival!" The dwarf was chattering to himself, in a voice that sounded like gravel being slushed around in the bottom of a bucket. "New boots. Mmph, a mite tight for my toes. This breastplate, just like the . . ."

The dwarf scowled and cocked his head, hearing a rustling in the bushes that unsettled him. The foliage on both sides of the path was thick with the new leaves of spring. He saw the branches of a lilac bush move, despite the lack of any breeze.

"Somebody there?"

"It's nothing personal." Silver scales glimmered like sun specks caught on the surface of a still lake as the draconian stepped into the open. His talons glinted like polished steel in the late afternoon sun. "You're just convenient."

"By the sacred breath of the Forge!" The dwarf's thick fingers flew to the hammer at his waist, his feet scrambling backward to buy him some space.

The draconian was quicker. Corded muscles bunched as the creature crouched and sprang. Arms shot forward slamming into the dwarf's shoulders, the impact driving the dwarf violently onto his back and knocking the breath from him in a gravelly "Whooff!"

"Stay still, dwarf, and I promise to make this quick. You won't feel anything."

"Cursed sivak!" the dwarf spat, as he found his breath and struggled to free his arms. "To the Abyss with you!"

"Stay still, I said!" The draconian's jaws opened wide, acidic spittle edging over his lower lip and dripping onto the dwarf's face. "I need your body," the creature offered as an explanation, his voice a sibilant hiss. "I cannot pass through this country looking as I do. Even the dragons hunt my kind now."

The dwarf screamed that the sivak ought to find another body, that his was too old, too fat. All the while he futilely struggled against the larger and stronger foe. The draconian regarded him a moment more, then dragged a razor-sharp talon across the dwarf's throat, ending his life in a heartbeat.

"I told you it would be quick," he said.

The sivak pushed himself to his feet and stared at the corpse. The dwarf was barrel-chested, with stubby arms and legs, fingers short and thick. The face was broad and weathered, deeply lined from the years. His beard was steel gray, streaked with white, and it was elaborately braided and decorated with metal beads.

"Definitely an old one," the draconian grumbled. "The last was an old one, too. Still, it will have to do."

He closed his eyes and let out a long breath, felt his heart rumbling. He urged it to beat more rapidly as he concentrated on the magic, sensing the warmth as his blood pumped faster through his veins. He felt his armorlike skin bubble, the scales flowing, muscles contracting. He felt his body fold in upon itself, wings melting together to form a cape, snout receding, talons becoming feet fleshy and thick. The draconian growled softly, the sensation of his transformation both gratifying and uncomfortable.

He flexed his new legs and opened his eyes, looking round now and perceiving the world a little differently. He stared down at the corpse that could pass for his twin.

"Your dress is too garish for my tastes, old dwarf, though there is nothing I can do about it." The corpse and he were both attired in an ornate gold breastplate with an anvil emblazoned on it and an artfully engraved hammer poised above the anvil. The leggings were darkly red like wine and stuffed into the tops of black leather boots that smelled new and had been buffed until they practically glowed. A cape made of an expensive black material hung from the transformed sivak's shoulders. Even though the draconian did not bother to keep track of the customs of civilization, he realized that the dwarf had spent considerable coin on his dress.

He tugged the heavy body off to the side of the road, concealing it amid a patch of broad-leafed ferns. He plucked the hammer from the dwarf's waist, considered for a moment carrying it, as the weapon was finely crafted and quite valuable. However, shaking his head, he dropped it. "I do not need their *things*," he hissed. He returned to the path, following it as it continued to wind toward the foothills.

The sivak was in the heart of dwarven country, on a well-traveled road that was twisting and at times steep. It was called Barter Trail, and it ran between dwarven towns all nestled amid the impressive, rugged mountains of Thorbardin. He'd been taking the forms of lone dwarves he killed along the road as a means to disguise himself as he cut through the Thunder Peaks and then along the lengthy Promontory Pass—a miner one time, young and filthy from the work; a wheezing, rash-ridden merchant another; and most recently a one-armed elderly dwarf with a dozen knives strapped around his waist.

Only one more village and then one small range to travel across—according to the map the merchant had been carrying. After that he'd be in the Qualinesti Forest, where, he'd heard, draconians were gathering to hide from the dragons and men.

He was nearing that last village now, not needing the sign he just passed to tell him so. He heard the gruff chatter of dwarves coming from around the curve ahead and what sounded like a drum being thumped in a peculiar rhythm.

"Neidarbard," the sign had said in rich brown paint. "Home of the Forge's Favored Dwarves." "And Kender" was scrawled in bright blue paint beneath.

The transformed draconian squared his dwarven shoulders and picked up the pace, rounded the bend—and came to an abrupt stop. The town that spread out before him was not like the others he'd passed through. Neidarbard was . . . oddly colorful. It seemed a ridiculously cheerful place.

The homes closest to him were covered in pieces of gray-blue slate, looking like big turtle shells with doors and windows cut in them. The trim was red and white, with various shades of green and yellow thrown in. Beyond those were more traditional dwarven homes, made of stone with thatch roofs, some with sod that had a scattering of wild flowers growing in them. There were even a few two-story dwellings of stone and wood—all of them with brightly painted eaves and shutters, many with window boxes full of daffodils and daylilies.

Each home had long, streaming pennants, a rainbow of clashing colors to assault the eyes. Thick, twisting ribbons ran between the turtle-shaped homes, and delicate parchment lanterns, unlit at this time of day, dangled on purple twine stretched between the tallest dwellings. Out of the corner of his eye, the disguised draconian saw two dwarves precariously balanced on a ladder, alternately drinking from a big mug of ale while they tried to add to the decorations. The sivak involuntarily shuddered at the entire festive scene.

There seemed to be no pattern to the streets. They did not radiate outward from the center, like the spokes of a wheel—the last two dwarven towns the draconian passed through were like that. The streets did not form a grid or any other geometric shape that dwarves seemed to be fond of. They were random and curvy, some a mix of cobblestones and earth, some paved with the same bricks used in the stoutest dwellings, some dead-ending into the backs of buildings.

In what the draconian surmised passed for the center of the town, a fountain topped with a statue of a warrior-dwarf bubbled merrily, the water spewing from the stone fellow's mouth. No, not water, he noticed on second glance. Ale. All around the edge of the fountain sat a mix of dwarven and kender musicians dressed in bright reds and yellows. The former were thumping long, slender drums that rested between their knees, and the latter had just begun to play flutes and curved bell horns that glimmered in the late afternoon sun. The smallest kender had tiny metal plates attached to her fingers, which she clinked together at what seemed—judging by the look of the other musicians' faces—the most inopportune times. A young female dwarf was attempting to direct them by waving an empty mug in the air. Her other hand gripped a full mug that she frequently sipped from.

In front of the musicians strolled a most portly dwarf. He was dressed in a shiny tunic, striped horizontally green and blue, which did nothing to help conceal the ample stomach that hung over his wide belt. Stroking his short black beard and staring at a piece of curling parchment he held in a meaty hand, he seemed to be practicing a speech.

"I, Gustin Stoutbeard, *hic* acting mayor of Neidarbard . . ." He cleared his throat and started again, the words slightly slurred.

The draconian's gaze shifted to the southern edge of town, where tables upon tables sat end to end. They were covered with red and green cloths and dozens of bouquets of spring flowers. Dwarven and kender women bustled around them setting out plates and mugs. A firepit was nearby, and a great boar was roasting over it, being turned by a dwarf with massively muscled arms. The scent of the meat hung heavy in the air and made the sivak's belly rumble.

"I, Gustin *hic* Stoutbeard, acting . . ."

The music swelled, drowning out the acting mayor, the clinking from the kender child coming at regular intervals now, and the drummers beating out a syncopated rhythm that did not sound altogether bad.

The draconian stood on his tiptoes, a considerable feat given the body he'd adopted, craned his neck, and looked through a gap in all of the decorations. There! The mountains beckoned beyond Neidarbard, part of the Redstone Bluffs. Beyond those mountains was the blessed forest, safety, and the company of his own kind.

Ignoring the protestations of his empty stomach, he took a deep breath and strolled purposefully down the main street and toward the fountain.

"Hey!"

The sivak scowled as he felt a tugging on his cape-wings. He glanced down and over his shoulder, spotting a kender with two topknots. The kender had a large book in his hands, opened to a page with an illustration of a dwarf. The kender looked at the picture, then at the draconian, hiccuped, releasing a cloud of ale-breath. "Hey!" He beamed. "It's Reorx! You are Reorx, aren't you? *Hic.*"

The draconian did his best to ignore the besotted young man and took another step toward the mountains, but the kender was persistent and hurried to plant himself in the sivak's path. "Where are you going, Reorx? Do you mind if I call you Reorx?"

The dwarf he'd slain had made some mention of Reorx, the draconian recalled. "If I say I am this Reorx, young man, will you go away?"

The kender's eyes widened, he hiccuped again, and he nodded vigorously.

"Very well. I am Reorx."

The kender was quick to scoot out of his path, stuffing the book under one arm, topknots bobbing as he ran toward the acting mayor—who had stopped at the fountain to fill his mug.

"*Hic.* I, Gustin Stoutbeard . . ."

As the kender tugged on the acting mayor's clothes the draconian continued on his way. He passed by the musicians, slowing for only the briefest of moments when the delicate strains of a flute stirred something inside him, then slipped between a trio of two-story buildings, the bottom floors of which were businesses. One had a bright yellow-orange sign out front in the shape of a beehive. "Best-Ever Honey," it read. The next was a baker's, and all manner of elaborately decorated cakes and cookies sat tantalizingly in the window. The draconian's stomach growled louder, and he urged himself along. The third was a barber's, and through the open window he spied a young dwarf receiving a beard trim.

The music swelled as he thrust all these chaotic trappings of society to the back of his mind and set his sights once again on the mountains. He renewed his pace and actually made it another few yards before his cape was tugged on again. Growling softly in his throat, he turned to meet the gaze of the fat dwarf, Gustin Stoutbeard.

"Are you really Reorx? *Hic.*"

The draconian scowled. "Yes, yes, I am Reorx, and I am in a hurry." He pointed a stubby finger toward the foothills. "So if you will excuse—"

"You are *really* Reorx?" The fat dwarf swayed on his feet and blinked, as if trying to focus. "*Hic.*"

"Yes."

"*Really, really* Reorx?" The fat dwarf hiccuped again.

"Yes. I am *really* Reorx. And you and everyone else in this town are *really* intoxicated. Now if you don't mind—"

"We's s'been celebratin' allllll s'day," a black-bearded dwarf cut in. One of the drummers, he had wandered over to listen in. "S'day of the s'festival, ya s'know. We's don'ts drinks much otherwise. 'Cept unless we's thirsty."

The acting mayor glanced at the kender, who'd come up behind him and handed him another mug. The kender pulled the book from under his arm, opened it, and pointed to a full-page picture of a dwarf. The acting mayor got a good look. The draconian squinted at the picture—the breastplate indeed was similar to the one he displayed, as were the cape and the boots. The leggings were not quite so bright a red, but that could be attributed to a printer's error.

"The Forge!" the acting mayor bellowed, as he dropped the mug of ale in surprise. He waved his arms, looking like a plump bird trying hopelessly to take to the air. "Everyone! The Forge has returned! *Hic!*"

The music immediately stopped, and the townsfolk, kender and dwarves alike, seemed to utter a collective gasp. Then instruments were hurriedly set down, plates left in a stack, decorations left dangling. All the residents appeared to be thundering the sivak's way.

"I really must be leaving."

"I, Gustin—" the acting mayor slurred.

"Yes, I know who you are. You are Gustin Stoutbeard, the acting mayor of Neidarbard."

Gustin's cherubic face displayed surprise. "You know who I am? *Hic. Hic.* You know that I am the acting mayor here? Well. You truly are Reorx. *Hic.*"

"Yes. Yes. I am Reorx. I've said that three times now. I am indeed Reorx, and I must be on my way." The draconian was breaking into a sweat. He could only maintain a form for so many hours, and he did not want be discovered. He needed to get out of this town and into the mountains, where the shadows from the peaks would conceal his silver body. "I've things to attend to, someplace I must be."

The acting mayor seemed not to hear him. "I, Gustin Stoutbeard, acting mayor of the fine village of Neidarbard *hic* proclaim the opening of the Festival of the Forge in *hic* honor of the greatest of Krynn's gods, Reorx!" He stuffed the parchment with the rest of the speech into his pocket and continued, his voice raising in volume and authority. "We have been *hic* blessed, my friends. . . ."

Behind him, the draconian muttered to himself, "God? Reorx is a god? Oh my. I only know of the Dark Queen. . . ."

" . . . for the gods *hic* have been absent since the Chaos War. There were some who believed the gods were gone forever, but we Neidarbardians knew the gods would return. We continued to honor them in festivals and prayers. We knew! *Hic!* Now we have been rewarded for our faithfulness. Reorx has chosen to appear before us! Reorx has returned! On this very day when we traditionally celebrate the Festival of the Forge, Reorx himself *hic* has returned!"

A cacophonous cheer went up as the dwarves and kender pressed themselves against the draconian. Some merely stroked his breastplate, which they oohed and ahhed over and said did not feel like metal at all. Others shook his thick hand, while some kissed the ground near his feet. Mugs clanked together and were quickly drained. Someone pressed a mug into the sivak's hand.

"S'I brewed this," an ancient dwarf drunkenly growled. "S'not been aged s'all that long, but . . ."

"To Reorx!" There was another great cheer.

The draconian stood dumbstruck. "I . . . I really must be going," he said after a few minutes. He tried to remember how long it had been since he killed the dwarf and how much more time he might have to possess this body. Perhaps another hour at best, he guessed. Maybe two if he was fortunate. The hand holding the mug was nudged, and he raised it and drank the ale. It was thick and bitter and tasted good.

"Going where?" It was another one of the musicians.

The draconian studied his polished boots while he considered his reply. Someone refilled his mug. "Why, I am going to summon the rest of the gods, so they can all return to Krynn!"

There was another cheer, wilder and louder than before. More clinking of mugs that had been refilled. One of the kender musicians had picked up his horn and was blowing it shrilly.

"So, you see," the draconian added, as he drained the second mug, "I must be going. I must not keep all the other gods waiting." He tried to take a step but found himself trapped by the crowd. He guessed there were nearly a hundred dwarves and a third that many more kender.

"Wwwhich gggods wwwill yyyou ssssummon fffirst? Hic."

The draconian stared mutely at the speaker, who wobbled only a little more than the acting mayor.

"Mmmishakal?"

"Yes, I believe I shall summon Mishakal first."

"Oh, good!" chirped someone buried in the crowd. "I shall drink to that! To Mishakal!"

"To Mishakal!" went up a cheer. "We'll all drink to Mishakal!"

"Then Solinari? The god of good magic?" It was a middle-aged kender who was clutching a blue crystal mug in one hand and a flute in the other.

"Well . . ."

"To Solinari!" Came another wave of cheering and toasting.

"What about Haba . . . Habbbaba . . . Habakkuk?"

"I intend to summon Habakkuk and then Solinari."

There was another great round of cheering and toasting and drinking.

"Stay for a meal first!" This came from a dwarven woman at the edge of the crowd. Her face was smudged with flour, and she was waving a big wooden spoon in her hand. Chocolate dripped enticingly from it. "Summon the gods after you've tried the roast boar."

The draconian's belly growled again. "I suppose I could stay for just a little while." Someone refilled his mug.

The whoops and cries of the dwarves and kender swelled to deafening proportions.

"I, *hic* Gustin *hic* Stoutbeard, acting mayor of Neidarbard, welcome Reorx the Forge to our feast!"

"I cannot stay long, you understand. Gods are very busy." The draconian found he must shout to be heard over the ruckus.

The acting mayor nodded and drunkenly gestured toward the tables. In response the crowd quieted a bit and backed away, like a wobbly wave receding from a beach. Gustin held out his hand, and for an instant the sivak considered bolting toward the foothills. Though he had the stubby legs of a dwarf, he had the strength of a draconian as well as the speed. There was now considerable space between he and the short townsfolk, and in their general state of inebriation, they would not be able to catch him.

However, the boar smelled very, very good.

He sighed and took the acting mayor's hand, the portly dwarf practically swooning at the honor. Then Gustin led the sivak toward the gaily decorated tables and directed him to the center and to the largest chair. The draconian suspected the chair had been intended for the acting mayor, as it was wide enough to hold his bulk, and "His Honor" was engraved on the back.

Someone was slicing the boar, releasing more of the wondrous scents into the air. A finely carved tankard was filled to the brim with the finest dwarven ale the sivak had ever smelled. It was clomped down in front of the transformed draconian. He downed the contents of his other mug, discarded the empty container, then took a sip from the tankard and found that it oh-so-pleasantly warmed his throat. Not so bitter as the other ale, this had a hint of sweetness. He quickly drained it.

The acting mayor squeezed into a seat to the right of the god, as one of the dwarven musicians took the place to the left. Within moments, the seats were all filled, and the air was buzzing with dozens of slurred conversations, all of them centering on Reorx and the gods.

The sivak's tankard was refilled by a primly dressed dwarven woman who tried to stuff a napkin into the lip of the god's breastplate. "Doesn't seem to want to go in there," she said, finally giving up and waddling off.

"Why did you pick our village?" The speaker was a child at the far end of the table. His mug was filled with cider, and the sivak noted that only the adults were allowed the privilege of consuming the ale. "Of all the towns in Thorbardin, Mister Reorx, why'd you come here?"

The sivak scrunched his dwarven face in thought, then took another pull from the tankard. His fingers seemed to feel thicker, as did his tongue. "Well, youngling, when I looked down upon Krynn from the heavens, I glimpsed Neidarbard and felt drawn to it."

"To Neidarbard?" The child seemed flabbergasted. "There are much bigger towns inside and outside the mountains."

The sivak nodded and stifled a hiccup. "Ah, youngling, there certainly are, but I could sense that the people of Neidarbard were fiercely loyal to the gods—

even though we'd been away since the Chaos War. I could hear your prayers as I looked down on Krynn."

"You could hear me?"

The sivak nodded and took another pull. He couldn't remember ever drinking anything quite so delicious.

The child gasped and clapped and jostled his table-neighbors in the ribs. "He heard *me!*"

A thick slice of meat was lopped onto the draconian's plate, and he nearly forgot himself as he went to grab it with his fingers. He watched the acting mayor wield a fork and knife, copied the gesture to the best of his ability, and fell to devouring the meal. In all the dwarven towns he'd passed through, he was certain he had never eaten anything quite so delectable. Of course, he'd never gone so long without a meal and been so hungry—and he'd never drank so much. He drained his tankard again as a second thick slice of meat was placed before him. He awkwardly gestured for a refill of the ale.

"Gustin's *hic* cousin *hic* slew *hic* the *hic* boar *hic* yesterday," an old dwarven drummer explained. "The largest *hic* boar we've *hic* seen in these *hic* parts in years. It must have been *hic* an omen of your *hic* coming."

There was warm bread topped with the sweetest honey the draconian had ever sampled. "Best-Ever Honey," he was proudly told. He ate it almost reverently and let a dollop of the honey rest on his tongue. He finally washed it down with more ale.

"It's harvested from the *hic* honeycombs of the giant bees just *hic* outside the village," Gustin explained, pointing roughly to the south. "Uldred, Mesk, *hic* Puldar, go to the hive and gather more for our most important guest. *Hic.* Honey for Reorx!"

There were bowls of blueberries sprinkled with sugar, more ale, yams drowning in creamy butter, cinnamon sticks, more ale. The air continued to buzz with praise for the god who had deigned to grace the town of Neidarbard with his lofty presence.

"Where'd Chaos banish all the gods to?" This from a woman with a chocolate-covered spoon. She hadn't been drinking as much as the others and was easier to understand. "Was it t'other side of the world? Or maybe not on this world?"

The draconian swallowed a big piece of boar meat. "I am not permitted to say, kind woman. Chaos *hic* bid that location be kept a secret from all mortals."

There were murmurs of "I understand."

"So why'd you return to Krynn? Did Chaos let you free?" The same woman.

The draconian speared a yam. "He did not *let* me."

There was a chorus of oooohs punctuated by clinking mugs.

"I defied him and escaped his secret place. I was too long away from *hic* Krynn and the company of dwarves and kender," he continued, puffing out his dwarven chest. The yam slid easily down his throat, followed by another swig of ale. "So I decided on my own to return. Chaos does not know I'm here. When he was not looking, I cleverly escaped. Hence, I must be going. If I am to summon the other gods, I must do so before he finds me out and tries to stop me. *Hic*. Perhaps, though, I shall have just one more slice of boar."

The draconian's gaze drifted from face to face between bites of boar and blueberries. Some of the musicians had finished their meal and were striking up a sprightly tune. The melody was pleasing to the sivak's ears. They were all so . . . happy. It was an emotion generally denied him, abhorred by him, a weak sentiment that had no place in the lives of he and his fellows. He couldn't recall that he'd ever been *happy* before. He found himself grinning like everybody else.

"Maybe you can stay for the dance tonight!" This from a young dwarven woman in a red gown trimmed with embroidered daisies.

"Stay? No." How long had it been since he killed the dwarf? An hour? Two? He needed to be leaving before he lost hold of this form and his sivak body returned. That would certainly put an end to the merriment, and possibly an end to his life, as several of the sturdiest-looking dwarves carried swords and hammers. Still, he did not feel the tingling that usually signaled he was soon to shed his form. Perhaps he was wrong about the time. Perhaps he could tarry. He felt for the cadence of his heart and found that it seemed to beat in time with the dwarven drums.

"For one dance?" She politely persisted.

"I really should be going. Gods to summon, plagues to end, *hic* dragons to deal with, and other important business I must attend to. . . ."

Another ale was thrust into his hand and quickly found its way down his throat. It all tasted so good. There was no tingling, no hint of the coming reversion to his beloved self. Perhaps there was something in this wonderful ale that was allowing him to retain this wonderful body longer—even forever.

"I want you to have this." An elderly dwarven woman swayed up behind him, placed a medallion around his neck. "My husband mined the gold it's made of. Gave this to me when we were young and when all the gods walked on Krynn."

"*Hic* I want *hic* you to have *hic* this." Gustin Stoutbeard was unfastening a badge from his tunic, a dark purple ribbon from which hung a gold charm hammered in the face of a dwarf. "It's a symbol of you. *Hic. Hic.* It was cast years ago and given to me by the previous *hic* mayor." The acting mayor turned, his belly bumping into the draconian and nearly knocking him out of his seat. He thrust the pin into the draconian's cape, where a cloak clasp would hang, not noticing the draconian cringe at being stabbed by the long sharp object.

"And this!" A small dwarven child passed her his doll. "It's my favorite."

"I can't accept these," the sivak protested. "Now I really *hic* must be leaving."

Another mug of ale was placed in front of him. The musicians were playing a slow tune now, rich with a complicated countermelody that sometimes drifted off-key. The sivak found himself humming along.

"You *hic* must *hic* accept our gifts!" the acting mayor returned. He looked crestfallen. "We revere you above all the *hic* gods. Reorx the *hic* Forge, the greatest *hic* of Krynn's gods. It was you who *hic* tamed Chaos to form the world, and it was you who created the stars by *hic* striking your hammer against Chaos."

"It is true," the sivak admitted, as he ran his thick fingers around the lip of the tankard. "I did indeed create the stars. *Hic.* My crowning achievement, I think. Of course, I am also rather proud of the mountains. I made them with a brush of my hand."

"You are the father of dwarves and kender, and we owe you our lives," said the young kender with two topknots whom he had met when he first entered the village. "You forged the Graygem. Without you, the Chaos War would have been lost. Krynn would be no more."

Mugs were clanked together in toasts to the Forge, and dwarves slapped each other on the back and swayed in their seats.

"Well, yes," the draconian evenly intoned. "The Chaos War would have turned out much worse had I not taken some steps to intervene and help mortals. Yes, I will happily accept your gifts."

The acting mayor instantly brightened and cleared his throat. "The most *hic* powerful of all the gods, we knew it would be you who came back to *hic* Krynn first. We knew that you would show yourself to your *hic* children, the dwarves and kender of Thorbardin. *Hic.*"

A cheer went up, and the draconian was passed another thick slice of bread with the last of the wonderful honey atop it. The boys would be back from the honeycomb soon with more, he was told.

Maybe I could linger for one dance, he thought. He'd never danced before. How long had it been since he killed the dwarf? It couldn't have been that long ago, he told himself. The time didn't matter anymore, did it? The ale was forestalling the transformation. He closed his eyes and savored the last few bites of the boar, felt the meal resting comfortably in his very full stomach. He listened to the band and the bubbling of the fountain, the slurred conversations of his new friends. They were much better company than his own kind, he decided. They loved him.

His expression grew wistful, and he pushed himself away from the table, tucking the doll under his arm and finding that it took a bit of concentration to stand without wobbling. He glanced over his shoulder toward the fountain, and noticed that the paper lanterns were being lit and that the sun was setting. "Yes, I believe *hic* I can stay for a dance or two before I must leave to summon Mishakal and Habbakuk, Solanari and the others."

"But not Takhisis!" cried the kender with two topknots. "Please don't summon Takhisis!"

There were hisses and softly muttered curses at the mention of the Dark Queen's name.

"No. Rest assured *hic* that I will not be summoning Takhisis." He grinned inwardly, as it was the first real truth he'd uttered since entering the village.

"Doyoureallyhavetoleave?" asked an elderly kender who was gripping the table to keep from falling over. "SummonthegodsfromNeidarbard!"

The acting mayor pushed away from the table and stood, wobbling from the effects of the ale. "Now, now, good folk of *hic* Neidarbard. We have been *hic* truly *hic* blessed this day. Never before has a god, *the* god of Krynn, set foot in our *hic* fair village. We must not be selfish, and *hic* we must not—"

"Help!"

The cry was soft at first, giving Gustin Stoutbeard pause. But it was repeated, growing louder as the dwarf who was screaming it from afar barreled closer to the village. The musicians stopped playing, diners ended their conversations, forks were dropped, ale abandoned. All eyes turned to the panicked dwarf.

He was covered in honey, a gooey mess that plastered his beard and his hair close against his face. His chest was heaving, and he was holding his side from running so hard.

"Help," he breathed. He gestured behind him and to the south.

The acting mayor quickly waddled to the dwarf's side. "What's wrong, *hic* Puldar?"

"Uldred, Mesk," he gasped. "They're trapped in the giant honeycomb. The bees. You told us to get more honey for Reorx. We thought the great bees were gone from the higher chambers and we climbed in. But . . ." He fell to his knees. "Gustin, the bees came, and Uldred plunged deep into the hive. Mesk followed him!"

All eyes shifted from the dwarf to the transformed draconian, who was backing away from the table, eyeing the mountains that rose invitingly at the far edge of the village.

"Reorx!" The kender with the twin topknots was practically standing on the table. "The Forge will save Uldred and Mesk!"

"The Forge!"

The sivak backed farther away, staggering a bit.

"You *hic* can't *hic* leave now!" The acting mayor waddled toward the sivak, hands flapping and resembling the plump bird again.

"The affairs of the gods are above the affairs of mortals," the draconian began. "If there will be no dance, I should leave now to *hic* summon the other gods."

"But, it's Uldred!" A dwarven woman was crying, the one who had served him the delicious boar. "And Mesk! Oh, please save them, Reorx!"

"Save them, and then we'll dance!" someone shouted.

The acting mayor took the sivak's thick hand and tugged him toward the southern edge of the village. "Please," he repeated, sobering a bit with the desperateness of the situation. "It can't take so long to save *hic* two young men, can it? Mishakal would understand, Solanari, too."

"Where is the honeycomb?" The words came out too fast, a sibilant growl, but the acting mayor in his anxiety paid the tone no heed.

The rotund acting mayor tugged the god along. The entire village was stumbling after them, and murmurs of "Praise Reorx" and "Bless the Forge" filled the air.

"The bees don't normally bother *hic* anyone," Gustin huffed as they went. "They ignore us, actually, as we don't harvest that much honey, but Uldred and Mesk must've spooked the bees."

Within moments the throng had passed beyond the last row of colorful houses, ducked under a string of merrily burning parchment lanterns, and now everyone was awkwardly racing toward a scattering of huge trees. There, stretched between two massive, ancient oaks, was a gigantic honeycomb. Even the sivak was astonished by the size of the construction. Nearly a dozen feet off the ground, each chamber was easily five feet across. The entire honeycomb was bigger than the biggest building in Neidarbard. A rope ladder dangled from one of the oaks, and the acting mayor quickly explained that the dwarves and kender climbed it to access the chambers and harvest the honey.

Three giant bees darted in and out of chambers at the top. They were bigger than draft horses, striped in stark bands of yellow and brown, their round eyes darker than a starless sky. Their legs were as wide around as healthy saplings, looking fuzzy with pollen. The buzzing that came from the constant movement of their wings practically drowned out the worried chatter of the townsfolk.

"Save them, please," Gustin implored.

"Uldred and Mesk. They're so young," someone at the front of the crowd added. "You're a god, *the* god, you could . . ."

The draconian was no longer listening to them or to the incessant buzzing of the giant bees. He was listening to his heart, which had begun to beat louder and louder. He felt his fingers nervously tingling. It was near the time.

Or, the sivak idly wondered, was he feeling heartfelt concern for these young dwarves? They had, after all, been sent to get the honey just for him.

"Please save them, Reorx!"

"How *hic* will you . . ."

Acting impulsively, the sivak dropped the doll and ran toward the giant honeycomb, stumpy legs all a tingle as they churned over the grass. As he ran, he tried to shrug off the wooziness of the ale and shut out the pounding of his heart. The oak's shadows stretched out toward him as he closed in, crouched, and, relying on his powerful leg muscles, sprang up into the air. Amid the startled ooohs and gasps of the Neidarbardians, he cleared the lower chambers and grabbed onto the honeycomb.

He thrust the sounds of his heart to the back of his mind and listened intently. Faintly he heard the young dwarves in the comb calling for help, their voices little more than echoes amid the buzzing of the bees, so loud here that it hurt his ears. The sivak clambered up quickly, just as the three giant bees darted down toward him.

The first bee closed in on him, as the sivak clung to the honeycomb, half-paralyzed by amazement. He saw his dwarven visage reflected in its mirrorlike eyes. Beautiful and horrifying and perfectly formed, its head swiveled back and forth, feelers twitching. The gust of wind created by its wings threatened to blow him off. The giant bee flew closer still, eyes fixed on him, and then he acted, slamming his dwarven fist hard against it. The great insect dropped, stunned, to the ground, and the next moved in.

The second giant bee he drove away with an impressive kick, banishing it to the highest branches of the oak, where it seemed to struggle, entangled. The third bee darted in, obviously intent on stinging the little intruder. The giant insect buffeted the sivak with his wings, then shot down and landed on his back, stinging and raking him with its barbed feet. However, the draconian, even in this form, could not be truly injured by a creature such as this. The biting and stinging mainly served to annoy him and help shake off the last dullness of the alcohol. His senses were clearing.

Below the townsfolk shouted their praise for Reorx.

"Only a god would not be *hic* harmed by the giant bees!" exclaimed the acting mayor.

Finally the sivak managed to slip into a chamber, pulling the third giant bee in after him. Out of sight of the

Neidarbardians, he swiftly broke the stupid creature's neck. There were other bees in the honeycomb. He could hear them, deep in the tunnel-like chambers, buzzing around deafeningly.

He scrambled out and skittered to the top row, where the last rays of the sun painted the honeycomb orange as a dying ember. He pulled himself inside one of the topmost chambers and crawled quickly toward the soft cries of the trapped dwarves. He tunneled down, becoming terribly sticky with honey. Deeper still, and the cries were a little louder now. He moved at a frantic pace, worried for the dwarves that had risked their lives just to gain a little honey for him, practically sliding as the chamber sloped steeply down. Suddenly the tunnel dropped, and he found himself sliding down a path of honey. He landed in a large honey-filled room occupied by giant bees. They were workers tending a queen as enormous as a hatchling dragon. He marvelled at them for untold minutes, taking it all in. "Amazing," he heard himself whisper.

The bees ignored him, as they ignored the two young dwarves wedged in the morass of honey below where the insects were toiling. Uldred and Mesk were stuck as if they'd sunk into quicksand. The two dwarves were calling to him now, shouting praises to Reorx, *the* god. He drew his attention away from the bees, and within moments he was at their side.

He managed to pull both of them up and out. They were so thoroughly coated with the gooey mess they could barely move. He decided it would be faster to carry them and tucked one under each arm. It took great effort to keep them from squirting out, for now he too was thoroughly coated with honey.

"Reorx!" the smaller cried. "We knew you would come save us!"

The sivak urged them to stay still as he scrabbled up into another tunnel chamber and listened for a moment to make sure no bees were in position to bar their way. He edged forward, the terrified and grateful dwarves under his powerful arms. His fingers were tingling almost painfully with the effort.

"You will be all right," the sivak told them. "Gustin Stoutbeard, acting mayor of Neidarbard, is waiting outside and he will—" He heard something behind him and craned his thick neck around. A bee, a very large one, was laboriously making its way through the tunnel behind him. It lowered its head and buzzed its wings, the sound incredibly loud in the confined space. The boys slipped from his grasp, one managing to scramble forward and out the honeycomb, the other screaming as he slid back toward the great bee.

"Reorx!" the sliding young dwarf called. "Save me!"

Faintly, the draconian heard the townsfolk outside cheer. Obviously the one dwarf had made it to safety. As for the other . . . He fixed his jaw determinedly and trundled toward the bee, which was gradually closing distance on the terrified dwarf.

"Mesk!" someone was hollering. The sivak thought he recognized the voice as belonging to the acting mayor. "Mesk! Climb down the ladder! Hurry! While the bees are still stunned." There were other voices, but the draconian couldn't make out what they were saying. His ears were ringing with the buzzing of the bee and the beating of his heart. His chest felt so tight.

It was long suspenseful moments after that before the other young dwarf finally clambered out of the honeycomb, coated with honey and trying hard to pull the gooey mass from his beard. Despite the sticky mess, both rescued dwarves were eagerly and noisily embraced by the relieved townspeople.

More suspenseful moments passed, as the townspeople waited.

"Reorx!" Gustin hollered. "Uldred, where's Reorx?"

Uldred shook his head, trying again to pull the honey out of his short beard, so he could speak properly. "The god saved me—us." He coughed up a gob of honey. "There was this ferocious bee, though, and he was wrestling with it, rolling back down into the depths. He yelled at me to go ahead. Told me he had to deal with that bee and then go summon all the other gods. That they were waiting for him. Then the bee and he just disappeared." Uldred added solemnly, "I feel quite confident that he got out and that even now he is busy on his very important mission."

"I'm sure you're right," said Gustin Stoutbeard with matching solemnity.

"Praise the Forge!" a kender cried. "He saved Uldred and Mesk. Praise Reorx!"

The shouts of gratitude continued as the crowd turned back to the village, where the band had started to strike up a tune again. Uldred paused and stared at something on the ground. A small rag doll.

He oh-so-gently picked it up and cradled it under his arm, slipped away from the crowd, and headed toward the mountains.

"It was nothing personal," the young dwarf said as he glanced back at the honeycomb. There was a hint of regret on his ruddy face.

The Bridge
Douglas Niles

It was a stone span, not more than two dozen paces in length. The bridge crossed a chasm carved by a churning stream, a rapid flow of icy water spilling downward from the lofty valleys of the High Kharolis. The roadway was smoothly paved and wide enough to allow the passage of a large wagon, albeit snugly. Low stone walls, no more than knee-high to a grown man, bracketed the right of way.

The bridge was dwarf-made, a fact visible even to a casual observer. No gaps separated the carefully cut stones, and the outer surface was smooth and virtually seamless. The central pillar rising from the gorge was slender and high, far taller than would have been possible for any human or elven construct. The span had a sturdy appearance of permanence, appropriate for a structure that had stood without a single repair for more than a thousand years.

The road to the bridge curled down a steep ridge from the mountains. After crossing the gorge, the route formed the main street of a small village. This was a collection of stone houses, sheltered under low roofs and set into the rocky hillsides on either side of the street. A few dwarves walked down the lane, carrying bundles of firewood, while another squat, bearded figure led a small pony up a trail on the nearby hill. The steady cadence of a blacksmith's hammer could be heard from the shed attached to a smoking smelter. Other than these signs of activity, and a few plumes of chimney smoke, the town was quiet.

All this could be observed by the watchers atop the nearby ridge. Three dwarves lay there, flat on their bellies as they reconnoitered the road and its lofty crossing. From their vantage they couldn't see the bottom of the gorge, but they could see enough shadowy cliff to know that the cut was several hundred feet deep.

"And no doubt the river's frothin' like dragon breath down there," muttered Tarn Bellowgranite.

Beside him, Belicia Slateshoulder nodded. "Judging from the current in the highlands, it'll be deep and too rapid to ford—even if we could get two thousand dwarves down the cliff and back up the other side."

Tarn nodded, looking over his shoulder at the horde of refugees waiting on the roadway behind them, carefully halted out of sight of the village. He knew they were counting on him to lead them to safety, as they had counted on him to hold them together during four months of exile. The last remnant of Clan Hylar, driven from their home under the mountain by the attacks of ruthless enemies, they had barely endured the summer and early autumn in the barren valleys of the higher elevations. Shaken and demoralized by life under the open sky, they had struggled to survive, followed him as he led them to valleys of game, followed him as he brought them down finally from the high country. They looked weary and exhausted, and as Tarn gazed at the deep gorge he understood that most of the tired, ragged mountain dwarves would never be able to make such a climb.

"It has to be the bridge then," he said.

He turned his attention once again to the village beyond the span. He studied the stone houses partially buried in the rocky slopes, saw the low garden walls, the sturdy construction and thick, slanting roofs. A large building, the source of the pounding hammer, puffed a column of black smoke from a sooty chimney. Like his own people, the villagers were dwarves—but at the same time they were different, for they were hill dwarves, bred under the sky. His own tribe, for generations, had called the caverns under the mountains their home.

Past the village they could see the promise of their destination: a swath of green fields, bright with sparkling lakes and great stretches of forest that were sure to provide game and forage aplenty. The Hylar refugees would be able to build huts there, maybe find a few snug caves, and with luck the majority would last the coming winter. There would be food in the lakes and forests and some respite from the brutal weather that would soon seize the high altitudes.

Tarn pushed back from the summit, joining his two companions in stretching, then settling down into a squat. He looked over the mass of huddled dwarves awaiting his decision. They had built no fires, made no shelters here beside the narrow road. Instead they lay where they had halted, sipping at waterskins or chewing on thin strips of dried meat. Some were armed, still hale and sturdy, but too many others were gaunt, sunburned, bent with weariness. The eyes that looked to him for some glimmer of hope were haunted and dark.

Behind the ragged refugees stretched the rugged ridges leading into the High Kharolis. Snow dusted all the slopes, and the loftiest peaks were buried beneath ten-foot drifts of soft powder. Plumes of wind-blown crystals trailed from these summits, proof that winter's winds would soon scour the valleys and chill the life out of anyone who hadn't planned ahead for winter.

"Let's quit wastin' time," growled the third dwarf, speaking for the first time. "I say we move on the bridge before the hill dwarves even know we're here. If they try to stop us . . ." He didn't finish the statement, but his hand, tightening around the haft of his great war axe, made clear his meaning.

"Wait, Barzack," Tarn cautioned. "Let's make a plan and stick to it. There's got to be a way to get across that bridge without people getting killed."

"Bah—they're hill dwarves! Who gives a whit if we have to cut a few of them to pieces?"

"You're forgetting—we might have to live nearby to this place for the whole winter. It'll be hard enough just finding food and making shelter without having to worry whether we're going to be attacked by a bunch of villagers intending to seek vengeance for a surprise ambush."

"Not to mention," Belicia added pointedly, "we don't know. Maybe they're peaceful folk."

Barzack snorted. Like Tarn, he was a shaggy fellow, with long hair and a bushy beard. Despite months of living off the land, his dark armor was clean and polished and rust free. His boots and tunic showed signs of wear, but his helmet fit tightly over his scalp. While Tarn and Belicia had demonstrated patience and leadership in keeping the mountain dwarves together during the months of exile, Barzack had proven capable and useful as a tracker, a hunter, and a fighter of admirable courage and skills. All the tribe had honored him when he had single-handedly slain a great cave bear. Using only his axe he not only destroyed a threat to dwarven lives, but he furnished enough meat for a grand feast and procured a pelt that had yielded a dozen warm cloaks.

"The hill dwarves can't seek vengeance if they're all dead," he pointed out with cold logic.

Tarn shook his head. "We're not looking for another war. Besides, considering the state of the world, I'd be surprised if that village is really as sleepy as it looks. Maybe they aren't pushovers."

The other male glowered. "Let 'em try and fight us—I tell you, we could use a little action."

"What about our elders and the children?" Belicia retorted with a gesture at the listless mob of Hylar. "Don't you think they'd appreciate having their warriors around for the winter?" She turned to Tarn. "Let me go down and talk to them, see if there's going to be any trouble."

"I think we should all go. That way they'll know that we mean business," Tarn said. "We should be ready to make a move if they prove balky."

"No reason to get them all alarmed," Belicia countered.

"If they see two thousand mountain dwarves waiting to cross their bridge, they'll prefer to talk—and they'll think twice before trying to stop us."

Although he grimaced in disgust, Barzack nodded his reluctant agreement. "It's bad enough living outside, having the sun beat down on us for a hot summer. Now we've got to kiss up to a bunch of hill dwarves, just to hope they'll let us cross the bridge and pass through their little town."

"Maybe you'd rather go back to Thorbardin?" demanded Tarn, his temper flaring.

For a moment all three were silent, overcome by grim memories. The Hylar had once been the proudest of dwarven clans, unchallenged rulers of mighty Thorbardin. They had been driven from their ancestral home during the past summer, victims of the treachery of dark dwarves. As if the traitorous attack of their neighboring clans wasn't enough, they had suffered an influx of demon creatures from Chaos that had wracked their home with unprecedented violence. Now these refugees were the only survivors of Clan Hylar. Their city was a ruin. No family had been left unscathed by the devastation—in fact each of the three leaders debating what to do on the bridge had lost a father in the brutal battles against dark dwarves and Chaos beasts. Tarn couldn't help feeling a twinge of shame as he thought how far his people had fallen. He knew there were worse dangers that loomed ahead, and he wondered if he was capable of coping with the obstacles.

"One day we will go back," he said, speaking to himself as much as to his two companions. "That's a promise . . . to you, to all of us."

"For now, let's see if we can get across that bridge," Belicia said, bringing their attention back to the present.

"Barz?" asked Tarn, looking back to the multitude of mountain dwarves resting on either side of the road.

"I'll bring 'em up," the burly warrior muttered. "We'll be ready to rush the bridge if they show any signs of stupidity."

"Wait until I give the word," Tarn said. He was grateful for Barzack's competence, a useful attribute in this increasingly problematic world, but frequently found his bellicose nature a challenge to reasonable authority.

The black-bearded warrior shouted at the main body, and the mountain dwarves once again fell into line. The sturdiest warriors took the front positions, though a large detachment of armed Hylar brought up the rear of the band to guard against surprise. Tarn and Belicia led the large column across the crest of the ridge and down the road toward the village. They saw immediately that the sleepy appearance of the hill dwarf community was deceptive. In plain view a troop of armed warriors appeared from a squat building and marched forth to straddle the bridge.

"Do you think they knew we were here all along?" asked Belicia.

"Who knows? I wouldn't be surprised if they keep a company on permanent guard duty."

The dwarfwoman nodded. Both of them knew that though the Storms of Chaos had been beaten back before they could consume Thorbardin, strange beings still lurked across this and every other part of Krynn. No doubt the hill dwarves had experienced some of the Chaos horrors—dragons of liquid fire, shadow wights that sucked vitality, life, even memory from their doomed victims, daemon warriors who feared nothing.

Of course, the schism between the dwarf clans existed long before the Chaos War. Still, it saddened Tarn to see that the rivalries and resentments that had marred the history of the hill and mountain dwarves had not been allayed by the arrival of a greater, supernatural threat. The residents of this little village couldn't have looked more hostile than they did now, facing fellow dwarves. To judge from the first words spoken when Tarn and Belicia had advanced to within hailing distance, an all-out battle was likely.

"That's far enough, cousins . . . these arrows have sharp heads, and no one's ever complained about our aim!"

The speaker was a brawny hill dwarf, a fellow who looked to be nearly a head taller than Tarn. He carried a massive, heavy warhammer, and was flanked by a row of doughty comrades, each of whom held a heavy crossbow raised and pointed. Even from a hundred paces away, the mountain dwarves could see the sunlight reflecting off arrowheads.

"We want to talk to you," said Belicia, holding up both of her hands, palms outward. Tarn remained silent, and made no move to draw his sword.

"Talk from over there, then," growled the original speaker.

"We come from Thorbardin," Tarn said. "We are of Clan Hylar, and we left our ancestral home, driven out by evil Chaos fiends."

"We know—and for all we care, you can go back there! Maybe a fire dragon will keep you warm this winter!"

"Please listen," Belicia said. "We are not looking for a fight . . . or even your help. All we ask is that our band be allowed to cross this bridge and pass through your village, that we may have a chance to reach safety of the lowlands before the onset of winter."

"We know all we need to know about mountain dwarves . . . maybe you recall the stories yourself? How once upon a time the world was coming to an end, and the Cataclysm was raining death across Krynn? We hill dwarves turned to the undermountain clans for protection. Do you remember what the mountain dwarf king said?"

"I remember," Tarn said, "and it is a memory that brings us shame."

"Well, we remember too," declared the hill dwarf, "and to us it's a memory that brings only hatred and bitterness. There was no room for us, your king said . . . go back to the hills and die, he said. Ironic, isn't it, when you think about what yer asking. Now that we have a chance to return the favor, you'll understand that we plan to make the most of it!"

"You speak of a time of evil and selfishness," retorted Tarn. "Those traits led to war back then—the Dwarfgate War, the greatest tragedy of our history."

"Think about the past, and have a new vision for the future!" Belicia argued. "Your actions today can lay the groundwork for lasting peace."

"We've had all we want of mountain dwarf peace! Now, go back to the high country or face our steel!" The speaker brandished his great hammer, while the ranks of crossbowmen aimed their weapons meaningfully.

Other hill dwarves lined the edge of the gorge. All were armed and—unlike the Hylar—they looked healthy, clean, well-fed. Though they were no match for the sheer numbers of the refugees, they had the advantage of defending a bridge, a narrow route that would inevitably negate the greater force of the Hylar.

"We can't go back to the heights!" Tarn declared, feeling his temper rising again. "If you don't let us pass in peace, then we'll have to try to do so by force—we have no choice! That will lead to a waste of lives that benefits neither of our tribes. For you should know this, hill dwarf—though some of my clan may die, your people's blood, too, will flow across the ground. Cousins will kill cousins, and many dwarves will perish!"

"I say let the killing begin!" sneered the village chieftain. "My father and grandfather and all my ancestors have told me of mountain dwarf treachery, of the hate that kept my people from safety during the Cataclysm. You are no kin of ours!"

Tarn felt his sword hand twitching as he started to reply. Before he could growl out a word, however, he felt Belicia's hand on his arm. As always, her touch calmed him.

"It's no good," muttered Tarn, glaring at the belligerent warrior on the bridge. " 'Stubborn as a hill dwarf.' I see that it's an apt phrase!"

Barzack stalked forward. "Let's fight them!" insisted the veteran warrior. He fixed his dark eyes on Tarn and set his jaw belligerently. "Let me lead the way if you don't have the stomach for it!"

"That's enough of that kind of talk," snapped Tarn, still in a foul temper, "or you'll be fighting me, not some upstart hill dwarf."

"Stop it, both of you," snapped Belicia.

"What are we going to do about this impasse, then?" demanded Barzack.

"I guess you're right," Tarn said after a long silence. "We'll have to fight."

"Go to war against our own cousins?" Belicia asked glumly.

"Do you have a better idea?" asked Tarn in exasperation.

"I might," Barzack offered. He studied the picket line at the bridge. "That big hill dwarf, the one making most of the noise—like he was spoiling for a fight, right?"

"Aye," Tarn agreed, wondering what the mountain dwarf was getting at.

"Well, so am I! Let's suggest a match—myself against him. If I win, we get to cross the bridge and move swiftly through the village and into the low valleys. If he wins, we go back—or, rather, you will, since I'll be dead. We'll pledge against the honor of Reorx, so there will be no duplicity on either side."

"I don't know," the Hylar leader said slowly. He looked at the strapping warrior appraisingly, remembered Barzack's prowess against the massive bear. "If I were a bettor, I'd admit I like your chances, but we—especially you—would be gambling with very high stakes."

"I'll win," Barzack said confidently.

"How can you be so sure?"

"This is why." The burly warrior reached into the tangle of the beard at his breast. He groped for a moment, then brought forth a glittering object dangling from a golden chain. Tarn saw a necklace, three gold disks linked on a single chain of gold. One of the disks was centered with a ruby, another with an emerald, and the third with a bright diamond.

"This is all that I have left to remind me of my mother," said Barzack. "She gave it to me before she left Thorbardin with my father . . . I was a wee mite, for this was long years before the Lance War. She said I should always carry her prized necklace, for I was her first son."

Tarn was surprised to see moisture in the warrior's eyes, to hear emotion choke the dwarf's voice.

"I never saw her again."

"Do you know what happened to her?" asked Belicia.

"Yes, my father told me." Barzack drew a deep breath, and once again his eyes were dry, his voice hard. "She was taken by hill dwarves . . . captured, enslaved, probably worked to death or killed outright."

Barzack glared at Tarn, as if challenging him to make an issue of the story. "That's why I'll win—in my mind, these hill dwarves are the same as those who took my mother. My hatred of them will carry me to victory. I assure you, this fight will give me a great deal of satisfaction."

"Still, it's taking a huge chance."

"The alternative is war," Belicia pointed out.

"I know." Tarn gestured to the vast band of mountain dwarves gathered on the road before the bridge. "If it comes to battle, though, I know we could win. We easily outnumber them."

"However, it is as you say. Too many Hylar would die. How many would die before we prevailed?" his mate persisted. "I think Barzack's idea has real merit."

"Let me fight him—for my mother, my father, for all of us. For Reorx himself!"

Tarn still didn't like it. He knew that Reorx was the god of all dwarves, clans of mountain and hill alike, and there was no guarantee that he would favor the Hylar cause.

"Do you have a better idea? Any idea at all?" growled Barzack. Tarn was forced to admit that he didn't.

So it was decided. Tarn, Belicia, and Barzack turned and approached the edge of the bridge, with the rest of the clan pressing close behind. The hill dwarf sentries still stood in line, blocking passage across the bridge, and with the approach of the whole column of mountain dwarves more of the town's residents had spilled out of their homes to gather at the far end of the gorge. The defenders of the village shouted and jeered at the refugees, hurling the cruelest insults they could imagine.

In contrast, the mass of mountain dwarves regarded the hill dwarves with grim silence, glowering darkly, fingering weapons, occasionally muttering among themselves in reaction to the harsh invective. Tarn knew that their silence was not an indication of cowardice—if anything, it was an advertisement of their stern purpose. To the Hylar, the bridge represented a route not only to the lowlands but to their chances of any future at all.

"Go back—or I warn you, we'll kill you!" blustered the hill dwarf leader. Now, to Tarn's critical eye, this sturdy hill dwarf looked every bit the equal of Barzack in size, weight, and even in the burning anger that shone within his dark black eyes. Tarn hated the prospect of a duel, but he was determined to cross the bridge, and this seemed the only way.

"That will not be easily accomplished," Tarn said. "We're in no mood to retreat, and our numbers will overwhelm yours . . . though it is unfortunate that so many on both sides will die in the fighting."

The hill dwarf laughed. "You yourself will never make it across the bridge—and before you've breathed your last, we'll have hill dwarves from ten more villages among our numbers. Already messengers have gone out, and the first reinforcements will be here within the hour."

The fierce chieftain could be bluffing—certainly they hadn't seen any messengers depart the village since they had first approached the bridge. Even so, Tarn despaired at the note of defiance in the other dwarf's words. Certainly any battle would result in a huge loss of life on both sides.

"Before there's any killing, let us talk for a few minutes more. There's nothing to be lost in that, is there? My name is Tarn Bellowgranite. My father was the thane of the Hylar, and now I lead the remnants of our clan."

"Any breath spent in speech with a mountain dwarf is a waste of air," retorted the other.

"At least he's still wasting breath instead of blood," murmured Belicia, speaking under her breath and tightening a grip on Tarn's arm. He drew strength from her touch, forcing himself to control the emotions that once again threatened to boil over.

"Waste a little more of it, then. Tell me your name," coaxed Tarn.

"I am Katzynn Bonebreaker—and my surname declares the fate of any mountain dwarf who meets my hammer!" He raised the heavy weapon, spinning it easily from one hand to the other.

"Make the challenge," growled Barzack, "or, by Reorx, I'll fight him without any ceremony!"

Tarn too was weary of the pleasantries. "Well, there is one among us who shares your sentiments—his mother was snatched and enslaved by your people. He never saw her again. So you both have a grudge, a blood feud."

"There are blood feuds throughout our clans," declared the hill dwarf. "What of it?"

"Just this: We are not going back to the mountains, not without a fight. A fight would kill many of you, as well as many of us. Instead, let our champion fight you or any hill dwarf you name. Let the winner decide his people's fate."

The hill dwarf scoffed. "None can last more than five minutes against me. That is my reputation. How do we know you will keep your word when your champion dies?"

Tarn flushed. "Don't be so sure who will die! Either way, let us swear an oath to Reorx. The loser will abide by the terms of the pledge, or the curse of our god will come down upon his tribe."

"Reorx . . . father god to *all* dwarves," mused the hill dwarf. "In truth, such an oath would be binding, for the consequences of breaking such a vow are too dire to comprehend."

"In that case, let the matter be fought!" declared Barzack, loudly, "if there is one among you with the courage to face me!"

"I'll be glad to fight you!" snarled the hill dwarf chieftain, "but first let us make this vow."

Katzynn Bonebreaker and another hill dwarf advanced to the edge of the bridge. Tarn and Barzack moved forward, and the oath was sworn. Barzack, Tarn, and two hill dwarves each placed their hands over the blade of a sword as terms of the fight were outlined: the duel would last until the death—or the almost inconceivable capitulation—of one of the contestants. No physical aid could come from any other dwarves, and the two contestants had to remain on the bridge until the fight ended.

"That should take about five minutes," said Katzynn Bonebreaker with a malicious grin. Barzack met his eyes fiercely.

The dwarves of both sides moved off the bridge as Katzynn and Barzack faced each other. The mountain dwarf bore his huge axe, while the hill dwarf faced him with his equally large hammer. Both were hulking and fierce fellows, splendid examples of dwarven warriors. As Tarn watched them, he was struck by the realization that there were more similarities than differences between the two combatants.

The two pair studied each other for several heartbeats as the crowds on both sides of the gorge began to call encouragement.

"Kill him, Katzynn!" cried one bellicose hill dwarf, a female.

"Feed him to the fishes, Barzack!" countered one of the mountain dwarf matrons. The shouts quickly rose to a roar, drowning out the river and the wind. Tarn felt the tension all around him, and his own blood began to pound. He raised his fist and shook it angrily, barely conscious of Belicia's grip tightening on his arm. This time her touch did not pacify him.

Barzack raised his axe and charged while the hill dwarf crouched and swung his hammer in a low arc. The two weapons met in an explosion of sparks, steel clanging against steel. Shouts and cries intensified from both sides, dwarven voices raised in a hoarse, bloodthirsty din. The force of the first contact knocked both fighters backward, but Katzynn Bonebreaker recovered quickly to rush forward, twirling the hammer in great circles around his head.

The mountain dwarf ducked under to slash viciously upward with his sharp-edged axe. Somehow his opponent spun out of the way, then Barzack had to fling himself forward to avoid a backswing that would certainly have crushed his spine. Their momentum carried the dwarves apart, and when they turned to face each other again, they had reversed positions. Mouths agape, they drew deep breaths of air.

More shouts of encouragement, building to a roar that rumbled like thunder through the mountain valley. "Kill him! Kill him!" Tarn found himself shouting the same, unaware that Belicia had released his arm. He shook both his fists, bellowing in a dry rasp.

Now it was Barzack who stood at the far end of the bridge, as if protecting the approach to the village, and Katzynn with his back to the mountain dwarves as he regarded his scowling opponent. The hill dwarf stepped forward slowly, swinging his hammer easily before him, while the mountain dwarf raised his axe defensively and took a step backward. Suddenly, however, Barzack lunged at his enemy, and there was another tremendous collision.

Neither fighter gave ground, legs spread, feet firmly planted as they bashed at each other again and again. Their faces were distorted, eyes narrowed to slits as sweat streamed down their foreheads and their heavy weapons rose and fell. One would lunge and the other yield, then one would push back and the other falter. The sounds of the clash echoed in the deep gorge, continuing as the combatants stopped once again to catch their breath. Both gasped for air now, the sweat trickling down their faces.

Tarn was jumping up and down, wrapped up in the frenzy. Like others, he drew his sword, waving the weapon in the air, hurling insults at the despised enemies across the gorge, shouting advice to the mountain dwarf champion. He wasn't aware of what he was saying, but it didn't matter. Words were swallowed up in the tumult of hate. All around him the Hylar were swept up in battle rage, in the fury and lust for blood.

Surprising Katzynn, Barzack got off a good swing, and though the hill dwarf stumbled away, blood oozed from a deep gash in his thigh. The wounded warrior had a look of shock on his face, and cheers resounded from the Hylar. On their side, the villagers gasped as their wounded favorite fell back, barely blocking a series of powerful blows. They had never seen Katzynn so harried. Finally the two duelists paused again to collect themselves. Now the shouts had faded somewhat, replaced by gasps, muttered prayers, and hoarse whispers of fear.

The two dwarves closed in to resume the terrible battle. They swung their weapons, then clutched each other, too close for axe or sword. They grappled and punched, clawing at each other's beards and eyes, kicking and jabbing. Katzynn managed to grab the slender gold chain that Barzack wore around his neck and pulled it tight, choking the Hylar. The mountain dwarf was able to break away, but his antagonist snapped the chain and the three jewels that decorated the gold disks went flying. Barzack, clawing at his throat to regain his breath, spared the jewels a mournful look as they scattered across the road.

First the hill dwarf had the advantage, then the mountain dwarf. They circled back to their original positions, then wheeled, fought, wheeled again, ending up sideways on the bridge, each with his back against one of the low side walls. Blood spilled down Katzynn's flanks and legs, pouring from several deep wounds, while Barzack staggered from the repeated hammer blows that seemed to cover his body with bruises. Both dwarves moved in a daze, using both hands to wield weapons that now seemed too heavy to lift. Impossibly, the fight had gone on for more than an hour.

Once more they broke apart and paused. Tarn no longer felt confident that Barzack would win, but there was no way he could intervene, having sworn the oath to Reorx.

Again the two charged each other, and again Barzack's axe carved a deep wound, this time in Katzynn's shoulder. The mountain dwarf, sensing victory, thrust forward, axe raised for a final, killing blow. The hill dwarf was slumping, his hammer dangling uselessly at his side, and the end seemed near.

But from somewhere deep inside himself Katzynn Bonebreaker found the strength to act. He managed to lurch away from Barzack's blow, bringing his hammer up and around with a powerful swipe. The steel head of the formidable weapon slammed full-force into Barzack's helmet, bending the metal shell, crunching sickeningly into bone and flesh.

Soundlessly Barzack fell, his skull crushed. Katzynn, bleeding from numerous wounds, swayed wearily over his vanquished foe, staring down at the fallen mountain dwarf.

The valley had fallen silent, the cheers fading away in the presence of death. Numbly, Tarn stepped forward, looking at the lifeless form of his champion, his friend. Echoes of the fight, of hatred and rage, left him feeling utterly drained. It didn't seem real, or even important, who had been slain—he believed he would have felt the same emptiness and shame either way.

Quiet sobbing came from his side. Belicia—he had forgotten her—was down on her knees. "He sacrificed himself," she said softly, "for nothing."

His eyes met the dull gaze of the victorious hill dwarf, who was also watching Belicia. Tarn pulled her to her feet, put his arm around her, and turned to head back, to the mountains, to certain death for his clan. An oath had been sworn.

He felt a strong hand on his shoulder and instinctively reached for his dagger. Another hand, Belicia's, kept him from drawing the weapon, and he was turned around by Katzynn Bonebreaker. Tarn was surprised to see tears in the victorious warrior's eyes. A scrap of gold chain still hung from his hand, and wordlessly the hill dwarf extended it to Tarn.

Tarn took the piece of chain as the hill dwarf stepped to the side, his expression twisted with pain and torment.

Then he threw his great hammer over the wall, saying nothing as the bloodstained weapon spun down into the depths.

Only when the hammer had vanished into the churning water did Katzynn make a gesture that invited Tarn and all his clan across the bridge.

Tarn's gratitude was also mute. He merely nodded, too drained to speak, and led his people forward across the bridge and toward the valley beyond.

Gone
Roger E. Moore

Day 0, night

Dromel had always struck me as one of those annoying entrepreneur sorts who wander the fringes of human society, looking for a secret door to fame and wealth. I had never considered the possibility that he was completely mad, but I considered it now.

"So, what do you think?" he finished. "Are you in?" It had taken him two hours to explain his plan after coming to see me uninvited. The candles had all burned out, and only the oil lantern's steady glow illuminated my small room. He leaned forward, waiting for my response.

My blank look and silence ought to have discouraged him, but didn't. "It can't fail, Red. We'll come in below the waves in my new ship. Nothing on the island will see us, not even the shadow wights, if they still exist. We can—"

"Wait," I said. "As I understand the tales, which may or may not be true, shadow wights can—"

"Ah!" He seemed to have expected my response. "They won't be a problem. My relics will keep them at bay while we do what we need to do. We don't have to worry about shadow-things."

"You don't seem to have much regard for them."

Dromel spread his hands. "Well, why should I? Who do you know who's ever seen a shadow wight? I've heard the same things you have, I'm sure, that shadow wights make you disappear as if you never existed, if they touch you, but where is the proof? This is going to work, I tell you. We'll loot the ruins on Enstar and be out of there in less than a week. We'll come back home with thousands of steels, a mountain of money. You could get out of this rat-infested warehouse and get yourself a real palace, knock elbows with Merwick's finest and blow your nose on their tablecloths. That's what you want, and you know it, and now you can have it."

Dromel didn't know whale dung about what I really wanted. It was true that the pragmatic but unimaginative folk of Merwick had prejudices against certain nonhumans, particularly very large and potentially dangerous races such as minotaurs, like me. I could wander the docks as I liked, but there were many places in town where I was not especially welcome and many estates outside the town's stone walls where I was not welcome at all. I could live with that, though. Being a good citizen of Merwick was not my ultimate goal.

On the other hand, ship captains in any port would hire me the second they saw my broad, maroon horns. Curiously, even bigoted humans assume that every minotaur is a master sailor and skilled warrior. On that score, they were correct. I knew the western isles of Ansalon like the end of my snout, and I could handle myself in any brawl or battle. What I really wanted was to get my own ship and sail the world of Krynn, explore it and master it, live free as the gulls on the high seas. I had always felt I deserved better in life, which I suppose every minotaur does, and Dromel had just unfolded a plan that might let me sink my hooves into that future and call it mine.

The only drawback was that it was a plan only the insane would consider.

Dromel's eyes glowed with his vision. "It took me months to work this all out, Red. I've covered every step, every possibility. I've talked to every sage and scholar who knows anything about Enstar or shadow wights. Tell me if you see a flaw in my plan."

An argument was pointless. "Where are these relics you found?" I asked, half out of curiosity and half from a lack of anything else to say.

He looked surprised, then quickly reached inside his shirt. He carefully drew out a long, daggerlike item attached to an iron-link necklace, all of which he held out for my visual inspection. The "dagger" was actually an elaborately engraved spearhead with a rag tied over its pointed tip. "This is one of them," he said with pride. "My good luck charm. I get poked by it now and then, so I usually wrap it up, at least the sharp part."

The spearhead's workmanship was superb. It was certainly a legacy of the days before the Chaos War, when ironworkers had the time, talent, and money to craft such fancy weapons. My gaze rested on the runes along the bladed edge. Had the runes seemed to glow for a moment? A prickling sensation ran over my skin. "Where did you get this?" I asked.

"Not every battlefield of old is marked on the maps," Dromel said with an enigmatic smile. "Let's say I got lucky on my last trip over to the mainland and brought back some nice souvenirs."

I hated myself for asking, but I had to know. "How do you know that thing is a real dragonlance?"

"How?" Dromel laughed. He took the necklace off and handed the spearhead to me.

I took the spearhead in my right hand . . . and I instantly knew he was telling the truth.

Dromel saw the look on my face. He grinned in triumph. "You feel it," he said.

I nodded dumbly. My broad right hand shivered with the power flowing out of the spearhead. My palm itched and burned, my clawed fingers twitched. It was Old Magic, from the days when there were real wizards and real priests, and magic was everywhere, like air. It was exactly as the old tale-tellers spoke of it, the ruined men mumbling in their cups, remembering a better and brighter time that had ended just before I was born. The weapon in my hand brought me a taste of all that I had missed. I thought I was awake and alive for the first time in my life. And the future I wanted was within my reach.

"By all the lost gods," I whispered.

"It came from a footman's dragonlance," Dromel said. "We're lucky there, as we'd never manage with one of the big lanceheads around our necks. Well, you could, but not me." He paused, then went on in an urgent tone. "This will work, Red. It can't fail. If there are shadow wights, they can't possibly get close to us, as long as we have these relics. So, are you in?" His mad, green eyes searched my face for an answer.

Was I in? Perhaps Dromel was mad, but with the spearhead in my hand, I believed in everything. If his plan worked, our troubles would be gone forever.

If anything went wrong—if Dromel was wrong about the shadow wights—then we, like our troubles, would also be gone forever.

Day 1, late morning

My kind is not prone to literary pursuits, but I am an exception and proud of it (as a minotaur is proud of everything about himself, you see). Hence, I keep this diary. I am aware that documentation of adventures has great value to other adventurers, and the more incredible the exploits, the greater the value. Dromel hopes to find steel coins stacked like mountains in the treasure room of a dead lord's manor on Enstar. If this whale of a dream turns out to be a little fish, perhaps this work will still bring me some acclaim and a modest income to salve my disappointment. Any steel is good steel.

I awoke at dawn to meet Dromel at Fenshal & Sons, a family-owned business that had once been a major shipbuilder in Merwick. The Chaos War and the coming of the great dragons broke the back of the sea trade, with so many ships and ports destroyed. Fenshal & Sons had barely survived, restricting the family talents to making fishing boats instead of being the excellent sea traders for which they were justly famed. I found Dromel outside a huge enclosed dry dock where once the labor had gone on even during bad weather and at night. I'd last heard the building was unused and deserted.

Dromel grinned the moment he saw me coming. "You're a prince, Red," he said warmly. "Ready to get down to work?"

I eyed the dry dock building. I clearly heard hammering and voices coming from inside it. "I did have a few questions," I began, scratching my muzzle. "On the issue of the shadow wights, do you have any evidence that—"

Dromel waved the question off with an anxious look on his face. "Uh, let's talk about all that later," he said, glancing furtively around us. "First, let's take a look at my ship. Say nothing to anyone about our destination." He gave me a big smile that was meant to be reassuring, then led me to a side door, opened it, and showed me inside.

Dozens of skylights were open in the long, high roof of the dock building, though it was still largely dark inside. The dim light revealed about two dozen humans, adults and children alike, working on what I thought at first was a broad, nearly flat ship's hull turned over. My eyes adjusted rapidly to the illumination, and I walked to the edge of the dry dock to get a better look at the object of the workers' attention.

I looked at the object for a long time. The wild enthusiasm I had felt last night was rapidly dispelled. When the shock had worn off, I went to find Dromel. He was talking with old Fenshal himself, each man holding one side of a large sheet of ship's construction plans. Dromel gave me a broad grin and a wave as I walked up.

"You *are* mad," I growled at him. "You are madder than mad."

"Red Horn!" said Dromel happily. "Berin Fenshal, this is my new first mate, Red Horn. He's—"

"Have you ever *tested* such a thing as this?" I could not control my tongue. "Do you have even the vaguest idea of the difficulties involved in underwater travel? Is this some kind of secret suicide plot you've cooked up for us?"

"So you like it, then?" Dromel said in a hopeful tone, looking past me to the bizarre ship in the dry dock. "Sort of like a dragon turtle shell, isn't it? I actually got the idea from thinking about dragon turtles a year ago. You know how they cruise along just below the water's surface so you can barely see them, with that nice, huge, protective turtle shell all around. That sort of thing."

Old Fenshal rolled his eyes as Dromel spoke. I snorted and walked off halfway through his patter, going back to the dry dock. The other Fenshals, working on the craft in the dry dock, tried to ignore me as they quietly went on with their work.

"I call it a deepswimmer," Dromel called out. "That big X-shaped thing at the stern, that's the propeller. It rotates when you turn a crank on the insi—"

"This is a *monstrosity*!" I roared. All work instantly ceased. "It's a nightmare! You want us to travel all the way to . . ." With terrible effort, I bit off my words. I rubbed my eyes and snout vigorously with my hands, shutting out the world. Then I sighed and stared again at the ship, the deepswimmer. I had forgotten about this part of his plan after he had showed the dragon-lance to me.

Work slowly resumed as I looked on. Dromel's undersea craft was not very large, certainly smaller than a merchantman. It had no masts or sails, just a smooth wooden surface over which a thin, gray substance, probably a waterproofing sealant, was being painted by a boy with a broad brush. Flat wooden panels like fish fins came out from the sides in several places, pointing in every direction. Strange objects poked up from the vessel's top. I guessed there would be enough room inside for not more than a half dozen men, but it would be a cramped journey.

As I looked on, my harsh attitude softened. The design of the deepswimmer was not unreasonable, if it were to accomplish the task Dromel had set for it. It was as well crafted as anything Fenshal & Sons had ever made. Small portholes around the sides of the craft allowed for clear if limited vision. Piloting the craft would be a challenge, however. The things like fish fins must be steering rudders, I thought, but the vessel would surely be clumsy and slow to respond. There was the obvious problem of getting fresh air into the craft. Then, too, it might take weeks for it to get to Enstar, if that propeller was its only propulsion.

"We'll have it towed," said Dromel, as if reading my mind. He was just behind me, his voice barely audible. "That's what the bow ring is for, right there. We'll cut loose from the tow ship after we cross Thunder Bay, then we'll move on to the island. The ship will wait for our return off Southern Ergoth. It'll be fast and safe, and best of all, nobody will spot us. Not even," he whispered, "shadow wights."

"Air," I said. "We'll need fresh air."

"That round thing toward the stern, on top there, that's a floating air vent. We've created a flexible tube to go from the deepswimmer to the surface, to that. We'll release that floating intake, eject any water that gets into the tube, then pump pure air into the cabin anytime we want. We'll be only twenty feet under the surface at most. Storms won't be able to touch us."

"Dromel, how did you *think* of all this?" I turned to face him in amazement. "You told me once that you didn't even know which side of a ship was starboard, but now you've . . . I don't see how you could . . ." My voice trailed off as I swept my hand in the direction of the strange vessel.

A muffled cough came from behind Dromel. He spun around. "Ah, Pate!" he cried, and he hurried over to a short, bearded figure standing nervously behind old Fenshal. "Red, I want you to meet the real designer of the deepswimmer, the genius who came up with every nut and bolt in it after I gave him the idea. This is Pate. He'll be the chief engineer on our voyage!"

I stared down at Pate, and my worst fears came to life. I understood in a flash how Dromel, who did not know port from starboard, now owned such a monstrosity of a ship. My disbelief gave way to rage, and I glared hard at the bald, bearded, diminutive genius Dromel introduced.

A tinker gnome, the lost gods save me. Pate stared back at me with fear-stricken eyes magnified by his thick gold-rimmed spectacles. He clutched a trembling armload of ship plans, sweating like a fountain—as disconcerted to lay eyes on me, no doubt, as I was to see him. I could tell he was only moments from fainting.

"Say hello, Red!" called Dromel happily.

"No," I said with a disgusted snort and left the building.

Day 2, evening

"Are you *deaf*?" I shouted. "No! Get out of here!"

"Red!" Dromel was literally on his knees on the filthy warehouse floor, blocking my doorway. "Red, you've got to go! I really need you for this! We've got to have someone who knows the sea, someone with real navigational skills, someone fearless, someone—"

"Someone stupid enough to ride in a boat made by a genuine tinker gnome!"

"Berin Fenshal himself went over the plans!" Dromel cried. "He went over everything that Pate designed! Berin said it would work! You can go ask him, Red!"

I glared down at Dromel with narrow eyes, resisting an urge to strangle him. "This little runt—Pate, you call him—you said he's going with us, right?"

Dromel was in agony. "He *has* to go! He designed the thing from my general specifications! He's a real shipwright and engineer. He apprenticed under Fenshal himself, and at the Sea Kings' shipyard under Wallers and Goss. Pate's not like a real tinker gnome, Red, he's a genuine troubleshooter, and he's got—"

"Who else is on the crew? Or are we it? Get up, you look like a fool."

Dromel swallowed and stiffly got up from his knees, dusting off his pants. "We . . . we needed an outdoors sort. I found a Kagonesti, a good hunter and tracker. That's even his name, Hunter, just plain Hunter, or so he tells me. You know the Kagonesti, don't you, those tattooed half-naked guys, the wildlands elves? He's really a fine fellow even if he's not very sociable, but none of them are, I know. You'll like him anyway."

"Elves are dogs." I started to close the door.

"He's not like a real elf!" Dromel shouted in panic. "He's good at what he does, he's not stuck up, and he can get food for us on shore because we can't store all that we need in the *Mock Dragon Turtle!* If we get lost, he can get us off the island! He's good with all sorts of weapons! He's a master of blades! You'll like him!"

"Where did you get that?"

"Hunter? He was in the marketplace a week ago, and—"

"No, that name. The *Mock Dragon Turtle*, is that what you call the deepswimmer?"

"Oh, yeah, that's the ship. You like the name? So, about Hunter—"

"Elves are dogs until there's a war, and then they're a pack of whining, floor-wetting mongrel pups."

"Yes, I know, but no, not this one! Hunter's head and shoulders above the rest! Everyone says so! He's not like a real elf!"

"And what in blazes am I?" I roared. "Do you tell everyone I'm not like a real minotaur?"

It took a terrible effort to get control of myself. Finally, I took a deep breath and let it out slowly. This argument was giving me a headache. Getting rid of Dromel was worse than getting rid of a giant tick.

"Is anyone else going along?" I asked.

"No, no, that's about it." Dromel fidgeted. He looked very uncomfortable. "Almost, anyway. We need one more hand, someone to help with things in case of emergency, someone without fear. We can fit one more aboard without losing any comfort. We might need just that one more. Maybe. I'll know by tomorrow."

Silence stretched between us.

"Red," Dromel pleaded, "I'm going to do it with or without you. If you don't go, I'll find someone else. This is the chance of a lifetime, the chance of ten lifetimes. I mortgaged my entire inheritance, all the lands my father left me, to build that deepswimmer and find those dragonlances. We can find out what happened over there on Enstar, find out where those islanders went during the Chaos War, and we can make ourselves richer than the ancient Kingpriest of Istar when we get to the lord's manor I found on the maps I took from the naval library. It's going to work, and I want you to be in on it."

I mulled it over. There was always a chance he was right, and I'd hate myself if it really was the chance of a lifetime. I was defeated. "I'll see you tomorrow," I said. "We'll talk then."

Dromel nearly collapsed in relief. "By the old gods, Red, I knew I could count on you. You're a—"

I shut the door.

Day 3, late morning

I awoke at dawn and once more went to Fenshal & Sons' shipyard. I found Dromel inside the dry dock building. Beside him was someone I knew instantly and instinctively was our new and final crew member.

"Oh! R-Red!" cried Dromel. His voice shook with ill-concealed terror. "Red, th-this is our—"

"*No!*" I roared, and left the building.

"Hey, you big cow!" shrieked a feminine voice behind me. "You got something against kender?"

Day 11, night

My cracked phosphor-globe has gone out at last, so I write this using Pate's globe. Our deepswimmer rests on the sea bottom now; I have no idea how close to shore we are, though Dromel guesses about a quarter-mile. All is blackness through the small portholes around us. We go ashore tomorrow.

It is very late, but Twig is awake as always, too excited to sleep. She looks endlessly through her myriad pockets. She hums to herself only two feet from my right elbow. Twig is a born talker. At least she no longer asks to read my journal. I refuse to let her see it, which infuriates her.

Dromel is awake, too. He plays with a phosphor-globe across from Twig, the pale green light leaking through his thin fingers. I cannot imagine what is whirling through his mind now that he's so close to the land of his big plans and dreams. He has been very quiet today, his false bravado gone. Oil-stained Pate snores faintly under his filthy blankets at the rear of our cramped cabin. He sometimes mumbles in his sleep exactly as he mumbles when awake. I have no idea how he can sleep at all; after four days under the waves, we stink so offensively as to trouble the dead. I had heard that gnomes have a marvelous sense of smell, thanks to their large noses, but perhaps Pate is an exception. Hunter huddles in a ball at the bow window. I cannot tell if he sleeps or not. He calls his sleep "reverie," like a half-conscious daydream. He cannot explain how it is different, but it does not matter. He is just an elf, as conceited as any other, but he doesn't talk much, a blessing on a voyage where we have no privacy for anything at all, and every slight is magnified a thousand times.

We will be so busy tomorrow, however, that we will forget our petty thoughts. As soon as we see light through the portholes, Pate and Dromel will work the propeller crank as I steer with the fins, and our deepswimmer will rise and move toward the island's shore. Our little adventure will finally begin.

What will happen then and what we will see not even the new magic users, the mystics, could tell us. If we survive, we might be famous, wildly famous, and possibly rich beyond imagining.

Yet I wonder if this is likely. This voyage was a fool's gamble from the start. Dromel knows it better than I do, I believe, but he always spouts childish optimism, plainly hiding his true fears. We might find nothing here but death. We might have only a few heartbeats left to us after we reach the shore. We might not even have the time to scream.

I wonder what that will be like, to have never existed. Time for sleep. More cheerful notes later.

Day 12, morning

Twig awoke us at dawn. I moved my stiff legs and grunted from the pain that ran through them. I cannot bear to be cramped in this mobile tomb any longer. The air is foul, even with the air tube, and I fear I would kill to escape confinement. Today must be the day we leave, no matter what awaits us.

Little Pate, mumbling unintelligibly, worked on the reflecting tube as the rest of us ate our miserable breakfast rations. To our astonishment, he managed to un-jam the gearbox, and he carefully ratcheted the long reflecting tube up to the surface, so we could view our surroundings. This gave me some concern, as I thought perhaps that shadow wights, if any were hovering in the air above us, could pass through the tube and enter our deepswimmer, destroying us easily in our marvelous undersea prison. No such event occurred, a point in Dromel's favor. Perhaps shadow wights truly do not move about in broad daylight, as he stated. I can only hope his wisdom and our luck hold out.

Pate turned the reflecting tube from side to side, then twisted the lens to enhance the focus. He froze, staring with a wide eye into the tube's lens.

We said nothing, dreading the news. Pate slowly drew back from the reflecting tube and motioned Dromel to view. Without warning, Twig thrust herself into line first and put her eye to the lens before anyone could say a word. Dromel shouted angrily at her, but she would not be budged.

"I don't see *anyone*," she complained. "They must be off somewhere fishing. We will just have to look inside those ratty little houses to find out when they're coming home."

It was a moment more before the impact of her words stuck the rest of us. We surged toward the reflecting tube to see the coast of Enstar for ourselves.

Few written records or spoken tales tell of the folk who once lived on the small, southern island of Enstar or its smaller companion, Nostar. We have excellent maps of them made by sailors over many centuries, and these maps show the usual features: villages and towns, roads and paths, legendary sites, a few small harbors. Most inhabitants were surely humans, but few were at all famous, and the islands merited little attention over the course of many centuries.

No records exist today to tell us what became of these people after the Chaos War, three decades ago. No one is known to have ever gone to Enstar and returned to report. However, mystics and scholars murmur disturbing theories about the possible fate of the island people once the shadow wights arrived. Gone, they say, the people are gone. Not fled, not living on the mainland or other islands under assumed names—just gone. The shadow wights did it, tales say, but of course there is no proof, as Dromel once said.

When I finally looked through the reflecting tube to the surface, I clearly saw the remains of a dock and three stone cottages, minus their roofs, on the not-too-distant shore. A half-collapsed barn stood farther behind them with a crude wooden fence before it. A light wind stirred the wild brown grass around the ruins. The eerie scene strained my nerves.

"That old map was right!" said Dromel. His face was pale, but he was ecstatic. "We found the correct fishing village, and Lord Dwerlen's manor should be just a couple miles away! We made it! We did it!"

The din from the others was almost unbearable, especially from the shrieking Twig, but thankfully it was brief. I share their excitement, but it would be unseemly to display it. In a short while we will set foot on Enstar, the first people since the Chaos War known to do so. At last I will be free of this wretched floating coffin, thanks be to the world.

Dromel is about to hand out the relics that will, with any luck, keep us safe while we explore this lost realm. We each receive one dragonlance head, fastened to a chain necklace. Dromel assures us that if shadow wights are about, the nightmare beings will be kept at a safe distance by the magical radiation from the spearheads. Twig constantly pesters Dromel with questions about our safety, which Dromel states is absolute. She asks about this every day, probably because the subject of the shadow wights distresses him so much and for some perverse reason she likes that. I like to see him so distressed, too, as I had warned him about kender as crew before we left.

I will write more from the shore if I am able. If I am not . . . it will not matter, and no one will care.

Day 12, midday
I have a few minutes to pass. It is about noon and warm. We are lucky that the sky is clear, though it is windy. We will retreat if clouds come up, as any such darkness would make it easy for shadow wights to travel about. We are in the abandoned village, a few hundred feet in from the shore. All that is left of the place are stone walls and fallen timbers from the roofs. Pate digs for treasure as I write this, using an old shovel we found though he is too short to use it properly. He has found nothing in an hour of digging. He keeps tripping over the dragonlance he is wearing, and he mutters complaints about the length of the chain, how it tangles his feet, and how unnecessary it is with no obvious threat in view. He threatens to take the chain and dragonlance off, though he has been warned he would be a fool to do so. I have enough reservations to keep my own relic safely around my neck.

Twig found a few cheap rings and necklaces, and she has probably found more hidden away but we won't know until we empty her pockets and pouches tonight on the deepswimmer. She finds only worthless things for the most part, and these she keeps anyway. I am bored with throwing aside debris, looking for little trinkets. We await word from Hunter, who is off seeking a trail to the manor of this Lord Dwerlen, whoever he was. Dromel has not been very forthcoming about this, chattering on only about treasure. He is exploring along the shore, patiently awaiting Hunter's return.

The village was once full of fishermen, this we believe. Maybe twelve families lived here. Scattered bits of old clothing can be seen in bushes, in cracks between stones, under logs. No bones anywhere. The place smells as if no human or elf has been here in years. I put one of the pieces of cloth to my muzzle and inhaled slowly. It smelled only like cloth, almost clean of sweat, perfume, or rot. I dropped it and wrinkled my muzzle. It disturbs me profoundly to think of it, even now. If this was once a thriving village, where are the bodies? Something should be left behind. Maybe everyone did flee the island, as I had always believed. Perhaps there are no shadow wights, or at least, none left.

Dromel is calling to us from the shore. I will write more later.

Day 12, midafternoon

Dromel has found five long fishing boats hidden in a shallow cave about three hundred feet to the left of the footpath leading up from the beach to the village. I started to walk into the cave, stooping over, when Dromel screamed, "Don't go into shadows!" He became overwrought in an instant.

I had forgotten. It seemed like a foolish precaution, but Dromel has read widely, so I consented and stayed out in the sunlight. When he had recovered, Dromel said he thinks it possible that shadow wights can inhabit any area in shadow, as they are believed to move about at night and settle in before dawn.

Twig found a decayed rope in the sand leading to one boat, and I seized it and pulled the boat out with ease before the old rope snapped. We then examined the boat, which was cracked through by the elements and no longer seaworthy. Dry seaweed clung to it, perhaps left by a storm wave that came up the beach. The other boats seem to be disordered within the cave, as if tossed about, but of course I cannot investigate. They are far back in the dark.

Twig looked through some old rags in the bottom of the boat. She found two sandals made from tree bark and twine, a seashell necklace, and what appear to be rotted trousers—no bones or other disquieting mementos. She kept the seashell necklace. I sifted through the remainder and found a complex steel bracelet and a decayed pouch of worn silver coins of an unfamiliar make. I gave them to Dromel for packing. We are not doing too badly now, though steel coins would be better.

We are waiting now on the beach for Hunter to return. Twig is chattering about fools she's known on sea voyages. Dromel is stretched out in the sun, seemingly asleep. Pate walked off to see the ruined cottages once more for himself. I do not look forward to packing the five of us aboard our little undersea ship again, but at least we have aired out our ship and ourselves for a few hours. I think the others find my body odor far worse than they do each other's. They probably think it is like an animal's, like cattle maybe. It would figure. Hunter gets utterly filthy and never notices it; Dromel is a compulsive washer but has foul breath. Our smallest companion is always spotted with oil from working with the deepswimmer's machinery. He—

Someone is shouting from the ruins. It sounds like P—

That was strange. I had a moment of confusion, probably from the day's tension and exertions. I cannot remember what I was going to write. Strange.

We are going to call it a day and board the deepswimmer before evening falls. I do not look forward to packing the four of us aboard our little undersea ship again, but at least we will smell more tolerable for a short while. Time to close until I continue tonight on the sea bottom.

Day 12, evening

We waded out to the deepswimmer and got aboard without incident, before twilight came. We have survived our first day on Enstar. I wonder what we did right. I wonder if we did anything wrong.

There was a curious incident once we were aboard. I remember that the air in the deepswimmer had an alien smell to it, though at first I did not mention this to my comrades, being unsure of the cause. Twig then went in search of a change of clothing, and while rummaging in the rear of the cabin brought out a dirty blanket and a cloth bag filled with small garments. None of it looked familiar to me; it seemed to be of human make, but sized for a child or a gnome. Dromel and Hunter frowned, examining the clothing in detail. Neither claimed it was his own. It certainly wasn't mine.

Out of curiosity, I pressed one of the items, a shirt, to my nostrils and inhaled. I did it again, then held the shirt up to my eyes in the dim phosphor light. It did not smell like any of the four of us, and the scent was fresh and strong, less than a day old. That was not possible unless—

"Someone has been aboard the deepswimmer while we were out," I said.

The other three were stunned. "The hatch was sealed," said Dromel, looking around. His face was notably paler even in the faint phosphor glow.

I tossed the shirt aside and grabbed for the dirty blanket, jerking it from Twig's fingers. "Hey, I was looking at that, you big buffalo!" she yelled. I ignored her protests and pressed the blanket to my muzzle, then inhaled deeply.

"It was a gnome," I said, sifting quickly through the odors. "A male gnome, who had machine oil on him. He has eaten our food." I drew back from the blanket. That gnome's scent was the alien element I had detected in the air when we had come aboard.

I moved slowly around the deepswimmer cabin, smelling the walls, the floor, and the machinery. The others moved out of my way, watching me.

"He was here among us," I said. "He has been among us for days." There was only one explanation, I thought. The gnome must have been invisible. We could not possibly have missed him. A gnome is not *that* small, and a tinker gnome would not know how to hide himself even if he had a book on the subject.

"A *gnome*?" shouted Twig. "A *gnome* got into our deep-swimmer?"

Hunter said nothing, only looking carefully around the cabin with his right hand on the long-bladed forester's knife sheathed at his side.

"A gnome," said Dromel. He seemed about to say something else, but fell silent instead. He looked down at the small, ragged pair of trousers in his hands.

"We'd better see if he took anything while he was here," said Hunter, with only a brief glance at Twig. "We could be missing valuables."

"Oh," said Dromel loudly. He smacked himself on the forehead. "I *am* an idiot. Please forgive me. *Nothing* is wrong."

"What? Nothing's wrong?" asked Twig in astonishment. "Someone sneaked aboard our deepswimmer and nothing is—"

Dromel waved his hands about, cutting the kender off. "Nothing is wrong at all," he said, with some exasperation. "No one sneaked aboard. This is probably my fault. I brought a few extra items aboard before we left. I wanted some extra clothing in case of emergencies, and I bought a load from the first person I saw, someone in the dock market, a peddler. I bet these are from that batch. She must have gotten them from a gnome. I never checked. That was foolish of me. I forgot all about it in the excitement."

There was a little silence here, broken by Hunter. He sighed with a trace of disgust. "Understandable," he said, making it clear that he would never have committed the same mistake. He took his hand from the grip of his knife and rubbed his face.

"Ooooohh." Twig was plainly disappointed. "So no one sneaked aboard? We're here all by ourselves?" Her eyes darted about the cabin, hoping to pick out the intruder and prove Dromel wrong. There was no one around but us, however.

I stared at Dromel, but he avoided my gaze. "We'd best get some sleep while we can," he said, his voice imitating confidence. "Tomorrow's going to be another day, and maybe the lucky one for us." He wadded up the small pair of trousers and tossed it behind him into the rear of the cabin, without a second glance.

I watched Dromel at the propeller crank, trying to lower the deepswimmer. He struggled with it in vain before asking for assistance. "I must have gotten weaker since we got here," he said. "It was easier the first time."

I turned the crank with one hand, with little effort. The *Mock Dragon Turtle* settled comfortably onto the sea bottom once more with a dull thump.

"We're safe down here, right?" asked Twig. "I mean, those old shadow ghosts can't find us here. That's what you told us, right?" She had no trace of fear in her voice, only natural kender curiosity—and an innocent desire to irritate.

"*Perfectly* safe," responded Dromel curtly. "Shadow wights cannot get to us here."

"Because they hate water, right?" continued Twig. "You said that those shadow ghosts don't seem to like water, maybe because they're cold inside and might freeze solid and get stuck that way. You said they hate fire, too, but we can't burn anything on the deepswimmer or we'll burn up, too. Best of all, the shadow ghosts don't even know we're here, they can't see us down here at all, and that's why we have a deepswimmer, so—"

Dromel's face betrayed his anger. "We are perfectly safe here, as I've told you many times," he said, his voice rising. "If we weren't, we would all be dead now. They would have killed us the first night we were here."

Twig's face screwed up in concentration. "I thought you said they didn't just kill people. You told me they came to Enstar and Nostar during the Chaos War and they made people disappear forever."

Dromel hesitated. He almost glanced toward the back of the cabin, his face radiating anxiety. "They are believed by some authorities to do something like that," he said quietly, "but there is no proof to it. The idea, actually, is that whoever shadow wights touch and slay is forever erased from the minds of the living. It is not just disappearing, it is erasure from all living memory, much worse than mere death. The victim is obliterated, wiped completely from mind and heart, gone, forgotten for all time. The body is evaporated, or turned to vapor, or something equally horrid. Only the . . . the clothing is left."

I thought then of the clothing that Twig found in the fishing boat. Had someone gotten into that boat long ago, foolishly hoping to escape the shadow wights by hiding in shadows?

"Gone," said Twig. She sighed. "That *would* be horrid. I can't imagine anything worse than nothing at all. That would be dreadful!" Her childlike face lit up with triumph. "But we have the *relics*! Relics from the *wars*!"

Dromel was preparing for bed. Hunter looked bored. He curled up at his usual place at the bow and drifted away into his elven reverie, or whatever it was that passed for his sleep.

Twig watched as I took out my diary, but she did not ask to read it. She merely frowned at me, sniffed, then began examining her pouches for her day's haul in little treasures.

I penned this entry, but it is very late. Everyone else is asleep. I stared at Dromel for a long time when I was done. I wonder if he knows or suspects something that he has not said aloud. I wonder if I will be able to sleep at all tonight, thinking about tomorrow.

Day 13, midday

We are ashore again. The weather has been in our favor; it is pleasantly warm, cloudless, and bright. Much has happened already. Hunter spotted an overgrown trail leading inland, one that appeared to have been well used once. We trekked past great fields and abandoned, rusting wagons on the way. Two hours later, we discovered the ruins of what Dromel says was Hovost, a coastal human town much larger than the fishing village. I write this as I sit on a stump outside what must have been the local tavern.

Hovost was once a well-organized and well-populated settlement. I believe two hundred or more families lived here, judging from the long rows of farmhouses lining the weed-covered roads into the town's heart. We swiftly found this tavern, several small temples to the old gods, many barns, and two granaries. Not a living thing stirs. The silence is very unsettling. Not even birds call out from the bushes and trees. Insects are about, but fewer than I would have guessed. I have not even seen a lizard.

Dromel cautioned us again to not enter any buildings. Shadows might house shadow wights, he repeated, and we cannot afford the risk of facing them. Twig appeared bored as he spoke, but Hunter listened gravely. Dromel ordered that we explore in pairs and search for valuables. I found this last comment amusing. Farmers are not commonly known to hoard great wealth.

Twig went with Dromel. Hunter seemed happy to join with me. He has said little on this trip, and at first I thought the elf merited little respect, as he was not a proven fighter. Still, he has never once complained on our trip, and that is worth a snort of respect, if nothing more.

Hunter and I were barely out of sight of the others when a curious thing happened. He spoke to me in a low, even voice. "Red Horn," he said. "Did Dromel ever tell you why you were chosen for this expedition?"

I glanced down at him. He did not look at me but at the weather-damaged buildings we passed instead. "He mentioned it, yes," I replied coolly.

"You are a masterful sailor, it is obvious," said Hunter. "Dromel told me how your advice caused him to alter some aspects of the deepswimmer before we left Merwick. He said you were not like a real minotaur, being easy to work with and trustworthy. It is equally obvious that you are fearless, withstand hardship well, and are far stronger than the rest of us put together. Were those the reasons he said he picked you?"

"What business would it be of yours, tattooed one?"

"None, but I found his selection of me to be curious.

There were few trackers better than I around Merwick, but I had the impression that was not entirely why he selected me. He questioned me about my friends, family, associates, everyone. I almost felt he picked me because I had so few ties, so few connections to anyone—because I was a loner, in short."

I blinked and looked down at the slender elf again. I had never heard an elf who did not instinctively feel he was superior in all ways to everyone else, but the last part of his statement was very unusual.

Interestingly, I thought of myself as a loner, too.

Hunter pointed. "If we are to return with riches, we would do well to look there," he said, the previous subject forgotten. I followed his gaze to a curious building on a distant low hill, visible to us as we rounded a ruined temple. It was a stone structure, probably once a wealthy manor. The roof had fallen in, and half the shutters had been torn loose, possibly by storms.

"I believe there we will find our lost Lord Dwerlen," Hunter said, "or at least what is left of his home."

We stopped to study the building. Hunter turned, taking in the empty town around us. "How long would you say it has been since this place was last inhabited?" he asked in the same even tone.

I had already considered that question. I inhaled slowly, drawing in the full texture of odors the surrounded us. I exhaled and reflected. The scent of humanity was weak, nearly drowned in many seasons of sun, rain, and snow. "A full generation," I said at last, "possibly two."

"Ah," said Hunter. "That would fit with the stories about Chaos and the war. It is told that Chaos drew the shadow wights from the far south and loosed them over these islands that year. If they fed upon these unlucky people, it must have—"

"It is more likely," I interrupted, "that most of the people here fled for other lands once the war began. I cannot believe an entire island of beings would vanish so utterly."

"Unlikely, I agree," said Hunter, unperturbed, "but the

year of the Chaos War was a year of unlikely things. I would add that not one but two islands, this and Nostar, were apparently emptied of many thousands of people, and no trace of them has ever been found."

"None has ever sought them, as far as I know," I growled. I already knew of these tales from Dromel.

"Still, as you say, tales of the Chaos War make it clear that chaos was its primary feature. Many thousands of people could have fled to Southern Ergoth to be later destroyed by the dragon Frost, or westward to be destroyed by his rival Beryl. It would not take much to make an island of farmers take to their boats." I sniffed the air once more, purely for effect.

"All could be as you say," said Hunter. "Yet I have not heard there was ever such a fleet in these impoverished isles as could carry away so many people in such a brief time."

I mulled over his words and the impertinence of his tone. If I were to strike him with a roundhouse blow, he would likely be dead before his body hit the ground. My right arm tightened, and the clawed fingers of my broad right hand curled into a knotted fist. He would barely have time to see it coming.

But . . . only four of us were here, and every hand was a needed one. Perhaps when we returned home to Merwick, there would be time for a proper accounting. Still, my muzzle flushed with shame, and I lowered my head. I was angrier now at myself for my weakness in not settling things before we went farther, but I was not as quick to deal out judgment as the rest of my people were. I could wait a bit before acting.

However, I admitted to myself, Hunter had a point. Too many people had lived on the two islands for all of them to have escaped thusly. It just did not seem possible.

"There was one other thing," continued Hunter. "It was very odd, but as we were walking through the fishing village, I found something near a collapsed cottage. It was lying on the ground, carefully arranged as if someone had put it there on purpose." He started to reach inside his leather vest.

"Let us reflect on that later," I interrupted. "We should get our all-knowing leader and return here if we are to explore that ruin and be out of here before nightfall."

So it would have been, except that we have not been able to find either the entrepreneur or the talkative kender. It is perhaps three hours to nightfall. Hunter has suggested we retreat toward the coast to be certain to get aboard the deepswimmer when twilight is near, and I think his words are wise even if he is just an elf. It is not cowardly, I believe, to live to fight another day. I am not interested in testing my warrior's skills against creatures that cannot be struck by normal weap—

Day 13, night

We are aboard the deepswimmer again. The others are asleep.

The afternoon went well at first for our two comrades. Dromel and Twig found a graveyard and a nearby building where burial preparations took place. The roof was gone, but this allowed them to explore the insides without fear of the shadows and things that might creep within them. Twig discovered a secret place behind a stone wall, a small treasure vault of some sort, and they used long timbers to scrape the treasures out of the darkness within. The materials recovered included a book and many items of jewelry. Dromel thinks the people who prepared the dead here were also thieves who removed valuables that were supposed to be buried with their owners. It is not unknown for this to happen among humans. The rotting book is a kind of accounting ledger, in which the treasures are cataloged with estimated prices in old Ansalonian steel pieces, the dates they were acquired, and from whom. Most thorough, these robbers of the dead. Dromel brought back most of the valuables, which were stored in a large sack strapped to his back.

As Dromel and Twig were leaving the building thus laden, they were accosted by a shadow wight.

Twig will not speak of the incident. She is not herself tonight, and her injured foot causes her much pain. Before we boarded, Hunter gathered a few plants that he said were painkilling herbs, and their ministration has let her sleep for a time. She clutched in desperation at anyone who was near her until her eyes closed.

Dromel told Hunter and me what happened after Twig was unconscious. The shadow wight was in a small shadowed area behind a pile of debris from the long-fallen roof. The debris formed a dark space against the wall by the doorway through which they had entered the ruin. Twig saw the horrible being first and cried out in fear. Dromel said he had never heard a kender make a cry like that. He had difficulty describing the shadow wight's appearance; he had previously said shadow wights could change their shape to fit whatever the viewer found the most disturbing. He vaguely referred to this one as a dead thing and added that it spoke to them both. Dromel was not able to go further. He buried his face in his hands and wept for many minutes.

A display like that from a human would normally bore me. Instead, I found it disturbing in the extreme, and it preys on my mind even now. Dromel had struck me as immune to deep emotions, always a source of false cheer and well-meaning lies, an eggshell without a yolk. Hunter comforted him as much as he was able. I kept to myself, pretending to inspect the dirt-covered platinum rings, steel coins, and silver combs that we now possess, though I feel increasingly numb to their value.

Upon meeting the shadow wight, Dromel and Twig fled the ruined building. At some point, Twig fell off a ledge or stumbled over a rock, spraining her left ankle. Dromel's account was confusing; I had the impression he was covering up for not having gone back right away to aid Twig. Indeed, I myself heard Twig's cries for help as I was finishing my previous journal entry. I caught Dromel alone, asked him where Twig was, and had to go back myself to find her and carry her to the deepswimmer. We had no encounters of any sort on the way. Twig was hysterical, alternating between depressed crying and an unnatural excitement like panic. Both she and Dromel often clutched at the dragonlances on their necklaces, which seemed to provide them with comfort.

It is uncertain what we will do tomorrow. Twig is starting to talk in her sleep. Among her stammerings she has cried, "Don't touch me!" and repeats the word "empty" and "nothing" over and over.

I cannot neglect to mention one last incident. Before Hunter went into his reverie, he reached into his vest and pulled out a dragonlance spearhead on a chain, holding it up for me to see. I looked closely and noticed that he was wearing a second one just like it.

"Where did you get the extra one?" I asked. "Did you steal it from Dromel?"

Hunter gave me a smile he would give to a fool. "O trusting one, I did not. This is what I was going to tell you about earlier. It is the thing I found outside a hut in the fishing village. There were footprints leading up to it and away from it, going into the ruins near some shadows. Someone else came here not long before us, and that person had the same idea we did, taking an old magical relic like ours to keep away the shadow wights. Only this person was not smart enough to keep the relic on him at all times."

I looked long at the dragonlance head. A small shiver ran through me. "We will not make that mistake," I said sincerely.

"I agree," he replied. "It is a shame about the fellow who had this one. Judging from the size of the footprints, I believe he may have been a gnome."

Day 14, late morning

Awakening and breakfast were conducted without discussion. Hunter eventually revealed his find to the others, who found it very odd that someone with a dragonlance necklace remarkably like ours had been in the area before. We decided it must have been the gnome

Gone

who had stowed away on our deepswimmer. His fate could not have been a pleasant one, we agreed. Dromel then cleared his throat.

"I am not sure it would be . . ." He broke off in a fit of coughing before continuing. "I was saying, I am not sure we should go back to the . . . um . . ."

"No," said Twig suddenly. She brushed hair from her face, looking Dromel in the eye. "I think we should. We should go back." Her voice was clear and calm. We stared at her in amazement.

"Your leg," said Hunter, pointing.

Twig shifted and stretched her legs out experimentally. She grimaced but shrugged it off. "I'm fine now, really. I don't think I could stand to be stuck in here while you were out exploring and having fun. We'll just . . . stay out of dark places."

Until that moment, I had not believed kender were worth the spit from a gully dwarf. I looked at her rather differently now. She talked like a warrior.

"There is a stone manor house," I said. "It's on a hill—"

"What?" Dromel's earlier anxiety faded a bit. "What did it look like?"

"Two stories high, with a central tower," said Hunter. "It is about a mile beyond the far side of the town." He smiled. "Isn't that what we're looking for?"

Dromel swallowed and nodded. "I . . . yes, of course. Of course, that's Lord Dwerlen's manor. We would find wealth enough for us all there. We *should* go back then, you know. We would be fools to come this far and not to get his money."

Perhaps it was his stuttering or the trembling of his hands that told me he was holding back.

"Who was this Lord Dwerlen?" I asked, leaning close to him. "You haven't told us about him. I want to know."

"L-Lord Dwerlen was just a . . . a tax collector or something for—"

I had my right hand around his throat in a second. *"Don't lie to me, damn you!"*

"Red!" Twig screamed. "Don't hurt him!"

"Tell me the truth," I whispered in Dromel's face. "Who was Lord Dwerlen? Why have you been so determined to find his place?"

"H-H-H-He was . . . a c-cartographer!" Dromel gasped, turning red. "I w-wanted m-m-maps!"

I released his throat. He fell back, inhaling hoarsely. "A mapmaker," I repeated. "You talked us into coming here for a bunch of maps?"

Dromel hesitated, then nodded, watching me with wide eyes. "He was rich," he wheezed. "He had every sort of map known. He retired to Enstar from the mainland decades ago, before the Chaos War."

I leaned away from him, relaxing. This sounded like the truth, more or less—not that I still wasn't thinking about killing him.

"So there's no treasure there, no coins or jewels, only maps," I said.

"No, that isn't it!" Dromel fairly shouted. "No, I think there is treasure there, tons of it, but as for me, what I really want is the maps. I've got to have the maps!" He took a shuddering breath. "The rest of you can divide what iron pieces we bring out, but I want the maps. Please."

"Well, I like maps, too," said Twig. "How about if—"

"You can have the maps, Dromel," I interrupted.

"Hey!" Twig fairly shouted.

"Shut up," I said, still looking at Dromel. "But I want to know why you want those maps, and not just half the story."

Dromel swallowed. "I like maps," he said.

I knew there was more to it, but I decided to be patient. Soon enough I would see the maps for myself. I already had a fair idea of what he had in mind. "Fine. So they're yours. The rest is ours to divide, but there had better be plenty of treasure there, as you've said all along."

"We may have to go indoors," said Hunter softly. "It may be dark in there. There may be more shadow wights around."

Twig shuddered violently. She wrapped her arms around her as if for warmth. "We have the relics," she said softly, "but we should not go indoors unless we can't help it. I'm still here and breathing, so the things obviously work, just as you said they would, right? We can go where we want if we have to, just not for long."

She was getting braver by the minute. She was a warrior after all.

"Is anyone good at locks?" said Dromel, rubbing his throat carefully, avoiding any looks at me. "I figure we'll need to get through some doors to reach whatever his lordship had for a vault."

Hunter wore an enigmatic smile. "I am." He held up a dragonlance spearhead. "I can use the tip of this if necessary."

We left the deepswimmer within the hour. I must finish this entry, as we have finished our rest break outside Dwerlen's stone manor and are preparing to enter. The weather has held for us so far on our trip, and the sky is clear. No clouds, no shadow wights. It is close to noon. My next entry will either find us triumphant or doomed. I wish I knew the outcome, but I do not.

Day 14, evening

We have built a great fire. We are burning everything in the town we can find. There is no time to get back to the deepswimmer before the sun is gone. No time to—

Day 15, evening

My hand is not as steady as it once was. It feels like it has been a year since I last opened this diary. I barely remember what I wrote only a day ago. My memory is riddled with fog.

Twig and Dromel are sleeping, their lips stained green from chewing painkiller herb. The dark red hair across my right arm, between my wrist and elbow, has turned silver-white in a splash shape. I feel nothing there; all sensation has been lost, as if the nerves were sliced through. The fingers on my great right hand tremble, and my handwriting is like a dying elder's.

I have only a bare recollection of what transpired when the three of us passed through the old entry arch into the stone manor. I remember the roof had caved in, partly, so there was some light. We cleared the doorway to make sure nothing would block our hasty retreat. Inside was a small greeting hall, with open doorways to a dining hall and several darker workrooms and store-rooms beyond. We lit two torches each, one per hand, and went in. Weapons were worthless here, though we took them with us anyway. Only fire had a chance of driving a shadow wight back here—fire and our relics.

I am not sure what went on after that. I have a con-fused memory of roofless rooms and rubble-choked passages, and a narrow stone staircase leading up to a missing second floor. We wandered farther, aimlessly, until we found a broad stairway descending to a great set of old, locked doors. It was a vault. We had found our riches.

Otherwise we had seen nothing of value in the ruined manor. The doors at the bottom beckoned. Like moths to a furnace flame, we responded.

My memory is not what it once was. I do not remem-ber who opened the doors, though I suspect it was Twig, as kender are all thieves, even those with warrior hearts.

Once inside, we were exploring the room when Dromel cried out. It startled us all, but he was unharmed. He had found a seaman's chest. He flung the lid open before we could utter a warning, and his hands carefully pulled forth long rolls of aged paper, preserved in the cel-lar over the decades. He did not explain to us what they were, but I knew he had probably found what he had actually come here for—the map collection of Lord Dwerlen. Dromel was no fool. A good map was worth more than steel. So many of the old maps had been lost in the Chaos War, so many cities and libraries burned, so many guilds gutted and ruined, that a single good map of our world was invaluable. Dromel swiftly put as many maps as possible into a sack that he tied to his back. One in particular made him cry out with delight when he found it, and this one he tucked into his shirt. He even allowed Twig to take a few after he had gathered his fill.

The rest of us were wasting time, and the end of the day was approaching. At the far end of the great underground room was another locked door. Again, one of us worked on the lock, though it resisted easy opening. I still have a strangely clear memory of standing in the room near the stairs out, keeping guard with my torches, hearing nothing but the moaning wind above in the fallen stones and walls. Cobwebs covered the dark timber ceiling. I remember thinking, this is a bad place to be. We should move on.

The bright warm sunlight falling on the stairs going down to us suddenly disappeared, and a chill flowed down through the air.

A great cloud had covered the sun. We had not been paying attention to the weather.

I turned to shout at my comrades. I was too late.

The shadow wights had waited for this to happen. They fell upon us like night.

I wrote the above lines and have done nothing else but stare at the page for a great while. My right arm tingles in a peculiar way around the area where the hair has turned white. I feel pain there, though not a normal pain. I wonder if the skin and bone are dead. I wonder if I will die soon.

A shadow wight came down the stairs at me. It spoke as it reached for me. I will never write down what it looked like or what it said to me. I struck at it clumsily with the torch, and my arm passed through its own outstretched arm by accident. I believe I screamed. I had never felt such pain as I did then. As I fell back, I saw one of the shadow wight's arms pass through the wall at the bottom of the stairs, as if the wall was not real and the shadow wight was. Even in my agony I remember thinking, it moves so smoothly, like water flowing. It approached me again, and I hurled both torches into its face.

I have no idea if the fire did any harm to the thing. I have no idea what happened after that. I ran, though. I ran, and I should be ashamed, but shame is such an irrelevant, trivial thing. Running was all there was left to do. Shadow wights blacker than darkness came through the doors at the far side of the room, through the floor, down from the ceiling. I remember that I grabbed for Twig, as she was closest to me. It is strange I grabbed for Twig, as only a minotaur warrior is worth saving, and she is only a kender, but I caught her up and ran for the stairs.

Many shadow wights had gathered around the stairway to block our flight. They were all around us, an army of black-smoke figures that reached for me but did not make contact. I believe I was quite insane for a time. The memory of this presses hard on my mind.

I remember Dromel had a dragonlance spearhead on a chain in his hands, and another around his neck, and I hissed, "Where did you get an extra one?" The question seemed to startle him, and he stared at it in his hand. "I thought you . . . or someone . . . dropped it back there," he said. Dromel swung the chain around his head, screaming as he did. He struck at a group of shadow wights, and they fell back from him, dissolving into nothing.

The chain. The dragonlance head. I remember looking around the room and seeing another, stuck into the lock in the doors across the underground room. Someone had left it there, perhaps while picking the lock. It was the kender's fault, I thought, and I charged for it and snatched it out. I put Twig in my left arm, and I began swinging the newfound dragonlance on the chain, swinging it at the other shadow wights. They fell back. I charged for the stairs out. They fled before me, their feet never touching the ground.

It was almost sundown. Dromel, Twig, and I ran into the open for Hovost, the town near the lord's ruined manor, and there we made our stand. As the sun fell below the horizon, I started a fire. We got a tremendous bonfire roaring and fed it with every stick of wood we could find. We burned everything that could burn, and the yellow flames crackled and snapped high in the black sky, holding back the army of darkness.

All around us, the shadow wights gathered and waited until they numbered in the hundreds, perhaps the thousands. They spoke to us. I clamped my hands over Twig's ears to shut it out of her mind, but she screamed and screamed again as they spoke. I remember looking around until I found a kind of plant that I once heard would kill pain and cause sleep. I made Twig eat that plant, and she screamed less, then collapsed. I wrapped my extra dragonlance and chain around her body to protect her. No monster would touch her then.

I had nothing to keep the words of the shadow wights out of my own ears, nothing to keep them out of my head. They urged us to come out, to join them. Dromel and I listened to them all that night long, and no one heard us scream but ourselves.

I do not remember how we got back to the deepswimmer. All I know is that we are here, and though we are probably safe, it comforts me not.

Day??

I have no idea what day this is. Twig and I have remained inside the deepswimmer, though only I have been conscious of late. I fed Twig too much of that painkilling plant earlier, and she continues to sleep without waking. I do not remember why we are waiting, or how long we have been doing so. I remember only that we two came to Enstar to get rich. Twig had some maps, I believe, and we got this deepswimmer, though I do not recall how we got it. I think Twig had a lot to do with things, as I do not remember setting up the trip myself. My head is clouded with the words of the shadow wights, urging me to join them. I was one of them, they said, one of the worthless. They told me to lay aside my dragonlance and join them. When I did so, I would be free.

It is difficult to write. I have never been under such a malady as covers me now. A melancholy has crept into my body and spirit, and tears fall from my eyes. I was a fool to come here.

Day??

I am more lucid now, though not by much. I found a curious thing by my side when I awoke this morning. It was a note, written in the common language. I have no idea how long it has been sitting beside me. Twig must have written it, though she is still unconscious and very pale. Perhaps she woke up while I was asleep, too.

The note says:

Red Horn,

I cannot resist the cry of the shadow wights. I do not have your willpower. I am going out to shore. I am sorry for lying to you. I chose you because you had no ties in Merwick, so if our adventure went awry, your absence would not be missed. I believe we may have arrived here with others in our deepswimmer, but they were lost to the shadow wights. I cannot be sure how many came with us, but their blood is on me, and I must atone for their destruction. I wish only that I knew who I wronged. I still remember you and the kender. I remember no one else. I have left my maps behind for you and Twig to use. I found Lord Dwerlen's Grand Map of Krynn, which had been lost for many years. He had sailed far and knew much that was lost of late. I heard many great tales of him in the memories of those who had met him, and could thus know to seek his greatest treasure. I had meant to build a fleet such as the world had never seen with what I found, as these maps would today buy a kingdom. But they mean nothing to me now, and I am ashamed for bringing you here to your doom. I beg your forgiveness. I must surface and go. The relics will keep you safe. I leave you mine, it is meaningless to me now.

Use the maps to find your own dreams. A book on the operation of this deepswimmer is in the stern, under the rations box. Please, Red Horn, remember me in your diary, and speak my name to the world, even if no one else remembers me, and I am lost forever.

—Dromel

A strange note. I tucked it into my diary. Twig must have been raving when she wrote it. I wish I could sleep. The voices of the shadow wights still whisper inside my head, and their words grow louder every moment. It is too much to try to get the deepswimmer going. I will shake free of this evil influence, this awful sadness that grips me, and start the deepswimmer tomorrow. We have already begun floating away from Enstar toward the open sea.

Day??

I must go. There is nothing left to live for. Twig has not awakened. I fear she may die of poisoning from the painkilling plants. It is my fault. I leave her my relic, all the relics that remain. Her body will be safe. She has a warrior's heart, and the shadow wights will never claim her for oblivion so long as she wears the dragonlances. Me, alas, whose soul was bled by foolishness within and darkness without, the shadows can have.

* * * * *

Day 1

Wow! What a great story! Wish I knew who wrote this. It must have been a present for me, since I'm in the story, but I have no idea who would have done it. Someone's got a great imagination.

I must have really tied one on a few days ago, because I have no idea what I am doing inside this weird boat. I must have borrowed it to take it out for a cruise or something. My head is killing me; this must be the worst hangover ever. No more redberry wine for me, that's for sure. I looked outside through the portholes, and there's nothing anywhere but water. I think I remember running around on an island looking for stuff, and there were monsters that looked like empty things inside busted buildings, but that's about it. What a tragedy! Here I've probably had an adventure, and I can't remember it. It would be a great story to tell back in Merwick.

I've been keeping myself busy reading a manual I found on how this boat thing works, and I think I know what to do. I think I remember seeing this boat thing at Fenshal & Sons. Maybe if I take it back, they won't be mad at me, and I can show them some of the great maps I found inside here. One of them looks like a map of the whole world of Krynn! It's incredible! I bet I could buy a fleet with that map, but of course I won't because it is much too interesting to part with, like these five spearhead necklaces I found around my neck. I wonder if they're really dragonlances. I seem to remember hearing somewhere that they were. Wouldn't that be a hoot!

I'm going to get cleaned up. I smell like a barn floor, and my mouth tastes like one, too. Then I'm going to figure out this boat, and then I'm gone. I want to see the world of Krynn, explore it and master it, live free as the gulls on the high seas, just like whoever wrote the stuff in this storybook said he wanted to do. I might make up my own story and write it down here, too, and maybe it would get published and I would become famous. It would be nice to do something that everyone could remember me by.

To Convince the Righteous of the Right
Margaret Weis and Don Perrin

The snowstorm blew itself out. For the first time in two days, the sun shone. The sun was pale and thin, as if it were a parchment sun set against a gray flannel sky, but it was a sun, and it was warm.

Seeing the sun sparkle on the snow like scales from a silver dragon, the troop of draconians left the shelter of the trees and, moving as a single body—a single, well-disciplined body—the draconians passed from the shadows into the wintry light. Weak though it was, the sunlight was welcome to the draconians. They flapped their wings to rid themselves of the horrible white fluffy stuff, they lifted their faces to the sunshine, basked in its warmth. Blood that had been sluggish as frozen swamp water began to flow again. One soldier tossed a snowball at another, and war was declared. Soon snowballs filled the air thicker than snowflakes, the draconians hooting and shouting.

Concerned at this breach of discipline, the officers looked worriedly at their commander, but Kang only grinned and waved a clawed hand. Let the men enjoy themselves for a few moments at least. They'd had little enough to enjoy these past few weeks.

The only draconians not involved in the snowball fight were those wearing the fur-lined knapsacks containing the treasure, the most valuable treasure ever to come to the draconians, a treasure that would be the salvation of their dying race. Small squeaks and the occasional squall could be heard coming from the knapsacks; a snout thrust out of the flap of one, snuffling the air. The baby female draconians felt the warmth of the sun. Perhaps, hearing the laughter, they wanted to join in the fun, but Kang worried that even with the sunshine, the air was still too chilly to allow the babies out in the open.

The babies were growing, they'd doubled in size during the five months since the draconians had rescued them from Mount Celebundin. The draconians and Kang in particular were extraordinarily protective of the little ones. The young were rarely permitted to leave their snug womblike knapsacks. The babies were intensely curious, they had no sense of danger or self-preservation, they viewed everyone as a friend. The one day he had permitted the young to be set loose, he'd regretted it.

Once outside the protective confines of the knapsacks, the young stood on wobbly legs, looked at everything with their bright eyes, and immediately took off in forty different directions. Kang was astonished. He had no idea little draconians could move that fast. Within seconds, the babies were into everything—rummaging through the rations, leaving slashing claw marks on the waterskins, tumbling headfirst into the creek. One sought to make acquaintance with a skunk with disastrous, odiferous consequences. Another baby cut her foot on a spear and wailed as if she had been impaled, sending the adult draconians into a panic until they eventually discovered that the wound was completely superficial.

After that the worst happened. They took a count, discovered one of the babies missing. The entire army turned the woods upside down searching for the young female. They found her at last, curled up sound asleep beneath an overturned shield. By the end of the day, Kang felt as though he had aged a hundred years. It had been the worst day of his life, and that counted innumerable battles against humans, dwarves, and elves. Compared to looking after these children, a fight with a mighty gold dragon seemed an idyllic respite. He vowed that from then on, the babies would be kept under close confinement and careful watch.

For the sixth hundredth and seventy-first time, Kang wondered if he'd made the right decision, taking the babies on this long journey. For the sixth hundred and seventy-second time, his inner self came back wearily with, "What else could you do? You couldn't stay in the valley. You tried to live peacefully among the other races, and it didn't work. Best to find a place of your own, far from the rest of civilization where you can retire from the world and its lunacy, make a home, raise your families."

Squatting on his haunches in the snow, Kang reached for the map pouch. He pulled out a well-worn map, hunched over it, studied it.

"I doubt if the city's moved, sir," said Gloth, peering over his shoulder. "Nope, there it is." He pointed a claw.

"Right where it was yesterday. And the day before yesterday. And the day before that—"

"Very funny," Kang growled. He spread his wings, so that Gloth couldn't see, and gazed at the map.

It had been drawn by dwarves, and he had to admit that the little creeps could do two things well in this world: make dwarf spirits and draw maps. He located the dot that marked the draconians' destination, their future, their hopes. A ruined city, abandoned, probably for good reason, for it was near Neraka, the former capital of the evil empire of Queen Takhisis. The dwarves reported that the city was filled with all sorts of terrible beings: undead, ghouls, skeletal warriors, perhaps even kender. What terrified dwarves, though, might not be so terrifying to draconians.

Whoever chased out the current inhabitants would have a ready-made city. All it would take would be a little fixing up, and Kang and his engineers were experts in that. The dot had taken on such importance that it seemed to glow every time he looked at it. He had known the trail would be difficult, for it led through the Khalkist

Mountains, but he had not expected the snows, which were early for this time of year. Kang leaned back, flexed his wings.

A buzz like an angry wasp—except that no self-respecting wasp would be out in this weather—ripped through the map. Had Kang been leaning forward, as he had been just a split second earlier, the arrow would have torn through a wing, come to rest in his skull. As it was, Gloth was staring stupidly at an arrow lodged in his thick, muscular thigh.

"Take cover!" Kang shouted. "We're under attack!"

The draconians acted with alacrity, their playful fight forgotten. Those carrying the young sought the shelter of the woods, their comrades fanning out to cover them. More arrows sliced through the winter air, some finding their marks to judge by the yells.

"You bozaks! Stay clear of the young!" Kang shouted.

The bodies of all draconians are lethal to their killers. The baaz turn to stone, entrapping the weapon that had killed them. Others turn to pools of acid. When a bozak draconian dies, he effects revenge on his killer. His bones explode, killing or maiming anything in the vicinity. The draconians entrusted with the babies were baaz, who changed to stone.

Kang reached out, jerked the arrow from Gloth's leg. A trickle of blood followed, but due to the draconian's scales, the arrow had done little damage. The story would have been different if that arrow had found its target— Kang's skull. He and the wounded Gloth sought shelter in the trees.

Kang studied the bloody arrow closely and swore bitterly. "Slith!" he yelled, hunkering down. "Where's Slith?"

"Here, sir!" Slith came sliding and slipping through the snow.

"Who's attacking us?" Kang demanded.

"Goblins, sir," said Slith, looking apologetic.

"I thought you said we'd left those bastards behind!"

"I thought we had, sir," said Slith. "We left their lands two days ago! Sir," he said, lowering his voice, and dropping down beside his leader, "have you ever known those lazy slugs to leave their warm caves and track an enemy through the snow when he's no longer a threat?"

"We never were a threat!" Kang protested. "I can understand the goblins wanting to protect their own territory, but we told them we were just passing through, and we passed through!"

"Yes, sir," said Slith respectfully. "That's what I mean. Going back to my original question about the goblins, have you known them to be this persistent, sir?"

"No," Kang admitted gloomily. He looked at the arrow he was still carrying, shook it as though it were personally responsible for nearly skewering him. "I haven't seen goblins carry well-crafted arrows like this before."

As if to emphasize his words, another arrow whistled through the tree branches, thunked into the bole of a tree next to where Kang was crouching. An explosion, far off in the woods, told him that one of the bozaks had departed this world.

"You men keep your heads down!" Kang bellowed. He looked worriedly around for the soldiers carrying the young, hoped they'd found adequate cover.

"These aren't ordinary goblins, sir," Slith stated, as he and Kang helped the hobbling Gloth limp farther back among the trees. "I think we have proof now, that these goblins are acting on orders. Someone wants us dead, sir."

"Now there's a surprise!" Kang grunted. "I don't have fingers and toes enough to count everyone who wants us dead."

"Goblins aren't usually among that number, sir," Slith argued. "Goblins are usually on our side. Those who hire them are on our side, if you take my meaning, sir. The cursed Solamnics wouldn't be likely to fund goblin assassins."

"Which means that someone *on our side* wants us dead." Kang was thoughtful. This introduced a totally new aspect to the situation. "But why?" He answered his own question. "The females."

"We're a threat to someone, sir. We know that Queen Takhisis—I spit on her name and her memory"—Slith matched his words with the action—"intended us to die out once we were no longer of any use to her. She feared us, and now it seems that even though she's gone, others fear us, too."

"But who?" Kang demanded impatiently, studying the arrow he was still carrying, like a talisman. "Who even knows about the babies?"

"Those dwarves know, sir, and they're certainly not above selling the information."

"Right," Kang muttered. "I forgot about them, drat their hairy hides. I wonder—"

"Where's the commander?" a voice was shouting.

Draconians hissed and pointed. Whenever a draconian moved, an arrow zipped his direction.

Kang raised up quickly. "Here!" he shouted. An arrow struck his back, lodged in his chain mail armor. Slith plucked it out, broke it in two, and cast it into the snow. Kang hunkered back down.

"Sir!" A draconian slid through the snow, halted beside Kang, bringing a storm of arrows in their direction. The draconians flattened themselves into the snow, waited for the onslaught to pass. "Sir!" the draconian continued, "we've found a large stone building. It's outside the tree cover, in the middle of the plains, about a mile away! It's right out in the open, sir, but the building's good and solid."

"Excellent!" Kang was about to tell his troops to move out.

"There's only one problem, sir."

"What's that?" Kang asked impatiently.

"It's a Temple of Paladine, sir."

A temple of Paladine. Their most implacable enemy. The great god of the righteous on Krynn. In the old days, no draconian would have dared set a claw inside a temple of Paladine. The wrath of the god would have fried the meat from his bones.

"Paladine's gone," said Kang. "From what we hear, he fled the world five months ago along with our cowardly queen."

"What if we heard wrong, sir?" Gloth asked. He had packed his wound with snow, and the bleeding had stopped.

"We'll have to chance it," Kang said. "Slith, you go on ahead, check things out. Take Support Squadron with you."

He could hear shouts, sounds of fighting. The goblins had given up shooting at them from afar and were now attacking.

"Yes, sir!" Slith was up and gone before the archers had a chance to target him.

"Fall back by squadrons," Kang shouted. "Support Squadron first. Gloth, can you hold the line?"

"Yes, sir," Gloth said and began to issue commands.

The wind howled through the sparse copse of trees, kicking up snow from the ground that stung the eyes and half-blinded them. The sound of fighting was far away, but that was a trick of the winter wind. His soldiers, the draconians of the First Dragonarmy Field Engineer Regiment, were only five hundred yards away through the sparse tree cover.

Runners went scrambling across the snow to relay the orders he had just given. Kang hurried to the rear to take a look at the temple himself. He paused in the shelter of the trees, gazed across the plains to the building that would serve as their redoubt. The forward companies were doing an excellent job of keeping the goblins occupied. No arrows back here, not yet—but it would be only a matter of time.

The temple was large with two levels, few windows and those were lead-lined stained glass. A dome surmounted it. The building was made of marble that gleamed whiter than the snow. A wall surrounded the temple. Behind the temple and along the wall were several outbuildings. Kang could just barely see their red-tiled roofs.

The snow wasn't nearly as deep on the plains as it was in the forest. The wind swept the frozen ground clean, sent the snow piling up in drifts in front of the temple wall.

He watched as Slith cautiously approached the temple's holy grounds, which could be just as dangerous to the draconians as goblin arrows. Nothing and no one attacked him. Kang could see no signs of guards on the walls. Slith kicked in the front gate.

Support Squadron, nearly seventy strong, came up behind Kang. He raised a hand, ordered a halt. Support Squadron had been tasked with keeping the young female draconians safe. Every one of them had sworn a blood oath to defend to the death the babies they carried. Fulkth, the Chief Engineer and commander of the squadron, came to stand beside Kang.

"Looks good," he said.

"It's a Temple of Paladine," Kang returned.

Fulkth's long tongue flicked out between his teeth. "Must be nigh unto six hundred goblins on our tail, sir."

Kang snorted, said nothing. Slith came out of the front, began waving his arm back and forth, the signal that all was well.

"Go!" Kang ordered and Support Squadron moved out, heading for the temple at a run. They passed Slith, who was returning to make his report.

"You think we can hold there, Slith?" Kang asked.

"Yes, sir. Support Squadron can fortify the doors and windows. That brick wall is good and solid. It'll give pause to the goblins. They'll think twice before they try coming over the wall after us."

"Just like they thought twice about tracking us through the snow," Kang muttered. "I'm sorry, Slith. It's not your fault. I'm in a bad mood, that's all."

"I know how you feel, sir," Slith said. He gave a shiver, his scales clicked. Normally, the dragon heritage of the draconians would protect them from the cold, but if the temperature dropped too low, the draconians couldn't adjust to it and faced the possibility of freezing to death.

The temperature was dropping.

"No problems inside?" Kang asked. "No holy force tried to prevent you from entering?"

"No, sir." Slith grinned, showing a row of sharp teeth. "The rumors we heard must be true. Paladine's long gone. No one else is inside either, at least that I could see."

"Fulkth will check the place out. I'll make the temple my headquarters. Let's go."

Kang and his small security detail of five baaz draconians raced to the temple. Support Squadron had already entered the gateway of the temple grounds. He could hear Fulkth shouting commands to search the buildings, secure the windows and the doors. Kang had reached the gate when one of his guards called his attention behind them. A runner was coming toward him, using his wings to hop and glide, letting the wind help carry him across the plain.

The runner skidded to a halt.

"Sir, Squadron Master Gloth reports that the goblins broke through his first line, but that he repelled the break and now the goblins have retreated three hundred yards. He thinks its only temporary, though, and wants to know if you want him to pull back to the temple, sir."

Kang looked at Slith. "What do you think?"

Slith shrugged. "They've got to pull back sometime, sir. Might as well be now."

"How's it looking up there?" Kang asked the runner.

"We've lost four or five of ours, but one was Kelemek, the bozak, and when he went, he took nearly twenty goblins with him."

"Hate to lose him, all the same."

Another one of us gone, Kang thought. Our numbers grow fewer every day. Maybe we should have stayed in the valley. . . .

"Sir?" Slith was regarding his commander in concern.

The runner flapped his wings and did a little dance to keep warm.

Kang blinked, rubbed the stinging snow from his eyes. "If First Squadron pulls back, it'll put all the pressure on

Second Squadron. That can't be helped. Churz, go back and tell Gloth to retreat to the temple, then go to Yethik and tell him to do the same. The length of time it takes you to move between one and the other will cause a delay between the two. Keep the squadrons moving back in echelon."

Yethik was new to the command of Second Squadron. He had taken command only two days before when a goblin arrow had pierced Irlihk's eye, killing him instantly. They had lost nearly thirty draconians since setting out from Mount Celebundin. There were just over two hundred left in the regiment.

The runner nodded, repeated the orders to ensure he got them right. Kang slapped him on the back and sent him off.

One of the baaz in the Security Detail pitched forward on his face. Slith rolled him over. There was an arrow in his back, lodged beneath his wings, a patch which the armor couldn't cover. Even as they watched, the body started to turn to stone.

Slith ran inside the temple. Kang left the baaz where he lay and entered the gates to the temple grounds. The rest of the baaz guards trooped in behind him. Inside it was eerily quiet. The wall kept out the wind. Maybe it would also keep out the goblins.

"Slith, make sure Support Squadron's ready to handle the defense. Oh, and get fires going. We're going to need heat. You four, fix me a post up on the second level where I can see the fighting. I want some torches brought up. Have Dremon report to me once you're set up."

The lead baaz saluted but hesitated before carrying out his orders. He looked back out to the body of his comrade. Snow was starting to pile up around it

"Yes, I know," Kang said, answering the unspoken question. "If we win this battle, we'll go back and retrieve him and bury him properly. Same with the rest of our dead, those that remain intact. If we lose, it won't make much difference where he lies, will it?"

"No, sir. Sorry, sir."

"Don't apologize, Rog. We care for our own," Kang replied. "No shame in that. Only credit. Now, off you go."

The four baaz moved off to do their commander's bidding.

Kang climbed the stairs, entered what had apparently been a living quarters for some of the clerics who served the temple. The room was small and exceptionally clean but completely bare. Only the bunks built into the walls remained.

Kang opened the shutters, looked out the window. The wind howled at him, but he could see First Squadron drawing near the temple grounds. Second Squadron was five hundred yards back. Neither was being pursued. He closed the shutters, sat down on one of the bunks.

A mistake. He would lie down, stretch out, take a nap. Just a short nap. He hadn't slept much in these past few days. He hadn't slept much in the past few months, or so it seemed. A nap wouldn't hurt anything. He'd done everything he could, the matter was out of his hands, Slith could deal with . . . with . . .

"Sir! Support Squadron reporting, sir!" A draconian materialized in front of Kang, saluted.

Kang sighed and opened his eyes. He wearily returned the salute.

Dremon, another sivak draconian, had been promoted to Chief Supply Officer when Yethik had taken command of Second Squadron. Dremon was the best reconnaissance soldier in the regiment, meaning that he was the best assassin, but he had broken his shoulder during one of the last raids at Celebundin and had never healed properly. He couldn't do the stealth work required of a reconnaissance soldier, but Kang had found other uses for him. He had put Dremon in charge of security for the young draconian females.

"How are the babies?" Kang asked.

Dremon shook his head. "There's something wrong, sir."

"What, damn it?" Kang was on his feet. Fear shriveled his heart.

"I don't know, sir." Dremon looked helpless. "I don't know anything about kids. The only kid I ever saw was a little human and, well, sir, I killed it. That was on that raid on—"

"Never mind about the damn raid!" Kang thundered. "What about the babies?"

"They're listless and they won't eat. We tried to give them some of the raw meat we've been feeding them but they just turn their heads away."

"Are they warm enough?"

"Yes, sir. We've got them tied up snug as a bug in the sacks. They're fretful, sir. All they do is whimper and cry."

"Are they sick?" Kang was sick himself, sick with worry.

"I don't know, sir. I really think you should come—"

"Sir!" One of Support Squadron entered the room. "Subcommander Slith said to tell you that the temple is not abandoned, as we first thought. We've found six humans, sir. Females. They were hiding in the cellar. They call themselves Sisters of Paladine, sir. The subcommander wants to know what to do with them."

Kang groaned. Just one damn problem on top of another. Clerics of Paladine! All he needed. He hoped to the gods that weren't anymore that they had lost their magical holy powers, just as he had lost his. If not . . .

"Did they attack?" he asked grimly.

"They tried, sir." The draconian grinned. "One of them—a real old and wrinkled-up one—shouted out the name of her cursed god and waved some sort of medallion at us. Nothing happened. The subcommander took the medallion away and told her to sit down and shut up. Her screeching was giving him a headache."

"Where are they?"

"Still in the cellar, sir."

"Sir!" Another soldier entered the room. "First and Second Squadron are inside the temple grounds, sir."

"What about the enemy?"

"Taking up positions outside the temple, sir. Looks as if they're preparing to attack."

"Man the walls. I know goblins. Their first attack will come too fast, before they're organized. Should be no trouble holding them off the first time. The second time'll be more difficult. Officers report to me in ten minutes."

"Yes, sir." The runner dashed off.

"The female humans, sir?" said the soldier.

"The babies, sir?" said Dremon.

Kang put his hand to his forehead. Females and babies? Females and babies . . .

"Females and babies!" he cried, triumphant. "That's it! Don't you get it?"

The two soldiers shook their heads.

"Females adore babies," Kang explained. "It's . . . it's born into them. Instinct." He strode rapidly across the room. The soldiers ran along behind.

"Even draconian babies, sir?" Dremon asked, dubious.

"All babies," Kang said firmly. "Baby lions, baby wolf cubs. Baby birds. Baby dragons. According to the bards, females—particularly human females—are always taking in baby animals and raising them. They can't help themselves."

"I hope the bards are right, sir!" Dremon said fervently.

So do I, Kang said to himself. So do I. All he said aloud was, "Bring the babies down to the cellar."

* * * * *

After a hasty meeting with his officers, he left them to their work and hurried through the main temple building. It was empty except for an altar with the image of the god carved in marble. The god was portrayed as a platinum dragon, fearsome, wise, and benevolent. At least that's how it must have appeared in the not-too-distant past. Now the statue of the dragon looked forlorn and slightly foolish. Or maybe bewildered, baffled. Kang gazed at it, experienced a moment of empathy. He knew how the beast felt. He himself was forlorn, bewildered, baffled. So much had happened in such a little space of time, so much had changed.

Kang patted the statue on the snout as he went by, not so much out of bravado, although the gesture would show his men that he wasn't afraid of it, as out of a feeling of brotherhood. They'd both been abandoned, he and the statue.

The soldiers led him through the temple proper to a large outbuilding located behind the main building. Here were more living quarters and an enormous kitchen. Behind the kitchen, a large double door built into the ground stood open. They could hear voices coming from below the ground level. Kang clomped down the cellar stairs. The cellar was warm and dry and filled with food smells. The smells were ghosts, however. The cellar was, for the most part, empty. A single sack of flour remained, along with some wizened apples, a sack of potatoes.

By the sunlight streaming down through the cellar door, Kang could see Slith standing in the center of the room. He held no weapons, did not look particularly threatening. Six human females were gathered at the far end of the subterranean chamber, as far from Slith as they could manage. One of the human females, the eldest—a tall, stringy female with hair the color of Kang's sword and a face so sharp it put his blade to shame—stood glaring defiantly at the draconian. The other females had gathered behind the elderly woman, whom Kang took to be their leader. She shifted her glare to Kang when he entered.

The females wore robes that had once been white but were now covered with dust from the cellar. Each wore around her neck a silver medallion, with the exception of the leader. Kang saw that Slith held her medallion in his hand.

Kang was nonplussed. He'd never had much dealing with human females before. He didn't find them all that attractive, as did some of his kind. The only female he'd ever really come to know had been a Knight of Takhisis, a soldier, like himself. He had been able to talk to her. He had no idea what to say to a female cleric.

Technically the females were his prisoners, but he needed their help, and he would not gain that help by reminding them of the fact. Nor would he be likely to gain their aid by threats and coercion. He may not know human females, but he could size up a fellow officer, and he could tell by the old female's proud and upright stance, her fearless gaze and defiant air, that this was not a commander who would be easily intimidated.

Outside he could hear his officers ordering their men to take up positions along the wall. That gave him an idea.

Kang marched forward. Removing his helmet, he held it under his arm and stood to attention.

"I am Commander Kang, ma'am, of the First Dragonarmy Field Engineers. What is your name and rank, ma'am?"

"What does it matter to you, Fiend?" the elderly woman said. "Kill us, and get it over with!"

"We have no intention of killing you, ma'am," Kang returned. "Your name and rank, ma'am."

The woman hesitated, then said grudgingly, "I am Hana, one of the blessed sisters of Paladine. I am head of our order. What's left of our order," she muttered.

"Sister Hana," said Kang with a brief bow, "you and the rest of the females may consider yourselves as being under our protection."

"As being your prisoners is what you mean!" countered Sister Hana.

"No, ma'am," said Kang, and he turned slowly and deliberately to face sideways, leaving a clear path to the cellar door. "You and the others are free to go, if you choose to do so."

The females appeared startled, distrustful.

"This is some kind of trick!" said Sister Hana.

"No, ma'am." Kang gestured. "Slith, the rest of you troops, stand aside."

Slith and the others shuffled sideways.

"I should warn you, ma'am," Kang continued, just as the females were starting to make a hesitant move, "that a large goblin army has this temple surrounded. It is possible that you and the rest might be able to slip through their lines and escape. You should know that goblins don't kill their prisoners. They enslave them."

One of the younger females gasped.

"Quiet, Sister Marsel!" the older female snapped. "I knew it!" She glared at Kang. "It *is* a trick. You let us go and then your allies capture us!"

"You are wrong, ma'am," Kang said quietly. "You have only to go outside and look to see that the goblins are not our allies. They are attacking us. We are outnumbered. We came here to use this temple to defend ourselves."

The sounds of battle could be heard clearly. Above the clamor of arms and the harsh shouts and cries of the draconians sounded a long, thin, high-pitched, spine-tingling wail. The elderly woman paled and, for the first time, her defiance wilted slightly.

"A goblin battle cry, ma'am," said Slith, standing at attention. "I take it you've heard that before."

"I was in the War of the Lance," Sister Hana said, more to herself than to them.

"As were we, ma'am," said Kang, adding politely, "on opposite sides, I believe."

She cast him a grim and dour glance. "The side of evil!"

"No, ma'am," said Kang. "It was you who were on the side of evil."

She drew herself up straight. "I fought in the name of Paladine!"

"And we fought in the name of our goddess. It all depends on your vantage point, doesn't it, ma'am?" Kang said. The yelling outside had increased, so had the clash of steel against steel. "I would enjoy discussing the issue with you further someday, ma'am. Now does not appear to be the time, however."

"Sir!" called Dremon from outside.

"Come down!" Kang yelled.

Dremon and the other members of Support Squadron came clattering down the stairs, their claws scraping on the wood, their weapons clanging and banging. The woman put out her arms, crowded the young women further back against the wall.

"Don't be afraid, ma'am," Kang said quickly, casting Dremon a rebuking glance that brought him and the rest of the men up straight and stiff. "These are some more of my troops. We carry with us a valuable treasure, ma'am. The greatest gift to come to our race. I ordered my men to bring the treasure down here, where it would be safe from harm during the ensuing battle."

Carefully, gently, Dremon and the other draconians took the knapsacks from their backs. They placed the sacks on the cellar floor and lifted the fur-lined flaps that covered the babies. Bright eyes blinked in the light, snouts twitched. Small mouths opened in yawns and whines. Kang's heart twisted. A week ago the babies would have squawked and squeaked and complained. Now they looked drowsy, listless, as Dremon had said.

"Oh, aren't they cute!" Sister Marsel cooed.

"The sweet little things," said another.

Kang cast Dremon a triumphant glance.

"Are they baby dragons?" asked Sister Marsel.

"Spawns of evil is what they are!" Sister Hana snarled. "Those are baby draconians!"

"Yes, ma'am," said Kang.

"But I didn't think draconians could have babies," said Sister Marsel. She looked at Kang and blushed. "Because . . . because there are no female draconians."

"That's true, ma'am," said Kang, his voice softening.

"Then how . . .?" Sister Marsel didn't seem to quite know where this sentence was going.

"The babies were given to us in payment. Our queen sent us—"

"Tricked us," Slith said beneath his breath.

Kang shrugged. "Perhaps she had a right. She was desperate. To make a long story short, we fought Chaos's monsters in the caves of Thorbardin and defeated them. Then we found the babies. We saved them from death.

We paid for their recovery with our blood. This is the greatest treasure we have ever been given. You see, ma'am, these children are *female* draconians. Once our race was doomed. Now, we will survive."

"Paladine prevent it!" Sister Hana cried.

"I don't think he has much say in the matter anymore," said Kang gravely. "Our queen left us here on our own and, from what we've heard, you've been abandoned by your god, as well."

"Our god is with us!" Sister Hana retorted.

"I don't think so, ma'am," said Slith. He tossed her medallion into the air like a gambler tosses a coin, causing it to spin and flip. He caught it with a quick, overhand snap. "If your god were around, would he let me do that to his medal?"

"That will do, Slith!" said Kang in a rebuking tone. "It is not our place to mock the faithful. Give the sister back her medallion and apologize to her for mistreating it."

Slith stole a glance at his superior to determine if he were truly serious. Seeing not the hint of smile, Slith sidled over to the sister and held out the medallion.

"Sorry, ma'am," he said, "for any disrespect."

The sister, white-faced, snatched the medallion from Slith and closed her fist over it tightly.

"Commander! Where's the commander?" came a shout from outside.

"Down here!" Kang bellowed.

A soldier dashed down the stairs, came up with a salute. "Sir," he said, "we have repelled the first assault. The goblins have retreated."

"Only to regroup," Kang said. "They'll be back, soon enough, and this time they'll be better organized. What do you think, Slith?"

"My guess is that they won't attack until morning, sir. It'll be dark soon. They'll be wanting to fill their bellies and get a good night's rest." Slith shrugged. "They know we aren't going anywhere."

"That's true enough," Kang growled. "Perhaps you're right. Set the watch. I want it doubled. I don't want those sneaky bastards slipping over the walls to slit our throats in the night. And I want the men to have a hot meal. Roast those deer we shot."

Sister Marsel made a sound. Sister Hana scowled, and the young female put her hand over her mouth. Kang noticed the pinched cheeks of all the women, the thin bodies. He glanced around at the near-empty cellar and guessed the truth.

"We will be pleased to share our food with you, ma'am," he said gruffly.

"And poison us!" Sister Hana said, casting him a scathing glance. "We are not hungry."

"Suit yourself, ma'am. Slith, you have your orders."

"Yes, sir."

Kang looked anxiously at the babies. Kneeling down, he chucked one under the chin, tried to make her smile. She whimpered and turned away. Kang sighed deeply.

"You're right, Dremon," he said. "There's something wrong. I'll be damned if I know what."

Kang cast a sidelong glance at the females. Sister Hana was leading them in a prayer to Paladine, speaking the words forcefully, loudly, and angrily, as if she was certain the god was around, he'd just chosen this moment to step outside. Four of the younger sisters were praying along with their leader, though they sounded hopeless and resigned rather than angry. One, Marsel, was only murmuring the words. Her gaze was drawn to the baby draconians.

Kang had been intending to wait respectfully until the prayer ended, but after the harangue had continued for almost ten minutes without pause, he felt he could wait no longer. "Uh, excuse me, ma'am," he said diffidently. "There . . . there seems to be something wrong with our little ones, here. We're soldiers, ma'am. We don't know anything about children. I was wondering if you, with your experience—"

"My experience! Hah!" Sister Hana turned her back on him. "We are going to keep praying, sisters! Pray that this evil be taken from our midst! Marsel," Sister Hana said sharply, "you will lead us in the next prayer."

"Yes, sister," said Marsel dutifully and shifted her gaze away from the babies.

"Commander, sir!" Someone else was yelling outside. "Where's the commander?"

"I've got to go," said Kang to Dremon in an undertone. "Leave the babies down here. They're safer here than anywhere else. Maybe the sight of them will soften their hearts."

"What hearts, sir?" Dremon returned.

Kang just shook his head and dashed up the stairs to attend to the disposition of the defense.

* * * * *

Night blew in on a cold wind. The strange new moon lit the snow with a sick, bleak light. The moon looked lost and lonely in the sky, Kang thought, gazing up at it. It looked as if it were wondering how it had managed to find itself in this situation. He knew just how it felt.

He made the rounds, saying a word to each soldier on guard duty, urging them to keep careful watch, for it was in his mind that with the moon at the full, the goblins might not wait until morning to attack. Looking out over the wall, he could see their campfires blazing brightly, dark figures passed back and forth in front of the light. Tempting targets, but the goblins were out of bow range, and Kang's men were short on arrows as it was.

The draconians were short on everything—arrows, rations. What food they had went first to the young. The deer they'd shot that morning would be the only real meat the men had eaten in a week. Kang was pushing them hard to reach their destination before the heavy snows of winter set in and blocked the mountain passes, leaving the draconians trapped, easy prey for the cursed Solamnic Knights.

"Excuse me, Commander," said a voice at his side.

Kang turned. It was one of the women, the young one, Marsel.

"You shouldn't be out here, ma'am," he said quickly, and taking her by the arm, he hustled her away from the walls and into the safety of the temple.

"But why?" she protested, peering backward, trying to see. "The goblins aren't attacking, are they?"

"Not *now*, ma'am," Kang said with emphasis, "but they're not above trying a lucky shot, and—no disrespect intended, ma'am—but in those white robes, you make a very fine target."

"I guess you're right," said Sister Marsel, looking down at her robes with a rueful smile. "Do . . . do you have a moment, Commander? I'd like to talk to you, if I may."

Kang heroically put aside thoughts of stretching out beneath a warm blanket. "Did Sister Hana send you?"

"No." Sister Marsel flushed. "She doesn't know I've gone. She and the others are asleep."

"Where I should be," Kang muttered, but only to himself. "What can I do for you, Sister Marsel? Would you like some venison?" He brought out a choice morsel, a meaty bone, he'd been saving for his own dinner.

Sister Marsel eyed it, swallowed, licked her lips and said, "No, thank you. Well, maybe just a taste . . . " She took the meat and began to eat ravenously. Halfway through, however, she paused, her face flushed. She handed the bone back to Kang. "I'm sorry. I took your supper, didn't I? No, you eat the rest. Really, that was all I wanted."

Kang ate what she had left him, tearing meat from the bone with his sharp teeth.

"The babies wouldn't eat," Sister Marsel said. "Your man offered them some food. They wouldn't touch it."

Kang suddenly lost his own appetite. He tossed the uneaten portion down on the altar. Later that night, the cook would come around, gather up all the bones, throw them into the soup pot for breakfast.

"Could I ask you a question, Commander?"

Kang nodded. "Yes, ma'am."

"What did you mean when you told Sister Hana that she was on the side of evil. Was that . . . was that a joke?"

"I'm not much given to jokes, ma'am," Kang said.

Sister Marsel looked perplexed. "Did you mean it? That we are on the side of . . . evil? I thought we were on the side of right."

"We thought the same, ma'am. We believed that what we were doing was right."

She shook her head. "Killing, murdering . . ."

"Your Knights have killed countless numbers of us, ma'am," Kang returned. "The graves of my men stretch from the Plains of Dust all the way to here."

"You really care about them, don't you?" Sister Marsel was astonished. "Sister Hana always said that caring was what made us different. That draconians and goblins don't care about each other, that evil turns in upon itself."

"I wouldn't know about that, ma'am," said Kang. "I know that I'm a soldier and that my men are my responsibility. During the War of the Lance, we fought for the glory of our goddess, just as your Knights fought for the glory of your god." Kang shrugged. "As it turned out, we were both duped. Our queen turned tail and fled, leaving us to die, the cowardly bit—female. Your god did the same, or so I hear."

"That's what some say, but I don't believe them," Sister Marsel returned. "I think . . ." Her voice softened. "I think Paladine has gone and left us in charge in order to test us, to see if we are able to take what he has taught us and use it wisely. He's not the overprotective father, hovering over his children every minute to make certain we don't hurt ourselves." She smiled.

Kang, who had been drifting off to sleep, was jolted to awareness. "I beg your pardon, ma'am. What were you saying about children?"

"That's really what I came to talk you about. I think that's what's wrong with the babies, Commander," said Sister Marsel. "You can't keep them cooped up in those sacks for the rest of their lives. You have to let them out to learn about the world, the good and the bad."

"We tried that," Kang said harshly. "They hurt themselves. One wandered off. No." He was emphatic. "They are too precious to us to risk."

"You sound just like my father." Sister Marsel smiled and sighed. "He said the very same thing about me. Do you know what he did, Commander? He sent me to live with the Sisters of Paladine. He sent me here, to this temple, where I would be safe and protected from the world. Am I safe, Commander?" she demanded. "Am I protected?"

Kang cleared his throat, embarrassed.

"The world finds us, Commander," said Sister Marsel quietly. "We can't hide from it, not even in the cellar of a temple. We have to know how to face it. I don't." She lowered her head. "I don't know anything. I'm stupid, and I'm afraid."

She cast a glance out at the blazing bonfires. Every now and again, a goblin battle shriek split the air. Sister Marsel shivered. "I'm afraid because I feel so helpless."

"I don't think you're stupid, Sister," Kang said, "not by a long shot."

"The babies could play in the cellar," said Sister Marsel. "They couldn't get into much trouble down there. They need exercise and fresh air."

"Perhaps in the morning," Kang said.

Morning. The goblins would attack in full force. Kang wasn't at all certain he could hold them off. In the morning he and his men and their young might be dead. He said nothing of his own fears to the young human, however, and he made a silent vow that she would not fall alive into goblin hands. He'd seen what goblins did to their human captives, particularly their human female captives. Maybe she was right. Maybe they had been on the side of evil, but then he'd seen what Solamnic Knights did to the goblins they'd captured, he'd seen goblin babies carried on the ends of spears. Kang would protect this female from that savage and horrific part of the world at least. He would end it for her quickly. He hoped she would understand and forgive him.

"I had better go back now," said Sister Marsel. "You're tired and I've kept you talking. Besides, if Sister Hana were to wake up and find me gone, Paladine alone knows what she'd do."

"Good night, Sister Marsel," said Kang. "And thank you."

He continued his rounds and then headed for his bed, taking one of the bunks in the upper room of the temple. He was looking forward to his bed. Kang was not one to lose sleep in needless worry. He'd done everything in his power to prepare. The morning would bring what the morning would bring. He did miss laying the burden of his problems in the lap of his Dark Queen. Now he had to shoulder the responsibility himself, he could not foist it off on his goddess. He thought over what Sister Marsel had said, about the gods leaving them to make of the world what they could. He wasn't certain he bought it, but it was an interesting idea.

On his way to his bed, Kang gave the snout of the platinum dragon a rub for luck.

* * * * *

"Sir! Commander! Sir!"

Someone was shaking him by the shoulder violently. Kang started to wakefulness, peered bleary-eyed into a bright torch blazing above him.

"What? What? Huh? Is it the attack?"

He sat up, groggy and still half-asleep. He had a vague recollection of someone else waking him in the night. Slith, or so Kang recalled. Slith had been excited about something. Wanted permission to do something. Kang couldn't remember what. He'd agreed to it apparently, because Slith had departed, but what it was he'd said or what it was he'd agreed to, Kang couldn't for the life of him remember.

"I always said I could give orders in my sleep," Kang muttered. "I guess it's finally come to that."

"Sir! Please! You have to come! You have to see this!"

The soldier had thrown open one of the shutters. Red streaked the sky, clouds massed on the horizon. There would be more snow today. Horns blared. His troops were shouting and clashing their swords.

Certain that he would look out the window to see a couple of goblin regiments bearing down on him, Kang could not for the life of him understand what was going on.

The goblins, it seemed, were moving backwards.

"What the—?" Kang blinked, rubbed his eyes.

"They're retreating, sir!" the draconian said.

"What? Why?" Kang was astounded.

The draconian pointed. "See their general, sir. The big hairy bastard riding that great, hulking warhorse."

"Yes." Kang squinted into the sun. "Not much of a rider. He's almost fallen off twice since I've been watching him."

"Yes, sir!" The draconian was enjoying himself hugely. "That's Slith, sir! He killed the general and took over his body! Slith's the one who's ordering the goblins to retreat!"

It all came back to Kang. Slith waking him in the night, asking for permission to carry out a raid. Kang had mumbled something. He couldn't remember what. Slith had taken his mumble for a yes, however, as Slith was wont to do. Slith had saved Kang's life more than once. He'd saved their entire force more than once. Now he had saved their race.

Kang watched, his heart swelling with pride, as Slith, magically attired in the body of the murdered goblin general, bounced up and down in the saddle and shouted orders in goblin for the army to run and keep on running. Fortunately, having fought with goblin troops for years, Slith knew exactly what to say to motivate them. Kang could not hear him, Slith was too far away. But Kang could imagine.

"It's a trap!" the goblin-Slith would be shouting. "There are thousands and thousands of draconians holed up in the temple. They're going to come out and cut off your ears and eat goblin meat for dinner! Run for it, boys! Run for your miserable lives!"

"Support!" Kang said suddenly, fumbling for his equipment. "We've got to support him! Make it look good. Quickly now!"

"Yes, sir," said the draconian. "We're all ready, sir. Look."

The gates of the temple opened. Second Squadron under Gloth's command rushed out, shrieking like demons freed from the Abyss. The sight and sound of the enraged draconians further panicked the goblins, who had probably not been too keen on this action in the first place. Those few who had been guarding the "general" threw down their weapons and abandoned their post, fleeing over the windswept ground in haste.

Their retreat was fortunate for, at that moment, Slith tumbled off the horse. Although a dumb animal, the beast was smarter than the goblins. It knew perfectly well that this being on its back was not its master. The horse kicked up its heels and galloped off. The draconian force surrounded Slith and, in case any goblins might be watching, Gloth made a good show of taking the goblin "general" captive.

"Mogu," said Kang, "go tell the human females that they're safe. The goblins have fled. You can give them the good news that we're going to be leaving, as well. And tell Dremon to let the babies out to play in the cellar this morning. This glorious morning!"

Kang stationed First Squadron at the temple gate. Second Squadron marched back to the temple in triumph. The goblin army probably wouldn't stop running until they reached Newsea. Slith was now starting to let loose of his goblin form, returning to his draconian self. Kang led the cheers when Slith entered.

"Brilliant idea, Slith!" said Kang, slapping his subcommander on the shoulder. "Absolutely brilliant!"

"Thank you, sir." Slith grinned. "I have to admit that I didn't really intend to do that, sir. I went out just to see if I could find their general, maybe bring him back as hostage. And then it came to me that if I killed him and took his shape, I could—"

"Sir!" A draconian, breathless and panting, came dashing up. "You have to come—"

Kang waved him to silence. "Go on, Slith."

"Sir!" The draconian ignored Kang's command, actually laid hands on him and shook him. "Sir! You must come! She's going to kill the babies!"

* * * * *

Kang had never run so fast in his life. He nearly pitched headfirst down the cellar stairs, caught himself in time. Reaching the bottom, he found a standoff.

Dremon stood on one side of the cellar holding Sister Marsel in a clawed grip, a knife to her throat. On the other side of the cellar Sister Hana held a sword over the heads of the draconian babies, trapped inside their sacks. The other females huddled in a corner, weeping and cringing. Draconians stood with their swords drawn in front of them.

"If she hurts a single scale on one of them, Commander, I'll slit her from ear to ear," Dremon said, as Kang entered. "We'll kill the rest, too!"

"Keep calm!" Kang ordered, though the words caught in his throat. The babies were enchanted with the sword that threatened to end their short lives. They squeaked with delight, reached out small clawed hands to touch it. The sword, Kang noted, was a draconian weapon.

"There'll be no killing if I can help it. Report!" he said harshly to Dremon.

"We received your orders, sir. I took off my sword and set it aside when I prepared to let the babies out. I never thought—" Dremon swallowed, then said, "She grabbed the sword before I could stop her, sir."

"Sister Hana," Kang said, speaking as calmly as he could manage. "I don't want *anyone* to get hurt. Put down the sword. We will take the children and leave you in peace. We won't trouble you anymore."

"Your kind destroyed all I had!" Sister Hana cried. "My home, my family. Why should I spare yours? These babies are the spawn of evil. I will see to it that evil ends here, this day!"

She regarded Kang with a raw hatred, a hatred he found appalling and for which he was unprepared. He remembered feeling such hatred himself once, the time the dwarves had burned down the village he and the others had worked so hard to build. He had killed dwarves with his bare hands, then. For a soldier, killing is just another unpleasant job, like digging latrines or standing guard duty, but in avenging himself on the dwarves, Kang had enjoyed the killing. This female would enjoy the killing now, too. Killing the innocent babies.

"You won't bring an end to evil, Sister Hana!" Sister Marsel cried. "Killing the children will only perpetuate it. These children have done nothing. They are innocent. Paladine teaches that every being on Krynn is given the choice of what path to follow—the path of darkness, or the path of light. It is not up to us to take away that choice."

"There is no choice," said Sister Hana. "Not for these fiends! They are born of evil spells cast by dark clerics and wicked wizards. They are made of the eggs of good dragons, whose children were destroyed in order to produce these monsters."

"What you say is true, ma'am," Kang said, hoping to keep the woman talking while he figured out what to do. He had little hope of changing her mind. "I could offer excuses. I could say that we were not responsible for our birth any more than you are responsible for yours. I could say that we were never given a choice of what path to walk. From the beginning, we were made to walk the path of darkness. Even as babies, we were forced to fight each other for food, in the belief that this would make us strong soldiers. We were taught to hate, taught to hate humans and elves.

"After the war, I came to realize that it was the hate that was killing us. Hate kills everything. The only way we had a chance to survive was to stop hating and start living. That's why I think the babies were given into our care.

"Dremon," said Kang, after a moment's pause. "Let the sister go."

"But, sir—" Dremon protested, anguished.

"I said let her go!" Kang roared.

Reluctantly, Dremon released Sister Marsel. She staggered, weak-kneed, and caught hold of a post for support. She stood with head bowed, trembling. Sister Hana watched, suspicious.

"I make you an offer, Sister Hana," said Kang, unbuckling his sword belt. "I am an officer. Perhaps I was the one who ordered the deaths of your family. Take your revenge on me, and welcome. Only let the children live."

Sister Hana glared at him. There was no life in her eyes, only dead darkness. The madness of hatred had almost completely devoured her.

"I will give myself into your hands," Kang continued, desperately. "You may slay me where I stand. I will not try to stop you. Slith, are you there?"

"Yes, sir," said Slith.

"You are in command. My final order and one that I expect to be obeyed is this: When I am dead, you will take the men and the children and leave. These sisters are to be allowed to remain in this temple in peace. Do you understand?"

"Yes, sir," said Slith quietly. "I understand."

"Now take the men out of here, Slith."

"Sir—"

"That's an order, Slith!"

"Yes, sir."

Claws scraped, weapons were sheathed. The draconians slowly and reluctantly climbed back up the stairs. Kang was on his own, he and the children and the human females.

Kang placed his sword and his armor, his boot knife and other accoutrements on the floor. Walking forward until he stood within a sword thrust of Sister Hana, he lowered himself to his knees before her and held out his hands in submission.

"I offer my life in exchange for the lives of the children, ma'am. Let them go. Let them have the choices I never had. I would warn you of one thing, though, ma'am. When I die, my bones will explode. You should order the other sisters to leave now and allow them to take the children to safety."

Sister Marsel started forward, reaching out her hand toward the babies. Sister Hana blocked her, cast her a vicious glance. "Don't come near!"

"Don't do this, Sister Hana!" Sister Marsel begged. "In the name of Paladine be merciful. Or has everything you taught us about Paladine been a lie?"

Sister Hana smiled then. A terrible smile. "Yes," she cried. "It was a lie. It was all a lie! The god lied to me, didn't he? He said my children died for a reason, and then he left. He betrayed me, he betrayed them. Death take us. Death take us all!"

She swung the sword.

Kang lunged to avoid the stroke, which would not only kill him but everyone trapped in the cellar, the babies included. He rolled over, to try as best he could to fend off the next attack.

He watched in astonishment to see Sister Marsel jump in front of him. She grabbed hold of Sister's Hana's arm, struck her a blow on her wrist. The sword fell to the dirt floor with a dull clang. Sister Hana sank down beside it, sobbing in anguish, her hands clenched.

Sister Marsel gathered up the female in her arms, cradled her, began to rock back and forth, murmuring soothing words.

Kang stood up awkwardly. "Sister," he began, trying to find words to thank her.

Sister Marsel looked up at him and shook her head. "You better go," she said. "Take the children."

* * * * *

Support Squadron carried the children out of the cellar. First Squadron raided the goblin camp, picking up food and weapons left behind by the fleeing goblins. They returned to report that they now had supplies enough to last a month. While the rest of the regiment prepared to march out, Kang and Dremon took the babies into the upper room in the temple and released them from their snug prisons. The babies looked around in amazement at their freedom, then perked up and began to play. Some discovered their wings for the first time and began to jump about the floor, delighting in their ability to fly for a few short hops. Others climbed up on the bunks and took to leaping off, causing Kang's heart to lodge in his throat. He valiantly fought back the desire to stuff them all back in their sacks again.

The draconian troops allowed the children to play until they were tired, then fed them hot soup made of the remnants of yesterday's venison. The babies ate well and were now content to return to their sacks, where they soon fell sound asleep.

Late that afternoon the First Dragonarmy Field Engineers lined up in the temple courtyard, prepared to move out, to continue their march. Snow had started falling again, but this time Kang welcomed it. The snow would hide their tracks, throw off pursuit.

Kang had a debt to repay. He could not leave without first thanking Sister Marsel. He found her in the temple, standing before the statue of the platinum dragon.

"How is Sister Hana?" he asked.

"She'll be all right. The others are with her." Sister Marsel crossed her arms over her chest, shivered. The fires had gone out. The temple was cold.

"You shouldn't stay here," he warned her. "The goblins might return."

"I know," she replied. "We should have left long ago, left when the rest of them left. But Sister Hana said that someday Paladine would return and he would be disappointed to find us gone. There's a village not far from here. They'll be glad to take Sister Hana in and give her and the others a home."

"What will you do?" Kang asked curiously.

THE SOULFORGE
MARGARET WEIS

The long-awaited prequel to the bestselling Chronicles Trilogy by the author who brought Raistlin to life!

Raistlin Majere is six years old when he is introduced to the archmage who enrolls him in a school for the study of magic. There the gifted and talented but tormented boy comes to see magic as his salvation. Mages in the magical Tower of High Sorcery watch him in secret, for they see shadows darkening over Raistlin even as the same shadows lengthen over all Ansalon.

Finally, Raistlin draws near his goal of becoming a wizard. But first he must take the Test in the Tower of High Sorcery—or die trying.

THE CHRONICLES TRILOGY
MARGARET WEIS AND TRACY HICKMAN

Fifteen years after publication and with more than three million copies in print, the story of the world-wide best-selling trilogy is as compelling as ever. Dragons have returned to Krynn with a vengeance. An unlikely band of heroes embarks on a perilous quest for the legendary DRAGONLANCE!

THE LEGENDS TRILOGY
Margaret Weis and Tracy Hickman

In the sequel to the ground-breaking Chronicles trilogy, the powerful archmage Raistlin follows the path of dark magic and even darker ambition as he travels back through time to the days before the Cataclysm. Joining him, willingly and unwillingly, are Crysania, a beautiful cleric of good, Caramon, Raistlin's brother, and the irrepressible kender Tasslehoff.

Volume One: *Time of the Twins*
$6.99 US; $8.99 CAN
8307
ISBN: 0-88038-265-1

Volume Two: *War of the Twins*
$6.99 US; $8.99 CAN
8308
ISBN: 0-88038-266-X

Volume Three: *Test of the Twins*
$6.99 US; $8.99 CAN
8309
ISBN: 0-88038-267-8